Kingdom
OF
Darkness

By Andy McDermott

Featuring Nina Wilde and Eddie Chase
The Hunt for Atlantis
The Tomb of Hercules
The Secret of Excalibur
The Covenant of Genesis
The Pyramid of Doom
The Sacred Vault
Empire of Gold
Return to Atlantis
The Valhalla Prophecy
Kingdom of Darkness

Stand-Alone Novel
The Shadow Protocol

Kingdom
OF
Darkness

A NOVEL

Andy McDermott

DELL
NEW YORK

A Dell Mass Market Original

Copyright © 2014 by Andy McDermott
Excerpt from *The Revelation Code* by Andy McDermott copyright © 2015 by Andy McDermott

Published in the United States by Dell, an imprint of Random House, a division of Penguin Random House LLC, New York.

DELL and the HOUSE colophon are registered trademarks of Penguin Random House LLC.

Originally published in the United Kingdom by Headline Publishing Group, an Hachette UK Company, in 2014.

This book contains an excerpt from the forthcoming book *The Revelation Code* by Andy McDermott. This excerpt has been set for this edition only and may not reflect the final content of the forthcoming edition.

ISBN 978-0-345-53708-9
eBook ISBN 978-0-345-53709-6

Cover art: Mike Bryan
Art direction: Carlos Beltrán

Printed in the United States of America

www.bantamdell.com

9 8 7 6 5 4 3 2 1

Dell mass market edition: May 2015

For Kat

Kingdom
OF
Darkness

Greece, 1943

The military convoy ground through the darkness toward its next destination.

In the lead car, a Kübelwagen utility vehicle, SS-Sturmbannführer Erich Kroll used a torch to check a map of the farmland around the town of Pella. His Waffen-SS unit, soldiers of Hitler's feared Schutzstaffel elite force, were on a mission direct from the Führer: to locate and round up any Jews remaining in the Nazi-occupied zone for deportation to the concentration camps of Treblinka and Auschwitz. The operation had by now been mostly completed to German satisfaction, but, Kroll mused, the *Juden* were as hard to eradicate as rats—and the task had been made harder by Jewish sympathizers among the local population.

The Nazis had their own sympathizers, though. Fascist collaborators had provided their new masters with lists of those suspected of harboring fugitives, and now the SS was checking each one. On this night, they already had five prisoners in the truck behind: two Jewish women and a boy found in a farm's loft, as well as the farmer and his wife. A good catch, but Kroll hoped to find more.

The blond man swapped the map for his list. The next

target was the property belonging to the Patras family. According to his information, they liked their privacy, keeping to themselves. That alone made them worthy of a visit from the SS; even if they were not harboring enemies of the Reich, they still needed reminding who was now in charge of their land.

The Kübelwagen's headlights picked out a crossroads ahead. "Go right," Kroll ordered the driver, Jaekel. The young storm trooper had already impressed the unit commander, shrugging off a vicious slash across his face from a knife-wielding Jew in order to bayonet him and the family he was protecting. The scar was still a raw red line, the stitches visible; in time, it would be a stirring reminder of his bravery and a magnet for women.

The car made the turn, the truck and half-track behind it following. The muddy road led up a hillside to an old house near its summit. Jaekel pulled up outside the front door. The truck jolted to a halt alongside, the half-track heading around the building to watch for anyone trying to run from its rear.

Kroll marched to the door and pounded on the wood with a gloved fist. "Open up!" he barked in Greek. He had studied the ancient form of the language in his youth; learning its modern derivation had not been difficult. "This is the Waffen-SS—we are here to search your property for Jewish fugitives. You are ordered to let us in, immediately!"

He stepped back and waited impatiently. Behind him, his men readied their weapons as sounds of activity came from inside. "How long do we give them?" asked SS-Obersturmführer Rasche.

"Thirty seconds," Kroll told his senior lieutenant. "Then we kick the door down."

Rasche smiled, manic eyes widening. "I hope they don't rush." One hand went to a dagger in a sheath on his belt, the hilt bearing the *Totenkopf* death's-head of the SS. "I always like to make an example of someone."

"Open the door at once!" Kroll shouted. He heard voices behind it; that the occupiers had not immediately complied suggested they were trying to conceal something. "You have ten seconds! Nine! Eight! Seven!"

The *clunk* of a heavy bolt, then the door opened. An elderly man nervously peered out. "What do you want?"

"You heard me," Kroll snapped. He shoved the door, sending the old man reeling back. "You are Alejo Patras?"

"Yes, I am," Patras replied.

"Who else is in the house?"

"My wife, Kaira, my two sons, and my elder son's wife and daughter. But we have nothing to hide here, we are just farmers."

"Five others," Kroll told his men before turning back to Patras. "Bring them all here, now. Anyone who is not here in one minute will be shot when they are found." He made a show of raising his left arm to check his watch.

Patras called out urgently. Before long, others filed into the hallway: an old woman and a couple in their thirties, the wife fearfully holding a six-year-old child. The German regarded his watch again. "Where is your other son? He is running out of time!"

"Dinos!" cried Patras, with an exhortation for him to hurry. Seconds ticked by, Rasche's malevolent smirk widening as he fingered his knife—then a door banged deeper inside the house. Running footsteps, and a man in his twenties hurried into the hall.

Kroll's cold gaze turned upon him. "Why were you hiding from us?" he demanded in Greek.

"I—I wasn't hiding," the young man insisted. "I was in the cellar, I didn't hear you."

"Search the cellar," Kroll ordered, not taken in by the protestation of innocence. "Look for hatches, hidden doors—anywhere people might hide."

Rasche addressed one of the troopers. "Rottenführer! With me." A squat, round-faced man named Schneider followed him out, putting a hand over his mouth to hold in a wet cough.

Kroll waited as his unit searched the house. One by one they returned, reporting no sign of fugitives. The elder Patras appeared relieved to be vindicated, but the Nazi commander detected a rising tension in his sons—particularly the younger.

Only Rasche and Schneider had not yet come back. "Oberst_urmführer!" Kroll called. "Have you found anything?"

A pause, then: "I'm not sure. Is Walther there? We need him to move something."

Kroll glanced at the huge storm trooper, whose head reached to just inches beneath the ceiling beams. "Sturmmann, go and help him."

Walther's arm snapped into a rigid Hitler salute, his fingertips brushing the plaster overhead. "At once, Herr Sturmbannführer!" Hunching down to fit through the doorway, he headed for the cellar.

There was now definite concern in the brothers' expressions—no, Kroll realized, the whole family's. "If you are hiding Jews down there, you will be treated just like them," he warned the group. "Give them up now, and I may be lenient."

The elder Patras shook his head. "This is a very old house, it has many cubbyholes. But we are not hiding anyone, I promise."

"I would prefer to see for myself," Kroll replied with a sneer. He listened as thumping sounds echoed up from below. Then—

"Sturmbannführer!" Rasche shouted. "Come quickly!"

"Bring them," Kroll snapped to his men. The prisoners were hustled along at gunpoint. The cellar entrance was a crooked door at the rear of a cramped pantry, stairs leading down a steep passage lined in whitewashed stone. A flickering lantern provided weak illumination below. The SS leader noticed the polished curve to each stone step; the passage either was regularly traveled or had been here for a very long time.

He reached the foot of the stairs. The lantern revealed a grotto-like space, sacks and boxes lining the walls. Grunts of exertion came from around a corner. Beyond it, Kroll found his three men at what appeared to be a dead end—except that Walther had managed to get his thick fingers into a gap that had been hidden behind some barrels and was pulling at it. Wood creaked with each tug.

"There's a mark from a hidden door," explained Rasche, pointing at a faint line arcing across the flagstones. "But we can't get it open."

Kroll drew his Luger and faced Patras as the family was pushed into the subterranean space. "How does it open? Tell me now, or I will shoot your wife!" He pointed the gun at the old woman's head. She gasped in fear.

A tense silence—then the younger son shoved his mother aside, lunging at Kroll—

The gunshot was deafening in the confined space.

Blood gouted across the cellar from a bullet wound in Dinos's throat, almost black in the low light. Kroll stepped back as the young man collapsed at his feet. His mother screamed.

"Open the door!" yelled the Nazi leader. The young girl shrieked in terror as the other SS troopers slammed her parents against the wall. "Open it, or I'll kill you all!"

"Wait, wait!" cried the horrified Patras. "I'll open it!"

His older son shouted in protest even as gun muzzles were jammed against him, but Patras scurried to the wall and pulled aside a stack of boxes. Behind them, at floor level, was a small nook. He slipped his hand inside, fingers curling around a concealed catch.

A *clack* came from behind the fake wall. "It will open now," he told Kroll. "Please, let my family go!"

"How many people are hiding?" the German demanded.

"None, there is nobody there. It is just a room. Take what you find and go, I beg you!"

Again his son protested. "Father, no! You can't let them into the shrine!"

The last word caught Kroll's attention. "What shrine?" he said, rounding on the elderly man. "What's back there?"

The conflict on Patras's face told him that the Greek did not want to give up his secret. "I . . . it is our family's heritage," he finally said. "We have protected it for many generations, many centuries."

Kroll regarded him for a moment, then addressed Walther. "Open it."

The big man slotted his fingers back into the gap. This time, there was little resistance when he pulled. The hidden door swung outward.

The Nazi leader shone his torch into the newly revealed darkness to find another set of steps heading downward. He directed his light to the bottom. There was a chamber below.

"Sir," warned one of the storm troopers, a thin-faced man named Gausmann, as Kroll began to descend. "If someone's down there, they could be armed."

Kroll stopped, shining his torch back at his prisoners. "If anyone is down there, kill the family," he said. Their lack of reaction told him that they did not speak German. "But I don't think he's lying. Rasche, follow me."

The second set of stairs seemed even older than the first, the irregular stones in the whitewashed walls held in place by the weight of those above them rather than mortar. But the room beneath had been built with more care, he saw as it came into view. Elegant columns supported the ceiling of the roughly circular space. Ancient Grecian architecture, Kroll thought, directing his torch beam over the nearest. But later than the classical period . . .

He turned his light into the center of the room—and froze.

"My God!" he gasped, astonishment reducing his voice to a whisper.

The shrine was filled with treasure.

Gold and silver glinted everywhere his torch beam darted. Coins, jewelry, statuettes, even armor and weapons; the spoils of several lifetimes. Among them was something that immediately seemed out of place—a clockwork mechanism, bronze or brass. He quickly dismissed the anachronism as a later addition to the collection, his gaze instead going to the figure at the chamber's far side. The marble statue of a man, flakes of colored paint still visible on the pale stone, watched over the room of wonders.

Kroll heard Rasche let out an exclamation, but he ignored the SS section leader, advancing on the statue. The light picked out a word on its plinth: ανδέρας—Andreas. A common enough Greek name, but what had this man done to arouse such adulation?

Rasche's own torch flitted excitedly over the gleaming riches. "It's a fortune!" he said. "It must be worth millions of marks. And those farmers were hiding it from us!"

"Not just from us," Kroll said as he examined some of the items in more detail. The inscriptions upon them were in Greek—*ancient* Greek. "These are thousands of years old." He illuminated a line of carved text beneath the name on the plinth. "It says, 'Servant and friend of the king Alexander' . . . Does it mean Alexander the Great? It must!"

"I'll take your word for it, sir," said Rasche. "I never studied Greek."

"You should always study the past, Obersturmführer," Kroll replied, reading on with growing intrigue. "It can teach you a lot. Especially when it concerns Alexander the Great. He was born near here, near Pella—it was the capital of Macedonia." He stepped back, almost reflective. "Alexander was my childhood hero, actually; he was the greatest military leader in history, never defeated in battle. He'd conquered most of the known world before he was thirty years old. If he'd lived longer, who knows what else he could have accomplished?"

"Sir," Rasche replied, with clear disinterest. He moved to prod at a pile of coins.

"Philistine," Kroll muttered as he read more text. It *was* referring to Alexander the Great, he was sure. "These dates, they're long after Alexander died. But this Andreas, the inscriptions say he knew Alexander personally . . ."

He regarded the statue. The man it portrayed was old, bald-headed with a long beard, yet still with the upright posture of youth. The remaining scuffs of paint on its face were enough to give the impression that it was looking back at him, expression almost challenging. "Andreas, Andreas . . . ," he whispered, searching his memory. The name was connected to Alexander's somehow, but the link was elusive—

Suddenly it came to him.

The rational part of his mind instantly dismissed the thought as ridiculous. It couldn't possibly be true! But . . .

His gaze fell upon something behind the statue. It was a pithos, an earthenware jar as tall as a man and a yard across at its broadest. More Greek text was inscribed upon it. He went to the vessel to read some of it, then stood on tiptoes to examine the wide spout. It had been sealed, black pitch around a silver stopper. The rim was silvered too, as if the jar's interior was lined with the precious metal.

"Silver," he said out loud. However ludicrous it sounded, the connection between Andreas and the Macedonian conqueror had now solidified in his thoughts.

"And gold," said Rasche, coins clinking from his fingers.

"Forget the gold—we may have found something even more valuable." Kroll turned, ignoring his subordinate's look of confusion. "The old man and his family. Bring them down here!"

Rasche shouted an order up the stairs. The surviving members of the Patras clan were quickly hustled into the hidden chamber, their dismay at their secret having been revealed mirrored by the amazement and raw greed on the faces of the Nazis. "Andreas," Kroll said to the patriarch in Greek, indicating the statue. "He is who I think, isn't he? Andreas the cook, from the *Alexander Romance*?"

The defeat and resignation in the old man's voice told Kroll that he was right. "Yes, it is he."

The commander's pointing finger shifted to the pithos. "Then the jar—it really contains what Andreas found in the Kingdom of Darkness?"

Patras's son gave his father a look of alarm. "How could he know?" he whispered. Rasche raised his dagger to the man's throat to warn him to be silent.

Kroll's sneer turned upon the prisoner. "You think we Germans are all uneducated thugs? You need to remember that Greece is no longer the center of civilization. Yes, I know about Andreas, and what he discovered. But I thought it was only a legend, another of the *Romance*'s chapters of fantasy."

"Andreas *wrote* the *Alexander Romance*," Patras replied, a certain pride entering his tone despite his fear. "He hid the truth inside the fantasy." A flick of one hand toward an unimpressive wood-and-metal chest. "A copy of his original is in there."

The urge to open the chest and read the ancient text rose in the Nazi leader, but he restrained it. There were more important answers he needed first. "Why did he hide the truth?"

"So that only someone who believed they were a worthy successor to Alexander could find it."

Rasche's impatience at being shut out of the Greek exchange reached bursting point. "Sir, what are you both talking about? We've found their treasure—what else do we need from them?"

"Information," Kroll told him. "That's how wars are won, not with tanks or bullets. I told you, you should learn from history." He returned to the pithos, signaling for Jaekel to join him. "Open the jar."

"Sir!" Jaekel snapped in reply. He raised his gun, flipping it around ready to smash the stock against the pithos's spout—

Kroll's yell of "No!" and the horrified cry of "*óchi!*" from Patras were simultaneous. "Idiot!" the Nazi growled. "Use your knife, not your gun! Take out the stopper."

The chastened storm trooper slung his weapon and unsheathed his combat knife. Kroll watched as he worked the plug loose, then turned his attention back to the Greeks. The adults all seemed appalled at the prospect of the great jar's opening—or was it apprehension? He looked back at the text upon the pithos. More mentions of Alexander, but from the perspective of history. Andreas may have known the great king, but these words had been written long after his death.

Which meant that if Andreas himself *had* been the author of the *Romance*, the pithos really might contain the stuff of legends . . .

A crackle as Jaekel worked loose a chunk of pitch. He tossed it aside, then jimmied away at the stopper itself. More of the black resin crumbled. A sharp rasp of metal—and the cap moved.

"Careful, now," Kroll warned, but Jaekel had learned his lesson. He used the knife to lever the stopper upward. It was indeed solid silver, but the Nazi leader was now less interested in the metal's value than in what the pithos contained. Waving Jaekel aside, he hopped up onto the statue's plinth to look down into the container.

Water shimmered gently in the torchlight. The jar was almost full to brimming, holding hundreds of gallons, maybe more. He leaned closer, briefly moving the torch away as he adjusted his balance.

The shimmering remained, even without light.

For a moment he thought it was just an afterimage. But the same thing happened when he lowered the torch again to check. "Jaekel, point your light at the floor," he ordered. "Rasche, Gausmann, you too."

The SS troopers obeyed. The chamber became almost fully dark as Kroll flicked off his own light. He looked back at the jar.

The water in the pithos was aglow, sparkling, but not with bubbles: with light.

It was faint, like moonlight reflected from a pond on a misty night, but definitely visible. "What is it, Sturmbannführer?" asked Rasche.

"Wait," said Kroll. He flicked his torch back on and cautiously dipped his little finger into the water.

The resulting sensation made him twitch. "Sturmbannführer!" Rasche said again, with concern. "Are you all right?"

"Yes, yes," Kroll replied, slipping his finger back into the pithos. This time, he was prepared, and did not flinch. His skin tingled, very slightly. The effect was not unlike a mild electric charge.

He withdrew his hand, thinking for a moment. Then

he scooped up some energized water in his palm and raised it toward his mouth—

"That is not for you," said Patras. Kroll looked sharply at him. Even surrounded by SS troopers, his family at gunpoint, the old man's attitude was defiant.

"Who are you to decide?" Kroll demanded in Greek.

"We are the descendants of Andreas—once a humble cook, and later the guardian of the Spring of Immortality. We have protected his shrine for almost two thousand years, and kept his secret from those who think themselves better than the great king. Is that what you believe, German? That you are a worthy successor to Alexander?"

Kroll bristled at the challenge. "The Third Reich will become the greatest empire the world has ever seen, yes."

"But you are not its leader."

"I act in the name of its leader, Adolf Hitler. Therefore I *am* worthy, since Hitler is the greatest leader in all of history." Kroll allowed himself a smug smile, pleased with his own irrefutable logic.

Patras was unimpressed. "You may believe what you wish to believe. But the water is not for you. Andreas first thought to keep it for himself rather than share it with Alexander, and though he soon regretted that decision, by then it was too late."

"Then the water *is* the same as in the *Romance*, yes?"

The old man nodded. "It is."

Kroll felt almost breathless with excitement. He had been right: the gold and silver treasures were nothing compared with the value of the water. "And . . . you know how to find its source?"

A firm shake of the head. "No. This is a shrine to the memory and works of Andreas, marking his birthplace—but it is not his tomb. He is buried at the spring." Another shift in Patras's attitude; now he seemed almost condescending, a schoolmaster looking down upon his pupils. "The path to the spring is hidden, but it begins here. If you truly think you are superior to Alexander, then perhaps you *deserve* to find it."

"Of course I deserve it," Kroll snapped. With that, he

brought up his hand and sipped the water. The faint tingling was stronger upon his tongue. He gulped down the rest. For a moment he felt nothing. Then . . .

"Are you all right, sir?" Rasche again, shining his torch into his commanding officer's face.

Kroll blinked in annoyance. "Get that damn light off me. Yes, I'm fine. I'm . . ." He paused as an odd feeling rose through him—almost *elation*, the tingle swirling through his veins to every part of his body.

"The water—it could be stagnant. Or even poisoned."

"I'm fine," Kroll repeated. The sensation passed, but somehow he knew that something good—something *remarkable*—had just happened to him. And his knowledge of the *Alexander Romance*, a Greek recension of which he had read as a student, suggested what it might be.

He made a decision. "Close the jar," he ordered Jaekel. "Put the stopper back in and find something to seal it with. I don't want to lose a single drop of what's inside."

"What *is* inside, sir?" asked Schneider, who was holding Patras's daughter-in-law and granddaughter. Even in the low light, Kroll noticed that he had wound his fingers into the woman's long dark hair and was slowly stroking the strands.

"Something that will make us very rich. All of us. Now listen. Gausmann, bring down the other men outside—I want the whole unit to hear this."

"What about the prisoners in the truck, sir?" Gausmann asked.

"Execute them. I know you have wanted to since we arrested them; now is your chance."

Gausmann was surprised, but pleased, a cold grin crossing his face as he saluted. "Yes, sir." He hurried up the stairs.

"If I may ask, sir," said Rasche, barely hiding his impatience, "what is this about?"

"It's about a long and rewarding life, Rasche," Kroll told him. He stepped down from the plinth and waited. Muffled gunshots soon came from above.

The prisoners flinched, the little girl beginning to cry.

Schneider slid his fingers into her hair. "Hush now, little one," he said, giving her a snake-like smile. She buried her face against her mother's neck.

The other troopers clattered into the shrine, gazing at the treasures with awe. "Oster, come on," said Kroll, waiting for the last straggler to enter. Then he stepped forward to address his men. "Attention!" All those not holding the Patras family snapped upright. "I want everyone to listen very closely. You've all seen what this room contains. It's full of treasure . . . and we are going to take it." Eyes widened in avaricious delight. "But the gold and silver and jewels are *not* the most valuable things here. The water in that jar"—he gestured toward it—"is worth the most of all. I will explain why this is later, but for now I need to make it clear that no one must know about this outside our unit. *No one.* Either you are with me, or you leave now."

He regarded them silently. He did not expect any departures, and there were none. "Good. Here is what we are going to do. We will close up the cellar and secure this house until we can arrange for the treasure to be transported safely—and quietly—out of the country."

Rasche gave Patras and his family a sidelong glance. "And what about them?"

Kroll stared hard at the old man—who looked back with equal intensity. "You know already. And so do they, I think." He switched to Greek. "We are going to take everything we have found here."

Patras nodded in resignation. "What about my family? Please, they have done nothing. My granddaughter— she is only a child. She at least deserves to live."

The SS commander regarded the girl, then frowned at Schneider, who reluctantly withdrew his hand from her hair. "Very well. You have my word," he told Patras, before speaking again in German: "Take them outside and dispose of them. All of them—including the child."

The troops encircled the prisoners, pushing them to the stairs. Patras spoke to his family, trying to reassure them, but with a leaden fatefulness they quickly understood. All four hugged and kissed the little girl as they were led away.

Rasche watched them go, then turned to Kroll. "Sturmbannführer, I agree that we should take the treasure, but I have to know: What is so important about the water? How can it possibly be more valuable than gold?"

Kroll smiled thinly. "Obersturmführer Rasche, which is more valuable to a person—gold, or their life?"

Rasche was puzzled by the question. "Unless they're a fool, their life, of course."

"Of course. Now answer this: How much gold would you give to live forever?"

"I don't know—a lot, I suppose . . ." He trailed off, staring at the pithos before snapping his gaze back to his commander. "Wait, you think—"

"I *know*," Kroll interrupted. "The moment I drank it, I knew. A long time ago, someone found the secret of immortality." His smile broadened. "And now it belongs to us."

1

Los Angeles

71 Years Later

The Lamborghini Aventador Roadster tore through the intersection, the bright-orange supercar's tires screaming. In its wake, two gleaming black Mercedes SLS AMG sports cars skidded around the corner, their V8 engines snarling like enraged beasts.

The gull-wing passenger door of the lead SLS swung upward. A man, face hidden behind a bandanna, leaned out. The malevolent little MAC-11 machine pistol in his hand barked, vivid spurts of flame longer than the weapon itself gouting from the barrel as he unleashed a spray of automatic fire at the Lamborghini.

The Aventador's driver jerked the steering wheel to the left. The convertible whipped into a lane of oncoming traffic as sparks and dust spat up from the asphalt alongside it. An SUV rushed straight at it—

The driver swept up onto the sidewalk. Pedestrians screamed and leapt for safety. The Mercs continued their pursuit, the second car's gull-wing opening to reveal another masked man . . .

Holding an RPG-7 rocket launcher.

Danger behind—and ahead. The street was blocked by a tanker truck.

No way around it . . .

But there was a way *over* it.

A panel van with a lowered rear ramp was parked at the curb, its interior empty save for some cardboard boxes. The driver swerved back onto the road, aiming his car directly at it—

"And . . . *cut*!"

The Aventador came to a rapid stop. Behind it, both AMGs also slowed, wheeling around ready for the next take.

Nina Wilde, standing beside a camera crane, responded to the action with a dismissive shrug. "Y'know, I don't think they ever got above thirty miles per hour," the redhead complained.

Her husband was rather more impressed. "Oh, come on," said Eddie Chase, eyeing the Lamborghini with distinct automotive lust. "You've got to admit, being on a movie set is pretty cool."

"Yeah, when something's actually happening." They had been on the imitation New York street for over an hour, and this was the first time the cameras had rolled.

Macy Sharif nodded in agreement. "Thank God for trailers," said the younger woman, indicating a large and luxurious mobile home parked at the end of the back lot. "Grant's is kitted out better than his own apartment. And he's got a *really* nice apartment."

"So you like life in Hollywood, then?" Eddie asked with a grin. "Being a model's better than being an archaeologist?" The Englishman glanced sidelong at his wife, the grin becoming more cheeky. "Always thought it must be." She jabbed him with her elbow in response.

"I still *am* an archaeologist," Macy insisted. "I got my degree—yay!—and I'm starting on my master's soon. But . . . yeah," she admitted, smiling, "being a model *was* cool. I'll show you the magazine later. I think you'll like it."

"I'm sure I will," said Eddie.

Nina gave him a teasing look. "You'd better not like it *too* much. You're wearing clothes in it, aren't you, Macy?"

"Of course I am!" she replied.

Nina looked her friend up and down. The dark-haired young Floridian was in cutoff denim shorts and a midriff-baring T-shirt, both garments tight enough to show off her toned figure. "More than you are now?"

A moment's consideration. "Maybe . . ."

The Lamborghini pulled up in front of them and its door scissored open. Grant Thorn climbed out and called to a man in a baseball cap. "How was that, Mikey?"

The director was reviewing various camera angles on a bank of monitors. "Lookin' good, lookin' good . . . yeah, print it."

"And you can see it's really me driving?"

"Yeah, Grant, we can tell it's you."

"Awesome." The tanned actor gave the director a thumbs-up, then embraced Macy, lifting her off her feet and spinning around with a "Hey, babe!" before turning to his guests. "So? What d'you think?"

"That was . . . cool," said Nina politely.

Eddie snorted. "Don't listen to her, she doesn't appreciate action movies."

"Hey! I like *good* action movies," she objected.

"Like mine, huh?" said Grant.

"Er—"

"So what happens next?" Eddie cut in before Nina could offer any film criticism. He gestured at the van. "Hit the ramp, jump over the truck?"

Grant nodded. "You got it, man. And one of the bad guys shoots a rocket, which hits the tanker, and the whole thing blows up while the Lambo's going over it. Boom! Obviously they're not using the real car for that, and the stunt guy's gonna be driving, but I'd totally do it if they'd let me."

Nina looked unconvinced. "Yeah, totally."

"Can't wait to see it," said Eddie.

"Afraid you'll have to, dude," Grant told him, with a slightly condescending chuckle. "It'll take them, like, four hours to set everything up. I'm actually done for the day—the second unit takes over from here."

"Wait, that's your whole day's work?" said Nina. "Driving a car down a fake street for thirty seconds?"

"No, man, I did more than that!" Grant replied, slightly affronted. "I did my in-car close-ups before you guys got here. Mikey wanted the right light so I'd look my best." He turned his head to show off his blandly handsome profile.

"Well, yeah, you definitely need a break after working your arse off like that," said Eddie.

As always, the sarcasm went clean over Grant's perfectly gelled hair. "I know, dude, I know. So, anyway, how are you guys? Macy tells me you're on a big vacation—like a world tour or something?"

"You could say that," Nina replied.

"Cool! Where've you been?"

Eddie started counting off places on his fingers. "So far? Vietnam, Thailand, Australia, Italy, France, Spain, saw my family in England . . . We just started a bit of a West Coast tour here in the States. Did the Grand Canyon and Yellowstone, and after LA we're going on to San Francisco and up to Seattle."

"That's a lot of travel, dude," said Grant, impressed. "So what made you decide to do it? You two are usually total workaholics. Well, *you* are, Nina," he added with a laugh.

She didn't return it. "We just wanted a break," she said quietly. The faint sigh underlying her words attracted a curious look from Macy.

The actor didn't notice, though. "And when did you kick all this off?"

"Two months ago," Eddie told him.

"Two months! Hope you remembered to get all your frequent flier miles!" Grant laughed again. "But while you're in LA, everything's on me, okay? How do you like the limo?"

The movie star had arranged for a stretch limousine to transport the couple around the city—though its styling was not what Nina would have chosen. "It's, ah, fine," she said. "Thanks for organizing it for us. It beats taking cabs everywhere. Or having a rental car."

Eddie huffed. "We could have been cruising around California in a Mustang GT500 convertible, but *nooo* . . ."

"Yeah, I remember how much you like your fast cars, man!" Grant said. "You know, that time you drove me through New York at, like, two hundred miles an hour? It actually helped my acting. When I did *Nitrous 2*, whenever I was driving I just remembered how it felt, Method-style! I got some great reviews for that, so thanks, dude."

Even the star's best reviews tended to feature the word *wooden,* so Eddie didn't want to imagine what his bad ones were like. "Don't you mean *Ni-two-rous*?" he asked, grinning. The predecessor of the movie currently shooting had been given the rather awkward moniker *Ni2rous.*

Grant waved a hand. "Don't get me started, man. Leno *and* Letterman both gave me crap for that when I was promoting it. I don't pick the titles."

"You can't pronounce them either."

"Dude, enough!"

"At least you won't have any problems with this one," said Nina. She indicated a stack of equipment cases, which were labeled simply NITROUS 3.

"Nah, that's just the working title," said Grant. "We're getting a focus group to decide on the coolest option. Oh, hey, what do you think? The two titles we've got are . . ." He paused for dramatic effect. "*Nitrous 3: Overdrive* Or alternatively . . . *Nitrous 3: Maximum Boost* Which one's best?"

"I don't think either of them fully captures the subtle nuances of the series," said Nina, arching an eyebrow.

"Yeah," Eddie agreed. "It should be something more like *Nitrous 3: Tits and Explosions!* With an exclamation mark."

"It's a PG-13, so no boobies, man," Grant said with regret. Macy gave her boyfriend a huffy pout. "I like the exclamation thing, though. I'll suggest that."

"*Nitrous 3: Balderdash,*" Nina added under her breath. "*Nitrous 3: Physics, Schmysics . . .*"

"Anyway," said the actor, "give me five minutes to get changed and we'll go have lunch. There's something I want to talk to you both about."

Husband and wife exchanged looks. "What is it?" Nina asked.

"Spoilers, man," Grant said with a cocky grin as he headed for his trailer. "You'll find out soon."

It was nearer ten minutes than five, but Grant eventually emerged, having changed from his character's costume of ultratight jeans and white T-shirt into a blue Italian suit and a pair of sunglasses. "Very stylish," said Nina approvingly. As much as she loved Eddie, his usual outfit of considerably cheaper and looser T-shirt and jeans, allied with a scuffed black leather jacket, was not exactly high fashion.

"Thanks," Grant replied, beaming. "Thought I oughta look smart if we're talking business."

Another exchange of puzzled glances. "What business?" demanded Eddie.

"I'll tell you soon. Come on, let's take a ride." Walking arm in arm with Macy, Grant led the couple to a golf cart. The actor at the wheel, they drove off.

Nina looked up at the building façades as they cruised past. "It's amazing. They look so real."

"They *are* real," Eddie said with a mocking smile. "They don't do everything with CGI yet."

"You know what I mean. They've done a really good job of distilling New York. I know it's just painted plaster, but it's still quite impressive how realistic it is."

"Hey, if you want to see something from New York that's *really* impressive," Grant piped up, "check this out." He turned at the next intersection, the freestanding four- and five-story mock-up buildings giving way to flatter frontages wrapped around the exterior of a soundstage.

Macy looked over her shoulder at Nina. "You'll love this," she said. "I couldn't believe it when I saw it. It's kinda freaky."

"What is?" Nina asked.

"You'll see," said Grant. The golf cart pulled up at a ramp leading to the soundstage door, outside which was stationed a uniformed security guard. "Hey, my man!"

called the actor as he climbed out. "Showing my friends the set. That cool with you?"

The guard's expression suggested that it wasn't, but within the walls of a film studio, nobody dared challenge the wanderlust of an A-list star. "No problem, Mr. Thorn," he said through his teeth as he proffered a clipboard. "If they'll sign in here, please?"

"Come on, come on," Grant said excitedly. Macy, Nina, and Eddie scribbled their names, then followed him inside.

A strong scent of paint and fresh sawdust greeted them, the *thwack* of someone hammering nails echoing through the cavernous chamber. Before them was a huge wall, a mass of wooden panels supported by metal scaffolding and beams of rough raw pine that stretched almost to the lighting gantry high above. Nina had to tip her head back to take in its whole height. "What is it?"

"You'll know when you see it. Come on, around here." Grant led them along the stage's side, passing several workmen. He waved to them in greeting. "My man! How you doing? Dude, good to see you. You too, guy. Hey, dude."

"You know them all?" Nina asked when they were past.

"Not a one," replied Grant with a shrug. "I do two or three movies a year, and there are, like, six hundred new people working on each of them. Keeps 'em all happy if I say hi, though." He paused at a set of double doors in the great wall. "Okay, this is it. Go on in, Nina."

Intrigued, Nina advanced through the doors, walking into—

"Oh, wow," she gasped.

For a moment, she felt a bizarre sense of dislocation, as if she had traveled over two thousand miles·in a single step. The room she had entered was very familiar: the lobby of the General Assembly building at the United Nations in New York. Three floors of elegantly curved white balconies overlooked the checkerboard floor of the public space, light through the tall ranks of windows opposite reflecting off the gleaming replica of Sputnik suspended overhead.

Only . . . it wasn't quite right. Everything was compacted, squeezed down in scale, and the view of Manhattan outside was frozen in two dimensions. The corridor behind the reception desk that should have led deeper into the building was abruptly truncated by a green curtain. Even the light from outside was subtly wrong, the harsh glare of studio lamps instead of the warmer, more diffuse tones of sunlight.

She looked back at her companions. Eddie appeared impressed by the replica, while Grant and Macy were grinning with anticipation. "So?" said Grant. "You like it?"

"Isn't it cool?" added Macy. "It's just like being in the actual UN!"

"Yeah, it's pretty amazing," Nina replied, turning to take it all in. "It's smaller than the real thing, though."

Grant nodded. "Yeah, they had to squish everything to fit it into the stage. It'll look fine on camera, though. Put the right lens on, and they can make a broom closet look like a ballroom."

"So what happens in here?" asked Eddie. "If it's for *Nitrous 3: Shit Explodes,* I don't suppose you'll be delivering any long speeches about world peace."

"Nah, nothing boring like that, dude," said Grant cheerfully. He pointed toward the main entrance. "I'm gonna smash through there in a Ferrari, then do a drift to knock down the North Koreans shooting at me. Then I run up the stairs after the mad general with the suitcase nuke. We have a big fight, he uses all these darts and guns and crazy shit built into his bionic arm, and I end up hanging from that thing up there."

"That 'thing' is the Foucault pendulum," said Nina icily, glancing at the gold-plated sphere dangling on a long wire above one end of the lobby.

"What, it's part of a clock?"

"No, it's—"

"Thought it was just some cool swinging ball dealie.

Anyway, there's a big electromagnet inside it, so I use it to deflect a bullet he shoots at me—"

Eddie normally let his disbelief be suspended very high when it came to action movies, but the former Special Air Service soldier couldn't let that go unchallenged. "Don't think so, mate. Magnets don't affect bullets."

Grant regarded him uncertainly. "You sure?"

"I've got some experience in that area, so yeah."

"Huh. Wouldn't have thought the writers would get that wrong. I'd better tell 'em—don't want people to think the story's stupid!"

"God forbid," sighed Nina.

"Still, it's a movie, so the rule of cool applies, right? Anyhow, he misses and I swing across and use the magnet to grab his bionic arm so that he's trapped, then I shove the detonator I took out of the nuke inside his arm, and just before I jump to safety I tell him, wait for it . . . 'Know what my favorite book is? A—'"

"*A Farewell to Arms?*" Eddie predicted.

"Yeah, that's right, good guess! And then his arm explodes. Awesome, huh?"

"It's certainly incredible," said Nina, struggling to restrain an eye roll that would have snapped her head back with its sheer momentum. "Although don't take this the wrong way, Grant, but it all sounds kinda . . . far-fetched."

"Nah, it'll be great. The writers know what they're doing."

"The same writers who think bullets are magnetic?" said Eddie, smirking.

Grant considered that, then dismissed the thought. "Anyway, it's cool, huh? It'll look totally like the real thing on film. Hey, maybe we could have the premiere at the real United Nations. You could put in a word, Nina!"

"I'll think about it," she said, having already done just that for the millisecond the suggestion deserved. She walked deeper into the set, looking up at the tiered balconies. The resemblance to the real United Nations building was indeed uncanny . . . enough to trigger an unexpected pang of emotion within her.

A mixture almost of homesickness—the feeling that this was where she should be—and *sadness*. Loss. Until two months earlier, the UN complex had been the focus of her work, her base of operations as an archaeologist with the International Heritage Agency. Now she knew it was unlikely she would ever return. She gazed at the facsimile, lost in reverie.

Footsteps behind brought her back to the present. "I'm going to miss this place," she said quietly, thinking it was Eddie.

It wasn't. "What do you mean?" asked Macy, stopping beside her. Another curious look, this time with concern behind it. "You're just taking a break from work, like a sabbatical . . . aren't you?"

Nina didn't reply, but the silence was broken by Grant. "Okay, dudes. Let's go have lunch. And talk."

His expectant grin told the couple that he had more in mind than social chitchat. "Talk about what?" said Eddie.

Nina glanced at Macy. "Do you know what he's on about?"

She tried to contain a smile. "Some of it. Trust me, you'll be interested."

Still beaming, Grant gestured for the others to follow him back to the golf cart, and they resumed their drive through the lot. "All right, Grant, come on," said Eddie. "What's the big thing you want to talk to us about?"

The actor appeared briefly conflicted. "I kinda wanted to wait until you met my business partner, but . . . ah, okay, whatever. I've started my own production company!"

"Really? Congratulations," said Nina.

"It's called Every Rose Productions," Macy added.

Eddie and Nina exchanged puzzled glances, before getting it. "Because Every Rose has its Thorn, right?" she said.

"You got it!" Grant replied, extremely pleased with himself.

Eddie groaned. "Jesus, I thought *my* puns were bad."

Grant ignored him. "I've done well as an actor, but I want more control, you know? More of a stake in the success. So I teamed up with this guy I've worked with before—you'll meet him at lunch—and we've got some projects up and running."

"What sort of projects?" Eddie asked.

"You ever heard of the Gabriel Payne books?"

"No," said Nina.

"Yeah," Eddie said simultaneously. "I've read some of 'em. Thrillers. They're not bad. Sort of Jack Reacher knockoffs."

"We bought the rights to the series," Grant told them. "I'm gonna play Gabriel Payne. Former Navy SEAL, tormented loner with a dark past who's irresistible to women—it's perfect for me."

Eddie gave the blue-eyed, fair-haired actor a skeptical look. "In the books . . . isn't he *black*?"

"This is Hollywood, man! Things change. If Brits can play Americans, why not this?"

"It's not *quite* the same thing," said Nina in disbelief.

Grant wasn't listening. "So besides that, we've also got *Rev Limit*, which is like *Nitrous* but on bikes—"

"Grant says I can be in it!" said Macy happily.

"Then there's *Taking Liberty*, kind of a *Die Hard* in the Statue of Liberty. And a great comedy called *First Baby*, dunno if I'll be in it or just producing, but it's such an awesome concept. Get this: The wife of the president of the USA dies in childbirth, but her last words to him are that he has to promise to raise their kid just like a normal dad. So he takes the baby to cabinet meetings, changes its diapers on Air Force One, that sort of thing. The script's a scream!"

Nina had no comment, her mouth frozen open. Fortunately, Grant couldn't see her. "I'm sure it'll make a fortune," Eddie said sarcastically on her behalf.

"Yeah, we think so too," Grant went on blithely. "Anyway, here we are."

He brought the cart to a stop outside the art deco commissary building. A line of people, some studio workers and others extras in an assortment of costumes, were waiting at the entrance, but he breezed straight past them, signaling for his guests to follow. "We've got a table in the dining room," he told the maître d' at the doors to one side.

The man nodded obsequiously. "Of course, Mr. Thorn. This way, please."

Eddie glanced at the large, busy cafeteria into which the queue was heading, then said, "How the other half lives," as he, Nina, and Macy followed Grant into a more tranquil and expensively decorated space. Large framed posters of the studio's past successes adorned the walls between the potted palms.

Seated beneath one of the pictures was a heavily tanned little man in his fifties, gray hair cut in a sharp, bristling style that made his head resemble a mahogany-handled shaving brush. He looked up at the new arrivals from behind a pair of oversized sunglasses, then stood to greet them. "Hey, Marv!" said Grant. "This is Nina Wilde and Eddie Chase. And you know Macy already. Nina, Eddie, this is my business partner, Marvin Bronze."

"Good to meetcha," said Marvin with a broad Chicago accent. He extended a walnut-brown hand to Eddie and Nina in turn. "Come on, siddown. Let's eat. And talk."

The five took their places. A waiter was summoned and orders taken, then conversation began in earnest. "So, Mr. Bronze—" Nina started.

"Marvin, Marvin! We're all friends here. Hopefully very good ones by the time we're done."

"So, Marvin . . . what do you want to talk to us about?"

Marvin and Grant swapped glances, Grant grinning with barely contained anticipation. "I want to talk to you about *you*!" said the older man.

"Us?" said Eddie. "What about us?"

"You're big properties!" Marvin proclaimed. "You, Nina, I know a publisher in New York offered you six figures to write a book about all those incredible things you've discovered. Like Atlantis and the vault of what-sisname, the Indian guy."

Nina was startled. "How did you know about that? They haven't announced it publicly, because I don't know how long it'll take to write—and they *definitely* haven't gone public about the money side of it."

He chuckled. "If there's a deal being made that could lead to a movie, Hollywood knows about it. There's only one thing they're short of out here, and that's ideas. They need a constant flow of new ideas for movies. And the best are the ones that come from real life." He leaned toward the couple. "Let me lay it out for you. Your lives would make fantastic movies. A whole series of movies, even. You two have got the potential to become a billion-dollar franchise!"

"Yeah, but who'd play me?" Eddie asked while his wife was temporarily dumbstruck. Grant's smile widened. "What? No! *You* can't bloody play me!"

"Nothing's set yet, dude—but I've been practicing the accent. Check this out." The actor cleared his throat. "Looook art, thurrs a lurd o' turrorists cooomin' o'er that 'ill. Boogeration an' foockry!"

Nina let out an involuntary yelp of laughter. Her husband was less amused. "That's nothing like me! And it's not even *close* to a Yorkshire accent. It's more like . . . I dunno *what* the fuck it's like. A Welsh South African Pakistani Martian, maybe."

"To be fair, honey," said Nina, "you can't do accents either." By the time Grant had realized the implied criticism of his efforts, she had already turned back to Marvin. "So—you want to buy the movie rights to our lives?"

"No, no," he replied, shaking his head. "I want to buy the movie rights to the *book* of your lives. Someone wanted to make a biopic about you, they wouldn't have to pay you a penny. You're both public figures."

"*I'm* not a public figure," Eddie objected.

"Your wife is," Marvin told him, "so you are too. That's how it works, like it or not. But my way makes it official. Gives the movie the seal of authenticity."

"But like I said, I don't know when the book will be finished," said Nina. "Or even if." Again Macy picked up on the resignation in her tone; the younger woman's expression became questioning, but she didn't interrupt. "And to be honest, I'm not entirely comfortable with Hollywood turning what I do into mass entertainment. I mean, it's my work—it's my *life*! And real people have died on my archaeological expeditions, friends of ours. I don't like the idea of moments like that being re-created for people to watch while they're eating popcorn."

"I understand, believe me," said Marvin. "But here's the thing: Like it or not, you *are* famous, and this is the time to capitalize on it ... before someone else does. You know how many scripts with the word *Atlantis* in the title are going around the studios? A dozen at least—and they're all riding on your back. Ancient myths and legends are big right now, and it's entirely because of the stuff you've dug up over the past few years."

"I think they were already big without me. I mean, they've been in the collective consciousness for thousands of years."

"That's just it, though. They've been there in the background, with nobody really paying any attention until you came along." He leaned forward again, hands spread wide. "You know what movies are? They're our modern-day myths and legends. The difference is that they don't evolve over time, they're manufactured, fully formed, like Athena born from the forehead of Zeus." Noticing Nina's surprise, he added with a sly smile: "What, just 'cause I'm a Hollywood producer I can't know my classics? You should see my art collection. I can bore for my country about Dutch Renaissance paintings."

"Oh, he can, man," said Grant, pressing fingers to his temple to suppress a headache-inducing memory.

"People believe in movies," Marvin went on. "And even if what's up on screen is total bullshit, it still gets taken in." His gaze became more intense behind his tinted glasses. "Nina, this is your chance to make sure that the story being told on that screen—your story—is true. What do you say?"

Feeling uncomfortably as though she was being bamboozled by an expert, Nina looked to Eddie for advice, but he could only manage an uncertain shrug. "I'll . . . think about it," she eventually said.

This seemed to satisfy Marvin for the moment; she was sure he would follow up with more persistence before long. "Good, great," he said as the waiter approached with their first courses. "Okay, now let's eat."

2

"That's the Hollywood sign?" said Eddie, disappointed. "It's a bit small, innit?"

He and Nina stood with Macy on Hollywood Boulevard, looking up the flight of stairs beside the Kodak Theatre at the distant landmark, its white letters shimmering in the summer heat. Grant and Marvin had stayed at the studio to attend another meeting. "Well, it is quite a long way away," Nina pointed out.

"I was still expecting something more impressive. I thought it'd be three hundred feet tall with spotlights and animatronic dinosaurs or whatever."

"When I first came here, I thought it'd be bigger too," admitted Macy. "It was kind of a letdown."

"That's Hollywood for you, I suppose," Nina said. "It all looks a lot more spectacular and glamorous on the big screen. Anyway, at least now you can say you've seen it."

Eddie took a photo with his phone, and they headed back toward their waiting limo. "Speaking of the big screen, what did you reckon to all that stuff Marvin was saying?"

"I dunno. I really don't. On the one hand, somebody wants to make a movie about my life. How flattering is *that*? On the other . . ." Nina sighed. "I dread to think what they might do with it."

"Christ, yeah," Eddie agreed. "For a start, Grant playing me? For fuck's sake! Maybe Jason Statham or Tom Hardy, someone like that, I could cope with. But not a bloody Californian surfer dude."

"And who'd play me? Some bimbo with huge fake boobs, probably."

"I'd pay to see that," he said, smirking. Nina slapped his arm.

"Hey, if they make a sequel about finding the Pyramid of Osiris, I could play myself!" Macy chirped.

The smirk widened. "That'll save 'em having to look for a bimbo with huge fake boobs." Nina batted Eddie's arm again; Macy took a moment to work out exactly what he had meant, then followed suit. "Ow."

"Serves you right," Nina told him, before taking his hand as they walked along. "I don't know," she said again. "I have to admit that I'm tempted. And assuming that Marvin was only *partially* bullshitting us rather than totally, it seems like the potential money from a successful movie is astronomical. But would it be selling out? Is it cheapening everything I've worked for?"

Eddie squeezed her hand. "Only you can figure that one out, love. Although the kind of money he was talking about *was* pretty mind blowing, even more than the book deal. You could fund your own expeditions, never mind going through the IHA."

She became downcast. "I won't get to go on them, though, will I?"

Macy suddenly stopped, taking Nina's wrist and pulling her and Eddie to a halt. "Okay, so what's going on?" she demanded. "That's the third time you've said something that sounds as if you're giving up archaeology. I know you, Nina—that'd be like you giving up . . ." She tried to think of a comparison. *"Breathing."*

"I don't really want to talk about it," Nina told her.

The younger woman snorted. "You know that now I totally won't give up asking until you do, right?"

Eddie recognized his wife's growing discomfort and

attempted to change the subject. "Hey, cool!" he cried, looking down at his feet. "I'm standing on William Shatner!" Set into the paving was one of the many pink marble stars along the Hollywood Walk of Fame. "That's made my day."

"Shouldn't you be standing on Clint Eastwood to say that?" said Nina.

"Clint doesn't have a star; I looked it up." He turned and swept an arm back at those they had already passed. "Can you believe that? Clint fucking Eastwood doesn't have a Hollywood star! He was Dirty Harry, the Man with No Name—and he was in my favorite film of all time!"

"Which one?" asked Macy.

"*Where Eagles Dare!* Absolute classic."

"Isn't that the one where he just, like, shoots hundreds of Nazis?"

"Like I said, classic."

"He bought a PlayStation 4 just so he could watch it on Blu-ray," said Nina with humorous despair. They continued back toward Grauman's Chinese Theatre, a short way down the street.

Guessing that Macy had no intention of dropping her line of questioning, Eddie decided to distract her again. "You know what, though? If they do make a movie about us, that means there'll be an Eddie Chase action figure! That'd be pretty cool."

"Yeah, but it'd look like Grant," Macy pointed out.

"What?" He scowled. "Buggeration and fuckery, it would, wouldn't it?"

"I'm also not sure that toy companies would want to make a figure whose catchphrase is *Buggeration and fuckery,*" added his wife.

They reached Grauman's, where their ride was waiting. Nina pursed her lips at the sight. "I know Grant wanted to do something nice for us, but did he have to hire *that*?" Their limousine was a gaudy, chrome-dripping Hummer H2, stretched to almost double its original not-inconsiderable length. "Everyone'll think I'm on my prom night."

"That's your big problem," said Eddie. "You actually give a crap what people think." He took a photo of the iconic cinema. "Okay, that's another one crossed off my list of things to see."

"It's in a great location," said Nina sarcastically. "Directly opposite a Hooters."

Eddie looked across the street at the chain restaurant. "I dunno, seems fine to me. Watch a film, cross the road, get some nosh and ogle girls in tight tops and hot pants . . ." He trailed off as he noticed something else.

"Y'know, most women would consider half the stuff that comes out of your mouth as grounds for divorce," Nina joked, before realizing that his expression had changed. With slight concern—she had seen the look too many times before—she followed his gaze. "What's wrong?"

"That Jeep there," said Eddie. A bright-yellow Jeep Wrangler had stopped at the curb about twenty yards behind them.

"What about it?"

"It's keeping pace with us. It was parked about that far away from the Shat's star, and I'm sure it was on the corner when we were looking at the Hollywood sign."

"You think it's *following* us?" Nina said, dubious.

As if the driver had realized he had been seen, the Jeep suddenly pulled out. Eddie watched it pass, but caught only a glimpse of a young blond man through the tinted windows. It reached the junction with North Orange Drive and turned left, disappearing from sight. "See?" she said. "He's gone."

"For now," said Eddie, still staring after it.

"Oh, come on. Why would anyone be following us around? Unless it was some rival producer to Marvin. I mean, pretty much everybody who's ever had a problem with us is dead. Except for ex-president Dalton, but since he got arrested I'd imagine he has bigger things to worry about than us."

"Yeah, like not dropping the soap in the shower." He tapped on one of the limo's windows.

The driver's door opened, and a young Hispanic man

in a shiny and slightly too tight uniform hopped out. "There you are!" he said, scurrying to open the rear door for them. "Did you see the Hollywood sign?"

"Thanks, Hector," said Nina, climbing inside. "Yes, we did."

"It was so bloody small we had to squint," Eddie added, joining her.

"Yeah, people always think it's bigger than it really is," Hector said. He waited for Macy to get in, then closed the door and returned to his seat. "So where you going next?"

"Rodeo Drive, please," Nina told him.

"Hey, Beverly Hills! You'll like it. Very classy. Very expensive." He put the oversized four-by-four into drive and carefully merged with the traffic.

"Good choice," said Macy. She opened her little Victoria Beckham handbag. "And gee, look! Grant loaned me his credit card."

"Poor bugger," said Eddie. He settled beside Nina on one of the plump scarlet bench seats running the limo's length. "Why do you want to go there anyway?" he asked her. "It's just shops."

Nina retrieved a pamphlet from her own bag. "I don't know if you've noticed, Eddie, but I'm a woman."

"That explains the nice soft curvy bits and the lack of hairy bollocks, then."

She laughed as Macy held in a giggle. "And as a woman, sometimes—not often, as I'm sure you're very happy about, but sometimes—I have the urge to look at things I don't need and can't afford in places I'd never normally go. And since we're in the same city as one of the most ridiculously overpriced shopping streets on the planet, this is one of those times."

"You live in New York!" Eddie hooted. "The IHA is six blocks from Fifth Avenue!"

"That's different. We're on vacation!" She unfolded the pamphlet to reveal a map of Beverly Hills. "Hector, how long will it take to get there?"

"This traffic?" their driver replied. "About twenty-five, thirty minutes."

Nina shook her head. "What is it about Los Angeles?" she asked Macy rhetorically. "No matter where you are, the place you want to go is always a thirty-minute drive away. And there's nothing interesting in between." She flicked a dismissive glance at the low-rise sprawl of office blocks and mini-malls outside.

"Good job we're in here, then," said Eddie. The limo was home to a well-stocked bar. "We don't have to drive, so we might as well get bladdered. You want something?"

"Ehh . . . why not?" Nina had already had two glasses of wine over the long lunch with Grant and Marvin, and briefly considered one of the miniature bottles of Perrier in the glass-fronted fridge . . . but they *were* on vacation. "What have they got?"

"Loads of spirits—tequila, brandy, vodka, rum . . ."

"A bit much for the afternoon. Any wine?"

He took out a chilled bottle of champagne. "This do you?"

"Perfect. Since Grant's paying for it."

Eddie unwrapped the foil, and a loud *pop!* echoed through the limo as he removed the cork. "Whoa, it's got a bit overexcited!" he said as froth gushed onto his hand. Nina hurriedly used a glass to catch it. "Thanks." He filled it for her. "Macy?"

"You are old enough to drink legally, aren't you?" Nina asked teasingly as Macy brought up a glass.

"Yeah!" she huffed. "I'm twenty-one now. Finally!"

Eddie poured a glass for himself, then put the bottle into an ice bucket. "Something to celebrate, then. Cheers!"

"Cheers!" the two women echoed. They all clinked glasses and took sips, though Nina's was by far the largest.

"Ooh, and I've got something else to celebrate," said Macy, retrieving a larger designer tote bag from the back of the cabin. "My photo shoot!" She took out a glossy men's magazine. "Grant knows the editor; he set it up for me. Here, check this out."

"Oooo . . . *kay*," Nina said slowly as she took in the double-page picture. Macy, pouting seductively at the camera, was posing atop a rock before a vivid-orange desert sunset. Her long dark hair had been tied back into a loose ponytail, and she had a gleaming pistol in each hand. The headline read: TRUE-LIFE TOMB RAIDER.

"Is that . . . are you dressed as *Lara Croft*?"

"Pretty good likeness," said Eddie with an approving nod. "You got the tight top and hot pants right, too."

"Thanks!" Macy replied.

Nina had already moved on to the accompanying text, her attention caught by a familiar name. "Hey, this mentions me." She took the magazine from Macy.

"Let's see," said Eddie. "Where . . . oh, there. 'As a student of famous archaeologist Nina Wilde, Macy discovered the long-lost Pyramid of Osiris deep in the Egyptian desert, and later uncovered the legendary El Dorado, City of Gold, hidden in the mountains of Peru. But as our sizzling shoot reveals, she's every bit as sexy as she is smart.'"

"You weren't my student!" Nina objected.

Macy gave an apologetic shrug. "Yeah, I told them that, but I guess they thought it sounded better."

"So what else did they get wrong?" Nina quickly read on, turning the page to reveal a second spread of similarly provocative portraits. " 'With a boyfriend like Hollywood star Grant Thorn and a screen career on the horizon, it would be easy for Macy to take the road to the high life. But the Miami native insists she's keeping her archaeological options open. She's no mere MAW, but a real-life Lara Croft whose future is as exciting as the treasures of the past she digs up . . .' What's a MAW?"

"Model, actress, whatever," said Eddie. "Chuck something out of the window around here and you'll probably hit at least two of 'em."

"Bimbos, basically," Macy added.

Nina was not impressed. "So it's kind of a demeaning term, then."

"Well, the article said I *wasn't* one, so . . ." She shrugged again. "Anyway, what do you think?"

"Very nice," said Eddie with a grin. "I keep asking Nina to get an outfit like that, but she won't have it."

Nina sighed, then turned back to Macy. "Modeling's not exactly my thing, but you obviously enjoyed it, so . . . good for you. And I'm glad that even with these other options opening up for you, you're planning to stick with archaeology."

"I worked really hard to get my degree," said Macy. "I'm not going to let it go to waste."

"You could be a model, archaeologist, whatever," Eddie suggested, grinning.

"Yeah! Actually, Nina, if there are any openings at the IHA, I hope you'll look at my résumé!"

She laughed, but Nina didn't respond in kind. "Macy, I . . ." She gave Eddie a brief look before continuing. "I don't work for the IHA anymore."

The young woman laughed again, but it quickly faded when she realized Nina was serious. "What? Since when?"

"Since two months ago. I resigned. I asked them to keep it quiet because I didn't want to deal with the publicity."

"Oh my God! Why? What happened?"

"Something bad happened to me. I can't tell you too much, because it's classified"—that was not strictly true; Nina had made the decision to keep much of what had transpired a secret even from the IHA itself—"but I was . . . poisoned."

Macy stared at her in horror. "Poisoned? Did—did you see a doctor, get an antidote?"

"There isn't one. Not for this. How much Norse mythology did you study during your degree?"

"The basics: Odin, Thor, those guys," said Macy, confused by the shift of topic.

"Did you learn about eitr?"

"Yeah, it's some sort of primordial poison—" She broke off as she made the connection. "You mean it's *real*?"

"Fucking right it is," Eddie rumbled.

"Yes, it's real," said Nina sadly. "We found it—well, we were trying to stop other people taking control of it. We did, but I got . . . contaminated. Infected. Macy, I'm . . . I'm *dying*."

"Holy Jesus," Macy whispered. "I'm so sorry. When—how long have you got?"

"It could be years," Eddie insisted. "Enough time to find a cure."

"Or it could be weeks," his wife countered.

"I'm not going to believe that until I absolutely don't have any fucking choice."

"I can't believe it either," said Macy. "There's got to be something *somebody* can do."

Nina shook her head. "The Russians were looking for a cure for fifty years, and they didn't find one. I don't think our chances are any better."

"So you're just going to *accept* it? You're going to give up? Is that why you quit the IHA?"

"I'm not giving up," she said firmly. "The reason I quit was so I could do everything else that I wanted to in the time I've got left. You'll probably think it's weird to hear me say this, but there's more to life than archaeology."

"I've been telling you that for years," said Eddie.

"And just this once, you were actually right." The couple swapped faint smiles. "But that's why we've been traveling—so I could see the whole world, not just what's buried under it. And it's also why I'm going to write the book. I want to tell people about everything I've discovered—and also that there were other people involved besides me. The IHA turned me into a kind of media-friendly figurehead, and unfortunately, at times I started to believe my own hype. So I want to set the record straight."

"Does that mean I'll be in it?"

"Do you want to be?"

"Um, let me think . . . *yes*! Duh."

"Good. You deserve to have people know what you did. And in more detail than this." She held up the magazine, then tried to return it to its owner.

"No, no, that one's for you," Macy told her. "I've got plenty more copies. Keep it."

"Ah . . . thanks." Nina put it on the seat. "But yeah, if nothing else, the book will be a kind of legacy." She turned to her husband. "And it'll mean I can take care of you even after I'm gone."

"You're talking about it like you're already dead," said Eddie with grim irritation. An awkward silence followed.

Macy broke it, covering her discomfort with an excess of enthusiasm. "So, uh . . . hey, look, we're in Beverly Hills!" She gestured at a street sign informing those driving along Santa Monica Boulevard that they had just crossed the boundary of the exclusive city-within-a-city. "I definitely want to go to the Chanel shop." She hurriedly drained her glass.

"Drinking and shopping?" said Nina, also keen to change the subject. "Are you sure that's wise?"

"Probably not, but it's more fun than doing it on Amazon." She indicated Nina's map. "I mean, they've got Ferragamo, Fendi, Gucci, and Prada all right next to each other. It's like I've died and gone to heav—like I've, uh . . . found my Mecca?"

"Good catch," Eddie said, with some humor returning.

Macy winced. "Sorry. The whole death thing, probably not what you want to hear right now."

"It's okay," Nina assured her. She polished off her own drink. "How about a refill?"

Eddie reached for the champagne bottle, glancing through the rear window as he did. "Ay up."

"What?"

"Look who's back." He gestured, and Nina turned to see a yellow Jeep in the neighboring lane not far behind them.

"Oh come on, Eddie," she said dismissively. "We're in California—there must be hundreds of Jeeps like that."

"No, it's the same one, I'm sure of it." He regarded the four-by-four with deep suspicion, then looked ahead. The traffic was slowing, flashing orange emergency lights visible a few blocks distant. "Hey, Hector, I want to take a detour—can you go up one of these side streets?"

"Only houses up there, nothing to see," said the chauffeur.

"Just take the next right, will you?"

"For God's sake," said Nina as Hector slowed. "You really think we're being followed?"

"We'll know in a minute." Eddie turned to watch the cars behind as the Hummer swung off the boulevard. The Wrangler cut clumsily across the lanes, arousing an angry honk from another vehicle, and followed. "Told you."

"Maybe he lives down here," Macy offered, though with little conviction.

"Hector, go left," Eddie ordered, seeing an intersection ahead.

Their driver wasn't happy. "That's not a proper street, it's just a back alley."

"Take it anyway."

The limo turned again, brushing a hedge before it straightened out and continued down the narrow lane. The three passengers stared through the rear window. Nothing happened for several seconds . . . then the Jeep reappeared and rounded the corner after them.

"Okay, so he's definitely following us," said Nina, now worried. "What do we do about it?"

"Ask him why," Eddie decided. "Hector, when we get to the end of the alley, go right and park when you can. I want to have words with this arsehole."

"You sure that's a good idea?" Nina asked.

"Well, normally I'd just shoot him and be done with it, but you wouldn't let me bring my gun."

The Hummer reached the next street and made another laborious turn before pulling over in front of a house. A sign at the lawn's edge stated that the property WAS PROTECTED BY STERNHAMMER RAPID ARMED RESPONSE; an elderly man looked up from inspecting some minor blemish on his immaculate grass to glare at the ostentatious vehicle.

Eddie opened the offside door and got out as the Jeep emerged from the alley and, as expected, turned toward him. He held up a hand as it approached.

It stopped behind the H2. A man jumped out. Eddie had been right: it was the same person he had briefly seen earlier. He appeared even younger than Macy, and was quite striking, with angular cheekbones and intense blue eyes.

It was his expression that immediately put the Englishman on alert, though. The youth was agitated, even desperate. He reached back into the Jeep to snatch up a leather satchel, then hurried toward the limo. "Please!" he called. "I must speak to Dr. Wilde at once!" His accent was strongly German.

At the sound of her name, Nina moved to the open door to look out, while her husband stepped forward to intercept the new arrival. "All right, mate," Eddie said. "What's going on? Why were you following us?"

The young man saw Nina. "Dr. Wilde!" he cried. "Dr. Wilde, I must give you this. They must not be allowed to raid Alexander's tomb!"

He tried to slip past Eddie, who blocked him—but his words had already drawn Nina out of the limousine. "What about the tomb?" she said. "Who's 'they'?"

The man fumbled open the satchel, taking out several sheets of paper. "These are their plans—they are going to break into the tomb and steal the statue of Bucephalus. You have to stop them!" He thrust the pages at her.

"I think you need to calm down, mate," Eddie said, making the threat in his voice clear. The youth quailed, but held his ground.

Nina reluctantly took the documents. The handwritten text was in German, a language of which she had only limited understanding, but there was an annotated illustration that she immediately recognized. "How did you get this?"

"What is it?" Macy asked, exiting the Hummer onto the sidewalk.

"It's a plan of Alexander the Great's tomb, in Egypt—and the only places it could have come from are either the Ministry of Antiquities . . . or the IHA." She looked back at the blond man. "What's going on? Who's going to raid the tomb? Eddie, let him past."

Eddie reluctantly stepped aside. "The Oberkommando," said the youth, moving to Nina. "They need the statue to lead them to the Spring of Immortality. They are—"

A shrill of brakes made everyone whirl. A black Cadillac Escalade EXT pickup truck skidded past the Jeep to stop beside the limo. Its front windows were down, revealing a scowling, shaven-headed man with a prominent scar across his right cheek.

He raised his arm—

A flash of steel in the newcomer's hand. *"Gun!"* Eddie yelled. He lunged, shielding Nina as he threw her bodily back into the limo. Macy shrieked and dived over the garden fence.

The automatic boomed three times, the bullets hitting the young man in the chest. Blood splattered over the Hummer's flank from ragged exit wounds. He crumpled to the asphalt.

The attacker hadn't finished, though. The gun came up again, locking on to Nina—and firing.

3

Eddie dived at the Cadillac and seized the assassin's arm, shoving the weapon off target. The Hummer's side window exploded, bullets whapping into the limo's seats and shattering bottles.

The Englishman tried to rip the pistol from the attacker's grip. The scar-faced man kept firing, a stray round hitting the Jeep and exploding its front tire—then the Escalade's engine roared and the pickup surged away up the street. Eddie was dragged along for several yards before self-preservation forced him to let go. He landed heavily, the EXT's rear wheels missing his head by inches as he rolled. The pickup sped away.

Nina ran to him. "Eddie! Jesus, are you okay?"

He sat up, wincing. "I'm fine. What about you?"

"I'm all right, he missed me." She helped him stand. The gunman had decided to flee rather than finish the attempt on her life, the Escalade still powering away. "Who the hell was that?"

"What the *fuck*, man?" Hector screeched, scrambling out of the Hummer and staring at the corpse. "What the fuck?"

"Get back in!" Eddie shouted. "We've got to go after him."

The chauffeur waved his hands. "No, no, man. Are you crazy? I'm not getting shot!"

"Then piss off and let me drive." The Englishman hurried to the limo and shoved him aside. "Macy, stay there," he barked, seeing that the young woman was about to return to the Hummer. The homeowner was already calling an emergency number on his phone. "Nina, you wait with her where it's safe."

"I'm not letting you go without me," she protested, scrambling into the back of the bullet-pocked vehicle.

After three years of marriage, Eddie knew she wasn't going to change her mind. "Okay, then hold on tight." He hopped into the driver's seat, ignoring Hector's objections.

"You're *chasing* him?" Macy called in disbelief.

A distant skirl of tires told him that the Escalade had reached the next intersection and made a high-speed turn. "He's getting away—but if we follow, we can guide the cops to him."

"I don't think a Hummer limo's the best pursuit vehicle," said Nina.

"Grant didn't lend us a Lamborghini, so it'll have to do." Eddie slammed his door, then jammed down the accelerator—and the Hummer leapt forward, leaving Macy and the yelling Hector behind. The stretched H2 still had its original mammoth 6.2-liter engine, and kept its four-wheel drive through the use of an extended driveshaft. "Hey, that's not bad!"

"Yeah, it'll be great—right up until you have to turn a corner," said Nina, taking out her phone. She had dropped the papers, which now swirled in the wind coming through the broken window. The open magazine was also fluttering. A bullet had ripped through the chest of the photo shoot's subject. "Ooh, Macy won't like that."

"Good job she's got more copies." Eddie kept his foot hard down, the speedometer needle surging past fifty. The Cadillac had gone left at the crossroads ahead. He had no idea how the thirty-foot-long SUV would fare around the same turn, but he was about to find out. "Hang on!"

Nina grabbed her seat with one hand, trying to hold the phone to her ear with the other as Eddie braked hard and spun the steering wheel. The limousine lurched, its back end sliding wide through the intersection with a wail of tortured rubber.

For a moment it felt as though the vehicle was about to flip onto its side. Nina shrieked, heels scraping at the carpet—then the limo crashed back down on all four wheels. The champagne bottle was thrown to the floor, spewing froth. The bottles of spirits clashed against one another, more of them smashing and showering their contents across the cabin.

"Nine-one-one emergency," said a faint female voice in her ear as she struggled back upright. "What service do you require?"

"All of them!" she gasped.

Knuckles white as he gripped the wheel, Eddie looked ahead to see that the Escalade had much less of a lead than he'd expected. The next intersection was of the peculiarly American four-way-stop variety. The EXT had been forced to make an emergency halt to avoid ramming into a pink Bentley Continental convertible crossing its path, ending up slewed diagonally across the road. The Yorkshireman accelerated.

Smoke gushed from the Escalade's wheels as the driver saw him coming and jammed down the gas pedal. The big truck clipped the Bentley's front wing as it weaved past. The Continental's driver, a thin blond woman in enormous sunglasses, stopped and clapped both hands to her face with a shriek of horror.

It was a sound that was about to get louder. The Bentley was blocking the line the stretched Hummer needed to follow around the corner. Eddie hammered on the horn as the limo powered toward the crossroads. The woman gawped at him; he waved for her to get clear. "Come on, move!"

Behind him, Nina was through to the police. "No, I don't know where we are!" she told the infuriatingly laid-back dispatcher. "It's—it's a street with palm trees in Beverly Hills!"

"That doesn't narrow it down, ma'am," came the response.

Nina forced back an obscenity—then another escaped her mouth as she looked through the windshield. "Shit! Eddie, we're gonna hit it!"

The blonde finally got the message, one pink stiletto flying off as she scrambled from the Bentley. "Brace yourself!" Eddie warned. He braked as he spun the wheel to follow the Cadillac, the limousine's rear swinging out into an uncontrollable skid—

The Hummer cannoned off the Continental's side, the luxurious convertible acting as a bumper to keep the limo on course. Even braced, Nina was still thrown across the cabin. There was a horrible shrill of steel as the two cars ground against each other, then the H2 was clear.

"God *damn* it, Eddie!" Nina cried as she sat up, senses reeling.

"You okay?" he called.

"Oh, super-fine, thanks! Look, stop this thing before someone gets killed!"

"I'm not letting that arsehole get away." The EXT had opened the gap again. Eddie accelerated. The new street headed south to rejoin Santa Monica Boulevard; at its far end, he saw the flashing orange warning lights he had noticed earlier.

But there was another vehicle much closer that could stop the pursuit. For a moment he thought the approaching Chevrolet Impala was a police car, before seeing the name STERNHAMMER emblazoned across the side and realizing that it belonged to the private security company. It swerved, trying to block the Cadillac's path, but the Escalade rode two wheels up onto the grass verge to get past. The patrol car made a noisy handbrake turn, reversing direction and pursuing.

"Christ!" said Eddie as the man in the Impala's front passenger seat leaned out and took a shot at the EXT. "They weren't kidding about rapid armed response."

Nina was still dealing with the police. "No, I *don't*

know what street we're on now. Just look for the Hummer limo with bullet holes in it!"

"This is LA, ma'am," the dispatcher replied. "I'm afraid that's still not specific enough."

The H2 was not the only vehicle with bullet damage. The security guard fired again, hitting the pickup's tailgate. The assassin responded to the new danger by sending two shots back over his shoulder at the patrol car. One cracked the windshield, the Chevy swerving as its driver flinched. The passenger reacted by unleashing another six angry shots at the Escalade. That confirmed what Eddie already suspected about the private patrolmen—they were trigger-happy show-offs, who had probably been rejected as real cops for exactly that reason.

The driver's voice boomed from a loudspeaker: "Pull over *right now,* dickhead!" The Chevy drew level with the Escalade, the guard taking aim at the truck's front tire—

The EXT veered, slamming side-on against the Impala. The guard jerked back inside just in time to save his arm from being crushed. The collision briefly slowed both vehicles, letting the limo close the gap. The rentacops swept over to the right to overtake on the Cadillac's blind side.

The chase was rapidly approaching the intersection with Santa Monica Boulevard, where multiple lanes of traffic were flowing in both directions. Eddie saw a recovery truck on the street corner, orange strobes pulsing; there had been an accident, a Mini Cooper being winched up the ramp onto its rear bed.

Sunlight flashed on polished metal. An eighteen-wheeler, a long tanker truck, crossed the intersection into the path of the trio of chasing vehicles—

The Impala drew alongside the Escalade again—and the heavy SUV slammed savagely against it.

The force of the collision hurled the patrol car helplessly off course. It hit the back of the Mini, sending the smaller vehicle spinning off the recovery vehicle. The Chevrolet was flipped into a corkscrewing roll off the ramp, scything away a chunk of the tow truck's cab before arcing back down—

It smashed into the tanker's side.

The truck driver stamped on the brakes, his rig juddering to an emergency stop. Fuel gushed from a rent in the gleaming steel. The Escalade, also braking hard, swerved past the trailer's rear with barely an inch to spare as flames burst from the Impala's mangled engine compartment.

A flash of horrified realization told Eddie that no matter how hard he braked or turned, the speeding Hummer would end up embedded in the burning tanker.

That left only one option.

"Hang on!" he yelled as he jammed down the accelerator.

"Eddie!" Nina shrieked, but the limousine was past the point of no return. She threw herself flat on the seat as it shot up the ramp—

The Hummer flew off the end and sailed over the tanker—as it exploded in a searing blast.

Churning flames swallowed the Impala and set the recovery truck ablaze. The fireball boiled skyward in a halo of thick black smoke . . .

Out of which hurtled the Hummer, lancing back to earth like a boxy javelin.

Eddie and Nina screamed as the limo's nose pounded down onto the road—and the entire vehicle bent in half, the extended chassis snapping and ripping open a ragged gap in the floor and lower body.

The flames clinging to the H2's skin rushed hungrily inside. They found the spilled spirits soaking the seats and carpet—and the alcohol caught light.

Nina jerked back, batting at the singed ends of her hair. The German's papers were also on fire. She snatched up the few she could reach in the hope of salvaging some clues to whatever the hell was going on.

But the blaze wasn't the only danger. Sparks and metal fragments spat up at her from the Hummer's ruptured underside. The driveshaft had broken along with the chassis, the jagged end still spinning furiously as it bounced off the asphalt. Apart from a few overstretched cables and pipes under the floor, the vehicle was now held together entirely by its roof, and even that was buckling.

She raised a hand to protect her face from the shards, belatedly realizing that she was still holding her phone. "We just jumped over an exploding gas tanker!" she shouted at the operator. "Is *that* specific enough for you?"

Eddie sat up woozily. As if the impact of landing hadn't been enough, the Hummer's air bag had fired. Even though it had protected him from a potentially fatal collision with the steering wheel, it still felt like a punch from a heavyweight boxer.

A car loomed ahead. He swerved to avoid it, finding that the H2's handling had gotten even worse. A look back to check on Nina revealed why. The limo was still mobile thanks to its four-wheel drive, even if only the front two were still working, but its half-severed rear end was now acting like an anchor as the floor's mangled leading edge scraped along the road.

"Put the fire out!" he cried, looking for the Escalade. Traffic had come to a panicked standstill following the explosion, and the hulking black truck was easy to spot as it headed south.

"Oh, thanks, I would never have thought of that," Nina shot back. She was already searching for an extinguisher, but if there was one, it was stored out of sight. Instead, she yanked open the fridge and pulled out the little Perrier bottles, cracking their tops to pour fizzy water over the flames. It had roughly the same effect as spritzing a forest fire. "The bubbles aren't helping!"

"Then get up here!" Eddie slalomed around stationary cars in pursuit of the Escalade. The street it had taken led into the Beverly Hills shopping district. Sirens sounded in the distance, but he couldn't tell from which direction.

Nina hesitated at the sight of the driveshaft thrashing like an enraged snake, but summoned up her courage and hopped over the widening split in the cabin. The limo creaked alarmingly as her weight shifted to its front half. She climbed over the partition into the seat beside her husband.

Pedestrians gawped as the broken-backed Hummer screeched past in a trail of sparks. Farther down the street, the Escalade had been forced to slow by dawdling traffic. The gunman dealt with the obstruction by swinging into the oncoming lane and ramming head-on into a car, using his truck's sheer muscle to force the smaller vehicle onto the sidewalk.

Other drivers made the sensible choice to clear a path for the madman—which in turn left the way open for the H2 to catch up. Fast. "Oh, you're not!" Nina protested.

"Yeah, I am!" They both braced themselves—

The Hummer plowed into the pickup. The EXT was a hefty vehicle, but the limo was almost twice its weight, sending the Cadillac into a spin that left it nearly perpendicular to its pursuer. Eddie recovered, foot back on the accelerator. If he could ram the truck broadside-on, he might flip it over, ending the chase—

Nina saw movement in the Escalade's cabin. *"Gun!"*

They ducked as the man fired. The windshield burst apart, fragments cascading over them. Eddie tensed, expecting further shots, but instead heard the roar of the Cadillac's V8 as their attacker raced away.

Nina raised her head. A green sign at the corner told her that he had turned down Brighton Way. She remembered the name from her map; it intersected Rodeo Drive. "Don't suppose this would be a good time to bug out and let the cops take care of things?" she asked. A growl from their own vehicle's engine gave her an answer. "No, thought not," she added as Eddie set off after the truck. The severed driveshaft chittered like a pneumatic drill as they rounded the corner, the Hummer's back half now flexing horizontally as well as vertically.

The new road was one-way, with no oncoming traffic, but it was also narrower than the last street. The Escalade swerved wildly to thread between other cars. Blaring the horn, Eddie did the same. Anguished creaks of metal came from the roof behind them. Nina glanced back. "This thing's gonna come apart any minute," she warned. At least the fire was dying down as the alcohol fueling it was consumed.

Eddie didn't reply, eyes fixed on the fleeing pickup. The sirens grew louder—the police were closing in.

No sign of them yet, though. For now, he was the only person who could stop the assassin. Ahead was Rodeo Drive. Traffic waited at the intersection, parked cars on each side blocking any way around. The Cadillac's brake lights flared as it was forced to slow.

This could be his chance. Foot to the floor—

The Escalade swerved abruptly to avoid a small van backing out of an entrance on the right.

Eddie hauled at the wheel, but the crippled Hummer was reluctant to turn. The word CHANEL filled his vision—

The H2 smashed into the van, sending it spinning like a top. Its rear doors burst open, and hundreds of perfume bottles flew out, exploding like scented grenades. Gallons of Chanel No. 5 sluiced over the bifurcated Hummer . . .

And ignited.

Choking and wiping her stinging eyes, Nina heard a deep and very menacing *whoomph* behind her. She turned to see the limo's entire rear end ablaze, the dying flames given a new and highly flammable source of nourishment. "Shit! Eddie, we're on fire! Again!"

Eddie too was gasping for air. Perfume was fine in small doses, but by the gallon it was more like the chemical attack training he had been forced to endure in the army. Blinking away streaming tears, he searched for his quarry. The Escalade had barged a car out of its way to make a skidding left turn down Rodeo Drive. He followed it. Metal shrieked as the H2's flaming back end swung wide, tearing the overstressed roof like paper.

He spun the steering wheel, just barely countering the flailing oversteer in time to stop the limo's trailing half from ripping free. But the vehicle was now held together only by a thread . . .

The engine misfired, sputtering. The fuel line under the floor had finally been severed.

He looked down Rodeo Drive. The Escalade was pulling away. The chase was over.

Wait . . .

Flashing red and blue lights some distance ahead. The police were setting up a roadblock.

The assassin reached another intersection and started to turn, only to swerve sharply back onto his original course as he saw that the cross street was also barricaded. He continued past the junction before braking hard, slewing around on trails of black rubber and lurching to a stop.

"They've trapped him," said Nina. "Okay, you can stop now!"

But Eddie didn't slow. The Escalade's door had opened, the driver jumping out, gun in hand.

He aimed it at the onrushing Hummer—

Nina dropped with a yelp as a bullet shattered what remained of the windshield. Eddie hunched down as more shots clanged against the radiator and engine block. If he turned to escape down the cross street, he would expose the limo's sides to the gunman—and the thin sheet steel was no protection against even a pistol bullet.

Instead, he aimed straight at their attacker.

The man instantly changed tactics, switching his aim to the Hummer's left front wheel as the limo reached the intersection. Two bullets struck the H2's bumper—then a third blew out the tire.

The steering wheel jolted in Eddie's hands. He tried to hold it steady, but the limousine veered at the central divider, where a chromed statue of a human torso stood on a plinth. Instead he yanked the wheel to the left, stamping on the brake to hurl the Hummer into a skid—

The limo hit the plinth side-on and was sliced in half, its burning rear end finally ripping loose and bowling down Rodeo Drive . . .

Straight at the gunman.

The scar-faced man's eyes widened in fear, and he ran—

The flaming wreckage smashed into the Cadillac. Pedestrians fled as gasoline sprayed from the Hummer's ruptured fuel line . . .

Both vehicles exploded, the blast shattering the front windows of the Louis Vuitton and Bulgari stores and setting palm trees ablaze. The cops at the roadblock dropped behind their vehicles as wreckage showered around them. Car alarms wailed, parked Ferraris and Range Rovers reacting in pain to the barrage.

The Hummer's front half ground to a stop at the bottom of the arcing pedestrian boulevard of Via Rodeo. Shoppers and tourists regarded what was left of the smoking limousine with shock and amazement, phones and cameras clicking.

Eddie sat up painfully, a smear of blood from a fresh cut slowly oozing down his forehead. "Ow, fuck . . ." he grunted, adding a wincing "Christ!" as a drip of perfume ran into the wound like an acidic bee sting. "Nina, you okay?"

"I think so." His wife had ended up in the Hummer's foot well. She blinked blearily at him, then sniffed her clothing. "Oh, that's . . . strong."

"Macy won't need to visit the Chanel shop after all—she can just wring out your sleeve." He was about to open the door—then froze.

The assassin had been knocked down by the explosion, but he was still alive, crawling through the licks of flame dotting the street toward a metal object.

"Shit," Eddie gasped. "He's going for his gun. Get out!"

Nina pulled at the door release, but it refused to move. "It's stuck!"

He tried his own door. It too was jammed, the frame twisted. The assassin had almost reached his goal—

"Police! *Freeze!*"

Two uniformed officers emerged from behind a shrapnel-dented SUV, weapons pointed at the crawling man. He looked at them in alarm, then back at the object in front of him . . .

And kept moving, one hand stretching out to grab it.

"I said *freeze*!" one of the cops screamed. "Stop or I fire!"

Eddie saw desperation on the killer's face as he finally clamped his fingers around the gun—only the Englishman now realized it *wasn't* a gun, but some sort of container, a flask—

Four gunshots echoed around the street, both cops opening fire. The man on the ground jerked and twitched, then fell still. Blood pooled around him. One of the cops ran up and fixed his gun on the unmoving figure as his partner kicked the container out of his hand. It *was* a flask, about the size of a paperback book, and looking for all the world like something an alcoholic would keep in his hip pocket.

But the assassin's attempt to retrieve it had cost him his life. Whatever was in the flask, Eddie realized, it was more than mere whiskey or vodka.

Running footsteps caught his attention. He hurriedly raised his hands. "Ay up," he warned Nina as she clambered out of the foot well. "Beverly Hills cops."

More officers rushed to surround the battered limo. Nina regarded the guns pointed at her in alarm. "So much for our vacation," she sighed.

4

"So, ah . . . what are you in here for?"

Nina suspected that the nervous young blonde had wanted to ask the question since being brought into the cell twenty minutes earlier, but something had put her off; possibly the redhead's disheveled appearance, or more likely the overpowering miasma of Chanel No. 5. "Me?" she said. "Take your pick: grand theft auto, reckless endangerment, destruction of property, and vehicular homicide. Oh, and"—she sniffed her sleeve—"air pollution." The girl's mouth slowly dropped open. "What about you?"

"I, uh, tried to take a purse from Versace."

"Riiight." They sat in silence. "Of course, there were mitigating circumstances," Nina eventually said.

The blonde perked up. "Oh, same with me! I don't suppose you could . . . help me think of some?"

Nina was spared from further conversation by the arrival of two cops at the cell door. "Wilde!" one barked. "Nina Wilde. Come with us, please."

The "please" was something new; her status with the Beverly Hills Police Department had apparently been upgraded. Had her phone call finally gotten results? She stood and waited for the cops to unlock the cell, then went with them to an office on a higher floor. A sunset sky was visible beyond the slatted blinds.

Eddie was already there. "Oh, thank Christ," he said as she entered. "You okay?"

"I'm fine," she replied as they embraced. She held him for a long moment, then eased her grip as she realized they had company: two stone-faced men in dark suits. "And you guys are . . . ?"

"Special Agent Daniel Beck of the FBI," said the older of the pair. He gestured to his companion. "This is Agent John S. Petrelli. Dr. Wilde, we're glad you and your husband are okay."

"*We* are, an' all," Eddie told him with a humorless grin as the cops exited. "So, now that Nina's here, maybe you can finally tell us what's going on?"

Beck seemed uncertain himself, which did not fill Nina with confidence. "First, all the charges against you have been dropped. We've been ordered to take you back to New York. A . . . situation has arisen."

"No shit," said Nina impatiently. "A man gets murdered right in front of me, then the killer tries to shoot me too? I'd call that a situation as well."

"Who told you to take us home?" Eddie asked.

"The order came direct from Washington," Petrelli told him. "From the State Department—but it was approved by the White House."

The Englishman turned to his wife. "You must've done a good job with your phone call. Who did you ring?"

"Seretse, at the UN. From what that young guy said just before he got shot, I figured the IHA needed to know. I never imagined Seretse would be able to pull strings all the way up to the White House, though."

"You got better results than me, then."

"Why, who did you call?"

Eddie looked sheepish. "Macy. Only person I could think of in LA."

"What about Grant? Or even Marvin?"

"You've got Marvin's business card, so I didn't have his number. And would you really want Grant with all the paparazzi who'd follow him down here?"

"Good point. Is Macy okay?"

"Yeah, she's fine. A bit shaken up, but seeing someone get killed right in front of you'll do that."

"I know," she agreed gloomily. "I thought I'd left this kind of thing behind me. I'd hoped I had."

"Maybe you should've let more people know you'd left the IHA. That kid might have given his conspiracy theory to someone else. What was in those papers, anyway?"

"Something about the dig in Alexandria. I didn't have time to see much, but he'd definitely gotten inside information—there was a plan of the outer tomb with specific archaeological notations on it." She turned to the FBI agents. "Where are the papers now? Some of them got burned up in the limo, and the cops took the rest from me."

"They've already been taken away for analysis" was Beck's reply. "They'll be brought to you in New York."

The couple exchanged glances. "Okay, what's going on?" Eddie demanded. "We blow up half of Beverly Hills, and then get to walk away as if nothing's happened? You said there was a situation—*what* situation?"

Beck passed a photograph from a manila folder to them. "Is this the man who tried to kill you, Dr. Wilde?"

Nina stared at the picture. Though the printout was new and glossy, it was clearly from an old source, the image a grainy, dirt-specked monochrome.

The face on it was instantly recognizable, however. Glaring into the camera was her would-be assassin, the scar across his face clearly visible. He was younger in the photograph—she guessed it had been taken about fifteen years earlier—but it was definitely the same man. "Yes, it's him."

Eddie nodded in agreement. "That's the ugly bugger, yeah. Who is he?"

"His name is Maximilian Jaekel," said Beck. "There's a standing arrest warrant on him from all international and US law enforcement agencies."

"Why?" Nina asked. "What did he do?"

"He's a wanted war criminal," Petrelli told her. "He

got into the country undetected, but when the Beverly Hills police took fingerprints from his body to check his ID, they were immediately red-flagged."

"So what did he want with me?" Neither agent had an answer.

Eddie looked more closely at the photograph—not at the subject's face, but his clothing. Only part of it was visible, the image cropped near the base of Jaekel's neck, but the top of a dark raised collar still showed. "You said he's a war criminal," he said slowly. "*Which* war?" To Nina, it sounded as if he already knew the answer.

Beck hesitated before replying. "World War Two."

"What?" said Nina, with almost a laugh of disbelief. "The war ended in 1945! This guy was late thirties, forty at most. Someone's made a mistake."

"That's what we thought too, at first," said Beck. "But the fingerprints are a perfect match to the ones on file, and everything else confirms it: dental records, the facial scar—even the SS blood group tattoo on his left arm. The body's already en route to Quantico for further testing, but it looks like the results will be the same." His expression became more grim. "The man who tried to kill you today was a Nazi war criminal . . . and was over ninety years old."

* * *

The flight back to New York brought Nina and Eddie into JFK airport in the early hours of the morning. A black SUV transported them and their FBI minders to the city.

Nina peered at the rising towers of Manhattan as they approached the East River. "I didn't think I'd be back here so soon," she said. Her body was weary, but her eyes never tired of the sight. Even after all her travels, New York was still home.

"Just hope we can get refunds for the flights we'd already booked," Eddie grumbled. They were taking the Queensboro Bridge to 59th Street; the United Nations complex came into view on the far bank, the glass tower of the Secretariat Building alight even in the predawn gloom. "And that we can get right back to what we were doing without any pissing about."

There was a pointedness to his words, but she decided to ignore it. For now. "Is Seretse already at the UN?" she asked Beck.

"He's there now, yeah," the agent replied. "He should be ready to meet you by the time we arrive."

"Good." She leaned back, rereading the file on the mysteriously youthful Maximilian Jaekel. "Did you look at this on the plane?" she asked Eddie.

He nodded. "Nice guy, him and all his SS mates. France, Yugoslavia, Greece; they committed atrocities in all of 'em. Scumbags. Can't believe that most of his unit managed to get away after the war."

"They bribed their way out of being sent to trial, apparently."

A disgusted snort. "There isn't any amount of money you could have paid me to let those Nazi bastards go. If I'd caught them, I would've shot 'em on the spot."

Nina was a firm believer in the principle of "innocent until proven guilty," but in this case, with the benefit of historical hindsight, she could entirely sympathize with the former soldier's viewpoint. "It's a shame someone didn't do that at the time. It would have saved that kid's life. Have you found out anything more about him?" she asked Beck.

"The victim had a US passport under the name Volker Koenig," said Beck, "but it was a fake. An extremely good fake—it held up when he arrived at JFK—but it means we don't even know if that's really his name. Jaekel also had a fake passport, from the same source."

"Koenig came to New York first?"

"And then traveled on to LA, yeah."

"Looking for you," Eddie suggested. The idea did not make Nina any more comfortable.

"Jaekel had been tracking him—we found texts on his phone listing the flights he'd taken," Petrelli noted. "We're trying to identify the sender, but it looks like they came from a burner. All we know is that they originated in Italy."

They continued across the bridge into Manhattan, then headed to the United Nations. Nina expected them to go to the Secretariat Building, home to the offices of both Oswald Seretse and the International Heritage Agency, but instead they stopped outside the much lower sweeping block of the General Assembly. The two FBI agents led the way in.

"Wow," said Nina as she entered, stopping in momentary disorientation. The previous day she had been in a replica of the visitors' lobby on the other side of the continent; now she was in the real thing. "It's like I never left."

"That's what I'm afraid of," Eddie muttered.

Nina was about to ask him exactly what he meant by that when someone called her name. A tall figure in a blue suit strode toward the group. "Oswald!"

"Good morning, Nina," said Oswald Seretse, shaking her hand. The Gambian diplomat, who in addition to his duties at the United Nations was acting as the IHA's interim director following Nina's resignation, was immaculately presented as always, despite signs of sleeplessness around his eyes. "I'm glad to see you again. Although obviously the circumstances are far from ideal."

"You're not kidding," said Eddie. "Hey, Ozzy."

Vexation and amusement fought for dominance of Seretse's expression, the latter just winning out. "Good to see you too, Eddie." The Englishman grinned and shook his hand.

"Late night?" Nina asked.

"There was a Security Council meeting concerning the Iranian nuclear program. As ever, these things do tend to drag on. I had to excuse myself to meet you."

"What happened to us must be a big deal, then," said Eddie.

"It certainly is. If you'll come with me, there's an office where we can discuss matters." He headed back across the lobby.

Eddie looked up at the Foucault pendulum as they followed. "Got to admit, Grant's version of diplomacy is more interesting than the real thing. Even if his writers know fuck-all about how bullets work."

"If you mean 'interesting' in the Chinese proverb sense, then yeah," said Nina. "I'd rather real-life diplomats stuck to sitting at tables talking things out, though."

"I dunno, sometimes you just have to shoot a bugger."

"That would explain the enormous backlog of IHA incident reports prominently featuring your name that I inherited from my predecessors," Seretse said as they reached the security checkpoint. IDs were quickly checked, and they went deeper into the building. "In here."

The windowless room was a secondary conference area, a place for the small print of treaties to be hammered out by functionaries while their masters argued the bigger picture in the far more impressive main hall nearby. "Before we start, Oswald," said Nina, "I want to thank you for acting on my phone call so quickly. If you hadn't gotten the State Department to intervene, God knows how long we would have been stuck in a police cell."

The normally unflappable diplomat looked uncomfortable. "I must make an admission, Nina. I did call the State Department after we spoke in the hope of intervening on your behalf, yes . . . but they still have not replied to me. I suspect that I had little, if anything, to do with your release."

"Then who did?"

"I don't know."

Eddie regarded the FBI agents. "You?"

"We got orders from the top," said Petrelli. "But who gave them . . ." He shrugged.

"Looks like we've got friends in high places," the Englishman mused. "Makes a change."

"So what else do we have?" Nina asked.

Seretse took several files from his briefcase. "I can give you as much as I know so far. First, concerning the apparent threat against the archaeological excavation in Alexandria: Is this the plan you saw in Los Angeles?"

He slid a sheet of paper across to her. Nina recognized it at once as the illustration of the tomb of Alexander the Great that Volker Koenig had thrust upon her. "Yes, although the one I saw had annotations. In German."

"German, eh?" said Eddie, raising an eyebrow. "There's a coincidence."

Seretse took back the plan. "This was sent to me by William Schofield in Egypt. It's the most up-to-date survey of the outer tomb, made in preparation for the opening of the inner chamber two days from now. It has not been released to anyone outside the IHA or the Ministry of State for Antiquities."

"Somebody leaked it, then," said Nina. She knew most of the IHA employees on the dig personally, and couldn't imagine any of them committing such a security breach.

"So it would seem." He opened another file, revealing several sheets of creased paper in protective plastic sleeves. "These are the documents you managed to save after your limousine . . . caught fire and broke in half." The pause was accompanied by a faint sigh, though Nina wasn't sure if it was disbelief at the outrageousness of the situation, or the same kind of *Oh no, not again* resignation that she herself had learned to adopt many years ago. "I had one of the UN's translators read them. What you told me on the phone appears to be correct—they are part of a plan to raid the tomb."

The archaeologist felt a chill. "Have you warned Bill and the others in Egypt?"

"Yes, we did so immediately. Unfortunately"—Seretse leaned back, steepling his hands—"we do not know *how* the raid is to be carried out. There are references to an entrance, but it must have been described on one of the pages that was lost."

"They can't just be planning to walk in through the front door, though," said Eddie. "There's a lot of security, isn't there?"

"Oh, yeah," Nina told him. "One of archaeology's greatest long-lost sites, right in the middle of an Egyptian city? The whole dig's been guarded from the moment the first tunnel was discovered. Half the country's population fancies themselves as freelance relic hunters, especially after all the political upheavals. And by 'freelance relic hunters,' I mean thieves," she added for the benefit of the two agents.

Beck shot her a sardonic smile. "I kind of got the picture."

"I think it wise that we not tell the Egyptian ambassador you said that, Nina," said Seretse. "However, I am sure that Dr. Assad will increase security still further in light of this threat."

"And what about security for Nina?" Eddie asked. "Whoever this lot are and whatever they're planning to do in Egypt, they came over here and tried to kill her too."

"Why, though?" said Nina. "I don't even work for the IHA anymore, so I'm not connected to the dig."

"Perhaps the FBI has some more information," Seretse suggested.

"We might," Beck replied. He opened a file he had been given after landing. "These are the preliminary results of Jaekel's autopsy. We rechecked the fingerprints and other biometrics; they're a match for everything the DoJ's Human Rights and Special Prosecutions Section has on record for him. He and the other surviving members of his unit were processed when they were captured at the end of the war, so we have mug shots, prints, and so on."

He laid out eight photographs in a row on the desk. Jaekel's was the first; the others were equally old and grainy. His finger tapped each one in turn. "Maximilian Jaekel, Garan Oster, Archard Walther, Herman Schneider, Steiner Henkel, Bren Gausmann, Ubel Rasche . . . and the leader, SS-Obersturmbannführer Erich Kroll." The final picture showed a hard-featured man with close-cropped blond hair, a wide, downturned mouth, and intense, malevolent eyes. "They committed war crimes across Europe—slaughtering civilians, murdering prisoners of war, stealing an untold amount of valuables—and Kroll was actually promoted for all of it just before the end."

"So what happened to them?" Nina asked, taking a

closer look at the faces from the past. None looked like anybody she wanted to meet.

"No one knows. After they bribed their way free, they disappeared."

"Until one of them turned up in LA and tried to kill us," said Eddie.

Nina shook her head. "It can't be the same guy. It's just not possible."

"The fingerprints say it's him," said Petrelli.

"Maybe he's a clone," Eddie offered. "Like in *The Boys from Brazil*? There might be a whole army of cloned Nazis goose-stepping around somewhere."

"Be serious, Eddie," sighed Nina.

"We did find something unusual," Beck admitted. "We don't know what it means, though." He took out another picture, this one in color. "The man who shot at you in LA, Jaekel—he died trying to reach this. BHPD thought he was going for a gun and took him down."

The image showed a flat silver flask lying on asphalt. "Yeah, I saw it," said Eddie. "I thought it was a gun too, from the way he was so set on reaching it."

"What was in it?" asked Seretse.

"Water," Petrelli replied, to his listeners' surprise.

"Water?" Nina echoed. "Seriously? You're telling me he was killed because he wouldn't give up his flask of water?"

"He was dying for a drink," Eddie said with a grin. "Dead thirsty."

She held in a groan. "Maybe the flask had some sentimental value."

Beck shook his head. "It's silver, so it's probably worth a few hundred bucks, but we didn't find anything special about it." He paused, as if trying to convince himself of what he was about to say. "What was *in* it, on the other hand . . ."

Eddie regarded him quizzically. "You said it was water."

"It was. But . . . it wasn't *normal* water."

"How so?" Nina asked.

The FBI agent produced a thick document. "I'm a

cop, not a chemist, so I don't understand half of this. But our analysts gave me a cheat sheet." He flicked through the topmost pages. "Here: 'The water sample contains a high level of colloidal silver, at over five hundred parts per million. Such levels run the risk of the user's developing argyria with prolonged consumption, though the initial autopsy report shows no evidence of such a condition in the deceased. In addition, the water was discovered to hold a small electrical charge, though as yet the cause and mechanism for this remains unidentified. Finally, the water was also found to contain molecules of carbon-60, also known as buckminsterfullerene or buckyballs—'"

"You just made that up!" said Eddie. "That's not a real name, surely."

Nina smiled. "Let me tell you about the problems archaeologists have with moronic acid sometime."

"I'm just reading what it says here," said Beck. "Okay, so: 'The concentration of these molecules is far higher than previously discovered in any natural water source, though there is none of the expected purple coloration associated with carbon-60 content. Carbon-60 is believed to have potential for various medical treatments, including inhibition of the HIV virus and antioxidant neutralization of free radicals, but all current research is still experimental.' Like I said, it's not normal water."

"With all that crap floating about in it, it sounds as bad as New York tap water," Eddie joked, before noticing his wife's thoughtful expression. "What?"

"We've seen something like this before," she said. "In Egypt—when Khalid Osir was looking for the strain of yeast that extended the lives of the ancient Egyptian rulers. The yeast we found in the Pyramid of Osiris had very similar properties."

"Life extension?" said Seretse. "You're suggesting that this water may have somehow slowed the aging process of these war criminals?"

"I don't know, but it would explain why this guy"—she indicated Jaekel's picture—"only looked forty rather than ninety."

"What, clones are out, but you're fine with magic water?" Eddie scoffed.

"Yeah," Petrelli agreed. "It sounds pretty far-fetched."

"You're the ones who insisted that the dead guy in LA is a wanted Nazi war criminal," Nina countered. "And the water's not magic—it just has unusual properties. It's not the first time we've encountered something like that."

Her husband's face turned downcast. "Yeah. Some of it pretty recently."

Seeing Seretse's inquisitive gaze—she had not told him the full reason for her resignation from the IHA—Nina quickly moved the subject along. "It'd also explain why Jaekel was so desperate to get the flask, even with cops pointing guns at him. If the water really does have some kind of anti-aging effect, then it would literally be his lifeline."

"But what does it have to do with what happened in Los Angeles?" asked the diplomat. "The murder of the young man, the attempt on your life, and these plans to rob the tomb of Alexander the Great?"

"I don't know, but—holy *crap*!" she gasped as an answer suddenly came to her. It was wild, even crazy, but it made a twisted kind of sense . . .

Seretse and the two FBI men stared at her, startled by the outburst. "Sorry," she said. "But I think I've found a connection!"

"What connection?" said Beck.

"Alexander the Great. As well as all the historical records we have of his achievements, there was also a text called the *Alexander Romance*," she said, mind racing. "In a way, it was the first-ever novel. Parts of it recounted his actual life and conquests in a semi-fictionalized, romanticized way—hence the name—but there were also chapters that were more fantastical. Alexander and his men went on adventures where they encountered strange beasts and monsters, races of giants, centaurs, plant men, that kind of thing. Alexander himself went to the bottom of the ocean in a diving bell and was carried into the sky by eagles, until the gods themselves ordered him to return to earth."

"Now, that's the kind of history book I'd want to read," Eddie said. "Better than boring lists of kings and queens!"

"I have read the *Alexander Romance*," said Seretse. "In the original Greek, of course—I studied it at Cambridge."

"Well, of course," said Nina, a little facetiously. "It loses so much in translation."

He ignored her veiled sarcasm. "As I recall, the most fantastical parts of the story came after the death of King Darius of Persia."

"That's right," she told him. "Alexander defeated Darius's armies, and in the historical accounts secured the Achaemenid Empire before moving on into India. In the *Romance*, Alexander took a detour and headed north to explore the lands around what he thought was an ocean, but is presumably the Caspian Sea, given his route. That's where he encountered all these weird creatures. But the main reason he went there was because he'd heard of a place called the Land of Darkness—which contains the Spring of Immortality."

"Like the Fountain of Youth?" Eddie said skeptically.

"Yes, although there aren't many details, because Alexander never actually found it. What happened was that Alexander's *cook*, Andreas, discovered it by accident—he put a dried fish in a stream to wash it, and the fish came back to life. Andreas drank the springwater himself, and even kept some of it, but was too frightened to tell Alexander what he'd found. By the time he eventually did, the army had moved on, and when they went back, they couldn't find the right spring. The secret of immortality was right there in front of them, but now it's lost forever."

"Sheesh," said Beck. "I bet Alexander wasn't happy about that."

"He wasn't. He had a stone tied around Andreas's neck and threw him into the sea."

"Maybe he just didn't like his cooking," Eddie joked.

"I doubt it was exactly haute cuisine, yeah. But because Andreas was now immortal, he became a spirit. Or so the story goes, at least."

Seretse regarded her thoughtfully. "Could there be *any* truth to it? It would not be the first time you have discovered that a legend was based on fact."

"I don't know," she said. "I mean, without some solid evidence, I'm certainly not going to buy in to the story that there really is a spring that gives you eternal life, even if this guy Jaekel apparently believed it. Was there anything else in those plans that might tell us more?"

He referred to a translation of the German text. "Perhaps. There is a passage here . . . 'According to the relics, the statue of Bucephalus is located in the inner burial chamber. Obtaining the statue intact is our primary objective: it holds the map to the Kingdom of Darkness. We must secure the map before we can find the spring.' Could they mean the Spring of Immortality?"

"Maybe," said Nina. "I don't remember anything about a statue of Bucephalus when I was at the IHA, though. Has anything like that been found in the tomb since then?" Seretse shook his head.

"Who's Bucephalus?" Eddie asked.

"Alexander's horse. He tamed him as a child, and rode him throughout his campaigns. He was so devoted to him that when Bucephalus was stolen by a forest tribe, he ordered his men to cut down every single tree and slaughter every last member of the tribe if he wasn't returned. He got his horse back very quickly."

Eddie's eyes widened. "Not surprised. That's a bloke who really loves his ride."

"There wasn't any sentiment involved," Nina continued. "When Bucephalus was killed in battle, I think against Porus in India, Alexander just found another horse and carried on fighting. Victory mattered more to him than anyone or anything else."

"Seems that Jaekel and his buddies feel the same way," said Beck. "They were willing to gun a man down in broad daylight to stop him from telling you about all of this, Dr. Wilde—and then they tried to kill you too."

"Why, though?" she asked. "This is nothing to do with me anymore."

"But the young man in Los Angeles was specifically looking for you," Seretse pointed out. "He must have been certain that you would help him prevent the raiding of the tomb. And this man Jaekel must also have considered you a threat—you said that he targeted you, again specifically. So it would appear that you are somehow connected, even if you don't know how."

"You could still be in danger," Petrelli warned. "We don't know how many more of these guys are out there. They might try again."

"Well, thanks for brightening my morning," Nina told him, exasperated.

"We must find out what is going on, though," insisted Seretse. "The Egyptian government is extremely concerned about the threat to the dig. Since the IHA is a partner in the excavation, they have asked us to assist in any way we can."

"Wait a minute," Eddie said, suddenly wary. "Who's this 'we'? If you mean me and Nina, we don't work for the IHA anymore, remember?"

"Yes, I know. However, considering the circumstances . . ." Avoiding Eddie's increasingly hostile gaze, the United Nations official faced Nina. "I would like to request your help in investigating these events, and securing the tomb of Alexander the Great from the raiders."

"What?" protested Eddie. "No, no fucking way. We've got better things to do than act as security guards for another bloody hole in the ground."

"Eddie, wait," said Nina.

He rounded on her. "No, you wait! We agreed, okay! We're doing what we're doing for a *reason*, remember, and the last thing you need is to get dragged back into the job that—" He almost blurted out *got you poisoned*. "That you wanted to leave in the first place."

"I didn't *want* to leave," Nina said quietly.

Seretse broke the uncomfortable silence. "If it makes a difference, the request does not come from the Egyptians alone. The State Department has also asked for your help, Nina."

"Oh, well then, how can we fucking refuse?" Eddie said, throwing up his hands.

"If there really are Nazi war criminals still at large, they've got to be found and brought to justice," said Beck. "And speaking strictly off the record, Mr. Chase— not as an FBI agent, but as someone with family who died in the war—I agree with what you said in the car, about the kind of justice these people deserve. If I were in your shoes, I'd do it."

"You're not in my shoes," Eddie snapped. "You don't have a clue about all the shit we've been through. We—"

"Eddie," Nina cut in, still speaking softly. "I've got to do it."

"*What?*"

"Agent Petrelli's right: They might try to take another shot at me. If we go to Egypt, it'll be harder for them to find us."

He stared at her. "No it won't, it'll be bloody *easier*— because you'll be in the same place they're planning to rob!"

"Yes—behind maximum security! You know Dr. Assad; he'll have the ASPS on full alert now that there's a definite threat. You've worked with them, you know they're good at what they do."

"Yeah, they are," Eddie said in a begrudging tone. "Which means they don't need us. We could just head back to the West Coast and stay out of the way until this all gets sorted out."

"They found us in LA," she countered. "Who even knew we were there? But that kid found us—and Jaekel found him." She addressed Seretse. "Oswald, I'm going to say right up front that I don't *want* to do this. Eddie's right: I left the IHA for very good reasons—which I'm not going to go into," she added. "But whatever all this is about—what happened in Los Angeles, this plan to rob Alexander's tomb—somehow, these people think I can stop them. And considering who it seems they are . . ." She gazed at the line of scowling monochromatic faces on the desk. ". . . I'd say it's my duty, as the former head of the IHA, and as a human being, to do just that."

"For fuck's sake," Eddie growled, shaking his head before pointedly looking away from her.

Nina sympathized, but she knew that in his current mood he would not be receptive to any apology. Instead she asked Seretse: "So, what do we do?"

"I can have you flown to Egypt to meet Dr. Assad and his people—"

"First class," she interrupted. "We just got off a long flight; we're not getting straight back on another one and sitting in coach for thirteen hours."

"Very well," said the diplomat reluctantly. "Once you get there, any help you can provide to ensure the safety of the excavation will, I'm sure, be very much appreciated. Then you can go back to what you were doing. Both of you."

Eddie, still fuming, gave no answer beyond a curt nod. "Thank you," said Nina. "Before all that, though, I really want to go home and have a shower."

Seretse's nose twitched. "I didn't want to comment, but . . . Chanel?"

"By the gallon, yeah."

He stood. "I will make the arrangements." He extended his hand. "Welcome back, Nina. Even if it is only temporary."

Eddie rose, turning away from the others as he headed for the exit. "Yeah. Fucking great to be back."

*　*　*

Nina stepped out of the shower, draping herself in a towel. She let it soak up the moisture on her skin, taking in the familiar surroundings of her apartment. It might have been an unwelcome break in the grand tour she and Eddie had planned, but still . . . it was good to be home.

It was also, she was forced to admit, good to be back at work, however unpleasant the circumstances. She wiped condensation from the mirror, looking into her reflection's green eyes. Two months away had recharged her batteries and given her a new sense of perspective—as well as taking her mind off her illness. Two months, traveling with the man she loved, no concerns except those inside her own head.

But now her concerns had become external, in more ways than one. The towel slipped off her right side as she worked it down her body. What she saw there made her pause. Two months of *denial*, of believing that somehow she was different from all the other victims of the black poison from the depths of the earth. That she could carry on as if nothing had changed.

Only now, that was no longer an option.

Another look at the face in the mirror. Strands of damp red hair framed it, cheekbones picked out by the overhead light. Was she more gaunt than before? Had the shadows under her eyes become deeper? Denial returned: No, it was just the unflattering lighting and the effects of jet lag, surely.

Surely . . .

Eddie's voice snapped her back into the present. "Okay, yeah, I'll talk to you again soon," he said as he approached the bathroom. "Thanks for ringing. Bye."

Nina hurriedly pulled the towel tight again as the door opened. "Don't you ever knock?" she said with a smile.

"This from the woman who just wanders in and out while I'm having a dump," he replied. "I never get a chance to read my iPad in peace."

"Maybe if you didn't spend so frickin' long reading it . . ." She glanced at the phone in his hand. "Who was that?"

"Macy. She wanted to check we were okay—and find out what was going on."

"What did you tell her?"

"Most of it."

Nina eyed him. "Are you sure that was wise?"

"I didn't tell her the part about Nazi war criminals hunting for the Fountain of Youth, if that's what you're worried about," he said, tetchy. "I still know how to keep secrets."

"Okay, okay. Is Macy all right?"

"Yeah. A bit pissed off that we left LA without seeing her, but apart from that, she's fine."

"Good. I'm glad nothing happened to her. It's bad enough that we got dragged into this business without our friends getting involved too."

"Speaking of business . . ." His expression became harder. "Are you still definitely wanting to go to Egypt?"

She drew the towel tighter. "Yes, I am."

"For Christ's sake, Nina! It's the exact opposite of what we planned!"

"What am I supposed to do?" she fired back. "Just ignore the fact that someone tried to kill me? Whatever's going on, I've been dragged into it, whether I like it or not! Besides, the inner tomb's going to be opened two days from now. If the Egyptians do that and secure everything without any trouble, then we can come back home and pick up where we left off. For all we know, just the fact that we know about their plan might stop these people from trying."

"Or if they've already gone to so much effort, they might try even harder to get what they're after. They don't need you there, Nina," Eddie insisted. "The world of archaeology doesn't fall apart when you're not in it!"

"It's two days, Eddie. Two days! That's all." Nina waved her hands for emphasis, the towel accidentally slipping away from her body. She quickly yanked it back—but it was too late.

Eddie stared hard at her side, gaze as piercing as an X-ray. "Let me see that." His voice was suddenly, oddly calm.

"There's . . . there's nothing to see," she told him lamely.

"Nina, I'm not fucking blind. Let me look."

Reluctantly, she drew back the towel. Eddie bent down to look at her side. He regarded the pale skin in silence, then let out a heavy sigh. "So when were you planning on telling me?"

"I . . . don't know," she admitted. "I didn't want to worry you."

"You didn't . . ." Another sigh, this time of disbelief and exasperation. "I'm your fucking *husband*, Nina. How could you not tell me?"

Revealed on Nina's flank was a line of ugly lumps, the largest almost half an inch across. They could easily have been mistaken for blisters, or warts—but both Nina and Eddie knew they were far more malevolent. "When did these appear?"

She couldn't meet his eyes, using the excuse of examining the blemishes to look away. "I don't know exactly," she lied. It had been close to two weeks. "The biggest one came out first; it started small, but . . . it's just been growing ever since."

"And you deliberately kept them *hidden* from me? Is that why you suddenly started wearing T-shirts to bed?" She nodded. "For fuck's *sake*! You should have told me!"

Nina looked back at him. "What could you have done about them?"

The simple, quiet question floored him. "About them? Not much," he had to admit. "But I could do things for *you*! Whatever you need, I'll do it."

"You already are, Eddie." She blinked away a tear. "You already are. But . . ."

"But?"

"There's nothing you can do about—about *these*." She jabbed at the lumps with sudden anger. "There's nothing anyone can do, nothing! We both know what's going to happen to me. These things are going to kill me, and I didn't tell you about them because the thing I need most from you is for you not to *worry* for me, and if I think about what's going to happen I get so *mad* because—because—because of all the things I'll never get to *do*! Like having a child—only now we daren't risk it . . ."

"The doctors don't think I can get infected."

"But the baby would be! We already know that . . ."

She broke down, letting the wet towel drop to the floor as she clutched Eddie tightly.

"It's okay, it's okay," he said, wrapping his muscular arms around her.

"It's not, though, is it?" she managed through her sobs.

He choked back tears of his own. "No, it's fucking not. If I hadn't already killed the fuckers who caused all this, I'd kill 'em again! Bastards."

Nina sighed. "Enough people have died already. All that death, and nothing to show for it. We found Valhalla, we found something that had been hidden for over a thousand years, but they burned it down. It's a waste." Anger flared in her once more. "The whole thing's such a *waste*, Eddie! I'm dying, and for what? I found something incredible, and they destroyed it!"

"Yeah, and we also found something horrible, and it's a bloody good job that got destroyed too," he reminded her. "We kept a bunch of arseholes from getting hold of the worst poison on the planet. And we stopped a nuclear war while we were at it."

"Saving the world again, right?" She managed a small, sad laugh.

Eddie made a similar sound of strained amusement. "Wouldn't be the first time. Christ, it wouldn't even be the second time."

"And this is what we get in return?" She felt her naked side again, disgusted by the tumorous excrescences. "This is why I want to go to Egypt," she said, looking back at her husband with renewed determination. "One last job, as the cliché goes. If nothing else, I can help make sure that Alexander's tomb is opened properly. Part of that legacy I talked about."

"What, finding Atlantis and Excalibur and El Dorado and everything else wasn't enough?" There was still an edge behind the words, even though his tone had lightened.

"I just don't like loose ends. Please, Eddie. Let me do this."

He took a deep breath. "Two days?" he finally said. "Two days, and then we're done. Okay?"

"Okay," she promised. "Let me see this through. As you like to say, fight to the end."

Despite his clear reluctance, he nodded. "Fight to the end."

5

Egypt

Nina opened the shutter to squint out of the window of the 747 at the blue Mediterranean below and the sandy shoreline on the horizon. She checked her watch; the flight had taken over twelve hours, yet on the ground it was a full day ahead of when they had left New York. "God, overnight flights always screw me up," she mumbled. "My body clock'll be so out of sync, I'll probably think we're meeting Alexander the Great in person."

Eddie was holding her Kindle. "Good, we can tell him he should be called Alexander the *Dick*."

"You've been reading about him?" Before falling asleep, she had used the ebook reader to refresh her memory of both the *Alexander Romance* and the historical exploits of the ancient leader.

"Yeah. I knew a bit about him—that he was a tactical genius who never lost a battle—but I'd no idea he was such a bloodthirsty arsehole. That story you told me about how he threatened to kill the entire tribe who took his horse; he would've done it, wouldn't he?"

"Yes, he would. Alexander preferred to show mercy to the rulers of the lands he conquered, as it made the transfer of power smoother if it seemed like they were voluntarily submitting to Macedonian rule. When it came to ordinary people, though," she went on with a grim shrug, "he could be completely merci*less*. It took his army months to win the siege of the city of Tyre, and when they finally broke through the walls, Alexander let his soldiers murder every man, woman, and child they found during the first few hours, as a reward for what they'd endured to get in there. After that, anyone suspected of being a defender of the city was crucified, and every surviving civilian was sold into slavery."

"Nice bloke," Eddie said sarcastically. "Doesn't sound much better than someone like Hitler, but he still somehow ended up being called 'the Great.'"

"History's written by the winners," she reminded him. "And Alexander was definitely a winner. He was said to rule 'the entirety of the known world.' Which isn't true, as there were plenty of places the ancient Greeks knew about that he didn't control—he didn't even rule the whole of Greece, for that matter. The Spartans wanted nothing to do with him."

He smiled. "Did they meet him and go, 'This! Is! *Spartaaaaarghhh!*'?" Other passengers in the first-class cabin looked around irritably at the noise.

"Words to that effect, I'm sure. But he still ruled the largest empire in history to that point."

"'Alexander saw the breadth of his domain and wept, for there were no more worlds to conquer.'"

She raised an eyebrow. "Is that from the book?"

"No, *Die Hard*."

"Well, wherever it's from, it's a misquote. The actual one's from Plutarch: 'Is it not worthy of tears that, when the number of worlds is infinite, we have not yet become lords of a single one?' Totally the opposite meaning."

Eddie snorted. "Who are you going to listen to—some old Greek, or Hans fucking Gruber?"

The aircraft's captain spoke over the intercom; they were now only fifteen minutes from Cairo. "Shame we couldn't get a direct flight to Alexandria," said Nina, stretching to make the most of her remaining time in the luxurious reclining seat. "I'm not looking forward to driving a couple of hours through the desert."

Her husband was less bothered by the impending slog. "At least somebody's meeting us at the airport."

* * *

Somebody was—though not anyone they had expected.

"*Macy?*" Nina said, wondering if the Egyptian heat was already affecting her.

It wasn't a mirage. "Hi!" Macy replied, giving the couple a perfect white smile. She was wearing what by her standards were quite modest designer clothes, though some of the locals waiting at the arrivals gate were still shooting disapproving—or lecherous, depending on gender—looks at the amount of tanned olive skin on display. "How was your flight?"

"Uh . . . fine, I guess. What are you *doing* here?"

"Waiting for you," the young woman replied, as if it were self-evident. "I came here to help you!"

"I'm not an invalid," Nina said.

Macy either didn't pick up on her irritation, or chose to ignore it. "My flight got in from LA about an hour ago, so I decided to wait for you. It'll save me catching a bus to Alexandria. Trust me, you do *not* want to spend any length of time on an Egyptian bus."

Nina glowered at Eddie. "How much did you tell her?"

"Nothing!" he protested. "I said you wanted to go to Egypt to sort out the dig, that's all. I didn't say what flight we'd be on or anything."

"Oh, Dr. Assad told me all that," said Macy.

Nina was surprised. "You spoke to Assad?"

"Sure! I phoned him and asked if I could come with you and Eddie. He remembered me from when we discovered the Pyramid of Osiris, so he said yes."

"What—he said it was okay for you to join a high-security dig, just like that?"

Her expression became sweetly evasive. "Okay, well I *might* have let him think that I was still working for the IHA. I didn't say I wasn't, and he didn't ask, so . . ."

Eddie chuckled. "Never mind archaeology, you'll go a long way in Hollywood blagging like that."

"Anyway, once he said yes, I persuaded Grant to pay for my flight. And here I am!"

"Macy, you can't just turn up and waltz into someone else's dig!" Nina spluttered.

"You mean, like when you beat Dr. Berkeley into the Hall of Records under the Sphinx?"

"That was different!"

"Not really. Anyway, what's the harm?" said Macy. "I wanted to make sure you guys are all right, and I'll be able to use this dig as experience for my master's. I mean, you'd rather see me become an archaeologist than a model, wouldn't you?"

The Englishman laughed again. "I saw your Lara Croft photos; no reason you can't do both."

The conversation was interrupted by a call of "Dr. Wilde!" The trio looked around to see a tall, neatly bearded Egyptian in a loose-fitting suit striding toward them.

"Ay up," said Eddie. "Who's this?"

"He doesn't look like an escaped Nazi war criminal, so I'm guessing it's our ride," Nina replied.

The young man reached them and extended a hand. "Dr. Wilde, welcome to Egypt. I am Deyab, from the Antiquities Special Protection Squad; Dr. Assad sent me. I will be your driver while you are in the country. And also your bodyguard," he added in a more conspiratorial tone, lifting his left lapel to reveal a holstered gun concealed beneath.

"Hello," said Nina. "Hopefully we won't need that side of your services."

"I am told you had some trouble recently, so it is good to be prepared." He turned to Eddie. "You must be Mr. Chase."

"I must," said Eddie, shaking hands.

"And you are Miss Sharif, yes?" Deyab went on, addressing Macy. Rather than shake her hand, he raised and kissed it, to her surprise. "Dr. Assad told me to expect you. Welcome to Cairo."

"Well, I'm expected," the faintly blushing Macy said to Nina as Deyab released her hand. "So I guess I'm coming with you after all."

"I guess you are," Nina echoed through a frozen smile.

"Ignore her," said Eddie, winking at Macy. "It's always fun when you're around. So, where's your car?" he asked Deyab.

The Egyptian's comfortable Mercedes C-Class sedan was waiting outside the terminal; the ASPS apparently had immunity to parking restrictions. Luggage was loaded, then they set off for Alexandria.

The drive was tedious, first negotiating the eternally choked roads of Cairo before heading along an increasingly desolate highway, the irrigated farmlands of the Nile delta giving way to barren desert. All four occupants were glad of the Mercedes's air-conditioning. By the time they reached Alexandria, the sun was wallowing toward the rippling horizon. Deyab guided his vehicle through the busy streets of Egypt's second-largest city, bringing them into the heavily built-up downtown area that had been the heart of the ancient port. "This is where the dig is?" Eddie asked dubiously.

"It's underneath all this," Nina explained. "The modern city's literally built on top of the old one. They only found Alexander's tomb by chance when they demolished an old building and started excavations for a new one."

"We *hope* it is Alexander's tomb," Deyab corrected cheerfully. "If it is not, we have gone to a lot of trouble for nothing, eh? But we will find out tomorrow."

"So nobody even knows if it's the real thing?" said Eddie. "Great, it'll probably just turn out to be Imhotep the Seventeenth's latrine or something."

"That'd still be a fascinating find," Nina insisted. She saw his expression. "Yes it *would*! But they're confident it really is the tomb of Alexander the Great, based on what they've discovered in the outer chambers."

"That is why the ASPS are here," said Deyab. "The

stories say Alexander was buried with many great treasures. It is our job to make sure they stay with him!"

He sounded the horn to encourage a dawdling van to
clear his path, then turned the Mercedes down a side
street. The buildings here were squeezed together even
more closely, but there was a prominent gap ahead. Tall
wooden boards and plastic road cones around a space
between apartment blocks marked a building site—but
the armed men in dark paramilitary uniforms showed
that there was more going on than normal construction
work.

Deyab gave another quick blast on the horn, this time
to alert the guards to his arrival. One waved, then rolled
aside a high metal gate. The Egyptian guided the Mercedes through.

The area beyond was roughly square, strewn with
dirt and rubble. Ragged trenches marked where the de-
velopers had begun to dig out foundations for the new
building—but it was a far more carefully excavated section that was the focus of attention. A shelter had been
erected over it, a pair of portable cabins nearby acting as
operations center and security post. More armed men
watched the new arrivals closely.

The car stopped. Deyab got out and spoke briefly to one
of his fellow ASPS, then opened the doors for Nina and
Macy while Eddie emerged from the other side. "Dr. Assad
and Dr. Banna are underground," he told them.

"Dr. Banna?" said Eddie. "You wouldn't like him
when he's angry." Macy giggled.

Nina was puzzled. "What?"

Her husband and the younger woman exchanged mocking looks. "Seriously, Nina?" said Macy. "You've never
heard of the Incredible Hulk?"

"Of course I have!" she replied, adding with a smile:
"I'm married to him."

Eddie feigned modesty, brushing the lapel of his leather
jacket. "Yeah, I am pretty incredible, aren't I? But Banner, Banna, they sound—oh, never bloody mind."

Deyab looked on with bewildered amusement. "This
way," he said, leading them to the shelter. They clomped

down a series of sloping wooden planks to the bottom of the covered pit. A ladder led into a hole in the ground. The floor of a tunnel was about eight feet below, faint inscriptions and images visible on the dust-covered walls.

Nina knew the dig's background from the files she had read while still at the IHA. The construction work had opened up a hole in the ceiling of a long tunnel running at an angle beneath Alexandria's street grid. Archaeologists had since discovered a complex of chambers at its far end, everything found within adding credence to the theory that this was indeed the long-lost tomb of Alexander the Great, but as yet the final barrier—sealing what was believed to be the burial chamber of Alexander himself—had not yet been opened.

That would happen tomorrow . . . assuming all went to plan.

Their Egyptian minder descended the ladder, then gestured for them to follow. Nina went first, taking the opportunity to examine the tunnel as she waited for Macy and Eddie. Lights strung along the wall revealed that in one direction the passage was blocked after about forty feet by rubble where the ceiling had collapsed long ago. In the other, it continued on for some distance until the line of lights dropped out of sight at a set of stairs.

She took a closer look at the wall. Cracks lanced through the surface, but she could still see what was left of the reliefs carved into it. Alexander's name stood out beneath a scene showing a group of men in battle against a far larger force.

The picture's focus was clear: a figure on horseback leading the group of soldiers, sword hand raised high. The Macedonian king had not been one to issue orders from a safe distance behind the lines.

Eddie joined her. "So that's the big man, is it?" he said, before indicating other bas-reliefs along the passage. "And that, and that . . . I can see why they think this is the tomb."

"Yeah, it's fairly compelling evidence," said Nina. Macy reached the bottom of the ladder, and Deyab led the way down the tunnel. "But I know why they're being cautious. Alexandria's riddled with ancient sites, and people have been mistaken about what they've found before. There are even fringe theories that the tomb isn't in Alexandria at all."

"How can you lose a tomb? It's a hole in the ground—it's not like they can go anywhere."

"No, but what's in them can," Macy piped up. "Some of the Egyptian rulers who came after Alexander moved his body to their own seats of power, so they'd look like his legitimate successor."

"That's right," said Nina. "He was supposed to be buried in Macedonia, his homeland, but Ptolemy—one of Alexander's generals, who took control of Egypt after his death—hijacked his body and buried it in Memphis, south of Cairo. Then his son Ptolemy the Second brought it to Alexandria after *he* took power."

Eddie shook his head. "So if Alexander's body was so important, how the hell did they lose track of it?"

"Alexandria hasn't exactly been the most stable place in history. Plenty of wars have been fought over it, and there have been natural disasters too—most of the old city was destroyed at one time or another. The most recent historical reference to the tomb was by Leo Africanus, in the sixteenth century, and even that only seemed to be a marker of its location rather than the tomb itself. The last person we know to have actually gone *into* the tomb was the Roman emperor Caracalla, who died in the third century. So there's kind of a long gap."

They reached the end of the passage, which dropped down a flight of age-worn steps. Deyab called out in Arabic. A reply soon came. "Dr. Assad and Dr. Banna are in here," he told his charges.

Nina, however, was less interested in who they were about to meet than where they were meeting them. "God!" she exclaimed as she reached the foot of the steps. "This is amazing!"

The space they entered was a rectangular room around fifty feet long and thirty wide, its arched ceiling supported by two rows of ornate columns. The walls were decorated with more reliefs depicting the life and conquests of the Macedonian leader. At the far end was a marble tableau, statues kneeling before a larger-than-life figure poised in an eternally heroic stance.

Alexander the Great.

The sculpture was similar to other representations of the king that Nina had seen: waves of thick hair flowing down around a handsome yet hard face with a broad, almost leonine nose. A noticeable change from other statues of Alexander was a greater sense of age—not of the stone, but the subject it had captured. This leader was near the end of his short but eventful life, weariness showing through his commanding presence in contrast with the almost boyish features usually portrayed.

"So that's him?" said Eddie as they passed two armed ASPS stationed on each side of the entrance.

"That's him," Nina replied. "Alexander of Macedon."

"Nice hair, I'll give him that much."

A young Egyptian man with a thin and patchy beard emerged from behind a pillar. "Dr. Wilde?"

"Yes, hi," said Nina, peering past him for the senior archaeologists they were there to meet. "I'm here to see Dr. Assad and Dr. Banna. Can you take us to them?"

The man's eyes widened, and he rose to his full height, affronted. "*I* am Dr. Banna!"

"Really?" she said, surprised. He appeared to be only in his mid-twenties, just a few years older than the recently graduated Macy, and nowhere near old enough to have earned a PhD. "I mean, of course you are," she quickly corrected as his expression of offense deepened.

It did not mollify him. "I should have expected nothing else from the *great* Nina Wilde," he said, the emphasis positively dripping with derision. "Why would you bother to find out who you are meeting? Everyone else is beneath the world's most famous archaeologist! And here you are, swooping in to take credit for someone else's discoveries, as you have done so many times before."

Eddie nudged Nina. "I *said* you wouldn't like him when he's angry."

She held up her hands to the scowling Banna. "Okay,

don't know what I've done to make you so mad, but we seem to have gotten off on the wrong foot. Is there a problem?"

"Oh no, there is no problem at all!" he said, shrugging as his sarcasm threatened to break the top of the scale. "You think I am some intern, some *child,* because I am young, but there is nothing wrong with that. Nor is there anything wrong with the IHA taking control of an Egyptian dig, and there is *especially* nothing wrong with you coming here to feast on the publicity of opening the tomb like some desert vulture!"

"All right, mate, that's enough," said Eddie, stepping forward.

Banna gave him a dismissive glare. "Who are you?"

"I'm her husband. And I'm also the bloke who's going to pop you in the face if you're rude to my wife again."

"I do hope that won't be necessary, Mr. Chase," came a booming voice from behind Banna. Dr. Ismail Assad, wearing dust-caked overalls, stepped into view. "Ubayy is simply full of the fires of youth."

Banna fumed, but under the level gaze of the country's chief archaeologist decided to say nothing more . . . for the moment. "Dr. Assad," Nina said, stepping around Banna to greet him. "It's great to see you again."

"And you too, Dr. Wilde. Mr. Chase as well—I last saw you in Switzerland, I believe? That was an exciting night." His smile widened, a twinkle appearing in his eye as he saw Macy. "And Miss Sharif, welcome back. The discoverer of the Pyramid of Osiris returns to the land of her ancestors!"

"*Co*-discoverer," Nina pointed out. Macy jokingly made a face at her.

Banna spoke sharply in Arabic to Assad, then said to Nina: "This is exactly what I mean! When you are around, no one else is allowed credit. You are like a black hole, except all the light you pull in comes from camera flashes."

By now, Nina had recovered from her initial startlement. "Hey, you listen, Doogie Howser," she said, jabbing a finger at him. "I don't know where you've gotten this idea that I'm some sort of insane publicity hog, but point one: The Egyptian government *asked* the IHA to assist on the dig; it didn't barge in and take over. And point two: I don't even *work* for the IHA anymore! I'm here entirely as a favor, again by request of the Egyptian government. And frankly, right now I'm not in a frame of mind to take crap from anybody. Okay?"

Banna bristled, but Assad intervened smoothly before he could reply. "Perhaps we should go and meet Dr. Schofield, hmm? You can see the final preparations for the opening of the tomb tomorrow."

"Yeah, I think that'd be a good idea," said Eddie.

Macy sidled up to him. "Whoa. She gets scary when she's pissed at someone," she whispered.

"Don't I bloody know it," he replied.

"What was that?" Nina demanded, eyeing the pair.

"Nothing," Eddie said with an innocent face.

Deyab stayed behind as Assad gestured for the others to come with him, heading for an opening in one corner. "This room is the antechamber," he began, his voice becoming oratorical. "Visitors would enter here to pay homage to Alexander. The most important visitors, or those who brought sufficient tribute, would be permitted to go through to the treasury and the burial chamber beyond, to see the body of the king in person." He gestured at the floor as they descended another set of stone steps. "Emperors and pharaohs have trod these very stairs."

"Not for a long time, though," said Nina.

"No indeed. We believe the tomb has been sealed since around 400 CE. There is evidence that a structure was built to mark its original entrance—which we have not yet located, as the tunnel to it is blocked. That would explain how Al-Masudi and other scholars of the Middle Ages could claim to have seen it, but until now, nobody has entered the tomb itself for at least sixteen centuries."

"No wonder the place needs a bit of dusting," said Eddie.

They reached the bottom of the stairs and continued

along a passage, rounding several corners before seeing bright spotlights illuminating a large metal door. A small group of people stood at the obstruction. "You know Bill, of course," the Egyptian said to Nina as they reached them.

"Yeah, I might have met him somewhere before," she replied with a wry smile as she shook the hand of Dr. William Schofield. Her former colleague was now on the short list of candidates to take her place as the permanent director of the IHA.

"Can't think where," Schofield said with a grin of his own. "Nina, hi. Good to see you again—although having heard what happened to you in LA, I'm sorry about the circumstances."

Assad completed the introductions. "And this is Dr. Youssef Habib, my associate from the ministry, and Dr. Dina Rashad." He gestured to a pair of Egyptians, the former a doleful middle-aged man, the latter a plump woman in her thirties with a brightly patterned head scarf over her long black hair.

Nina recognized her name. "Did you write a paper on the tomb of Queen Hetepheres a year or two ago?" she asked.

Rashad smiled, blushing slightly. "Yes, I did. Thank you! I am honored that you would remember it, Dr. Wilde."

"It was a very thought-provoking paper. I always remember things that interest me."

Eddie smirked. "You written anything Nina'd remember?" he asked Banna.

"Eddie," Nina chided.

Banna scowled. "I have written three very highly regarded papers, as a matter of fact. My monograph on the founding of Alexandria is the reason I was put in charge of this dig."

"He is very good," said Assad, adding with a tiny smile, "for a man so young. Now," he went on, before Banna could complain, "will this door be opened tomorrow?"

"I think so," said Schofield. "We've finished checking

the lock with the fiber optics." He nodded toward a laptop and endoscopic camera on a bench.

"The lock is a simple latch," Rashad added. "Once we release it, we should be able to pull the door open."

Assad nodded. "Good, good. So what do you think, Dr. Wilde?"

"Very impressive—and very exciting," she said, examining the door more closely. As in the outer passage, reliefs had been worked into its surface. The figure of Alexander was at the center, standing tall above the supplicants around him. "It'll be an incredible find."

"As long as nobody tries to take it from us," the Egyptian said with dark humor.

"Anyone trying to break in here'd have a job," said Eddie. "The only way in or out's down that long corridor, and you've got, what, a couple of dozen blokes with guns at the top?"

"That many—that you can see," said Assad. "The whole street was being watched, even before this new threat. The ASPS guard the tomb, inside and out, twenty-four hours a day."

Habib spoke up. "This threat, I cannot believe it is serious. You would need an army to break in here! We are worrying about nothing."

"It was serious enough for a man to kill someone to stop them from telling me about it," said Nina. "And serious enough for them to try to kill *me*, even though I'm not even with the IHA anymore."

"Perhaps they did not know that," suggested Rashad. "I did not know you had left until Dr. Assad told me."

Banna faced Nina, radiating both disdain and skepticism. "Dr. Assad also told me what these raiders are supposedly trying to steal. A statue of Bucephalus?"

"That's right," she told him. "We managed to save some of the plans, which say it's their primary objective."

"But we have found no such statue in the outer tomb." He thumped his fist against the imposing bronze barrier. "This door has been closed for centuries. Nobody could know what is inside. And there are no mentions of a statue of Bucephalus in the texts describing the tomb. I know this for a fact; I have read every one of them."

"Then maybe they've got a text you haven't," said Eddie.

He folded his arms. "I doubt that. And why would they want to steal this one statue alone, and ignore the other treasures?"

Nina hesitated before answering, unsure how much she should reveal to the Egyptian archaeologists—and to Macy, for that matter. But she decided that since they could be at risk if the raiders carried out their plan, they had a right to know. "From what we've learned, they think the statue will lead them to the Spring of Immortality."

The revelation produced different reactions from her audience: puzzlement from Macy, surprise from Rashad, a look of uncertainty from Habib. But it was Banna's response that was the most clear and forceful. "*Hra!*" he scoffed in Arabic, drawing a disapproving glare from Assad, before continuing: "You believe the *Alexander Romance*?"

"I don't believe or disbelieve it at this stage," Nina insisted. "The point is, whoever these people are, *they* believe it. And since they're willing to kill for what they believe, I'm taking the possibility seriously. And so should you."

"The *Romance* is fiction, a fairy tale!" said Banna. "It is not even correct on simple historical facts." He searched his memory for an example. "Like the role of Ariobarzanes."

"Who's he?" Eddie asked.

Nina knew the name. "In the *Romance*, he was one of the men who killed Darius, the last ruler of the Persian Empire. Alexander wanted to capture Darius alive, but his own people murdered him first."

"So says the *Romance*," Banna continued. "But according to the actual chroniclers of history, Ariobarzanes was killed by Alexander and his men at the Battle of the Persian Gates, half a year before Darius died!"

"Well, that depends which chronicler you're reading,"

Nina countered. "He was killed in battle, *or* he and his officers surrendered to Alexander, *or* he survived the Persian Gates and was killed while trying to return to Persepolis. Those are all from accepted historical records—but they're also all mutually exclusive."

"But what you are talking about is fantasy, not history. Giant crabs! Invisible men with whips! Six-eyed horses! It is all nonsense—amusing nonsense, yes, it is very entertaining. But it is not true."

"The people who tried to kill Nina obviously think it is," said Macy, defending her friend.

Assad intervened once again. "There is a simple way to find out. When we open the tomb tomorrow, if there is indeed a statue of Bucephalus inside, then perhaps we should give the possibility more thought."

"It would prove nothing," insisted Banna. "I will be surprised if there is *not* a statue of Bucephalus in the burial chamber. Alexander and his horse were almost inseparable." He shook his head. "The world's most famous archaeologist"—the words oozed with disdain—"believes that the Spring of Immortality is real. What is next? Noah's Ark? Pandora's Box?"

"I dunno, maybe Atlantis?" Eddie said sarcastically. "Oh, wait, Nina's found that already. Or Hercules—no, hang on, she found his tomb an' all."

"And the Pyramid of Osiris," Macy added. "And the city of El Dorado, and King Arthur's tomb . . ."

Assad chuckled at the younger Egyptian's growing annoyance. "I think Dr. Wilde has proven her credentials, don't you, Ubayy?"

Scowling, Banna spoke in tight-lipped Arabic to the government official. Assad grudgingly conceded some point, then faced Nina. "You know that I will always listen to you, Dr. Wilde. But Ubayy reminded me that this is his dig; I put him in charge myself! So when the burial chamber is opened—"

"I never wanted to step on anybody's toes," said Nina, raising her hands in conciliation. "My number one concern is to protect a major archaeological site—and my own life, of course! But it looks like you've got everything covered."

"I certainly hope so." Another exchange in Arabic, then Assad checked his watch. "It is getting late, and I'm sure you are tired after such a long journey. I suggest that for now, we leave Dr. Banna and his team to continue their preparations, and return here tomorrow morning to observe as they open the tomb. Deyab will take you to your hotel, and anywhere else you wish to go."

"That sounds good," said Nina, nodding. "I could use something to eat."

"Yeah," Eddie agreed. "Last thing I ate was on the plane, and even in first class it doesn't really count as food."

"You will not have trouble finding a good meal in Alexandria," Assad assured them. "And while you are eating, I am sure you will have much to talk about."

6

"The thing with the *Alexander Romance,*" said Nina, gesticulating with one hand while she stabbed a fork at her plate with the other, "is that it's impossible to know which parts are the original and which were added by later authors. Even the so-called A-text, which is the earliest known complete recension, comes from at least five hundred years after Alexander's death. We don't even know the identity of the original author—it's usually accredited to a figure known as pseudo-Callisthenes, the real Callisthenes being a historian who accompanied Alexander on his campaigns. But Alexander had him executed"—she chopped her fork and the piece of lamb impaled upon it through the air to illustrate—"five years before his own death, and besides, the writing style doesn't match. So we know it wasn't—"

Macy, whose eyes had begun to flicker wearily during the meal, slumped forward in her seat, snapping awake just in time to prevent herself from face-planting into her tahini salad. "Guh! Sorry, it's okay, I was listening," she mumbled apologetically. "What was that about the A-Team?"

Eddie laughed. "Now you know how I feel every time

Nina goes off on one." Deyab, who had eventually been cajoled into joining the group for dinner, tried to hide his amusement.

"It's not my fault if you don't want to pay attention," Nina objected. "But even though the more fantastical elements of the *Romance* aren't included in the A-text, that doesn't necessarily mean they were added later. They could have been excised precisely because they felt out of place in what that particular version's editor considered a serious account of Alexander's life . . . Eddie, you're not funny."

Her husband had lolled back in his chair, tongue hanging from the side of his mouth. He straightened and gave her a devilish grin. "Couldn't resist, love. But seriously, we're knackered after flying halfway around the world. Give the archaeology stuff a break, at least until morning. Once they open the tomb, if they find that horse statue you can tell Banna *I told you so* as much as you like."

"Oh, all right," she said irritably.

Eddie picked up on her mood, but didn't comment on it. "Are you sure you're okay, Macy?" he asked instead.

The younger woman rubbed her eyes. "I'm fine, but . . . yeah, I'm really tired."

"Jet lag and two glasses of wine, not a good mix," Eddie told her. "You should go to bed." He looked out at the street. Darkness had fallen, but figures were still milling on the busy thoroughfare outside the restaurant. "Deyab, will she be okay going back to the hotel by herself?"

"I'll be fine," Macy protested, through a yawn.

The bodyguard was less certain. "It would be better if I went with her. A young woman on her own at night could attract bad attention—especially an American woman. But you have not finished your food yet, and I am supposed to stay with you . . ."

"We'll be all right," Nina assured him. "Take Macy to the hotel."

"You will wait for me here?"

"Yeah, yeah," Eddie said with a nod. "Go on, Macy, we'll see you tomorrow."

With a mixture of reluctance and relief, Macy stood. Deyab accompanied her. "I will be back as fast as I can," he assured them.

"Make sure you wake me up," Macy said over her shoulder. "Don't let them open the tomb without me!"

"I'm sure you'll be there," Nina called out. She waited for the door to close, then added to Eddie: "I doubt I could get rid of her if I tried! Jeez, I couldn't believe it when we got off the plane and she was waiting for us."

"She's keen, I'll give her that," Eddie replied. "Is that why you're in a mood? Because Macy's here?"

"I'm not in a mood." She gulped down the forkful of lamb.

"Yeah, you are. You got all stroppy just now. I didn't want to say anything about it 'cause we had company."

"But now we're on our own, it's fine?"

"See, you're getting stroppy again. What's up?"

"Nothing's up!" Nina insisted. "I was just . . . Okay, I enjoyed getting to talk shop again. It was great to go down into the tomb, even if that kid Banna was a condescending little asshole. How old is he anyway? Twelve?"

"Twenty-six," said Eddie. "I asked Assad."

She was surprised. "Only twenty-six? Wow, he's even younger than I was when I got my PhD. And they put him in charge of a dig this big already? There must be some nepotism there."

"Or maybe he's just really smart as well as being a bell-end. I mean, you were only twenty-eight when you found Atlantis."

"Yeah, and now I'm thirty-four, and . . . and I'm probably not going to see thirty-five." She sighed, a deep expression of gloom. "This is the last archaeological dig I'll ever be involved in. And I've missed it, Eddie. I miss the work. I miss the IHA, and the discovery—and I really miss being able to talk about it with people who actually care."

She put more sharpness than she had intended into

those last words, and Eddie bristled. "Just 'cause I'm not an archaeologist doesn't mean I don't care," he snapped. "I care about it because *you* care. But we agreed, Nina. We were going to do more with however much time you've got left than let you hide in some hole in the ground."

"I'm not hiding! It's what I *do*, Eddie. It's my passion—it's my *life*."

"Your life is more than your bloody work, Nina!" he said, loudly enough to draw the attention of other patrons. "I'm part of your life too, remember? And I want to spend the time we've still got together with *you*, not getting dragged back into working for the IHA or listening to you drone on about Calisthenics the Boring or whatever the fuck his name was."

Nina stood, snapping her fingers to draw a waiter's attention. "Check, please."

"Okay, bad choice of words, I didn't mean 'drone,'" Eddie hurriedly backpedaled, but by now his wife was heading for the door. "Bollocks! Okay, how much was that?" he asked the waiter, fumbling for his wallet and counting out Egyptian banknotes until the man nodded. He handed over the money and hurried after her. "Fuck's sake, I could probably have bought an entire flock of sheep for that. Nina, wait!"

"Not boring you, am I?" she said frostily as he caught up outside.

"No, but you're worrying me. They gave us a bodyguard for a reason, remember?" He surveyed the street. Nobody appeared to be paying the couple any untoward attention, but that didn't mean they weren't being watched. "We should have waited for Deyab."

"I wasn't going to sit around in there until he got back. The atmosphere had suddenly gotten rather unpleasant."

"Okay, okay. I'm sorry, all right? That's not what I meant." They walked on for some distance before he spoke again. "Look, you know I'm not exactly William Shakespeare when it comes to stringing words together—I could have phrased that better."

"No shit," Nina replied.

"But still, you know what I meant. The whole point of us going away and seeing the world—the world *now,* not the one from thousands of years ago—was because we didn't know how much longer we'd have together. And now . . ." He looked mournfully down at her side, where the tumors were hidden beneath her clothing. "It might be less time than we'd thought. And I don't want to waste any of it."

"That's just it, though. I don't think this *is* wasting it. I'm . . . I'm *achieving* something, Eddie," she said. "It's important to me. Maybe I'm not going to go on any more expeditions, and I'm never going to make another find like Atlantis or the Garden of Eden or any of the others. But at least I'll have helped protect someone else's discovery—even if that person is a jerk like Banna." She stopped and faced him, tears glistening in her eyes. "We've been together for six years, Eddie; you must know me fairly well by now."

"I like to think so."

"Then you also know that yes, there *is* more to my life than my work—there's you, for a start. You mean more to me than anything. But ever since my parents died, and even before then, archaeology has been what's *driven* me. It's . . . it's defined me, Eddie. I can't just give it up, any more than you could give up being British. You understand that, don't you?"

He looked back at her, drawing a long breath before answering. "I can understand it, yeah. It doesn't mean I like it or agree with it, though. I want the time we've got to be about *us,* not people who died centuries ago. *You* understand that, right?"

"I do, Eddie. I do. But this . . . It'll be over tomorrow, after they open the burial chamber. One more day, okay? Please? Let me see this last thing through."

Eddie sighed, but reluctantly nodded. "Okay, yeah. One more day."

"Thank you, Eddie. Thank you. I really—" She broke off, sensing a sudden change in his bearing. "What's wrong?"

"We should have waited for Deyab," he said quietly, taking hold of her arm. "Come on, we need to move."

"What is it?" she asked, worried.

"Someone's following us."

"Are you sure?"

"Two blokes. They're not Egyptians. I saw 'em when we came out of the restaurant—they started following us, then stopped when we did."

Fear prickled through Nina's body. "Who are they?"

"Don't know—one young guy, one older one." He looked through the pedestrians at the crawling traffic ahead. "Shit, no taxis. We need to get off this road."

"They wouldn't try anything with so many people around, surely?"

"They did in LA. This alley coming up on the right, we're going down it."

The side street was narrow, and dark. "Are you sure?"

"If they're going to try and kill us, they'll do it wherever we are. At least down here there won't be any civvies in the way."

They turned to enter a trash-strewn warren of alleyways between run-down tenement buildings. The only light came from a few windows on higher floors. "Eddie, I don't like this," said Nina, her fear deepening. "They'll know we've seen them now—and we don't even know if there's a way out of here!"

"We'll get out, even if we have to go through them." He guided her into another passage to the right, looking back as he made the turn. The two men appeared at the end of the side street, having increased their pace to catch up.

"They're definitely after us," he warned Nina. A television blared from an open window somewhere above. "You keep going." He released her arm and pushed her onward.

"What are you doing?" she demanded, ignoring the prompt and turning to see him duck into the shadows beside an overflowing garbage bin.

"I'm going to have words with 'em. Go on, move!"

"Eddie, no! We need to—"

"Go!" With deep reluctance, Nina hurried away into the darkness.

Eddie watched until she turned a corner, then hunched down. Over the sound of the TV he picked out the scuffle of footsteps. Two sets, moving at a brisk jog.

The first man rounded the turn, hesitating as he found that his targets had disappeared. He was ten feet away. Eddie clenched both fists into tight balls, ready to strike.

Whispered words from the leading man to his companion as he caught up, then the former set off again. He reached the bin—

Eddie sprang up, whirling to drive a fist into his pursuer's face.

It didn't connect.

The young man dodged reflexively, snapping sideways to avoid the blow. With all his weight behind the swing, Eddie was suddenly unbalanced, having braced himself for an impact that didn't come. He staggered as he tried to correct for his mistake—

The edge of a palm knifed at the Englishman's throat.

He glimpsed the pale blur rushing at him, but with one arm outstretched and the other thrown back as a counterweight, all he could do to protect his windpipe was jam his chin down hard against his chest. The blow hit his mouth. He tasted blood.

His attacker's hand drew back, then whipped at his face again—

The Yorkshireman twisted, taking a painful blow to his jaw—then, with a roar, charged and tackled his opponent.

Both men crashed against the bin, scattering garbage. Eddie pressed his attack, driving a fist into his assailant's abdomen. It was a hard blow, and even though the other man's muscles were solid as stone, he still grunted in pain. Eddie shoulder-barged him against the wall, pulling back his arm to deliver another punch—

The edge of a boot slammed against his shin, grinding agonizingly down the bone to knock his leg out from under him. Eddie tried to grab his adversary's clothing for support, but it was too late. His knee barked against the ground, and he fell.

The man loomed above him, raising a foot to stamp on his face—

"*Chadal!*"

The descending boot froze an inch from the tip of Eddie's nose before swinging away. The attacker drew back, almost standing at attention. The second of the two pursuers came into view, a faint wash of light from a window above revealing concern on the older man's face.

He reached down. "Mr. Chase, my apologies. Are you okay?"

Eddie glared at him. "Who the fuck are you?"

"A friend—although I can understand why you wouldn't believe me. But trust me, I am on your side. Here, let me help you."

The Yorkshireman ignored the proffered hand and pushed himself upright. "What the fuck's going on?" he demanded, recognizing the man's accent. "You're Israeli?"

"Benjamin Falk." He tipped his head in greeting before indicating his younger companion. "My overzealous associate here is Jared Zane."

"Eddie?" called Nina, peering nervously around the corner. "What's happening? Are you okay?"

Her husband spat out a red glob, forcing himself not to show any discomfort as he straightened his leg and felt a raw pain where Zane's boot had scraped down it. "I'll live."

"Is it safe? Who are these guys?"

"You are quite safe with us, Dr. Wilde," said Falk.

She drew back, disconcerted. "You know who I am?"

"'Course they know who we are," growled Eddie. "They know who *everyone* is. They're from fucking Mossad."

"The Mossad?" Nina echoed. She knew of the Israeli intelligence agency by fearsome reputation, but had never encountered anyone who worked for it; at least not that she had been aware of.

Zane was surprised to have been identified. "How did you know that?"

"That Krav Maga martial arts bollocks you were doing, I've seen it before. I met Mossad agents when I was in the forces. Bunch of arrogant fucking twats."

The young man scowled at him. "What did you say?"

Falk held up a hand. "Jared." Zane's offended frown remained, but he made an effort to lower his hackles. "We should get back to the main street, or your bodyguard might miss you when he returns from escorting Miss Sharif to your hotel."

Nina warily joined her husband as he brushed dirt off his leather jacket. "I guess you really do know who we are. So why are you following us?"

The Israelis started back toward the street. Eddie and Nina followed cautiously. "You encountered a man named Maximilian Jaekel in Los Angeles," said Falk.

"If by 'encountered' you mean 'were shot at by,' then yeah," she replied.

"Jaekel was an escaped Nazi, although I'm sure you already know that," Falk went on. "But the Mossad has an . . . *arrangement* with both Interpol and the American government—the British government too," he added, glancing at Eddie. "The moment his fingerprints were identified, we were alerted. It didn't seem possible—the dead man appeared far too young. But fingerprints do not lie. So my unit was reactivated to investigate."

"*Re*activated?" said Eddie.

Falk nodded. "My current role at the Mossad is irrelevant, but I was formerly in charge of the Criminal Sanctions Unit. The reason the CSU had been deactivated was simple: It had run out of criminals to pursue."

"*War* criminals," said Nina, realizing the unit's true function. "You're Nazi hunters?"

"Yes." They reached the street and the two Israelis stopped under a light, giving Nina and Eddie their first clear view of the pair. Zane was in his mid-twenties, tall and lean in both face and figure, with a neat mane of tight black curls framing his intense features. Falk was a good three decades older, his hair and bristling mustache gone to gray. Despite his age, however, he seemed as fit as his younger companion. "The CSU has not had a field operation in almost seven years—until now. As former head of the unit, I was recalled from my other duties."

"And him?" Eddie asked, jerking a thumb at Zane. "He doesn't look like he'd even have finished school seven years ago."

"I've got personal reasons for wanting to join the CSU for this operation," said Zane, dark eyes regarding the Englishman coldly. "My family comes from Greece, from Macedonia. Most of them were slaughtered by the Nazis. Jaekel was one of the men responsible. If he survived, others from his SS unit may have too. If they did, I want them to see justice."

"Well, can't argue with you on that one."

"So okay, you're hunting for the rest of these Nazis," said Nina. "Then why are you following us around Alexandria? And why did you attack Eddie?"

"He attacked *me*," Zane pointed out brusquely, putting a hand to his stomach where Eddie had punched him.

"We have been observing you ever since you arrived in Egypt," said Falk as the group started walking again. "We knew you were coming, so I decided to keep watch on you. Just in case."

Nina regarded him warily. "Just in case of what?"

"We're their fucking *bait*," Eddie realized. "They think that since one Nazi went after us in LA, another might take a pop at us here—and they want to catch him if he does. That's it, isn't it? That's the only reason you're keeping an eye on us—to see if someone tries to kill us!"

"We would do as much as we could to stop them," Falk said, not exactly reassuring the couple. "But yes, that is why we are here. Whoever Jaekel was working with wants to obtain the horse statue from inside Alexander's tomb, very badly—and they believe you are a threat to their plans. Since you are now here, they may make another attempt—and we will be waiting."

"How did you know about the statue?" Nina demanded, before the answer came to her. "This arrangement you've got with the US government—the Mossad gets access to more than just fingerprints, doesn't it? How high up does it go?" Falk and his partner remained silent, though the former had a faint smile that suggested any level Nina imagined would not be as high as the truth.

Eddie's expression was anything but smiling. "*You* got us out of jail, didn't you? You had words with somebody at the Justice Department, because you knew that if Nina came to Egypt, you'd be able to use her as your fucking canary. And if you knew anything about her at all, you also knew that she *would* come out here." He gave his wife an *I told you so* look, which was not well received.

"Yes, we expedited your release," confirmed Falk amiably. "Ideally, you would never even have known we were here, but unfortunately you chose a restaurant that limited our options for observing you covertly. It's hard to run a surveillance operation with just two people."

Eddie made a sarcastic sound. "Short-staffed, are you? Mossad's murder squads using up all the budget?"

Again Zane bristled at the insult to his organization, but Falk took it in his stride. "Even the Mossad has its limits—although we prefer that our enemies don't realize it. But don't worry. You won't see us again . . . unless we're needed."

"We don't need you," Eddie said firmly. "You want some friendly advice? Fuck off and don't come back."

"Anytime you want to finish what we started, Chase . . . ," rumbled Zane, stepping closer.

Falk sighed and shook his head. "Young men and their machismo! They learn, in time—if they don't get themselves killed first." He spoke to his companion in muted Hebrew, causing Zane to retreat and lower his head, then addressed the couple again. "Anyway, I can see your bodyguard coming back, so we shall leave you in peace. Until we meet again, Dr. Wilde, Mr. Chase." He gave them a cheery wave, then headed away down the street, Zane at his side.

Nina watched them go, still slightly bewildered by

events, then looked around at Deyab's slightly alarmed voice. "Dr. Wilde! You said you would wait at the restaurant."

"Change of plan," Eddie told him. He gave the street's other denizens a cautious once-over, Falk's revelations now weighing on his mind, but nobody showed the remotest interest in the two foreigners. "Did you get Macy back to the hotel?"

"Yes," Deyab assured him. "But you should have waited for me. I could get into trouble for leaving you—"

"It's okay, we won't tell anyone," Nina assured him. "And nothing happened." She noticed that he was staring at the dirt on Eddie's jacket. "Except that Eddie had too much beer and tripped on the sidewalk."

Deyab looked perturbed. "But you only had two drinks."

"Guess I can't take my booze," said Eddie. "Come on, then. Now you've found us, let's go back to the hotel."

"Good idea," said Nina. As they set off, she glanced back for any sign of Falk and Zane, but the two Mossad agents had vanished into the crowd.

7

"So, what's your big problem with the Mossad?" Nina whispered to Eddie.

The pair were in the back of Deyab's Mercedes, Macy up front with their driver. The bodyguard had the radio on, listening to a mix of news and traffic reports, but Nina still kept her voice low. Deyab was, after all, an Egyptian government operative, and while Egypt and Israel had for the most part left behind the conflicts that led to war in 1973, she still didn't want to find out how he would react to the revelation that she and Eddie had been in contact with Israeli agents.

"Don't get me fucking started," Eddie muttered. "They just waltz in and do whatever the fuck they want without giving a damn about how it'll affect anyone else—even their allies. I was on a mission in Iraq where we were supposed to recover an Iraqi chemical weapons specialist—"

"I thought they didn't actually have chemical weapons?"

"They didn't have chemical *WMDs*, that was all bollocks, but they still had some nasty shit left over from the Iran–Iraq War that they could use on a small scale.

But we managed to meet this guy and guarantee his safety, and were about to bring him in—when Mossad fucking assassinated him, right in front of us!"

"My God!" said Nina. "What happened?"

"We were coming out of a house when they popped him with a sniper rifle. Blew his head right off. We went after the shooter—we didn't know who'd done it—and we found these four Israeli tossers chilling out half a mile away, waiting for us. They gave us some code word and told us to pass it on to our command, and when we did, we were told to let them go, just like that."

"Seriously? The Israelis murdered someone the SAS was protecting and got away with it?"

The Englishman made a sound of deep disdain. "Mossad do whatever the hell they want, wherever they want—and the American government looks the other way 'cause the pro-Israel lobby in Washington is so powerful."

Nina was uncomfortable about the turn the conversation had taken. "I'm not disputing what you've just told me, but that sounds . . ." She tried to phrase it in a nonconfrontational way, but struggled to find any suitable term. "Kind of like anti-Semitic paranoia," she was forced to finish.

"Yeah, and that's what happens," Eddie said, frowning. "You say Israel's done anything bad, you're immediately accused of being anti-Semitic. But a government isn't a race or a religion—and neither's an intelligence agency." He leaned deeper into the seat. "Not that I'm saying *everything* they do is bad. Having a Nazi-hunting unit is something I can totally get into."

Macy glanced over her shoulder. "What can you get into?"

"A big woolly sweater with a cat on it," he told her, instantly switching his expression to a grin.

She gave him an uncertain look. "Okay, sometimes I just don't understand British humor."

"You're not the only one," Nina assured her, relieved that the awkward moment had passed.

The excavation site came into view ahead. "We are here," Deyab announced.

"Looks like there's even more security than yesterday," said Nina.

"We are taking no chances," said the Egyptian as he approached the gate. Unlike the previous day, the Mercedes was waved to a stop. He pressed the trunk release so one of the ASPS could check the back of the car, while another cast a stern eye over its occupants before waving to a comrade. The gate was opened; Deyab waited for the trunk to be slammed shut, then drove into the compound.

More ASPS stood watch inside. Deyab pulled up. "There is Dr. Assad."

The Egyptian official was talking to Habib outside the cabins. "Ah, good morning!" he called as the visitors emerged from the car. "This is a very exciting day."

"It is," Nina said, greeting him. "Thank you for letting me be a part of it. A small, non-interfering part," she added as Banna came out of the cabin. The bearded young man gave her a dirty look, but said nothing to the new arrivals, heading straight for the shelter.

"Dr. Schofield and Dr. Rashad are already inside," Assad told her. "Did you have a good evening?"

"It was . . . interesting," she said as they moved toward the entrance. "But yes, we did, thanks."

"Good, good. There is no hospitality like Egyptian hospitality!" He reached the ladder. Banna had already descended, but did not wait for the others, instead stalking away down the tunnel. "Mind your step."

Assad went down first, Nina following. "How long before they open the door?" she asked him.

He glanced after the retreating Banna. "Not long. Ubayy was working down here very early this morning. If I had not told him to wait, I am sure he would have opened it himself by now!"

"The lad's keen," said Eddie.

"It is how he has reached such heights so quickly. I am sure you were once the same, Dr. Wilde."

"It seems such a long time ago, I can hardly remember," Nina replied wistfully.

"Ha! Wait until you get to my age," said Assad as they started walking. "*That* is when the achievements of your youth seem so far away!"

Eddie gave his wife a reassuring squeeze as he saw her downcast expression, then they followed the Egyptian through the antechamber and around the twisting passage to the great bronze door. Schofield and Rashad were already talking with Banna. More equipment had been set up since the previous day; a motorized winch was braced by scaffolding against the floor and ceiling, and the dig's leader was fussing with a contraption mounted on a bench.

"Christ," said Eddie. "Looks like it was built by Professor Branestawm."

Nina didn't get the reference, guessing that it was excessively British, but it was easy to guess what he meant from the device's makeshift appearance. A set of thin steel arms rose from a geared mechanism with a crank handle and entered a narrow slot at one side of the barrier, the endoscopic camera's flexible lens tube also disappearing inside the opening. The monitor screen had been duct-taped to the door beside the apparatus. "That'll open the lock?"

"It will," said Banna, not deigning to look around at her. "Unlike some people, who gain entry to sealed archaeological sites by crashing helicopters into them, I do not want to risk damaging the tomb's contents."

"Hey, that only happened once," Eddie objected. "Or was it twice? You lose track after a while."

"Thanks for the help, hon," said Nina with a thin smile. "Bill, hi. Seems you're all set here."

"Just about," Schofield replied as he finished typing on a laptop. "I know that thing looks a bit Rube Goldberg, but it should lift the latch. Once that's done, we can start winching the door open."

"How much does it weigh?" Macy asked.

"We reckon about two tons. I wouldn't stand in the way while it's swinging open!" The sandy-haired man chuckled, then became more serious. "Have you heard anything more about this potential threat?" he asked Nina. "Are we still safe to proceed?"

"We *will* open the burial chamber this morning," Banna insisted before she could answer. "The site is like a fortress now. Nobody could possibly get in."

"Let's hope nobody even tries," said Eddie. "Sooner whatever's inside is safe, the sooner we can go home and get on with our lives again."

Nina decided to ignore his pointed remark, settling instead for watching the final preparations. Banna tweaked his elaborate lock pick for a good fifteen minutes, examining the endoscopic display with laser-beam intensity until he was satisfied. He spoke in Arabic to Assad, Rashad, and Habib, then added as an afterthought: "I am ready."

"Don't let me hold you up," said Nina.

"I won't." He looked at Schofield, who had set up a video camera on a tripod. "Are you recording?" The American nodded. "Good. I shall begin."

Banna reverted to Arabic, giving a short speech to the camera for archaeological posterity, then turned with a theatrical flourish to his apparatus. He took hold of the crank handle and carefully rotated it, delivering a hushed running commentary as he watched the screen. The display showed pristine steel gently shifting among dull bronze.

Everyone stared, the observers holding their breath in anticipation . . .

One of the bronze levers shifted upward. A faint *clink* came from within the door.

"Wait, that's it?" Eddie complained after Banna smugly reported success. "All that bloody buildup just to move a little piece of metal? I could've done it with a coat hanger."

"Archaeology is not all about exploding airliners and crashing submarines," said Banna. "Now we can use the winch."

The next twenty minutes was spent dismantling the lock pick so that the winch's steel cable could be secured to the door. At last, Banna concluded his careful examination of the hook and spoke to Schofield's camera again. Rashad used a cell phone to record events from a second viewpoint. "You might need to move back a bit," Eddie whispered to her, getting a puzzled look in return. "So you can fit his ego in." She tried to suppress a smile.

Banna kept talking. "Ubayy?" Assad gently interrupted. "The door? It is perhaps time to open it."

"Yes, yes," said Banna, flicking a dismissive hand. "This is a great and very proud moment," he announced to the camera. "The tomb of Alexander the Great has been lost for centuries, and we are the ones who will open it again. The hidden secrets of one of the most important figures in history shall again be revealed to the world."

With that, he activated the winch.

Nina had half prepared herself for something awful to happen, but the machine started up with a muted electric whine and slowly began to wind in the cable. It did not take long for the slack to be drawn up and the line to become taut.

Macy cringed at a scraping rasp from the ceiling. "That's not going to come down, is it?" she asked as the end of a scaffolding pole crunched against the ancient stone.

"That bracing should hold up to four tons," Schofield assured her.

"It's still causing some damage," said Nina as dust dropped to the floor.

"Not as much as if we had blasted the door open with explosives," Banna sniped over the winch's noise. Assad sighed and said something in Arabic; from the younger man's irked expression, Nina guessed it had been a rebuke.

But she was no longer interested in Banna's snide remarks, all her attention now on the door. A deep moan echoed through the passage, the noise of metal reluctantly sliding over stone. Puffs of dust wafted from the edges of the great barrier as, with almost painful slowness, it began to move.

"It's coming!" said Schofield unnecessarily. Unpleasant shrills filled the tunnel as the door ground over the floor.

"Christ," Eddie grumbled, putting his fingers in his ears. "I'm already half deaf, and that's not bloody helping."

Nina, however, moved closer as an opening appeared. More dust swirled out as air flowed freely through the underground tunnel for the first time in sixteen centuries. "Get some more lights on it," she said.

Assad preempted another stinging comment from Banna. "That *was* part of our plan, Dr. Wilde," he told her with a gentle smile. "We have been preparing for this for quite some time."

"Okay, okay," she said, reluctantly stepping back. "And you can wipe that grin off your face," she told Eddie without looking around at him.

"I'm not grinning," Eddie lied. Macy giggled.

Another minute passed—then Banna suddenly cried out in Arabic as something gave way. The door jerked open wider before crunching to a halt, wedged against an uneven paving slab. He hurriedly switched off the winch. "Is it damaged?" Schofield called, going to the machine.

"Forget the winch," said Nina, trying to control her breathing in her excitement. The gap was now wide enough for a person to fit through. "It's open, the door's open."

Banna recovered his composure. "I shall enter first," he said, going to a box of equipment and taking out a large LED lantern. "Dina, Bill, we must record this." Schofield detached the larger camera from its tripod.

Macy tried to peer through the gap. "Can you see anything?"

"The back of Banna's head," said Eddie. He watched as the Egyptian raised his lamp, then cautiously slipped through the new opening. "Okay, three, two, one—*kashung!* Death trap."

The archaeologists all gave him unimpressed looks. "That's not funny, Eddie," Nina told him.

"Tchah! If there is one, don't blame me, then." By now, the other Egyptians and Schofield had collected their own lights and made their way to the door, Nina following suit. Eddie shrugged and joined Macy at the back of the line. "Okay, what's inside?"

Nina waited for Schofield to maneuver through the gap, then squeezed after him. "Ah . . . a lot of impressive stuff," she called back in awe.

Banna's belief about what lay beyond the bronze door had been correct. They had entered a treasury, a space to display the tributes paid to the dead king. The entrance was in one corner. The room was almost as large as the antechamber, more rows of pillars supporting its vaulted roof—and everywhere the eerie blue-white glows of the lanterns reached, they revealed wonders.

Statues gazed back at the new arrivals, the figures of men and animals surrounded by weapons and armor, furniture, chests, and vases . . . all of it glinting with gold and silver, multitudes of inset gemstones winking like stars. "Whoa," Macy whispered, astounded.

"Whoa indeed," said Assad as he advanced. His light revealed clear paths through the carefully arranged treasures. Banna was already following one across the vault, turning up a wide central aisle. At the far end was a broad flight of stone steps leading to a large and ornate opening in the wall. Statues holding spears and swords stood guard on each side.

He was about to ascend the stairs when he paused to examine something, then brought his light around to survey other parts of the gleaming display. "You see?" called the Egyptian, looking back at Nina with a mocking smile as he pointed out a statue of a horse. "Bucephalus." Another jab at a different sculpture. "Bucephalus." And another. "Bucephalus. The treasury is full of them."

"That doesn't mean these people aren't after one in particular," Nina replied, but Banna was no longer listening.

Rashad and Schofield spread out to catalog the incredible sight on video, while Habib peered at his reflection in the gilded face of a replica of a Macedonian warrior. "It is more incredible than I ever imagined," he said. "A find for the ages."

"Yes," Assad agreed. "Well done, Ubayy! Well done! This is truly one of the greatest discoveries of our time."

"I would say *the* greatest," Banna answered, "and it is entirely an Egyptian find."

Schofield gave Nina a look of long-suffering amusement. "What am I, chopped liver?"

Assad chuckled. "It is something to be proud of, that is for sure. Another wonder of the world to add to our collection! But we have not even seen the greatest wonder of all." He waved a hand toward the dark passage at the top of the stairs. "The burial chamber of Alexander the Great. Lead on, Dr. Banna!"

Banna puffed out his chest in pride and went up the steps, stopping at the top. "Dina, Bill, come on! This must be filmed."

"No point making an amazing discovery if you can't put it straight on YouTube, is there?" Eddie said as the group marched up the central aisle.

"He's probably going to take a selfie with Alexander's body," said Macy.

Assad smiled. "I know he can be very . . . what would be the best word? Intense."

"Not the word I'd have picked," said the Englishman.

"But he is very dedicated, very thorough, and very knowledgeable. I would not have put him in charge of the dig if he were not. Just because he is young does not mean he does not deserve respect."

Macy blushed. "Sorry." Eddie merely shrugged.

"Dr. Banna is right, though," said Habib. "There are many statues of Alexander's horse. If somebody really does plan to raid the tomb, which one do they want to steal?"

"I don't know," Nina told him, "but they seem to have knowledge of the tomb that even we don't. I'd guess they know specifically which one they're after. And there's still the matter of how they got hold of the map of the outer tomb—or rather, who they got it from."

"It is troubling, yes," said Assad. "You are certain it was an up-to-date plan?"

"I'm positive. It showed more detail than the last version I saw when I was still at the IHA."

"Too bad you didn't manage to keep it," said Schofield. "They're time-stamped; we'd be able to work out who accessed it from our server."

"Yeah, too bad. It was kind of on fire, though."

They headed up the stairs to meet the impatient Banna. He was already shining his light into the new tunnel, its walls decorated with reliefs. Unlike those in the outer tomb, these were painted, adding rich and vivid detail to the carved scenes. "At last," he said. "Now, I want both cameras to follow me so they see the inner tomb as I do."

Nina peered past him. "You're not going to make a complete survey of the treasury first?"

"There will be plenty of time to do that once we have found Alexander. Now, the cameras." He clicked his fingers. Schofield and Rashad took up position behind him. "It is time to meet the great king."

"Not playing up his part or anything, is he?" Eddie said to Nina in a fake whisper.

Banna set off, lantern raised high. "I can see another room ahead," he narrated. "It is smaller than the treasury, but . . . it is definitely the burial chamber." Excitement rose in his voice. "I can see the coffin!"

His pace quickened, everyone else hurrying to keep up. Banna crossed the threshold and stared for a moment at what his lamp revealed, then turned to the cameras with an expression of almost child-like joy. "It *is* Alexander! We have found him!"

Nina entered the chamber with the rest of the group, and was struck by the same amazement as the young Egyptian. The room was dominated by a dais, on which stood an ornate sarcophagus. Unlike the solid stone or metal of the coffins of Egyptian pharaohs, this was made of a greenish glass, the individual panes supported by a gilded framework. The surface was far from smooth, distorting the view of what lay within . . . but it was still clear enough to reveal its occupant.

"It's really him," she gasped, creeping closer to get a better view through the rippled crystal. "It's Alexander."

"He doesn't look so great," Eddie commented. The body had been preserved in the ancient Egyptian manner, mummification, but was not wrapped in bandages. Instead the wizened figure was clad in silk robes of deep Tyrian purple, with parts of a suit of scale armor covering the shoulders and lower body. The corpse's hands were crossed over its stomach, gold rings visible upon the fingers.

Nina saw Greek text upon the frame of the glass sarcophagus. "'A tomb now suffices him for whom the world was not enough,'" she translated.

"Oh, he was a James Bond fan?"

So thrilled he struggled to speak, Banna gestured for Schofield to film the coffin's occupant. "The . . . the breastplate is gone, just as the records said—stolen by Caligula. And look, look—the nose is missing." He pointed at the dead king's face, below the golden band encircling the forehead. Even through the lid's distortions, a dark hole was clearly visible.

"Broken by Augustus when he bent down to kiss the body," said Nina. Banna looked at her in mild surprise. "I did my research too."

The young archaeologist was too enthralled to continue his rivalry, at least for the moment. "The coffin, glass, just as was written—the original golden coffin was melted down by Ptolemy the Ninth Lathyrus."

"Why did he do that?" Macy asked, torn between fascination and distaste at the sight of the eyeless, shriveled corpse.

"To turn into coins," Nina explained, gazing at the king's remains. "However much they venerated Alexander, the rulers who came after him still needed money, wherever they could get it."

Eddie surveyed the rest of the room. A selection of treasures, even more impressive than those in the chamber below, surrounded the dais. "A lot of this other stuff's gold, as well as everything outside. Why'd he leave all this alone?"

"Ptolemy Lathyrus ruled until 81 BCE," said Banna, reluctantly turning away from the coffin. "But the tomb remained open for centuries after. These tributes must have been placed here later."

Macy was keen to look at something other than a dead body. "Hey, Nina. There's another statue of Alexander's horse here."

Nina's interest was immediately drawn by the statue. It was about two feet long, sculpted so that the horse appeared to be in mid-gallop, with its head held high and proud. Even from across the room, she could tell that the workmanship and detail were exquisite.

That was not what had caught her attention, though. It stood out because of its lack of ostentation. The other tributes around it dripped with gold, silver, and gemstones, but this was content to be merely a beautiful piece of art rather than an extravagant display.

"Let me see," she told Macy. Rashad took her place to film the coffin as she joined her friend.

"You found something?" Eddie asked.

"I'm not sure." Nina knelt, bringing her light to the statue. It was made of fired clay or ceramic, the surface delicately painted and then glazed to seal in the colors. Threads of gold picked out the animal's tack, but beyond that it was unadorned . . .

She squinted, leaning nearer. There was something written *on* the tack, Greek text inscribed in tiny letters along the bands of the bridle and reins.

Macy peered over her shoulder. "What does it say?"

"It's really hard to read, especially in this light . . . Does anyone have a magnifying glass?"

There was a faintly embarrassed silence from the other archaeologists. "Seriously?" said Nina. "Nobody's brought a basic tool kit with them?"

Assad chuckled. "It would be a good idea to edit this from the video, yes?"

Habib headed back to the tunnel. "I will bring one from the cabin."

"No, it's okay," said Nina as an idea came to her, but he had already gone. She took out her phone. "This can magnify, hold on . . ." She activated the camera and zoomed in until the text on the screen became legible. "Here, I can read it."

"Well, what's the story?" Eddie asked after a few seconds.

"Jeez, give me a chance!" Nina moved the phone slowly over the statue's surface. "It says, near enough, 'No one could hope to match the sagacity and bravery of Alexander . . .'"

"Whoever made that had a pretty high opinion of him."

"They wouldn't be the only one. Although I wonder if it says who *did* make it?" She checked the rest of the statue.

"Why are you so fascinated by that one piece, Dr. Wilde?" asked Banna. "Alexander the Great himself is here, in this room, but you are more interested in his horse!"

"I'm interested in his horse because the guy who tried to kill me was interested in it too," Nina said. "Okay, here's another line . . . 'The riddle of the Gordian Knot outwitted all, until Alexander's wisdom found the answer.'"

"The Gordian Knot?" said Eddie. "That's the one where he couldn't unfasten it, so he just chopped it in half, right?"

"That's right," Nina answered, reading on. "'Only such great wisdom will solve the riddle of Bucephalus and reveal that which leads to the Spring of Immortality.'" That aroused intrigued looks from the others.

Most of them, at least. "I shall continue to examine the body of Alexander the Great," Banna announced huffily and to nobody in particular. "Keep the camera on me!" Rashad, who had turned to watch Nina, hurriedly brought her phone back to the expedition leader.

"Where's this riddle?" asked Eddie.

Assad joined Nina. "There must be more text."

She reached for the statue, then hesitated, looking at the Egyptian for approval. He nodded. As carefully as she could, she lifted it. "It's really heavy," she reported.

Assad supported the statue's underside with one hand. "Ten kilograms, at least. It must be solid." He tapped softly on the horse's flank with a knuckle, producing a dull *clonk*.

"Sounds that way," Nina agreed. "Okay . . . I can't see text anywhere except on the reins. Let's see what the rest of it says." They lowered the sculpture, and she brought her phone back up.

It did not take long to read the rest of the inscriptions. "Well, that's a little weird."

Eddie came over. "What is it?"

"You remember the story in the *Alexander Romance,* where Andreas the cook accidentally discovered the Spring of Immortality?"

"Yeah?"

"According to the text, this statue was *made* by Andreas. He put it in the burial chamber to honor his king." Now even Banna looked up from his examination of the coffin to listen. "It also says that when he did that . . . he was over three hundred years old."

"Impossible!" Banna snapped.

"I'm just reading what it says. Andreas found the Spring of Immortality again after Alexander died. The statue can show the way to it—if you solve its riddle."

"But what *is* the riddle?" asked Macy.

"I don't know." Nina checked the horse's belly, but found no more text.

"On the feet, perhaps," Assad suggested. He and Nina gently turned the statue over. Again, there was nothing visible, even on the underside of the hooves. "Or hidden in the hairs of the tail?"

"What are you *doing*?" hooted Banna. "Ismail, this is the greatest find in years, and you are ignoring it!"

"No, I am not ignoring it," Assad told him as he put the equine sculpture back on its feet. "But I am paying more attention to a *threat* to it. This statue must be the one Dr. Wilde's attackers plan to steal. So, to ensure the safety of the rest of the tomb, we need to take it to a secure location." He straightened. "I will return to the antechamber and bring the ASPS so that—"

The chamber shook, a single sharp pulse jolting the floor. The treasures rattled as a low, forceful *whump* rolled around the space.

Eddie's gaze whipped toward the exit. "That was a fucking bomb!"

Banna gawped at him. "A *bomb*? But—"

Another sound thundered through the tunnels, a tearing crunch of falling stone and rubble. The golden tributes juddered again, dust dropping from the arched ceiling. Banna gasped and splayed his upper body over the coffin to protect the figure inside.

The echoes of the impact faded, to be replaced by new noises in the distance.

Gunfire—and screams.

8

"Jesus!" cried Nina as the horribly familiar chatter of automatic weapons reached her. "They must have blasted their way in!"

"Who?" demanded Banna, wide-eyed with confusion and fear.

"If they're the same lot as the bloke who came after Nina, they're fucking *Nazis*!" Eddie pulled his wife to her feet. "We've got to get out of here, or we'll be trapped. Oi, Hulk!" he added to Banna, who was still trying to shield Alexander's remains. "It's not him you need to worry about."

More gunfire howled down the passage, the pitch and tempo different. "The ASPS are shooting back!" said Assad.

"Yeah, but it doesn't sound like there's as many of 'em."

"Where are we going?" Nina protested as everyone ran into the tunnel. "There's only one way out of here."

"Sounded like they blew another one." Eddie listened to the battle. Even though his hearing had been degraded by years of exposure to loud, explosive noises, it was the higher frequencies that had been affected the most; he had no trouble picking out the roar of bullets being fired. "Jesus, it must be a fucking slaughterhouse."

"Are the ASPS winning?" Nina asked. His grim expression gave her an answer. "Oh, crap."

They reentered the treasury. It was much darker than before. The reason became clear once they descended the stairs and could see the entrance past the pillars: The spotlights were off. "They have cut the power," reported the worried Assad. "What do we do?"

"We can't fight 'em," Eddie replied. The firing had stopped—and the last shots he had heard were from the invading force's guns, suggesting that the defenders had been overrun. "If we can shut the door, we might be able to hole up in here until backup arrives."

"It weighs two tons!" Banna protested. "And the winch is on the other side. We will never be able to move it."

"Won't know unless we try. Come on! Bill, Dr. Assad, give us a hand." Eddie ran to the doorway, the other men following.

"What about us?" Macy asked, even beneath her fear sounding a little offended on behalf of the three women. "We can help too!"

"Not being sexist, Macy, but you weigh as much as a crispbread. Find somewhere to hide." He rounded the great bronze door. "Bill, help me push it. You two, pull from the inside."

The Egyptians took hold of a handle behind the lock and hauled at it as Eddie and Schofield pressed their shoulders against the door's face. "Shit!" gasped the American. "It's not moving!"

"It's wedged on the floor—push harder!" The bronze barrier shifted slightly as the four men strained, its corner rasping against the stone slabs. A shadow obscured the light from inside the treasury. "Nina!" said Eddie as his wife ran through the opening and joined him. "Get back inside!"

"You won't close it in time without help," she replied through clenched teeth.

"It won't matter if it's shut if you're on the wrong side of it!"

Nina was about to reply when she heard a noise behind her. "Someone's coming!"

Running footsteps echoed down the passage. "Shit, they're here," Eddie growled. Despite their efforts, the gap was still wide enough for a person to fit through. "Go and—"

"Wait!" said Assad as shouts reached them—in Arabic. "It is one of the ASPS!"

Eddie twisted to look down the dark tunnel. A jittering shaft of light appeared from around the last corner. The approaching man had a torch, the beam swinging as he hared down the passage—but the noise of more runners warned the Englishman that his pursuers were not far behind. "We'll never get this door closed," he realized.

"Do we keep pushing?" Schofield asked.

"No point now—get inside and hide. You too, Nina." He straightened, glancing back as Nina and Schofield ducked through the gap. The running man reached the corner—

The stuttering orange of a gun's muzzle flash silhouetted the Egyptian against the walls—which were discolored by splatters of blood. The man fell.

Time was up. "Shit! *Go!*" Eddie barked, following the others through the opening. He heard a shout from behind. The attackers had seen him. "Find cover!"

He dived behind a statue—as more bullets tore through the air above him, smacking into the stone pillars beyond. The door rang like a gong as stray bullets struck it. He scrambled along the floor until he was clear of the danger zone, then jumped up. "Hide and turn out the lights!"

Another sustained burst cracked against the stonework. Assuming that anyone inside the tomb could be armed, the attackers were using overwhelming firepower to deter them from shooting back. But the suppressing fire had also cut Eddie off from Nina. She and the others had gone toward the burial chamber, while he—and Macy, whom he glimpsed climbing into a large metal chest—were isolated at the opposite end of the treasury.

More shouts from just outside, spears of light stabbing through the opening. The archaeologists hurriedly switched off their lanterns, Eddie and Nina's eyes meeting for one last desperate moment before she too disappeared into the darkness. He muttered a curse, then crouched and felt his way through the ranks of tributes in what he hoped was Macy's direction.

Something flashed through the probing torch beams and clanked loudly on the floor. Eddie guessed what it was, closing his eyes and clamping both hands over his ears, but there was no time to warn the others—

The stun grenade exploded with a piercing bang and a blinding flash. Schofield and Rashad had instinctively turned toward the noise when it landed—and both screamed as the detonation overpowered their senses.

Men swarmed through the opening, golden visors shielding their eyes. Powerful tactical lights mounted on their guns pierced the darkness as they searched for targets.

They found two, reeling helplessly from the stun blast.

Guns blazed, short but deadly bursts. The archaeologists were cut down, tumbling bloodily amid the ancient treasures.

Nina had found cover behind a golden sculpture of Bucephalus, kneeling and protecting her eyes—but the grenade's crack still hit her like a physical blow. Ears ringing, she struggled to rise . . .

A bright light pinned her. Still dizzy, she squinted into the glare—and saw a gun taking aim—

A sharp command, and the weapon withdrew, though the spotlight under its muzzle remained locked upon her. Figures marched past, more beams scouring the shadows. She picked out snatches of speech as her hearing returned, but didn't understand the words. The language sounded familiar, however. German?

Someone moved in front of her, partially shading her from the pitiless light. Nina looked up at an unsmiling man in dark overalls, his eyes hidden behind a visor. The gunman spoke, again in German; the black-haired new arrival replied dismissively, then removed his face shield.

Nina felt a chill of recognition. She had seen him before—at the United Nations. It was Rasche, one of the men whose photographs the FBI had shown her. A wanted Nazi war criminal.

But like his comrade from Los Angeles, he was too young. The man staring down at her with intense, dangerous eyes had aged since the mug shot was taken, but still appeared to be only in his early forties, not much older than Eddie.

He spoke to the gunman; Banna's name was mentioned. That snapped her back to full awareness. Where were her companions, and what had happened to them? Where was Eddie? She looked around. Other intruders were moving through the treasury, hunting for the rest of the group. One huge hulk had already located Assad, hauling the older man to his feet. Another black-clad man dragged the dazed Banna out from behind a pillar.

"You are Dr. Nina Wilde?" She looked back at the mad-eyed man.

"Uh . . . yeah, yes I am," she mumbled.

He gazed unsettlingly at her as if examining a specimen under a microscope, then surveyed the treasury. "Anyone else who is here, show yourself now!" he shouted. "If you do not, you will be killed on sight." The command was repeated in Arabic, but stiffly, the phrases learned by rote.

Two more intruders, both young men, called out. Nina shuddered as she saw Schofield and Rashad's blood-splashed bodies in the beams of their lights. Rasche stared at Nina again. "Are there more people with you?"

She forced herself not to glance in the direction where she had last seen her husband. "No."

"If you are lying, I will kill you." There was distinct anticipation in his voice at the prospect.

"This is all of us, I swear."

It was evident that he didn't believe her, but seconds passed with no reports from the other searchers. "Very well," he said eventually. "Where is the body of Alexander the Great?"

She gestured toward the stairs. "Up there."

He nodded. "You will come with us."

The gunman yanked her to her feet and shoved her toward Banna and Assad, who had been corralled in the main aisle by their captors. Nina counted twelve men altogether, all armed with submachine guns and wearing webbing holding extra magazines. Some had other equipment too: more stun grenades, lethal hand grenades, even blocks of plastic explosive.

She risked looking back for any sign of Eddie, or Macy. Nothing. At least two of the intruders had searched the area where he had been, so he must have found a hiding place . . .

The gigantic man holding Assad—Walther, another of the escaped war criminals—regarded Nina with a hard expression. "Dr. Wilde," he said, "take us to the statue of Bucephalus."

"Which one?" she asked, playing for time. If their attackers could be delayed in the tomb, it would give Egyptian reinforcements a chance to respond. "There are several." She indicated a couple of the nearest examples.

Rasche snorted—then lashed out with a gloved fist, knocking her to the floor. Banna flinched, while Assad stiffened in outrage. "Do not waste my time. You were given stolen plans of this operation; that you are here proves you know what we seek." Nina glared up at him, a hand to her cheek.

"I—I am in charge of this dig," said Banna, voice pitched high with fear before he cleared his throat and managed to lower it. "If you want anything, speak to me. She is only an observer; she is no longer even a member of the IHA."

Nina saw Walther and Rasche exchange looks. Had they expected her to be an official part of the excavation? "Then *you* will take us to the statue of Bucephalus," said Rasche, pointing his gun at Banna. The young archaeologist shrank back. "The one in the burial chamber."

"Do as he asks," said Assad. "Nobody else needs to get hurt."

"Good. Now move." Rasche issued more orders, and five of his men started back toward the entrance. The rest pushed the three prisoners to the stairs.

* * *

In the darkness at the other end of the chamber, the lid of a bronze chest opened slightly. Eddie peered through the gap, the start of a creak from the hinges deterring him from lifting it higher. "Bollocks!" he whispered. "They're taking Nina up to the coffin. Assad and Banna too."

A strained squeak came from beneath him. "Eddie, your elbow's right on my chest!" Macy gasped.

"It's okay, you've got plenty of padding there."

"What? You *asshole*!"

Eddie smiled faintly, but the brief levity vanished as he saw that some of the attackers were positioning themselves to guard the entrance. The nearest man was twenty feet from him. His hiding place was not in their direct line of sight, but he doubted he would be able to get out of the box without making a noise—and drawing their fire. Farther away, Nina and the others climbed the steps to the burial chamber. "Shit," he muttered.

Macy squirmed beneath him. "What's happening? Are Nina and the others okay?"

"For now, but I doubt they're going to let them go. And Bill and Dina are dead."

"Oh my God! They're—they'll kill us too!"

"Stay calm," he told her, changing position to take as much of his weight off her as he could. "I won't let that happen."

His assurance calmed her, a little. "What are you going to do?"

"Buggered if I know."

"Y-yeah, that helps."

"First things first. I need to figure out how to get out of this fucking box without them hearing me." He shifted until he was able to put his hand down beside her neck, then carefully levered himself up, raising the lid again until it began to creak.

The guards hadn't moved, watching the door—and Nina and the others were now out of sight.

* * *

"There," said Banna as the intruders pushed the surviving archaeologists into the burial chamber. "There is the statue. Please, take it. We will not stop you."

Most of the torch beams turned to where he was pointing, but some explored other parts of the room. Walther whistled appreciatively as he shone his own light over a large golden vase decorated with multicolored gemstones. The huge man made a suggestion, which drew chuckles from some of his companions.

Rasche did not share their amusement. Nina guessed from his impatient reply that he was telling the others they were only there for the statue. The younger men responded to the rebuke by straightening and issuing apologies, but Walther was more relaxed, shaking his head in wry amusement. He spoke again, Nina understanding a few words: *"Wir brauchen mehr Gold, Rasche"*—we need more gold, Rasche.

Rasche spoke again, with more anger. Walther shrugged, but acquiesced. He crouched and clamped his massive hands around the sculpture, lifting it as easily as though it were a bag of sugar.

"So you've got what you came for," said Nina, fear rising. Now that they had the statue, the Nazis had no reason to keep their prisoners alive. "What are you going to do with us?"

Rasche did not respond at once, instead gazing at the desiccated figure inside the crystal coffin. "So this is Alexander . . ."

"You are interested in the great king?" asked Banna.

Rasche shook his head. "Not I. But our Führer has a fascination with the man. Which is fortunate for us, as otherwise we would not—" He caught himself, as if about to give away some secret. "It is a shame we cannot take the body. He would like to possess it, very much."

"Egypt will pay anything you ask to ensure the safety of Alexander's remains," said Assad. "I am the senior archaeologist of the Ministry of State for Antiquities; if it is necessary, I will act as a hostage during negotiations."

"There will be no negotiations," Rasche said sharply. He nodded to Walther. Cradling the ceramic horse, the big man headed into the tunnel. The leader regarded the mummy once more, then made a silent decision. "Take them into the treasure room," he ordered.

The other men shoved the prisoners back down the painted passage. "What are you doing?" Nina demanded.

"Our Führer would be . . . *unhappy* if anything happened to his hero," Rasche replied, a veneer of disdain telling her that he did not share his commander's concerns. "So I will make sure that the burial chamber is preserved."

"By killing us outside it, right?"

The German smiled, but there was nothing except cruelty behind it. "You are a clever woman, Dr. Wilde."

They descended into the treasury and headed down the central aisle. Nina glanced around in growing fear, searching the shadows for her husband, but there was no sign of him. "Eddie, where *are* you?" she whispered.

* * *

Inside the metal chest, Eddie watched Nina and the others with growing desperation. The archaeologists' expressions—Banna was close to tears—warned him that they didn't expect to leave the room alive.

He *had* to do something. But even if he got out of his hiding place without alerting the guards, he was still unarmed . . .

The silhouette of a nearby treasure caught his eye as the procession passed behind it. That gave him a weapon, however impractical—if he could reach it.

Rasche held up his hand. The group stopped, Walther putting down the statue. Macy felt Eddie's muscles tighten. "What is it?"

He watched helplessly as the three prisoners were pushed into a line. "They're going to kill them . . ."

* * *

"Wait!" Nina pleaded as she was shoved between Assad and Banna. "You don't have to do this. You've got what you came for—just take it and go!"

None of the faces looking back at her showed any inclination toward mercy. Rasche could barely contain a rat-like smile of anticipation as he raised his gun.

"Good-bye, Dr. Wilde," he said—aiming at Nina's heart.

9

"No!" cried Assad, lunging forward—in front of Nina. The bullet ripped into his chest, the burst of blood almost aglow in the glare of the tactical light. The Egyptian fell to the floor. His eyes met Nina's, trying to send her a last silent message . . . then they rolled back as life left his body.

Banna stared in disbelief at his mentor, then wailed in shock and despair. Nina looked up—to see Rasche's smoking gun still pointing at her.

His finger tightened again—

A crash from the darkness made him whirl.

* * *

The gunshot's echoes had not even faded before Eddie fought past his horror and threw open the chest to leap out and run for his weapon.

It was a sword, over-ornate and gaudy, but beneath the hilt's gold and jewels the two-foot curved blade was still honed. He snatched it up without breaking step as he rushed at the nearest Nazi.

The man's attention had been on his commander, his hearing momentarily overpowered by the gun's blast—but now he caught a new sound from behind.

He turned—

Eddie slashed the sword at his throat with a two-handed swing. There was a flat *chut* of tearing flesh and a crack of bone—and the Nazi's head tumbled off his shoulders with a gush of arterial spray. The nerveless body crashed onto a pile of treasure.

The Englishman dropped his blade and grabbed the dead man's gun. It was a SIG Sauer MPX-K, an ultra-compact submachine gun so new that it was the first time Eddie had seen one in person. Its sales were supposed to be restricted to military and law enforcement agencies, but he had no time to wonder how the raiders had obtained their sidearms.

Instead, he used it.

Another guard spun at the noise, only to take a three-round burst to his face. But the men in black were well trained, and fast. Even as the second Nazi fell, the others near the door were already diving behind pillars and larger relics.

Eddie glanced at the group holding Nina and Banna as he too pulled back into shelter, switching off his weapon's tac-light. Rasche shrieked orders, his men moving to face the new threat, then whipped around, gun raised to kill his two remaining prisoners—

Another burst from the stolen MPX forced him to scurry back. "Nina, *run*!" Eddie roared.

Nina pulled Banna after her as Rasche ducked behind a column to avoid her husband's bullets. "Come *on*!" she yelled. The young Egyptian was in a helpless daze. She practically had to drag him around a pillar.

The German fired again—but hit only stone. He cursed, then shouted more commands to his men.

Eddie peeked around the column. He now had an advantage, however small: The intruders' positions were being given away by their tactical lights, while he was concealed in the shadows. There were three men near the door, the rest spread out in the center of the chamber.

He spotted something else in the sweep of a tac-light: the statue of Bucephalus where the giant had left it in the aisle. That was what the attackers had come for—so if it were taken away from them, they might leave . . .

He switched the MPX's selector to single-shot—and fired.

A thumb-sized chunk of the horse's mane shattered into splinters. He adjusted his aim to compensate for the stubby weapon's recoil and locked on to the statue's head. Take out the ancient text inscribed on its reins, and the bad guys had nothing—

Rasche had reached the same conclusion. He bellowed an order—and the chamber lit up with multiple muzzle flashes as the intruders opened fire on the Englishman.

"Shit!" Eddie gasped, jerking back as shrapnel spat past. Bullets clanged off gold and bronze, pottery exploding in the darkness. He heard Macy shriek as a ricochet whined off the bronze chest.

The light beams shifted. His attackers were heading for the door. He risked a glance down the length of the chamber, seeing before another onslaught drove him back that Nina and Banna had found cover—but also that Walther had grabbed the statue once more and was hurrying toward the exit.

⁂

"Are you okay?" Nina asked the hyperventilating Banna. "Dr. Banna!"

He struggled to focus on her, jabbering in panicked Arabic before slowing and switching to English. "I, I am okay, yes. But Ismail and the others, they—they killed them!"

"We're still not safe," she warned. "When I tell you, run for that pillar—the farther we are from them, the better our chances." She indicated the next-closest column to the burial chamber, then peered back toward Rasche.

He and the rest of the main group were moving away from her. A moment of relief—which was short-lived as she realized they were keeping Eddie pinned down while Walther escaped with the sculpture of Bucephalus. "Run, now!" she shouted over the echoing gunfire. Banna didn't move. "Dammit, go!"

"I—I can't!" he gasped. "I don't want to die!"

She felt a flash of contempt for him—which was immediately replaced by guilt at her own arrogance. Her own reaction only a few years earlier would have been a similar terror. "Okay, then get down and stay out of sight," she said instead.

Another look at the retreating Nazis. The younger men had formed a protective cordon around Walther and his precious cargo, backing toward the exit as they kept up their assault on Eddie's position. Rasche shouted more orders, one of the group near the door taking something from his webbing.

A yell of *"Granaten!"* warned her what it was. The word was easy to translate.

"Eddie!" she cried. "They've got—"

* * *

"Grenades? *Fuck!*" Eddie yelped. NATO training exercises during his military career had taught him danger warnings in multiple languages. He looked for shelter, but the dancing shadows cast by the strobing muzzle flashes made it impossible to pick anything out amid the visual confusion. "Macy, shut the lid and stay down!"

He had no idea if she had heard him—and no time to warn her again. All he could do was *run*—

Eddie burst out from his cover. Blazing guns swung after him, chunks of statues and spalls of gold exploding in his wake. But he also heard hard metallic clacks as two grenades hit the floor behind him.

Something large and low to his right. He dived over it, rolling and pressing himself against its base—

Both grenades detonated, a lethal blizzard of steel shards shredding the treasures around them. Sculptures toppled and smashed on the floor.

* * *

Rasche looked out from behind a column as the echoes faded, seeing no movement except drifting smoke and dust. "Pull out!" he ordered. "Protect the statue!"

Walther was first to the door. The big man had to turn

sideways to fit into the gap, making maneuvering the statue through it tricky, but after a few seconds he managed it. The others slipped out of the treasury behind him. Rasche cast another glance back, gun raised, but nobody challenged him. A small, nasty smile, and he followed his men.

*   *   *

Nina lowered her hands from her ears. Even halfway across the large room and with solid stone at her back, the explosions had still knocked her down.

The chamber was now completely dark. "Eddie?" she called, before hearing someone close by. "Banna, are you okay?"

"My ears . . . ," said the Egyptian, voice quavering.

"Did you get hit?"

"No, I—I do not think so, but my ears, they hurt so much . . ."

"Stay still for now." She got shakily to her feet. "Eddie!"

No reply. A new fear rose within her. "Eddie, can you hear me?"

A metallic clang from the blackness. "Nina, is that you?" came a female voice.

"Macy! Are you okay? Where's Eddie?"

"I dunno, I'm not even sure where *I* am. Hold on, I've got a light . . ." A corner of the room lit up as Macy surveyed her surroundings. "Holy crap! They've blown the hell out of the place!"

"Just find Eddie!" Nina said, picking her way toward her friend. Shrapnel crunched underfoot. She found one of the abandoned lanterns in the wash from Macy's own light and switched it on. "Come on, Eddie, I know you're here somewhere, you've *got* to be . . ."

A moan came from the shadows. "Over here!" Macy shouted. "I see him, he's here!"

Nina went toward her, rounding a heavy marble bench to find Eddie sprawled against it. Blood stood out on the dusty floor around his head. Frightened, she touched his neck, searching for a pulse. "Eddie, wake up. Please . . ."

"Oh God," Macy whispered. "Is he . . ."

"Am I what?" came a Yorkshire-accented grumble.

The younger woman let out a sigh of relief. "Okay, not dead, then!"

"No, I'm not dead, but it fucking feels like it. Jesus *Christ*, my head hurts!"

"You've been cut," Nina warned him. A crooked gash had been sliced into his scalp.

"Yeah, grenade frag, probably," he said, face scrunching as he sat up. "Ow! Shit, it's got my arm too."

Macy brought her own light closer. "There's a big rip in your sleeve—I can see blood underneath."

His frown deepened. "Buggeration. This was a new jacket!"

"This is *new*?" She regarded the battered black leather dubiously. "But it looks like it's been dragged under a bus."

Nina gave her a sardonic smile. "Yeah, don't get me started. We've had discussions about his taste in distressed clothing before. Can you stand?"

"Yeah." He picked up his gun and rose. "Got some new bruises, but I'll survive. Where's Banna?"

Nina pointed. "Over there. I think he's okay, just shaken up."

"I'm guessing from the way we're not being shot at anymore that the bad guys have gone."

"Yeah, and they took the statue."

He eyed her. "You sound like you're pissed off about that."

"Well . . . kind of, yes. It could have led to an amazing find."

"And it could've led to us all getting killed!" He saw Banna crawl out from his hiding place. "Go and help him," he told the two women, before hurrying to the entrance.

"What are you doing?" Nina called after him.

"What do you think? I'm not letting a bunch of fucking *Nazis* get away with all this!"

"Eddie, wait!" she cried, but he had already gone.

10

Eddie ran back through the tomb, finding the ante-chamber littered with the bullet-torn corpses of the defending ASPS. No sign of the Nazis. The passageway through which he had originally entered the tomb was now strewn with debris, the long tunnel blocked after about thirty feet by tons of earth and rubble. *Nice work,* he thought grimly; the explosives that had blasted a six-foot hole through the ceiling had also collapsed the passage behind it, letting the intruders get in and out while preventing the ASPS still on the surface from providing backup.

Several ropes dangled from the new opening's ragged top—the Nazis had initially rappelled into the tomb—but two aluminum ladders had been their means of escape. Eddie moved underneath the hole, gun raised in case they had left a guard. Nothing moved above. He scaled one of the ladders.

The entrance had been blown through the floor of an apartment, all its windows shattered by the blast. He swept the room with his gun at the ladder's top, but there was nobody there.

Nobody alive, at least. He didn't need to see the bodies of the apartment's former residents in an adjoining room to know they were there; the buzz of flies told him the Nazis had taken their dig site by force.

He clambered out. Most of the floorboards had been ripped up to give access to the ground below. The air was still hazy with dust from the explosion. He held in a cough, then looked for an exit.

An open door led into a lobby, where he found a middle-aged Egyptian man slumped dead against the wall. The sound of weeping reached him. A woman was curled up tightly outside another apartment, shuddering with grief. The man must have come to see if anyone had been hurt—gas explosions were not unheard of in Alexandria—and been shot for his trouble.

"Bastards," Eddie growled, but there was no time to offer any comfort. The door to the street was open. He checked outside.

The rumble of slow-moving traffic greeted him. The road was busy, vehicles crawling in both directions. The sun's angle told him it ran roughly north–south, but he didn't know where he was in relation to the archaeological dig's entrance; probably a couple of streets away.

No sign of the tomb raiders—but a conspicuous gap between the parked cars suggested they had left in a van or small truck. They couldn't have gone far through the congestion—but which way?

He darted onto the narrow sidewalk, gun raised. That turned out to be a mistake. The MPX immediately prompted panic from bystanders, mobile phones hurriedly summoning the police.

Muttering a curse, he looked for the robbers, but there was too much traffic in the way. He needed a better view.

The apartments above all had balconies . . .

Eddie ran back inside. There was a narrow flight of stairs past the crying woman. He clattered up them to the first landing, then went along the hall.

The door to one apartment was open; the occupants had fled after the explosion. Eddie entered. The balcony door was ajar, a shutter half lowered to let in a breeze while keeping out the heat of the Egyptian sun. He ducked under it.

The street spread out below him, four lanes of traffic crammed into a thoroughfare meant for two. There was barely enough room for pedestrians to squeeze between the jostling vehicles, so intense was the competition for space. Horns parped and bleated.

The most insistent blasts came from a knot of cars to the north. A long-wheelbase white van was shoving through them, using its size to intimidate some of the drivers, and bullbars to barge others aside in a more physical manner.

It had to be the Nazis—they were using brute force to get away with their prize. How could he stop them?

A rapid check of the vehicles below, then he hopped up onto the balcony's railing—and leapt from it.

He landed with a bang on top of a van. A shocked yell came from inside. Eddie ignored it, sliding down the windshield and jumping onto the car in front.

Shouts rose in his wake as he vaulted from roof to roof, using the crawling cars as stepping-stones. He saw the white van ahead. It was not far from an intersection with a wider road, where traffic was moving more freely.

He had to keep them from escaping. But how?

A dirty green garbage truck was just what he needed.

He scrambled over an elderly Renault that was trying to slip past the larger vehicle, then grabbed the truck's door handle and yanked it open. "Morning!" he said, pointing the gun at the startled occupants. "I need to take out some trash."

The garbagemen practically fought each other in their haste to exit through the other door. Eddie swung himself into the driver's seat, then experimentally shoved down the heavy clutch and revved the engine. It roared in response. "Okay, make way for the Perfume Wagon!" he called, slamming the truck into gear.

It lurched forward—faster than he had expected. He swung the wheel hard, but still swiped the car in front. "Whoops, sorry," he said with a grimace.

Horns shrilled as he cut in front of other traffic. He

kept up a harsh tattoo on his own horn, which did the trick; those in his path somehow achieved the impossible and cleared a lane. Even so, he drew more howls of rage as the truck's hefty bumpers screeched along the sides of cars and clipped off wing mirrors.

But he was closing on the van, a blank-sided Mercedes Sprinter. With no windows in the rear, they might not realize he was chasing them until it was too late.

The van was at the junction, about to make a turn. He accelerated, swinging to catch it at an angle as it pulled out—

The collision threw him against the steering wheel. But the truck far outweighed the van, ramming it onto the sidewalk. Pedestrians scattered as the Sprinter was mashed sidelong into a streetlamp. One of the rear doors burst open, a crate tumbling out and breaking apart on the pavement.

Eddie jumped down from the cab. Gun in hand, he circled the wrecked Mercedes.

The first thing he saw was the statue of Bucephalus. It had been in the crate, protected by rolls of foam padding, and now lay on its side among the remains of its container. He considered shattering it with a gunshot, but noises inside the van warned him that he might need all the bullets for live targets.

He raised the MPX and looked through the open door—to see angry faces glaring back at him.

The van had no seats in the rear, the raiders having piled in with the crate. The crash had thrown them all against one another, but they were already recovering. Their own MPX-Ks came up—

Eddie fired—remembering too late that he had switched his gun to single-shot. It was still enough to catch the Nazi nearest the door squarely in the chest, sending him flying backward into his comrades.

The confusion gave the Englishman a few seconds of grace. He ducked back, about to switch his weapon to full auto and perforate the entire van—

He nearly stumbled over the broken crate, his left palm landing on the statue as he caught himself.

His plan changed. He didn't know why—some connection with Alexander's history, Nina's archaeological obsession rubbing off on him, or simply the urge to deny the Nazis their prize—but he clapped his free hand around one of the horse's legs and hauled it from the smashed container. It was heavier than it looked, but its compactness at least made it merely awkward rather than actively difficult to carry.

And as long as he had it, his enemies might think twice about shooting at him . . .

Eddie fired again as he backed around the garbage truck. The bullet clanked against metal, but there were no screams, just shouted commands in German.

The collision had brought traffic on the wider road to a standstill. He ran between the stationary vehicles toward an alleyway opposite. Alexandria's back streets, he knew from the previous night, were tight and twisty mazes. With enough of a start, he might be able to escape into the labyrinth—

The crack of a gunshot served as warning that the odds of that were not good. He dropped lower behind the cars. Men spilled from the van, guns raised.

One of them saw him, took aim—

"*Nein, nein!*" Rasche yelled furiously at his surviving team members. "*Sie werden die Statue zu schießen! Nehmen ihn am Leben!*"

Statue was German for "statue," then—and Eddie guessed that the rest was an order not to shoot him in case it was damaged. His gamble had paid off and given him a bargaining chip, however small.

Whether he got a chance to play it was another thing. Still bent low, he ran into the alley.

The Nazis raced after him.

* * *

After making sure that Banna was okay, Nina left him with Macy and sprinted after her husband. Once she scaled the ladder and left the apartment building—with a moment of shock as she saw the dead man in the hallway—the shriek of horns and the crunches of collid-ing vehicles made it easy to follow Eddie's trail.

She ran along the sidewalk, shoving past bewildered pedestrians. A much louder crash told her that some-thing serious had happened ahead. Apprehension turned to fear as she heard gunshots.

The Egyptians on the street were fleeing, forcing her to clamber onto a stalled car to avoid being knocked down. From her elevated position, she glimpsed Eddie vanishing down an alley with the statue.

Black-clad men charged in pursuit, Walther and Rasche among them. The latter yelled orders, gesturing at an-other alley nearby. Walther and about half of the raiders veered away to take the parallel route, while Rasche and the rest continued after Eddie.

They were going to try to trap him between two forces.

She jumped down and ran to the intersection. A third narrow passage ran between the buildings, closer to her. There was a chance she might be able to catch up with her husband.

If he didn't turn away from her—and if he wasn't killed first.

◆ ◆ ◆

Eddie was already regretting taking the statue. It had seemed manageable at first, but now it felt heavier with each step. He should have just smashed the thing and been done with it . . .

He glanced back as he rounded a corner. One of the Nazis had pulled ahead of the rest, running with me-chanical determination after his prey—and gaining fast.

"Where's Jesse Owens when I need him?" Eddie said as he searched for escape routes. There were none; he was between two large apartment blocks, the next inter-secting alley a good forty yards away on the right.

Pounding footsteps closed rapidly from behind. His pursuer was about to tackle him—

Eddie leapt, twisting to make a half turn in midair. He landed facing the Nazi—and threw the statue upward.

The young blond man skidded to a halt, unsure whether to kill or catch. His orders won out, and rather than attack the Englishman he lunged for the falling figure.

It landed in his arms with a solid *thump*. Relief crossed his face—

Which turned to pain as Eddie kicked him hard in the groin. The man convulsed and crumpled to the ground.

Eddie snatched back the horse and ran once more. He heard shouts as the rest of the Nazis rounded the corner. No gunfire; they were determined to take the statue in one piece.

But it was both his protection and his ball and chain. If he smashed it to keep it out of their hands, or even abandoned it to gain speed, they would kill him the instant they had a clear shot.

He reached the alley and turned down it, finding to his dismay that he was about to put civilians in danger. A little street market had been set up between the buildings, stalls selling vegetables and clothing and bootleg DVDs. Smoke wafted from a cart cooking potatoes.

"Move, move!" he shouted as he weaved among the startled shoppers. The sight of the gun caused most to jump away in alarm, but he still had to barge a couple of laggards aside.

German yells joined the Arabic. The Nazis had reached the alley. Even without their star sprinter, they were still catching up.

Eddie reached the food cart, seeing charcoal flames licking up from a grill. With a shout of "Fire!" he swung the statue at it. Potatoes scattered—as did burning wood, which landed on a neighboring stall. Cheap clothes instantly caught light. Eddie kicked the stall as he ran past. It collapsed, spilling its burning wares across the alley. People shrieked and ran in panic as the fire spread to other stands and awnings on the sides of buildings.

Eddie swerved through the throng, looking back to see that the blaze had forced the Nazis to stop. Rasche glared impotently after him over the burning cart. The Yorkshireman hurried on down the alley.

There was a small square at a crossroads ahead, more stalls clustered in it. If he took the right-hand alley and headed back in the general direction of the dig, he might be able to find the ASPS and get backup—

Walther and his men rounded the corner.

"Buggeration!" Eddie gasped as the huge Nazi pointed at him and bellowed an order. Guns came up—but didn't shoot. Walther knew that the Englishman was caught in a pincer, and as soon as Rasche and the others got past the fire, they would close it . . .

A doorway led into one of the apartment blocks. Eddie ran at it, hoping it wasn't locked—

The door burst open at his kick. He stumbled inside, finding himself in a stairwell. A door led deeper into the building, but a warning sign in Arabic with the stylized symbol of a key suggested that it was locked. Not wanting to waste precious seconds trying it, he charged up the steps instead.

He had reached the second floor when the outer door banged. A glance over the banister; Walther glared up at him. The German barked another command, and his men streamed past him in pursuit.

Eddie kept climbing, legs burning from the effort of carrying the statue. The doors to the internal hallways had the same warning sign as on the ground floor—but the fourth floor was different, a line of sunlight coming through a second, half-open door to one side. Keep going up, or out?

He chose the latter, barreling through to find himself on a small terrace. Any hope of jumping to a neighboring block faded as he saw that the nearest building presented only a blank wall, and a rooftop opposite was too far to reach. He peered over the edge. The floors fell away below, the sheer drop broken only by awnings over the windows.

The echoes of stamping feet grew louder. The Nazis were right behind him—

Eddie went to the terrace's railing—and held the statue out over the edge.

The first of his pursuers burst through the door, then

froze. "Get back!" Eddie shouted as a logjam of black-clad men built up behind the new arrival. "Get the fuck back, or I'll let it go."

Some of the Nazis retreated. But they weren't obeying Eddie; instead, they were responding to Walther's orders and clearing a path as the hulking man reached the landing. He filled the doorway, aiming his gun at Eddie's chest. "If you drop it, you will die," he said.

"And you'll never get your Fountain of Youth." Eddie looked down at the intersection again. People were still running from the fire, but it wouldn't be long before Rasche's group cleared the obstacle . . .

Red hair among the black and head scarves. Nina ran into the square. He yelled her name, seeing her stop to look for him—then caught movement in his peripheral vision. "Oi! Back off, Adolf," he snarled as the nearest Nazi crept toward him. The young man pulled away, but only by a couple of steps.

Walther emerged fully into the open, more of his men slipping onto the terrace behind him. "You have nowhere to go. Give us the statue, and we will let you live."

"Yeah, right," Eddie replied sarcastically. He checked below. Nina had seen him at last and was staring up at the balcony, unsure what to do.

"You do not believe me?"

"You're an escaped Nazi war criminal, mate. You've got a bit of a credibility problem."

"It is your only hope of staying alive." Walther nodded at the two men nearest Eddie. They slowly advanced on the Yorkshireman.

"You want this statue, then you'll all fuck off back down the stairs," Eddie snapped, but he knew that his bargaining chip was becoming less effective by the moment. They were going to rush him . . .

"Okay, okay," he said with a defeated sigh. One of the Nazis hesitated, but the other stepped closer, reaching out to take the statue from him.

Walther smiled. "Good. You are making the only possible—"

With another cry of *"Nina!"* Eddie whirled and flung the statue off the roof.

It spun through the air, arcing down toward his wife. Walther and the others stared after it, frozen in shock—

Eddie grabbed the nearest man by the front of his dark overalls, yanked the Nazi toward him—and rolled backward over the railing.

11

The Nazi screamed as he and Eddie plunged toward the ground—

They struck an awning, the black-clad man taking the brunt of the impact. But it barely slowed them, the pair wrenching the frame from the wall as they dropped.

*   *   *

Nina saw the statue whirling toward her and instinctively darted out of its path—before the rational part of her mind countermanded the reaction. If the statue hit the ground, it would be destroyed. She had to save it. But it weighed enough to seriously injure her . . .

A stall beside her sold rugs, heavy rolls of woven cloth stacked upon it. She snatched one up and held it across her chest, moving to intercept the falling treasure—

Even with the thick padding, the impact felt as if she had been kicked in the chest by a *real* horse. She fell on her back, the landing knocking the breath from her lungs.

But the statue had survived.

*   *   *

More awnings ripped away as Eddie and the Nazi kept falling, fabric flapping around them. Three, two, only one more left before they hit the ground—

The last sunscreen held.

For a moment—then its frame snapped. But it took the two men's weight just long enough to slow them before tearing loose.

They dropped the final ten feet with the younger man underneath Eddie. There was a harsh snap as the Nazi's ribs broke. The Englishman bounced off him and rolled, winded, against the wall.

* * *

Nina was also gasping for air. She opened her eyes, flinching in fright at an unfamiliar face glaring down at her. But it was an Egyptian man, not one of the Nazi raiders.

She thought he was going to help her up, but instead he frowned and said: "You have ruined my rug! You break it, you bought it. Four hundred pounds."

"*How* frickin' much?" she wheezed, before remembering first that he meant Egyptian pounds, not British, and second that she had much bigger problems than an irate street trader. She heard shouts—and down an alley saw Rasche and his men kicking a burning obstruction aside. "That guy'll pay for it," she said, straining upright.

"What guy?"

"The one with the gun." She took hold of the statue, then got clumsily to her feet.

The trader grabbed her arm. "Hey, hey! Four hundred pou—"

A bullet smacked against the building behind his stall.

"Consider it a gift!" the Egyptian decided, diving for cover.

"Shit!" Nina shrieked, pain and breathlessness instantly vanishing in a surge of panic-fueled adrenaline. She ran for a side alley, the heavy statue already weighing her down.

* * *

The gunshot jolted Eddie back to full awareness. Wincing, he started to rise—only to see Rasche and his men charge into the square less than twenty feet away. He had dropped his gun during the fall, leaving him defenseless . . .

But none of them looked in his direction. Instead, they all ran around a corner, heading north. He felt a moment of relief . . .

Until he realized who they were chasing.

He stood. His impromptu crash mat was sprawled at his feet. Blood bubbled from the young man's mouth with every feeble breath; he had punctured a lung.

Eddie had no sympathy. He collected his MPX-K from the ground and started after Nina and her pursuers.

* * *

Nina hurried through another narrow maze, every step a flat slap as the sculpture's weight passed down to her feet. The last time she had stood on a set of scales, she had been around 120 pounds; the figure of Bucephalus probably added a fifth of her entire bodyweight. And she was already feeling the strain of carrying it, each breath like sandpaper inside her throat.

But she couldn't stop. Fear drove her on; the sure knowledge that if the Nazis caught her, they would kill her. She could hear them closing in. Her breathing grew harsher, more desperate . . .

She rounded a turn and saw a busy street at the alley's end, a blue-and-white tram clanking past. A major road; there could be cops there, even soldiers.

"Dr. Wilde, this is your last chance!" Rasche shouted as she pounded toward it. "Surrender or die!" He fired a single shot over her head for emphasis.

Nina kept going, ducking around the corner—just as another bullet cracked against the wall, concrete fragments stinging the back of her neck. People nearby ran. She went with them, searching for help.

She was on one of Alexandria's main thoroughfares.

Several lanes of traffic ran in each direction, tramlines down the center of the road. Keeping low, she ducked between parked cars and ran alongside the line of empty vehicles, looking for somewhere to hide—

A siren wailed behind her.

Nina looked over her shoulder. A police car was weaving through the lanes in her direction. The cops were responding to the gunshots; Egypt's recent political turmoil had left the authorities on high alert. If she could attract their attention, she had a chance . . .

She put the statue down on a car's trunk and waved her arms. "Hey, police! Help me! Over here!"

Rasche and his men emerged from the alley. The Nazi looked toward Nina, then the source of the siren. He shouted an order and the group split up, two men pursuing the archaeologist as the rest raised their guns—

More screams filled the street as gunfire echoed across it. Bullets ripped into the police car and the two men inside. It crashed into an oncoming taxi and spun to a standstill across the tramlines.

Horrified, Nina grabbed the statue and ran once more. People hurriedly abandoned their vehicles and fled. She scurried among the stalled cars.

The two Nazis came after her. She tried to run faster, but the statue's weight had exhausted her reserves.

A loud bang from behind as one of her pursuers jumped up onto a car roof and vaulted onto the next. *Bang, bang,* and he was upon Nina, about to leap down and tackle her—

More gunshots—but from *ahead,* not behind.

The Nazi hit the road behind her with a nerveless *thump.* The second man hurriedly dived for cover as more shots cracked past. Rasche and the rest of his team scrambled back into the alley. "Dr. Wilde!" a man shouted. "Over here, keep down!"

She followed her savior's advice, scuttling onward until she caught sight of him. It was Falk, the Mossad agent.

He smiled at her, the expression incongruous among

the chaos. "Here, quick!" he called, signaling for her to join him behind a white Toyota four-by-four.

Another roar of gunfire. Falk's younger associate, Zane, was on the SUV's other side. He sent two more bursts from a submachine gun at Rasche's position, then slapped it down on the hood and took a grenade from his jacket, pulling the pin and hurling the bomb in a single smooth movement. The gun was back in his hand before the grenade reached the end of its arc. Nina flinched, expecting an explosion, but instead there was a flat thud. Thick smoke gushed from where it had landed, swirling around the abandoned cars and blocking her attackers from view.

Sightlessness did not deter them, however. Glass cracked and metal cratered as more shots ripped into the traffic, the Nazis firing blind through the gray cloud. Nina shrieked as a round clanked off a van behind her. Falk responded by sending a couple of pistol shots back at its source. "Good to see you again, Dr. Wilde," he said, as amiably as if they were chatting over coffee. "I told you we'd be ready if you needed us."

"That's great, thanks," she replied, "but any chance you could get me the hell out of here before half of Alexandria gets killed in the crossfire?"

"I will. Although first . . ." He peered out from behind the Toyota, calling in Hebrew to his partner, then moved past Nina. "Stay behind me."

"You *think*?"

Falk shrugged off the sarcasm with another smile—then his expression suddenly became intense. He advanced to the car ahead of the SUV, crouching to peer underneath it—and abruptly snapped up to fire a single shot. The second of the Nazis chasing Nina slumped to the asphalt in front of the car, a gory starburst surrounding a bullet hole in his forehead.

Another Hebrew command, and Zane resumed his suppressing fire, sending bullets into the smoke cloud. Falk hurried to the dead man and frisked him, taking a wallet and cell phone before returning to Nina. "Okay, now it is time to go!"

"No arguments there," Nina replied. She hefted the statue and moved to the SUV's rear door—

One of the Toyota's windows exploded, spraying them with glinting fragments.

"Ben!" yelled Zane, ducking in response to a new threat. "More of them—corner, seven o'clock! It's Walther!"

The hulking Nazi and his men had reached the main street, emerging from an alley half a block behind the Israelis' SUV. They spread out, using cars and street furniture for cover as they fired on the Mossad agents. "Dr. Wilde, we'll have to move," Falk snapped. "Get to the buildings over there." He pointed across the street, then glanced at the statue. "You'll go much faster if you leave that behind."

Even under attack, Nina was unwilling to be patronized. "No shit, Sherlock. This is what they came here to steal; after all the people they've killed, I'm not going to let them waltz away with it."

Zane rounded the SUV. "Ben, if we don't leave now, they'll box us in." The smoke was clearing, revealing Rasche's group resuming their advance.

Falk regarded the statue, then looked back at Nina. "Okay. Bring it. But you will have to carry it—we need to shoot!"

"Fine by me," Nina said, though with a weary sigh as she shifted the sculpture's weight in her arms. "Which way?"

"Behind the van, then cross the tramlines and go around that red car. Stay low and head for the building with the yellow awning. Are you ready?"

"As I'll ever be."

"Good. We'll get you out of here, Dr. Wilde." He smiled again. "Okay, now—"

"*Grenade!*" cried Zane, diving on top of them.

A metal egg clunked off the roof of a nearby car—and exploded.

Every window within fifty feet of the detonation blew out, shrapnel punching thousands of holes through steel. The SUV rocked on its suspension with the force of the blast.

Ears aching, Nina raised her head. Zane's face was tight with pain from several cuts on the back of his head and neck, but the wounds did not slow him; he was already back on his feet as he searched for their attackers. "They're coming," he warned. "From ahead and behind."

Falk rose to a crouch. "How many?"

"At least three with Walther. Rasche has another two."

The older man pulled the magazine from his pistol to check how many bullets remained, grimaced, then slotted it back in place. "The odds could be more in our favor," he told Nina with an apologetic shrug, before looking back at his partner. "Do me proud, *areyh tes'eyer.*"

The normally stoical Zane's face broke into a surprisingly boyish grin. "Have I ever done anything else, *alter kocker?*"

"Far too often." Another smile, then Falk peered cautiously down the street. Rasche and his group were scurrying toward them between the empty cars. "You take Walther and the ones behind, I will . . ."

His voice trailed off—not in fear, but surprise. Nina followed his gaze, seeing a tram clanking down the road at speed. That it was not in the hands of a normal driver was made instantly clear as it rammed the bullet-pocked police car aside and thundered toward her.

A figure leaned out of the open door, right arm raised—

* * *

Eddie let rip with the MPX on full auto, spraying the startled Nazis with bullets as the tram—its controller handle held in place by a bag abandoned by a fleeing passenger—charged past them. One man fell dead under the onslaught, a second reeling as a round clipped his upper arm. Rasche flung himself behind a car as shots plunked into its bodywork.

The Englishman ducked back inside as the enraged survivors returned fire. The tram's windows shattered,

splintered wood flying through the cabin. But the intervening seats stopped any bullets from reaching him.

The smoke from the grenade explosion rolled past. He
wasn't far from Nina's position. He pulled the bag off
the controls and shoved the lever back. The whine of the
tram's motors died down, and the little train began to
slow. He waited for the shooting to stop, then jumped
out and rolled to land behind a pickup truck. The empty
tram coasted on past him.

Where was Nina? A glance over the pickup's hood revealed a damaged white SUV about twenty yards back
the way he had come, Zane hunched beside it.

"Bloody Mossad," he muttered as he moved around
the truck, about to call to the Israeli—

Someone yanked him off his feet.

Eddie looked around in shock to find himself staring
into Walther's angry face. The huge German had hauled
him off the ground with just one hand—using the other
to tear the MPX from his grip.

"Englander, hey?" Walther growled, slamming Eddie
violently against the pickup's side. "I hate Englanders!"
He pulled him back, about to pound him into the truck
again—

Eddie drove his fist into his opponent's jaw. "Yeah,
and I fucking hate Nazis!"

The blow would have taken down any normal man,
but Walther was not a normal man. He bellowed like a
bull, and Eddie found himself flying through the air as
the giant hurled him down the street. He crashed down
on top of a car, buckling the roof.

The Nazi shouted orders. His troops moved in, closing the circle around Nina and the two Mossad agents
as Rasche and his remaining man advanced from the
other direction . . .

More sirens screamed.

Walther whirled to stare down the road. Three police
cars tore out from a side street, followed by a pair of
military jeeps and an open-backed truck carrying a
squad of soldiers. He hesitated; then, realizing the Nazis
were outnumbered, issued more commands. He and his

group ran to rejoin Rasche and the other man, and they all disappeared into the maze to the south.

Eddie lifted his aching head to watch their retreat, then saw Nina running toward him. "Oh my God, Eddie!" she cried. "Are you all right?"

"Just lying around," he groaned.

"What happened? I thought they'd caught you—you were up on a balcony!" She started to help him off the car.

"I took the quick way down after I chucked you that horse. It worked for Jackie Chan, so I thought I'd give it a shot—before I *got* shot." Wincing at the protest from his bruised muscles, he clambered down. "Speaking of the horse . . ."

"It's over there," Nina told him, gesturing toward the SUV. Zane was standing beside the statue, warily keeping watch.

"Great. Let's secure the fucking thing."

Falk met them at the Toyota. "Mr. Chase, hello again!" he said cheerfully. "I'm sure you're as glad to see me as I am to see you."

"Wouldn't put money on it," Eddie told him. "But . . . you watched out for Nina, so I've got to give you that, at least." The Mossad agent smiled and extended his hand. Somewhat reluctantly, Eddie raised his own to complete the handshake.

Falk smiled. "You see? We are not as bad as you think. Jared, Mr. Chase just saved us—you should show some gratitude."

Zane had the expression of a child being forced to thank a relative for a horrible sweater. "I wouldn't say he *saved* us," he objected. "He . . . helped."

"Glad to be of service," said Eddie sarcastically. But he held out his hand . . . then stiffened in alarm as Rasche reappeared at the end of the alley, aiming his MPX at Zane.

The young Israeli saw the Englishman's reaction and spun to find the threat as Eddie pushed Nina to the ground—

A gunshot echoed across the street.

But Rasche's round didn't hit its intended target. Falk threw himself in front of the younger agent, taking the bullet in his back. He crumpled to the ground. Blood gushed from the entrance wound.

"Ben!" Zane screamed, eyes wide in horror. He fired at Rasche, but the war criminal had already run back into the alley. One last futile shot, then he crouched beside his fallen comrade.

Eddie was already trying to help the downed man, but bitter past experience told him there was nothing he could do. "The bullet's still in there," he told Zane all the same. "Put pressure on the wound, we might be able to—"

"No!" said Falk breathlessly. "Jared, the phone, the wallet—you must take them and follow any leads. And . . ." He coughed, producing specks of bloody spittle. "And take everything else. You have to leave me."

Zane shook his head. "No, I can't—"

"You must! You know the rules." His eyes flicked beseechingly toward Nina and Eddie. "The Egyptians cannot know I am from the Mossad. We may be at peace, but they are not our friends. And they cannot take you, either," he went on, a warning note entering his voice even through the pain. One hand fumbled inside his clothing. "Here, here." He produced the wallet and phone and tried to pass them to the younger man, but they slipped from his grasp.

Zane caught them. Anguished, he leaned over his partner and spoke pleadingly in Hebrew. Falk shook his head, a tear running from the corner of one eye. "You know the rules," he repeated. "You must . . . accomplish the mission. *Tzeth'a leshalom veshuvh'a leshalom, areyh tes'eyer . . .*"

He began to smile, but it froze on his lips. The old man fell still.

Zane's fists clenched, his whole body shuddering. He opened his mouth as if to cry out . . . but then forced it closed again. Quickly and coldly, he ran his hands through Falk's pockets, taking out every form of identification, every personal possession. Grim task completed, he looked up at the couple. "Say nothing to the Egyptians." It was as much threat as request.

"We won't," Nina promised, feeling his loss. Eddie nodded.

Zane choked back his emotions, then hurried off through the stranded traffic. Within moments he had vanished, slipping away from the arriving cops and soldiers.

Eddie looked from Falk's body to the statue of Bucephalus. "That fucking thing had better be worth all of this," he rumbled.

"I hope it is," whispered Nina.

12

The statue rested on a tabletop in a government office, the survivors of the tomb's opening standing around it.

Habib was first to speak. "This may not be the best time," he said, "but . . . with the death of Dr. Assad, the responsibility for dealing with this situation is mine."

Banna gave him a sharp look. "I am in charge of the dig."

"The dig, yes, but this statue clearly has a wider importance. It must be dealt with by the ministry—it is now a government matter, not simply archaeological."

"The IHA is involved too," said Nina. "That makes it an international issue."

The reminder did not sit well with either Banna or Habib. "You are no longer part of the IHA," said the former.

"I was asked to come here by the United Nations, at the request of the Egyptian government. The IHA representative on site—and my friend—is dead. Until someone higher up tells me otherwise, I'd say that makes me the ranking IHA representative. Wouldn't you agree?"

It was clear they did not, but neither had a compelling rebuttal at hand, or for that matter the willingness to argue. Banna shrugged, then returned his attention to the sculpture. "Very well."

"The statue should be removed to a more secure location," Habib insisted. "I will take it to the ministry in Cairo."

"Make your arrangements," said Banna with a dismissive wave. "We have work to do." The irked official took out his phone and left the room. "Dr. Wilde, it is time you told me everything. Who are these raiders, what do they want, and why is this statue so important to them?"

Nina took a deep breath before launching into an account of what she had learned about the escaped Nazi war criminals, and events from her encounter in Los Angeles onward—minus any mention of the Mossad agents. "I'm still as dubious as you look to be about the Spring of Immortality really existing," she concluded, noting the Egyptian's skeptical expression. "But I've now seen three of the SS men who escaped after the war. They should be in their nineties, or even older—but they're not. That suggests they've found *something* that slows the effects of aging . . . and their being willing to take such extreme action to get their hands on this"— she indicated the statue—"means they're convinced it can lead them to its source."

Eddie nodded, then winced; the cut to his scalp had been stitched up, but was still painful. "If you're an escaped Nazi who's managed to stay hidden for seventy years, you don't stick your head out of your hole unless it's for something *really* important."

"It's not just the original guys, though," said Macy. "You said there were, what, eight of them? The people who attacked us were like a small army. And most of them were young."

"*Boys from Brazil,* like I said," Eddie told Nina.

"They're *not* clones," she replied. "But they knew the Bucephalus statue would be in the burial chamber with Alexander, so they had information we didn't. Presumably, they also knew that it would tell them what they needed."

"The riddle of Bucephalus," said Banna. He used a magnifying glass to examine the tiny letters inscribed upon the horse's reins. "But what *is* the riddle? We have read all the text, and there is nothing that could be a puzzle."

The writing had been translated into both Arabic and English. Nina picked up a transcript. "Well, let's see what we've got. According to this, Andreas the cook made the statue to honor Alexander."

"Three hundred years after Alexander died," Macy reminded her dubiously.

"It's not as crazy as it sounds. We've got bad guys who are half a century younger than they should be, looking for something that's linked to the legend of the Spring of Immortality. Maybe it's more than just a legend."

"Wouldn't be the first time that's happened to us," noted Eddie.

"Whether or not it was made by Andreas, most of the text is in praise of Alexander." Banna recited an example from the Arabic translation. " 'None could hope to match the wisdom and bravery of Alexander; he was and shall ever be unique in all of history, a true giant among mere men whose greatness will never be equaled.' The rest says that solving the riddle of Bucephalus will lead you to the Spring of Immortality. But there is no riddle."

"Maybe it originally had a base with more writing on it," Macy suggested.

"There would have been marks on the feet where a base was attached, but there aren't any," said Nina. "It's a single sculpted piece. A very good one too."

"The workmanship is beautiful," Banna agreed, admiring its lines. "A priceless artifact." He ran a fingertip along the horse's neck, stopping at the ragged bullet hole in the mane. "Even with this damage," he added, giving Eddie a disapproving glare.

The Englishman was unrepentant. "If I'd hit it a couple of inches lower, I would've blown the whole thing to bits and all this would be over."

Banna muttered something in Arabic that Nina doubted

was complimentary. "Brute force has no place in archaeology," he went on.

"Yeah, I've been telling him that for six years now," she said.

Eddie made a face at her. "Funny, I seem to remember it working for us quite a few times. It's like that whole Gordian Knot thing—Alexander just chopped it in half. Problem solved! If you can't figure something out with brainpower, sometimes you've got to take the direct approach . . ."

He trailed off, staring at the statue with sudden intensity. "What?" Nina asked.

"I think I've just solved the riddle of Bucephalus." He picked up the statue—

And before anyone could stop him, dashed it to pieces on the floor.

Banna gawped at the broken remains. "You—you *maniac*! What have you done?" He ran to the office door, shouting for security.

"Eddie, Jesus Christ!" Nina cried. "Why the hell did you do that?"

"Because that's what it said to do." He crouched and picked through the debris. "Something like 'Only Alexander's wisdom could find the solution to the Gordian Knot, and to solve the riddle of Bucephalus you need wisdom like his,' wasn't it?"

Several members of the Antiquities Special Protection Squad rushed into the room. Banna stabbed an accusing finger at the Englishman. "Arrest him! He has destroyed a priceless relic!"

"Yeah, and I've found an even more priceless one," Eddie announced as the uniformed men surrounded him. He raised one hand to show he was not a threat—and in the other held up a metal object. "See?"

"Wait, wait," Nina said urgently. "Dr. Banna, look! He's right—there was something *inside* the statue."

Banna hesitated before issuing a command for the ASPS to stand back, but not withdraw. "Give it to me."

"You're welcome," Eddie said sarcastically as it was

snatched away. Banna gazed at the new discovery, Nina joining him.

"It's a fish," she whispered. The hidden treasure was around nine inches long and half an inch thick, a flat bronze lens shape with a small triangular tail attached by a hinge to one end. Lines of tiny Greek text were inscribed around the artifact's outer edge. A circular hole at the head, half an inch in diameter, represented the fish's eye. A slot ran down the centerline, some sort of measuring scale marked along it. Standing proud of the slot was a metal pointer, which could apparently move; glimpses of a mechanism were visible through the opening. "Turn it over."

Banna did so, revealing several bronze cogwheels on the underside. The largest two were solid disks marked with Greek numerals, while the others resembled the inner workings of an analogue watch. The Egyptian cautiously rotated the biggest cog, causing some of the others to move in turn. The pointer in the slot shifted position slightly. A turn of the second disk set other cogs into motion, the end result also being translated to the pointer. "It is a machine," he said, anger replaced by wonderment.

"Yeah, but a machine to do what?" Macy asked.

"I guess this'll tell us," said Nina, pointing out the text. "We need to get it translated, as soon as we can."

"Yes, yes," Banna said, nodding absently. "It resembles the Antikythera mechanism. Not as complex, but similar precision in the workmanship."

"The what?" Eddie asked as he stood. The ASPS were still regarding him with suspicion. "It's all right, lads, I don't think he's bothered about me breaking the statue anymore."

"It would have been better if you had let us x-ray it first," said Banna, "but yes, I think this is the true treasure."

"So do I," Nina told him. She reluctantly shifted her gaze from the artifact to her husband. "The Antikythera mechanism was found in a shipwreck from the first century BCE," she explained. "Our best guess is that it was a kind of astronomical calculator—basically, an early computer. It seems that you could enter dates using the dials, and it would tell you the positions of the planets at those times."

"So what does this one do?" Macy asked.

"Tells you how to find the Spring of Immortality, at a guess," said Eddie. "Although it'd be a lot easier if Andreas had just painted a little map on the horse."

Nina looked back at the text. "He didn't do that because . . . because it's meant to be a *challenge*," she said. "You have to prove that you're as smart as Alexander in order to reach it. 'Those who believe themselves Alexander's equal shall learn the truth if they have the wisdom and bravery and endurance to follow the path to the spring.'"

"Sounds a bit ominous," said Eddie.

Banna also peered at the inscriptions. "I think this describes a landmark," he said, pointing out one line. "It says the Gate of Alexander is found on a mountain. But it does not say which mountain."

"That's the challenge," Nina realized. "You have to use the mechanism on the fish to work out the route. It looks like a pretty complicated procedure, so it's a test of your intelligence as well as your navigational skills." She continued reading; a word caught her eye. "It mentions a gnomon here . . ."

"What's a gnomon?" Macy asked.

Eddie grinned. "Gnome drugs."

"Huh? *Ohhh*," she added with a groan as she got the joke.

"It's part of a sundial," said Nina. "The stick that casts the shadow—wait, is that what this is? A way to navigate by using the sun?" She poked the tip of her little finger into the fish's eye. "If you put a gnomon in here and aligned the slot with the shadow at midday, you could use it to work out your latitude . . ."

"There is a height written here," Banna said with sudden excitement. "One *dichas*—half a foot."

"A gnomon that tall would be enough to produce a shadow, yeah. But how would you deal with seasonal changes in the sun's inclination?" The answer came to both archaeologists simultaneously. "The dials! Turn it over!"

The Egyptian flipped the relic to reveal the mechanism. "One dial for months, another for days, perhaps?"

Nina examined the metal cogs. "I think you're right. It's a way to set the date."

Habib reentered the room. "Why are they here?" he asked as he regarded the ASPS with concern—then his expression turned to shock on seeing the statue's remains. A high-pitched burst of Arabic, then: "What is going on? What happened to the statue?"

"The statue is not important," Banna told him almost absently, his focus on the bronze fish.

The official seemed on the verge of panic. "Not important? *Not important?* But I have told the minister that I will bring it to Cairo . . ."

"The raiders weren't after the statue," said Nina. "They wanted something hidden *inside* it. That." She gestured at the object in Banna's hands.

Habib finally noticed the relic. "Inside the statue?" he asked.

"Yeah. It's a sort of treasure map. We don't know where it leads yet, but we will, given time."

"I see, I see. Then yes, I suppose the statue is not important." He nodded slowly, as if trying to convince himself of his own words. "But the—a fish, is it? The fish should still be taken to Cairo. It will be safer in the ministry than here. Even you must see that, Dr. Banna."

The Egyptian archaeologist was annoyed at having his authority challenged again, but conceded the point. "I . . . yes, it will. But we must arrange secure transport— I will not have you drive it there in your glove box!" He put down the artifact and spoke to one of the ASPS before having an exchange with the increasingly unhappy Habib, Banna countering some objection with a dismissive wave. "The ASPS will arrange an armed convoy to Cairo tomorrow morning," he finally told Nina. "Until then, the Andreas relic will remain under guard here. I shall continue to examine it."

"I think," Nina said gently, "it might be better if you took the rest of the day off."

"What do you mean?" he asked, almost affronted.

"I mean that . . . you almost died today. And people you know, your friends, *did* die. You might think that pressing on regardless is the best way to deal with it, but it's not. Trust me, I know. Ignoring what's happened isn't the way to honor Dr. Assad, or Bill Schofield and Dina Rashad, and all the others who were killed. Right now, you need time to process what's happened."

The young man seemed about to object, then looked down at the broken sculpture. "You are right," he said at last. "A lot has happened, and . . ." He tried to find the right words to express his feelings—or to admit to them. "I cannot pretend that it has not. You are right," he repeated.

"Is there anyone you can be with?" Macy asked.

"In Alexandria? No, my family are all in Qena. I will . . ." His face turned downcast. Nina realized the person he had probably been closest to was the late Assad. "I will go to my apartment. I will be okay," he went on quickly, raising a hand to forestall any further suggestions or sympathies. "I just want to be on my own, to think."

"If you need anything . . . ," Nina offered.

Banna shook his head. "I will be fine. But yes, we shall begin again tomorrow."

"Will that thing be safe here?" Eddie asked.

"The ASPS will protect it; this building also has soldiers guarding it. And the men who attacked us are now fewer in number, thanks to you."

"Doesn't mean they've given up. If they're that desperate to get hold of your clockwork fish, they might try again."

"I am sure the ASPS and the army will protect it," said Habib. "I shall contact Cairo and tell the minister when to expect our arrival." He left the room, signaling for the ASPS to follow.

"We should go too," said Nina to Eddie and Macy.

Her husband nodded. "Yeah. It's been one hell of a day."

Nina was about to exit when Banna spoke, his voice surprisingly hesitant. "Dr. Wilde?"

"Yes?"

"I perhaps . . . underestimated you. You were right about the danger to the dig."

"I never expected anything like what happened," Nina told him. "Nobody could have."

"Maybe not. But I did not take you seriously, and . . . and now, people have died."

"It wasn't your fault."

"I have told myself that. But . . . it is still a difficult thing to accept. How do you deal with it?"

"The hard way."

His face fell further. "I had hoped you would have advice for me on how to make it easier."

"There is no easy way. I'm sorry."

"Yes, that is what I was afraid of." He stared at the artifact. "Dr. Wilde . . . would you be willing to work with me on the relic?"

She was surprised by the offer. "As an individual, or as a representative of the IHA?"

"Both."

"You're not in the IHA anymore," said Eddie, with a subtle tone of warning. "And we've got other plans, remember?"

"I know, I know," she said, before turning back to Banna. "But . . . this wouldn't be a long-term commitment, would it?"

"No, no," Banna replied. "Only until we have translated the text and understood the working of the mechanism."

Macy raised a cautious finger. "Ah . . . just to remind you, the Antikythera mechanism was found over a hundred years ago, and nobody knows exactly how it works yet."

"The Antikythera mechanism is missing some pieces," Nina said. "This isn't. And it's even got instructions written on it." She moved back to the table and gazed at the metal fish. "A couple of days should be enough . . ."

"Nina." There was no subtlety in Eddie's warning now. "That's not what we agreed."

"I'm still doing what Seretse and the Egyptian government asked me to do," she insisted.

"No you're not. What Seretse asked you to do was help the Egyptians secure Alexander's tomb. Well, that's done."

"Yes, but the thing those Nazis came for is *right here,*" she said, jabbing a finger at the relic. "And it leads to something incredible."

"It *might* lead to something incredible. Or it might lead to absolutely bugger-all—I mean, he said yesterday"—Eddie gestured at Banna—"that the *Alexander Romance* was full of crap."

Banna did not want to be drawn into the argument. "If you want to help me, Dr. Wilde," he said, "then call me. Here is my number." Avoiding Eddie's glower, he handed her a business card.

"Thank you. I'll talk to you later; I think Eddie and I should have the rest of this discussion somewhere else."

"Yeah, that way I can swear more," her husband rumbled. "Deyab's waiting to drive us back to the hotel. Macy, you coming?"

Macy looked apologetically between the couple. "Thanks, but . . . I'll take a cab. You two might want to talk in private, you know?"

13

"We are almost at the hotel," said Deyab, with considerable relief.

"Good, great," growled Eddie. Privacy, even the relative kind, had not brought his and Nina's increasingly bitter argument any closer to a conclusion. He turned back to his wife. "So that's it? What I think—and what we both agreed on before—doesn't matter now you've got a chance to chase after another piece of archaeological bollocks?"

Nina tried unsuccessfully to contain her frustration. "It's not 'bollocks'—this is *important* to me, Eddie! This is what I do, this is what I've spent my whole life doing. And it's not that big a deal. It'll only be for a day or two."

"Only a day or two," he echoed. "And what if it takes longer? Macy said they haven't worked out what that Antique-tick-tock mechanism does after a century, so what if you and Banna *can't* just do a Robert Langdon and figure everything out in five minutes? Are you going to stay working on it for a week? A month?"

"I don't know! Maybe, maybe not."

"And how long have you got left? You're going to use up a chunk of that time sitting in a bloody lab translating ancient Greek!"

"For God's sake, Eddie! It's just a few days."

"A few days, yeah—out of how many? If you're going to live to be ninety, that's not a big deal, but if you only live to thirty-fou—" He stopped abruptly, fear refueling his anger. "For fuck's sake, Nina! You're *dying,* but you'd still rather spend time with people who are already dead than with me!"

"That's not true!" she cried.

Her hurt expression warned him that he had overstepped the mark, but he was in no mood to back down. "That's what it feels like, though. You could have told Seretse to piss off and let the Egyptians handle it, but you had to come here to see for yourself. And even though a bunch of Nazis, actual out-of-World-War-fucking-Two *Nazis,* just tried to kill us both, you still want to go chasing after another bloody legend!"

"It might not *be* a legend, though."

"That doesn't make it your problem."

"No, but it's my *choice.* I *want* to follow up on this, Eddie." She folded her arms across her chest.

"Decision's made, is it?" he said. There was no reply; Nina was not even looking at him. "Jesus Christ," he muttered.

Deyab broke the chilly silence. "Here is the hotel!" he said, even more relieved than before. He stopped the Mercedes and got out to open Nina's door. "If you need me for anything else, just call."

"Thanks, Deyab," she replied as she exited.

Eddie emerged from the other side. "If you hear shooting, it'll probably just be the two of us."

They entered the hotel in single file rather than side by side. Eddie was about to follow Nina to the elevators when someone caught his eye. "Ay up," he said as Zane beckoned to him from across the reception area. "Somebody wants a word."

Nina hesitated, not in the mood for company, but there was a sadness around the Israeli's eyes that his stoical mask could not fully conceal. Zane went to a corner seat; they joined him. The cuts to his head and neck were now covered by Band-Aids. "Are you okay?" she asked.

"Yes, I'm fine," he said brusquely, before adding in a slightly softer tone: "Thank you."

"What's up?" Eddie asked.

Zane glanced around to make sure that none of the other patrons was listening. "We got some information from the phone Ben took from the dead man."

"By 'we,' you mean Mossad, right?"

The younger man's eyes twitched in aggravation. "Yes, and don't shout it out across the room. We checked the phone's memory, and got our friends in America to track down the contact numbers."

"Your friends at the NSA, I'm guessing."

A small nod. "It was a prepaid phone, and most of the calls were to other burners—probably belonging to the other members of the cell. None of them is active anymore, so the raiders must have disposed of them when they realized they'd been compromised. But one number was different. A landline."

"Someone phoned home?" said Nina.

Zane shook his head. "If we'd located their base, the Criminal Sanctions Unit would already have been fully reactivated. All I have is a potential lead. The call was to a man named Leitz, Frederic Leitz—he's from Luxembourg, but lives mostly in Italy. He's been on the Mossad's watch list for a long time."

"The guy in LA had been in contact with someone in Italy," Nina recalled.

"What's this Leitz done?" Eddie asked, becoming intrigued in spite of himself.

"He's a middleman, arranging money transfers for anti-Israeli and extreme right-wing organizations. And individuals too; he has some very powerful and very wealthy clients, all of them known anti-Semites."

"So you think this guy might know where these Nazis came from?"

"I do, yes. The dead man having contacted Leitz can't be a coincidence. I want to find out what he knows."

He regarded the couple with an expectant expression.

"Sooo . . . ," Nina said, after a few seconds of silence, "you want us to . . . what?"

"I want you to help me do that," he replied. "Or rather," he went on, facing Eddie, "I want *you* to help me. No offense, Dr. Wilde, but you don't have the skills I need. I've read your husband's file, though, and I know he does."

The Englishman let out a dismissive laugh. "Wait, you want *me* to go with you? And, what? Beat the truth out of this bloke?"

"If that's what it takes, yes."

"Why do you need Eddie?" Nina demanded. "You're in"—she dropped her voice—"the Mossad. You must have other agents."

"We do, but they're all in other divisions. Ben and I were the CSU's only currently active field agents. It could take days to recall someone else." Zane's youthful face suddenly became harder, older. "I don't want to wait that long. I want answers *now*. But . . . I can't do it by myself," he said, the admission difficult. "Leitz takes his security very seriously. That's why I need you, Chase. On my own, it would be very hard to get to him. But with two of us . . ."

Eddie shook his head. "And why the fuck would I want to do that?"

"Because you owe me. Both of you."

"How do you figure that?" asked Nina.

"We saved you from Walther and—and Rasche." Anger rose in the Israeli's voice as he named his partner's killer, but he quickly covered it. "Without us, the Nazis would have the statue."

"I don't care about the statue," said Eddie. Nina shot him an irritated look.

"But you care about your *wife*, don't you?" Zane snapped. "Without us, she'd be dead."

"She was doing okay when I turned up."

"No, that's . . . probably true," the redhead was forced to admit to her husband. "The Nazis had me cornered. He and his friend took out two of them and held the others off . . ." She hesitated, seeing the Mossad agent's expression flicker. This time, the emotion he was trying to conceal was not anger. "Are you all right?" she asked in a gentle tone.

"Yes, of course," Zane replied. The muscles around his mouth were drawn tight.

"No you're not. Mr. Falk—Ben; he was more than just your boss, wasn't he?"

The young man was obviously reluctant to open up on the matter, especially before Eddie, but after a moment of conflict he admitted, "Yes. Ben was . . . my mentor, I guess. He taught me everything." A lengthy pause. "More than that. He saw something in me that nobody else had, not even me. If it wasn't for him . . ."

"You wouldn't be who you are now?" Eddie finished for him with a new understanding, even sympathy, in his voice. "I'm sorry. I know what you're going through."

Zane shook his head. "I doubt it."

"You're not the only one who's lost someone like that."

The Israeli regarded him with surprise, but then shook his head again as if to dismiss the subject. "I need to get that information from Leitz."

"And you want Eddie to help you get it?" Nina said.

To her concern, Eddie did not dismiss the idea out of hand. "Whereabouts in Italy is this guy?" he asked Zane.

"He has a villa south of Naples. Just outside Amalfi."

"Amalfi? I know the place."

"You do?"

"We just visited it," said Nina, her alarm growing. "Eddie, you're not seriously—"

"I *am* seriously," he cut in.

The Mossad agent was surprised again; apparently he had not expected it to be so easy to convince the Englishman. "You are?"

"You *are*?" Nina echoed, appalled.

"You'll make the arrangements, right?" Eddie said to Zane. "Flights, cars, all of that?" The Israeli nodded. "Good. Then I'll go with you. Get us on the first flight to Naples—and make sure everything we'll need is waiting for us at the other end."

"I know what I'm doing," said Zane with an edge of annoyance. "But—you're really willing to help me?"

"Those bastards tried to kill us, twice now. That deserves some payback. Plus," he added with a cold grin, "I've always wanted to beat the shit out of some actual Nazis."

"That's because you've watched *Where Eagles Dare* too many times," Nina told him. "And no, you're not jetting off to Italy!"

"Yes I am," Eddie said. He turned back to Zane before she could respond. "Call me here at the hotel when it's time to go. I'll be ready."

"Okay." Zane stood. "Dr. Wilde," he said with a polite nod before leaving.

Eddie also got up, heading for the elevators. "I'd better start packing."

Nina hurried after him. "What the hell do you think you're doing, Eddie?"

"I think I'm going to Italy to track down those twats who've been trying to kill us. Thought that was pretty much decided."

"*I* didn't decide it!"

"Yeah, and *I* didn't decide that you were going to sit around in Egypt puzzling out some fucking two-thousand-year-old treasure hunt." The doors opened and he stepped inside, jabbing the button for their floor.

Nina followed. "Oh, so that's what this is about? You're mad that I want to see this through, so you're dealing with it by going Nazi hunting?"

"No, I'm mad because you've apparently got better things to do with the rest of your life than spend it with me!" He looked past her to see a tourist regarding them from the lobby. "Going up? Don't mind us."

"It's okay, I'll . . . you know, the next one," the embarrassed man replied, flapping a hand at the neighboring elevator before hurriedly sidestepping out of sight.

"That's *not* what I'm doing, Eddie," Nina insisted.

"It's what it feels like." The doors closed, and the lift ascended.

She tried to control her anger. "I don't want you to go to Italy."

"And I don't want you to stay in Egypt to decode that bloody fish." A long silence followed, broken by the ping of the bell announcing that they had reached their floor. "I don't hear you saying you won't."

"No, you don't," said Nina as the doors opened. "And I don't hear you saying you'll stay here."

"Nope." Eddie stepped onto the landing.

"So that's it? You're going and I'm staying? We're not going to talk about this?"

"You made it pretty clear we already had. You coming?"

She didn't move. "I guess not."

They regarded each other with sullen displeasure. The doors rumbled shut. Neither did anything to stop them. They banged closed, and the elevator started its descent.

14

Deyab led Nina from the hotel's side entrance to the waiting cars. Macy stood outside the middle vehicle, a Toyota minivan; she regarded the pair with confusion. "Where's Eddie?"

"He's not coming" was Nina's curt reply. She clambered into the van, finding Banna and Habib already occupying the back row of seats, and took a place in the middle row.

"What? Why not?"

"He's doing something he thinks is more important. And no, I don't want to talk about it," she added to forestall the inevitable follow-up questions.

"Uh . . . okay," Macy said, clearly aching to know more. But she managed to keep quiet as she got in beside Nina. Deyab took the wheel and waited for the Mercedes he had been driving the day before, now leading the convoy, to pull away before following. Behind, a Toyota Fortuner SUV took up the rear position. The accompanying vehicles were occupied by the ASPS, acting as guards for both the archaeologists and the contents of the case in the minivan's rear.

Banna was also intrigued by Eddie's absence. "Good morning, Dr. Wilde," he said. "Is your husband not joining us?"

"No, he's not," said Nina.

"After what happened yesterday, I am surprised that he would leave you alone—"

"Something came up that he felt he had to deal with," she cut in with irritation. "Okay?"

Habib gave her a concerned look. "Is it anything to do with the relic?"

"Yes, I guess, but . . . not directly."

"Then I will not need to change the security arrangements?" The Egyptian raised a hand as if about to take out his phone.

She shook her head. "No, it's fine. He got a potential lead about the people who attacked us, so he's gone to check it out."

Habib's expression of mild relief was replaced by one almost of shock. "He has found them?"

"No, like I said, it's only a potential lead—we don't know if anything'll come of it."

Deyab looked back sharply. "Dr. Wilde, if you have information about the men who attacked the dig, you should have told us."

"I will, as soon as I know anything definite. But for now, I don't even know if I can trust the source of the information. We'll have to wait until Eddie tells me what he finds out."

"And when'll that be?" asked Macy.

Nina shrugged. "Hell if I know." The driver was unhappy at having been left out of the loop, but didn't push the issue further, returning his attention to following the Mercedes.

A rustle of paper from the rear seats prompted her to turn. Banna was reading what she could tell even upside down was Greek. "Is that the text from the fish?"

"Yes," he replied. "I am translating it into English for you. It will be finished soon."

"Thank you," she said, slightly surprised.

"You saved the tomb—and my life. It is the least I could do. And now we are working together, you need as much information as possible."

"When did you do all that?" Macy asked.

"I came to the government office very early this morning to start work. Actually, it was still night," he admitted to Nina. "You said I should take time after what happened yesterday, but . . ."

"That's okay," Nina told him. "I totally understand."

"Yeah," said Macy with a small laugh. "A workaholic archaeologist—that sounds familiar!"

The convoy continued through the city. They soon entered one of its main arteries, heading southward through the urban sprawl before finally reaching the long highway that would take them to Cairo. Once clear of the Alexandrian traffic, they picked up speed. Settlements and irrigated farmland rolled by, the desert encroaching more with each passing mile.

"Well then?" said Macy after a while, nudging Nina.

"Well what?" she replied.

"You and Eddie. Come on, spill! You were about to start a big argument yesterday, and it obviously didn't stop there. So what's going on? Are you both okay?"

"Oh, we're super-fine," Nina snapped sarcastically, before softening at her friend's wounded look. She glanced at Banna and Habib to make sure they weren't eavesdropping before lowering her voice. "We just had a . . . difference of opinion."

"About what?"

"You know, you ask a lot of questions, Macy."

The younger woman grinned. "Hey, you were the one who told me to sit up front with the teachers instead of having fun at the back with the jocks."

"Huh, I must be getting old if I've managed to become someone's mentor . . . No, we're both okay. We had a fight; wasn't the first, won't be the last. At least, I hope it won't. Not because I enjoy fighting with Eddie, I mean, but because of what I told you about in Los Angeles."

"Your . . . illness?"

"Yeah. I want to find out more about the Andreas relic, but that means spending a few days working on it here in Egypt. Eddie wasn't happy about that."

"Yeah, I guessed. But I can kind of see why," Macy added. "If you don't know how long you've got, then the way he sees it, it's like work's taking away some of the time you've got left together. I'd be pissed too."

"Straight to the point, as always. Have you been taking subtlety lessons from him?"

Another grin. "No, I've always been like this. Drove my parents crazy! But I always felt, why waste time dancing around what you want to say—or what you *need* to say? Hashtag YOLO, you know?"

"I'll . . . take your word for that," said Nina, feeling even older as she realized she had no idea what Macy meant. "But, yeah, my deciding to stay in Egypt definitely wasn't what he wanted." She leaned back, running through the argument in her mind. "Did I do the right thing?"

"You're asking *me* for relationship advice?" Macy sounded as if she couldn't decide whether to be honored or shocked.

"Who else am I going to ask: those two?" She looked around again to make sure the men behind her were still not listening . . .

Some wary part of her brain issued a warning: A silver SUV trailing their rear escort had also been there the last time she looked back. She decided to dismiss it. They were on the main highway between Egypt's two largest cities, and another car might travel with them for a long time.

"Okay, since you asked, I'll tell you everything you're doing wrong with your life." Macy gave her a devilish little smile, making Nina wonder what she had let herself in for, but she was only joking. "No, I wouldn't do that. Not here, anyway. Maybe in a bar, after a couple of Fuzzy Navels!" She giggled. "But I know what you're like, Nina. Remember when we were at Abydos, trying to work out how to find the Pyramid of Osiris? You told me archaeology wasn't just a job to you—it was something you *had* to do, like a calling. And that hasn't changed, not even after what's happened to you."

Nina remembered the day. "I suppose not," she said. "It's part of me."

"Yeah, but so's Eddie," Macy went on pointedly. "And you're a part of him too—a *big* part. That's why he was so upset about you wanting to go off and do your thing. He loves you, and he doesn't want to be without you, not even for a couple of days."

"You're right," Nina admitted after a moment. "I wasn't thinking about it from his point of view. I . . . I just wanted to use the time I've got left to make one last big discovery, you know? Is that being selfish?"

"I think that's something you've got to decide for yourself. And then tell Eddie, when you see him again."

Nina nodded. "Yeah, you're right again."

Pleased with herself, Macy settled back into her seat. "So, where's he gone?"

"Italy."

"*What?*" she yelped. "You mean he's not even in the *country* anymore?"

"Nope. He left hours ago."

"So he was mad at you for wanting to go off and do your own thing, and then *he* goes off and does his own thing?"

"That's about the size of it," Nina told her, though with an amusement that would not have been there earlier. "I tried to change his mind again before he went, but . . . well, *he* tried to change *my* mind, and you can guess how well that turned out." She felt a flash of regret for being angry enough not even to say good-bye, never mind give him any expressions of love, and resolved to remedy that the next time they spoke.

"I can't believe he did that! Man!" Macy threw up her hands. "And after I just totally defended him. Why's he gone to Italy?"

"Like I said, he's following a lead. There's a guy there who might know something about the people who attacked us, so he's going to—"

"Dangle him over a cliff until he talks?"

Nina smiled. "Hopefully it won't come to that."

"I don't know." Macy became more solemn. "I mean, those bastards deserve it. How did he find out about this Italian guy?"

"We got some help from . . ." Nina glanced at the Egyptians, not wanting them to know about her contact with the Mossad. Deyab was focused on the road ahead, a seemingly endless straight line disappearing to the shimmering horizon. Behind, Banna and Habib were talking in Arabic, the latter seeming on edge and distracted—

A flash of sunlight on silver caught her eye. The SUV she had noticed before was still tailing them. It had pulled out to overtake a truck that the little convoy had just passed, but was maintaining the same distance as before.

Most people would have dismissed the vehicle's continued presence as mere coincidence, but recent events—and past experience—had made Nina more paranoid. She stared intently at the SUV as it pulled back in behind the Fortuner. "Is something wrong, Dr. Wilde?" asked Habib.

"I don't know. Maybe. A car's been following us."

Deyab looked in the mirror. "Which one?"

"The silver SUV. It's been behind us for miles now."

The Egyptian spoke into a walkie-talkie. "The rear guard has seen it," he reported after getting a reply. "They do not think it is anything to worry about; it is just going at the same speed. We do have speed limits here in Egypt, even if you do not believe it!" he added with a chuckle.

"Most of them *do* kinda drive like psychopaths," Macy whispered.

"Humor me and slow down, just to see what he does," Nina said.

"You think it's those Nazis?" Macy asked, adding: "Huh. That sounds so weird saying that."

"I'd rather not find out."

Habib snorted. "You are worrying about nothing."

"I am surprised, Youssef," said Banna, in a faintly jabbing tone. "You are the one who insisted that we take the relic to Cairo, and you arranged the security—if anything goes wrong, it will be on your head! We should not take any risks."

The annoyed official had no comeback to that. Deyab spoke into the radio again. "Okay, we are slowing down," he announced after the other cars responded.

Nina looked back as the convoy reduced speed. The object of her suspicion remained blocked from view by the Fortuner . . . until it pulled out sharply and powered past. She tried to see who was inside, but the windows were too darkly tinted.

"He is not following us, then," said Habib as the big SUV, a Volkswagen Touareg, swept away down the highway.

"I guess not," Nina replied. But she couldn't shake off a feeling of worry. The SUV could have overtaken them at any time, so why had it waited until now to pick up speed? "Deyab, is there anyone else behind us?"

"Nobody is following us!" exclaimed the agitated Habib. "How could anyone even know we are transporting the relic? Our journey is a secret."

"The plan of the tomb was supposed to be secret too, but the Nazis got hold of it somehow," she reminded him.

The Egyptian responded with anger. "I have started a full investigation into the leak! Whoever was responsible, I will find them."

"That should not take long, should it, Youssef? The list of suspects is very short," said Banna. Bitterness flooded his voice. "Shorter now, after yesterday."

"How many people had access to the tomb plan?" asked Macy.

"Not many. Myself, Dina Rashad, and Bill Schofield at the dig; Dr. Assad at the ministry, of course . . ." He looked at the man beside him. "And you, Youssef."

"I do not like your tone, Dr. Banna," Habib said, frowning deeply. "If you are suggesting that I—"

"I am not suggesting anything," Banna insisted, though

it was obvious that now the idea had been planted, it was not going to leave.

The government official looked away, affronted—to find the two women giving him looks that were, if not outright accusatory, at least questioning. Tight-lipped, he turned to watch the desiccated plains slide past.

Nina regarded him for a long moment. Banna was correct: The number of people who could have accessed the detailed map given to her by Volker Koenig was indeed small, and several of them were now dead. But in the absence of evidence, she decided to give him the benefit of the doubt. Besides, the same finger that might point at Habib could equally be directed at Banna himself.

She checked the highway ahead. There was little to be seen on this stretch but sandy scrub. Vehicles going to Alexandria flicked past on the other side of the concrete central divider, but even with the road narrowing from four lanes down to three, there was almost no traffic.

The silver SUV was still there, though, visible past the convoy's leading car. It had slowed again, matching their speed a few hundred yards distant. Nina eyed it. Was it just a coincidence that it was keeping pace with them, or . . .

The Touareg suddenly pulled out. The reason for its swerve came into sight as the leading Mercedes also moved over: a pickup truck with a shredded rear tire was slewed at an angle in its path, blocking the inside lane.

The convoy leader's voice crackled from Deyab's walkie-talkie. The Egyptian acknowledged, pulling out to pass the stranded truck. "Shouldn't we help them?" Macy asked.

Deyab shook his head apologetically. "We need to get to Cairo on schedule." Ahead, the first car was about to pass the pickup. "But I can call the traffic police and—"

The truck and the Mercedes both vanished in a flash of flame.

The deafening crack of an explosion hit the minivan a fraction of a second later. The front windshield shattered, fragments spraying its occupants. Eyes squeezed shut, Deyab stamped on the brake. The van skidded across the highway—and crashed into the mangled remains of the convoy's lead vehicle.

Dazed, Nina sat up—and felt heat scouring her face. The Merc had been flipped on its side and set aflame by the car bomb, blocking the two outer lanes. The minivan's nose was buried in the wreckage. Fire was already spreading to the Toyota's bodywork. "Deyab!" she cried. "Go back, reverse!"

The Egyptian brought up an arm to shield his face from the blaze, fumbling for the gear selector with the other. Through the flames, Nina saw sunlight flash off silver and glass. The Touareg had swung around to come back toward them—

Gunfire!

She twisted, looking past the dazed Banna and Habib to see that the Fortuner had stopped behind them. One of the ASPS jumped out—only to be cut down by a burst of bullets from another van. Black-clad men scrambled from the newly arrived vehicle and opened up with automatic weapons. The Egyptian guards thrashed and flailed as rounds ripped through their bodies.

Horrified, Nina desperately pounded a fist against Deyab's shoulder. "Go, get us out of here! It's an ambush!"

The bodyguard floored the accelerator. The engine whined, but the minivan could only manage a crawl, its front bumper entangled with the Mercedes. He jerked the steering wheel in an effort to shake it loose.

The Touareg stopped on the other side of the burning barricade. More men jumped out—Rasche among them. "It's them, it's the Nazis!" Nina yelled. "Jesus Christ, *go!*"

Guns raised, the attackers ran toward them—

The minivan broke free. It lurched backward, swerving off the road before Deyab regained control. He braked hard and shoved the gear selector into drive.

The van scrabbled through the sand. The Egyptian

spun the wheel to round the blockade—and charge at the gunmen. Some of the Nazis had to dive to avoid being mowed down.

"Everyone duck!" Nina yelled, seeing guns being brought to bear. She dropped low, pushing Macy's head down. But the expected assault didn't come.

Which meant the Nazis wanted them alive . . .

The minivan swung past the Touareg, tires shrilling as it bounded back onto the asphalt. Still shielding himself from the licks of fire coming through the broken windshield, Deyab hauled the Toyota back into line with the highway—

The side windows burst apart.

Rasche fired a long burst from his MPX-K, raking bullets along the Toyota's flank at head height. Deyab screamed as a grazing round ripped across his temple, instinctively bringing both hands up to the wound.

The van veered toward the concrete divider. "Deyab!" Nina shrieked. He realized the danger and grabbed the wheel again—

Too late.

The Toyota hit the unyielding slab at an angle and was flipped into a roll. Engine screaming, it crashed down on the divider, flank grinding along it before toppling back onto the road—upside down. The remaining windows shattered. The minivan screeched along the tarmac before, top-heavy, it rolled again and landed on its side.

The seat belts had saved its occupants from serious injury, but now the same restraints trapped them inside the overturned vehicle. Nina struggled to find the release, but Macy was slumped on top of her. "Macy, wake up!" she cried.

The younger woman moved weakly, but had been left stunned by the crash. Nina reached around her, grabbing her friend's seat belt and following it to its buckle. She stabbed at the button, and with a yelp Macy dropped from her seat, tumbling over the redhead to end up in a heap. Nina found her own button and thumped down beside her.

"Come on, get up!" she said, wriggling clumsily around in the confined space. "We've gotta go!" Banna and Habib were still belted into the rear seats. The young archaeologist had a deep cut on the side of his face. "Banna! Ubayy, can you hear me?"

Banna's face screwed up in pain. "Yes, yes," he managed to say.

"Hold on, I'll get you loose." She reached out—

"Nina!" Macy cried in alarm. Nina turned—and through the now vertical slot of the windshield saw men encircling the overturned Toyota. All were armed.

"Shit!" Nina gasped, moving with a new, fear-driven urgency. She and Macy unfastened Banna's seat belt, pulling him upright before releasing Habib. "They're surrounding us. I don't know what—"

"Dr. Wilde!" called a voice from outside. Rasche. "Do not try to escape."

A deeper voice told Nina that Walther was also among their attackers, the hulking Nazi issuing orders. A young man peered in through the van's rear window, giving its occupants a cursory glance before spotting the case. He dragged it into the open.

Rasche appeared at the front window, narrowing his eyes as he saw Deyab still buckled into the driver's seat. The bodyguard groped for his gun—

Lips curling into a cruel smile, Rasche shot him in the head. Blood and brain matter splattered across the seat, and the Egyptian's body went limp, twitching. Macy screamed.

Someone climbed onto the minivan. Dazzling sunlight flooded in as the door above the two women was pulled open. "Get them," Rasche said, gesturing with his gun.

Hands reached down, roughly pulling Nina out. "You didn't have to kill him!" she shouted at the Nazi leader. Rasche merely shrugged. Macy was lifted into the open, then Banna and finally Habib. The four stood in a line beside the wreck, fearfully regarding the hard, impassive faces staring back at them.

The young man who had retrieved the case called to

Rasche and held up the bronze relic. He frowned at the prisoners. "Where is the statue?"

"It was destroyed," Nina replied. The Nazi's expression darkened further. "But we found that hidden inside it."

Walther joined him and spoke in German. Rasche was still not pleased, but nodded. "Then it is fortunate that our orders were already to take you alive," he told Nina. "We have use for archaeologists. Especially one with a reputation for finding the unfindable."

"What use?" she demanded.

He ignored her, watching the other man return the relic to the case before moving to Habib. "Thank you for all the information you gave us, Youssef. You have been most useful."

Habib's expression became that of a rabbit trapped in headlights. "You—you promised you would keep my helping you a secret!"

"*You* gave them the tomb plans?" cried Nina. The enraged Banna tried to lunge at him, but one of the Nazis shoved him back against the minivan.

"I needed the money!" Habib gabbled. "I did not know anyone would be hurt, I swear to Allah!" He turned to Rasche, frantic. "Why did you tell them? They will tell the police—I will go to prison!"

"We are going to take them with us, so they will not talk to anyone," Rasche replied. "Come over here. I have the rest of your payment."

He backed to the roadside. Habib followed, offering a stammering apology over his shoulder to Banna. It was not well received. Shamefaced, the government official turned back to Rasche—

The German's gun was pointed at his heart.

Habib barely had time to register the betrayal before Rasche pulled the trigger. He staggered, held upright by sheer disbelief, before collapsing onto the tarmac. Macy screamed again and turned away, Banna frozen in horror. Another wave of cold disgust hit Nina.

"*Gierige kleine Ratte,*" muttered Walther. He issued

an order, and the case was taken to the Touareg. "Move," he told the prisoners.

"Where are you taking us?" Nina demanded as she, Macy, and Banna were hustled to the Nazis' van.

Rasche's malevolent smile returned. "To the home of the New Reich."

15

Italy

"Well, this is ironic," said Eddie. "Me and Nina sat right here not that long ago. If we'd known there was a bad guy just over there, I could have sorted him out before any of this started."

He and Zane were in the heart of the small town of Amalfi, on Italy's west coast. On their visit some weeks earlier, Nina had been entranced by the beauty of the medieval port, and even Eddie, not normally given to gushing over matters aesthetic, had agreed that it was "really pretty." Elegant old buildings of pale stone surrounded the busy square, leading the eye to the baroque cathedral towering over it. Beyond the striped marble structure, the ragged cliffs that for centuries had acted as natural fortifications formed a stunning backdrop.

But his interest today was not scenery. The two men were in one of the piazza's pavement cafés, keeping a sidelong watch on another establishment: more specifically, a patron. Seated in the shade was a lean, pale-skinned man in his fifties, his features further protected from the sun—and observers—by a broad-brimmed white hat and a pair of rectangular sunglasses. Despite the rising heat, he wore a full three-piece suit of a white cloth so clean and fine that it looked almost like porcelain.

Frederic Leitz.

Eddie had not seen the Mossad file, but the Luxembourger matched the description Zane had given him on their journey from Egypt. In his youth, Leitz had been a member of the Luxembourg army before broadening his horizons beyond the tiny state by joining the French Foreign Legion. For the past twenty years, however, he had taken on a civilian role as an information broker and middleman; handling transactions for assorted far-right-wing organizations, if the Mossad was to be believed. He was apparently very good at what he did, since he had never been charged with any crime.

He took his personal security as seriously as his secrecy. Zane had told Eddie that their subject had a morning routine of enjoying a coffee and a glass of local orange and lemon juice at the café before returning to his villa. However, he was not doing so alone. He had arrived shadowed by two younger men, both with slight bulges under their clothing that to a trained eye were identifiable as handguns. One of the pair was at another table, from where he could observe his patron and the surrounding square, while the other had stationed himself at the nearby fountain, keeping watch from behind its statue of St. Andrew.

"He also has another man at the villa," Zane told his temporary partner. "There is always at least one man guarding it. The villa itself has surveillance systems covering the main road above it and the jetty at the bottom of the cliff below."

"You know a lot about him," Eddie noted. "Been on Mossad's radar for a while, has he?"

"We take an interest in anyone connected to anti-Israeli organizations. But"—Zane's gaze flicked toward the broker—"so far Leitz has been smart and careful enough not to do anything that would justify direct action against him."

"Until now."

"That's what we're going to find out. If he really is

working for these Nazis, then the Mossad *will* act. But first, we need confirmation."

Eddie finished his own delicious citrus juice. "And how are you planning on getting it?"

"If I can reach his computer, it doesn't matter what security it has—I can still access it." He touched a small satchel on the table.

"That's what the bloke at Naples airport gave you? Some sort of hacking gizmo?"

"A gift from the Mossad's friends at the NSA," Zane told him. "All I have to do is plug it into his PC's USB port, and it'll take control of his system through a back door. He won't even know anything has happened."

"So if he's here, why aren't you at his place doing this already?"

"Those surveillance systems I mentioned? They're very good. We can't just jump over the fence."

"How are we supposed to get inside, then?"

Leitz finished his coffee and tossed some coins onto the table, then got up and left. The two bodyguards followed, smoothly filtering into positions behind him. Zane waited until they reached one of the piazza's exits before rising. "That's a good question. I'm hoping you'll be able to help me find an answer. Come on."

* * *

"I remember this road," said Eddie as Zane followed Leitz's BMW, keeping a few other cars between them. "Drove along it with Nina. It's a bloody nightmare to get past anything." He looked out to the left across the glittering sea, then added: "Great views, though."

The main westward route out of Amalfi was a narrow road halfway up the coastal cliffs, steep rock walls above and below. Despite the tight confines, the roadside was still home to numerous parked cars and wheelie bins belonging to locals, making overtaking almost impossible. Inevitably, this resulted in traffic jams; equally inevitably, this being Italy, the jams were accompanied by car horns and emotive gesticulation as arguments erupted over who would be forced to back up first.

Zane slowed the Lancia Delta as another knot of traffic built up ahead. A bus was coming the other way, forcing westbound vehicles to crawl along hard over against the cliff face. "Views here are expensive. Leitz paid a million euros for his villa, and that was over ten years ago."

"He's made a few bob from what he does, then."

The Israeli nodded. "His standard fee is twenty percent. His clients are willing to pay that much, because he is able to keep their secrets."

"Even from Mossad? He must be worth the money, then."

A cacophony of horns broke out as the bus found itself unable to squeeze past a car that had refused to pull all the way over. Zane brought the hatchback to a stop. After several seconds in which the jam remained unmoving, he drew in a slow, deep breath. "*Sav'lanut, areyh tes'eyer* . . ." he muttered.

"What was that?" Eddie asked.

The younger man hesitated before answering. "It was something Benjamin used to say to me. A lot, to begin with. It means 'Patience, young lion.' "

"Young lion? Was that what he called you?"

Zane nodded. "I had a nickname for him too. *Alter kocker.*"

"What does that mean?"

The younger man appeared almost sheepish. "The nearest translation would be . . . 'old fart.' "

"Kids these days, no respect," Eddie said with a grin. "Sounds more like he was your dad than your boss."

"He *was* like a father to me," said Zane, with an insistence that surprised the Yorkshireman. "He trained me, he helped me become who I am today. Without his guidance, I would have been . . ." He waved a hand as if trying to pluck the right word from the air. "*Nobody.* Just another aimless kid. He gave me a purpose. But . . ." His cheek muscles tightened with barely suppressed emotion. ". . . now he is gone."

"I'm sorry."

The Israeli gave a small nod of thanks, then his expression became curious. "In the hotel, in Egypt: When

I told you Ben had been my mentor, you said that without him, I wouldn't have been *who* I am. Not *where* I am. Why did you phrase it like that?"

"Because I know what you're feeling right now."

"How?"

"You said you'd read my file. Figure it out."

The Israeli's smooth brow creased slightly in thought. "Your commander, in the SAS . . ."

"Yeah," said Eddie. "I know what it's like to lose someone who . . . who made you what you are, someone who kicked your arse into line when you needed it most. Especially when they were taken away from you by being shot in the back."

"That part wasn't in your file," said Zane.

"I didn't get time to do any paperwork afterward. Seeing as I was wanted for murder."

"You went after the man who did it?"

"Yeah."

"Did you kill him?"

"Yes, but . . . it wasn't revenge. I was trying to find out who he was working for, but he pulled a gun on me. I didn't have a choice."

"I already know who Rasche is working for," Zane said, his face becoming cold once more. "When I find him . . . I won't try to capture him. *Ayin tachat ayin.*"

"What does that mean?"

"It's from the Talmud. 'An eye for an eye.'"

Eddie nodded. "I'm not Jewish, but I can totally get behind that."

Zane seemed about to say more, but a shrill bleat from the car behind told him the traffic was moving again. "Can you see Leitz?"

"Yeah, whenever I bang my head. No, he's still there," Eddie added, seeing that his companion did not share his sense of humor. "In front of that Ape."

"What ape?" Zane scanned the road. "I didn't know they had monkeys here."

The Englishman laughed. "Not a bloody monkey! The little three-wheeler van, there." He pointed ahead. Behind Leitz's black 7 Series was a tiny pickup truck, whining along at the head of a stream of blue smoke from its puny two-stroke engine. The Apes, in both three- and four-wheeled form, had been a constant source of amusement on his previous visit, as the diminutive utility vehicles always seemed laden with far more than they could possibly carry.

"Then why didn't you just call it a van?"

"Because that's its bloody name, a Piaggio Ape. Anyway, we haven't lost him. How far to his villa?"

"About two kilometers."

Eddie let the rest of the journey pass in silence, watching the beautiful scenery glide by. It only took five minutes, even with stoppages, to reach their destination. "There it is," Zane announced.

The BMW pulled across to the top of a driveway on the left, an electric gate rolling out of its way. The drive dropped away steeply beyond it, giving Eddie a glimpse of a red-tiled rooftop below. Leitz's driver went through the barrier the moment he had enough clearance, the gate immediately reversing direction to close behind the car.

"Don't draw any attention to us," said Zane as the Delta passed the entrance and continued along the rising road.

"I wasn't going to fucking lean out and take a picture," Eddie shot back. He did, however, pay close attention to their surroundings. "He's not short of cameras himself, though. I see three—no, four, at least."

"Those are just the ones we're supposed to see," Zane said ominously. "According to our information, he has thermal detectors and motion trackers as well as CCTV."

Eddie looked back as the road curved around a headland, giving him a slightly better view of the villa. From what he could see through the high metal fence, the house was built directly into the rock of a small promontory overlooking the sea. He also spotted more cameras. "Okay, so going in from the road's out. Did you say there was a dock down below?"

Zane nodded. "I'll pull over so we can see."

That turned out to be easier said than done, but eventually he found a space. Zane collected a pair of binoculars, then the two men went to the low wall along the edge of the road to get their first clear view back at Leitz's villa.

Eddie immediately saw that it was worth the money the Luxembourger had paid for it, and probably more. The large three-story building was painted a soft sandy orange. Several windows on the upper floors had balconies overlooking the ocean, and a patio ran the width of the lowest level, chairs and shaded tables set out along it—enough seats for at least a dozen people. "Is he planning a barbie?" he wondered aloud.

Zane was more interested in the flight of steps that zigzagged down the cliff from the patio to a jetty at sea level. A suited man in sunglasses stood at the bottom, looking for all the world like a doorman expecting guests. "Down there: one of his guards. If there's one at the dock, that only leaves two watching the house."

"Think you might need to check your intel." Eddie could see another two figures at the top of the drive . . . and a third had just emerged from the house onto the patio. None was Leitz. "Your man's got visitors," he added as the gate opened again. A large black Mercedes with dark windows negotiated the tight turn from the road.

The two guards watched as it descended the steep slope, the gate sliding closed behind. A figure in white stepped into the sunlight. "There's Leitz," said Zane. The broker waited on the villa's pink marble steps for the new arrival. The Mercedes pulled up, its uniformed driver getting out to open the rear door.

The passenger emerged. From this distance, Eddie couldn't see much beyond that he was male, gray-haired, and somewhat overweight—but Zane had a much better view through his field glasses. "Szőko!"

"Bless you," said the Englishman.

The Mossad agent was too fixated on the scene to acknowledge the joke. "No, Zoltan Szőko—he is one of

Leitz's clients. He is Hungarian, a businessman with connections to the country's biggest anti-Semitic party. He is openly anti-Israeli; we have been watching him." The young man lowered the binoculars. "Why is he here?"

"Maybe he wants to work on his tan."

"That's not what I mean. People like this do all their business at a distance; they never meet in person."

Szőko and Leitz shook hands, then the Luxembourger guided his guest into the villa. "Well they are now," said Eddie. "Must be a special occasion."

"The Mossad has nightmares about the occasions these people think are special." Zane noticed something at sea level. "Szőko isn't the only visitor."

The guard below advanced to the end of the jetty. Numerous pleasure craft were cruising along the coast in both directions, but one was heading toward the private dock. Zane locked the binoculars onto it. "It's Takis Metaxes!"

"I'm guessing he's on Mossad's shit-list too?"

Zane nodded. "Another rich businessman who likes to put his spare cash into neo-Nazi organizations. Only he's Greek, not Hungarian."

"There must be more coming—he's got plenty of chairs set out." The Englishman watched as the motor launch came alongside the jetty, one of its crew tossing a mooring line to the waiting man. "Maybe Leitz is hosting a *Klaus* barbie."

"Something big is going on," said Zane. He regarded the house thoughtfully. "We have to get inside."

"Well, that was kind of why we came here. But it might be better to wait until things quiet down."

"No, they've come here to discuss something major. I need to find out what. It's the only reason they would meet like this—Leitz is the host, but he would never organize something on his own. He always acts on behalf of a client."

"And you think those arseholes from Egypt are the clients?"

"Maybe they intended to sell the statue they were trying to steal from the tomb."

"The buyers'll be disappointed, then." The mention of the statue made Eddie think of Nina. He now felt somewhat guilty about his abrupt and ill-tempered departure. She would be in Cairo by now; he considered phoning her to make peace overtures, but the sight of a second arriving car distracted him. "Another one's just turned up."

"We have to get in there," Zane insisted. "But how?" He surveyed the upper fence through the binoculars. "There's no way in from the road without being seen. And the dock is guarded."

Eddie leaned over the wall, looking at the cliffs below. They were steep—extremely so, in places—but for the most part not actually sheer. From where he and Zane were standing, he could see past the promontory on which the villa had been built to the coastline beyond.

He could also see that unless an observer was at the very end of the jetty, the other side of the rocky outcrop would be blocked from their sight . . .

"Think I might have found a way," he announced, catching Zane's attention. "You ever been free-climbing?"

* * *

The Israeli's satchel contained more than hacking gear. Among its contents were several wads of high-value euro banknotes—one of which had been given to a surprised but delighted man in Amalfi harbor for the no-questions-asked charter of his small motorboat. Eddie and Zane then set out back along the coast for Leitz's villa, the journey rather quicker by sea than by road.

"Okay, over there," said Eddie, pointing at the cliffs. They were on the promontory's eastern flank, one side of the orange house overlooking them about eighty feet above—but crucially, the guard on the jetty was out of view on its far side.

Their pilot regarded the base of the outcrop unhappily. "Is too rough, we hit rocks." Even though it was a calm day, waves were still churning noisily against the ragged shore.

Zane produced another wad of euros. "If your boat gets scratched, that should cover it."

"Hell, that'll buy you a whole new boat," said Eddie.

"I maybe *need* a new boat!" the man protested. But he took the money anyway. "Okay, you better be fast."

"All right." Eddie tensed as the boat edged toward the shore, the swell of the waves kicking it up and down. He put both hands on the gunwale, the hull's edge, to steady himself. "I'll go first, then you—"

Before he could finish, Zane stood—and used the gunwale as a springboard to leap across the eight-foot gap. He barely made it, his feet catching the rocks just inches above the water.

His exit set the boat rocking violently. "Jesus!" Eddie yelped, crouching to lower the craft's center of gravity. "Patience, young lion!"

Zane glared at him. "Don't call me that. Only Benjamin called me that."

"Then don't go fucking jumping out of boats before anyone else is ready."

"You should have *been* ready. And why aren't you ready now? Hurry up." The Israeli started his climb.

"Fucking kids," Eddie said loudly. He waited for the boat to stabilize before rising again. The driver pulsed the outboard to get as close as he dared to the cliff. "Okay, hold it steady, hold it . . ."

He waited for the boat's shoreward side to roll upward—and jumped.

Even though the gap was only just over six feet, he didn't quite clear it. He slammed against the wall, both hands finding grip on the rock, but his feet splashed into the water. "Shit!" he growled, pulling himself upward to find dry footing.

Zane stopped and looked down. "Did you get your feet wet, old man?"

"Old man, my arse," Eddie said, glowering at the Israeli. "Go over to the left; those plants above you won't take any weight."

"This isn't my first climb." The younger man resumed his ascent.

Eddie shook his head, then started after him. The boat turned back out to sea, and the pair were left alone.

It didn't take long for Eddie to catch up with Zane, though to his annoyance he realized it was because the Mossad agent had deliberately slowed down. "Okay," said the Yorkshireman, "wait here for a sec."

"Why, are you out of breath?"

"Piss-taking little bastard . . . No, I want to find the best route so we don't get stuck—or climb up right in front of one of his guards." Eddie cautiously leaned backward to survey the cliff. The villa's lowest floor was about sixty feet above, a wall marking the patio's eastern end. If anyone looked over it, the climbers would be visible, but the chances of that happening were low . . . he hoped.

Besides, the patio wasn't his destination. "We should be able to reach one of those balconies on the top two floors," he said. "Okay, so if we keep going straight up, then when we get level with that bush go right and then back around toward the house where those vines are, we'll avoid that really steep bit." He indicated a near-vertical chimney that rose from the sea almost to the villa's foundations.

"That takes us the long way around," Zane complained. "We should go left before we get to the bush. It'll be much quicker."

"It's an overhang! The whole point of doing this was that we wouldn't need ropes and pitons to get up there—never mind having to be fucking Spider-Man."

"I know *I* can make it," the Mossad agent sniffed. "Come on. We're wasting time."

"For fuck's sake," said Eddie, but his companion had already started climbing again. With a rumble of irritation, he followed.

They picked their way upward. Thirty feet above the water, Eddie peered over his shoulder. There was a risk that somebody on a passing boat might spot them and draw the attention of the watchers on the shore, but the vessels were all some distance out, and those aboard were focused on their own pleasures.

He looked up again. Zane was clambering toward the villa with apparently zero effort despite the seventy-degree slope. "Christ, the kid's a fucking gibbon," Eddie grumbled as he searched for his next handhold.

The Israeli was indeed taking the quicker route, heading for an overhanging arch sixty feet up. Small stones dropped from a crevice as he moved his foot from it, forcing Eddie to shield his eyes as they pattered down onto his head. "Oi! Fucking watch what you're doing," he said, stopping to brush away the debris. "That almost—"

Dirt crumbled—and his feet slipped.

He gasped as he dropped, free hand snatching desperately at the bare rock—

His nails found a crack and he jerked to a stop, all his weight taken by his fingertips before he found new support with the edge of his sole. "Jesus Christ!" he gasped.

"Chase! Are you okay?" asked Zane.

"Yeah, fucking wonderful!" he snapped back. "That's what happens if you knock stuff down onto people underneath you. You fucking bell-end," he added.

"Sounds like you're okay," said the Mossad agent. "But I'll be more careful."

"You'd bloody better." Eddie carefully checked his hand. His palm had acquired a nasty graze, and his fingers were throbbing, but beyond that he was unharmed. He had been lucky.

Zane had already set off again. Eddie allowed himself a few more seconds to recover from his fright before following. "I still think we should go the easier way," he said, keeping his voice low now that they were potentially within earshot of the people above.

"We'll be okay," the younger man replied. "If you get stuck, don't worry—I'll help you up."

"Funny kid," Eddie muttered. He paused to survey the cliff again. From this angle, the overhang looked more treacherous than ever, and to complicate matters further, the wind had picked up.

Zane was still heading for the arch, however. Eddie sighed, glancing over one shoulder as he started after him—

A launch was angling toward the jetty.

"Hey!" Eddie said. "There's a boat, keep still! They're more likely to see us if we're moving."

No response. Zane hadn't heard him over the wind. The Israeli had reached the overhang, his bare hands the only thing keeping him from a long fall as he clambered along its underside. Eddie moved higher and tried again. "*Zane!*"

The other man looked back. "What?"

"There's another boat coming in! Keep still or they'll see us!"

Zane twisted to look, and let out a Hebrew curse. He stopped his advance, digging his fingers into a crevice on the underside of the rock.

Eddie reached a secure position. The guard on the dock was now in view, walking to meet the incoming boat. Three men were aboard the small but expensive-looking craft: two crew in the front, and an older passenger. All were watching the guard, but if they looked along the cliffs . . .

"Chase!"

The cry from above was almost strangled, Zane desperately trying not to shout. Eddie looked up. His companion was still suspended from the overhang . . . but the cliff face beneath it was too friable for him to brace himself with his feet.

And his hands were slipping.

The boat slowed as it lined up with the jetty. The guard went to the edge of the dock to receive a mooring line. The passenger gazed up at the villa—putting the two climbers in his peripheral vision. If they made any big movements, he would see them . . .

"Chase!" Zane gasped again, now with fear. "I can't hold on!" He tried to pull his legs toward the rock face—but the movement tore his right hand loose from its grip.

The guard caught the rope and wrapped it around a metal cleat. The passenger looked back at him—

The Israeli scrabbled frantically for a new handhold, but found none. He hung for a moment, suspended only by the fingertips of his left hand . . .

Then he fell.

16

Z ane plunged straight down—

Eddie's outstretched hand clamped around his wrist.

Pain flared in the Englishman's other hand as his clawed fingers took Zane's full unsupported weight. "Don't—fuckin'—*move*," Eddie rasped.

The boat was now tied up. The passenger stepped onto the jetty.

"Chase, I'm slipping!" Zane gasped. Eddie felt the Israeli's sweat-drenched hand sliding through his. He squeezed more tightly, but knew he was about to lose him . . .

The new arrival rolled his head to work out a crick in his neck, then spoke to the guard. The man replied, the visitor nodding. For an agonizing moment they remained still . . . then the pair started for the steps.

The crewmen turned their attention back to the boat. Eddie waited, still straining to keep hold of Zane's hand. The instant the two men on the jetty passed out of sight, he hauled the younger man upward. "Get a foothold!"

Zane's feet scrabbled at the rock, finding a small protrusion. He pushed himself higher. Eddie shifted to bring his companion's free hand within reach of the cliff. The

Mossad agent grabbed it, letting out a loud gasp of relief. "You safe?" Eddie asked.

"Yeah, I . . . I got it," Zane replied. "I think . . . maybe the easy route is a good idea."

"No fucking kidding."

They recovered their breath, then started to climb again—along Eddie's suggested path. The Israeli's ascent was considerably more cautious than before. They soon drew level with the patio. Voices warned them that more of Leitz's guests had arrived and were enjoying the view, though fortunately across the sea rather than down the cliff.

They continued up to the next floor. Eddie shimmied across until he reached a little balcony with an open door and peered warily into the room beyond. The contrast between the bright sunlight outside and the shade within limited what he could discern, but he immediately picked out the glowing rectangle of a computer monitor on a desk. He climbed onto the balcony and moved to the door, back against its frame as he looked inside.

Nobody was there. As his eyes adjusted, he made out several tall bookshelves, their contents a mix of large leather-bound ledgers and black box files. Lined up beside the monitor were a laser printer and three telephones, one of which he recognized as a scrambler unit. Leitz apparently liked to keep certain conversations private. Everything was fastidiously neat, even the small amount of paperwork perfectly aligned with the desk's edges.

A closed door led to the rest of the villa. "Okay, it's clear," he said as he entered. Zane clambered onto the balcony behind him. "You all right?"

The Israeli was still breathing heavily. "Yeah, I'm fine," he replied. He went to the desk, seemingly examining the papers on it—but Eddie noticed him holding one hand just above the polished surface, fingers slightly splayed. They were trembling; only a little, but enough for the Englishman to spot.

"It's okay to be shaken up," Eddie told him quietly.

Zane hurriedly closed his fist. "What?"

"You were seeing if your hand was shaking."

"I was checking Leitz's mail," the younger man insisted. He opened the satchel. "Watch the door."

Eddie shrugged, knowing all too well how reluctant men in their twenties—and beyond—were to reveal weakness. He listened at the entrance. Indistinct voices reached him, but none were close. "We're okay."

Zane nodded, then took a small device from his bag and plugged it into a USB port on Leitz's computer.

"How long will that take?" Eddie asked.

"Not long, I hope." He watched the screen—while making another surreptitious check on his hand. "Okay," he said after thirty seconds, reclaiming the USB device. "I can access everything on his computer—"

Eddie raised a hand in warning. "Someone's coming."

Zane scurried to join the Yorkshireman as he flattened himself against the wall behind the door. A conversation in German grew louder outside. For a moment, Eddie thought the approaching men were going to enter the office . . . but then they continued past, going down a flight of stairs.

"One of them was Leitz," Zane whispered. "He said, 'Now that everyone is here, we can start.'"

"Start what?"

"That's what I want to find out." The Mossad agent produced a compact and rather ugly matte-black handgun from his satchel.

Eddie eyed the weapon, an Israeli SP-21 Barak. "Don't suppose you brought one for me?"

"Sorry." He flicked off the safety. "Leitz probably has a weapon hidden in here."

"And you're going to give me time to look for it, right?" the Englishman said sarcastically as Zane opened the door and peeked out, then exited. Annoyed, he followed.

They emerged onto a landing running around three sides of a spacious marble-floored hall. Sunlight from the patio's entrance gleamed off the stone—revealing growing shadows inside the bright rectangles. Eddie and

Zane both ducked as two elderly men entered the hall, but they didn't go toward the staircase, instead heading for a set of dark wooden doors.

"That guy's American," Eddie muttered, overhearing snippets of discussion as they passed below.

Zane nodded. "From Florida. His name is Thomson Holmes—another rich man, and another Jew-hater."

"Thomson Holmes? Sounds like a property developer."

"He is." They exchanged looks, then Zane continued: "The man he was with is English. He's a member of your aristocracy. Charles Hertsmore, also known as the eighth Baron Winderhithe. His grandfather was a personal friend of Adolf Hitler before the war."

"Apples don't fall far from the tree, then." Eddie watched in disgust as the pair went into the next room, then tilted his head. "I can still hear them talking. Where's it coming from?"

"Through there." At the end of the landing, directly above the double doors, was another entrance. It was ajar. Keeping low, Zane moved to it and cautiously looked through before gesturing for Eddie to join him.

The large room beyond was a mixture of library and lounge. The door opened onto a narrow gallery overlooking the main floor. Windows opposite looked out along the coast, though the focus of attention was not the view but a big flat-screen television. A camera had been mounted on top of its bezel.

Zane crept to the edge of the gallery to look down between the wooden railings. Eddie joined him, getting his first view of Leitz's assembled guests. All were male, well into middle age or older. Even though they were chatting, there was a definite lack of humor among the group. Everyone present took themselves very seriously indeed.

The agent's gaze flicked from one man to another. "I know them all," he whispered to Eddie. "They're some of Leitz's biggest clients. There isn't one of them worth less than fifty million US dollars." A hard edge entered his voice. "And they're all known anti-Semites, supporters of fascism."

"Didn't bring a hand grenade, did you?" Eddie asked. "One bomb chucked down there'd be doing the world a big favor."

The group below looked around as someone else entered the library. White suit, white hair, rectangular glasses: Leitz. "Gentlemen, good day," he said in clipped, accented English. "Now that Mr. Haas is here"—he gestured to the man who had arrived by boat while Eddie and Zane were scaling the cliff—"we can begin. If you will take your seats?"

The dozen men found places facing the screen. Leitz lowered blinds, then turned to the TV. "Computer, screen on," he said. It came to life, the giant display replicating what was on the monitor in the office. "Computer, conference." A window opened in response to his voice command, showing the dashboard of an encrypted videoconferencing program. He took up position beside the television. "As I am sure you all know, there have recently been changes in the ranks of the so-called global elite. The disappearances, and presumed deaths, of the Bull brothers, Rudolf Meerkrieger, and Travis Warden, as well as several others in their circle, have created a power vacuum at the highest levels of commerce and politics."

"Oops," said Eddie under his breath as Leitz continued speaking.

"What do you mean?" asked Zane.

"The people he's talking about? Basically the secret rulers of the world?"

"They are? What about them?"

"Me and Nina kind of . . . blew them up. In a volcano."

The Israeli regarded him in disbelief. "A volcano."

"What can I say? That's how we roll. Although don't blame us for whatever's going on here," he added hurriedly. "We were in the middle of saving the world, so we were kind of preoccupied."

Zane waved him to silence. "This has created a unique opportunity," the middleman was saying, "for those with a certain vision for the world. You and I all share that vision, as does my client." A chime from the TV, where a flashing message announced an incoming call. "He is offering you a way to ensure that you will not only see this new world come into being, but also enjoy it for a very long time." Leitz stepped back from the television and said, "Computer, accept." The dashboard disappeared, replaced by a live feed. "Gentlemen, I present to you: SS-Obersturmbannführer Erich Kroll."

Eddie stared in amazement—and a sense of horror—at the screen. Kroll was recognizable as the man whose photo he had seen at the United Nations . . . but only just. In the seventy years he had been in hiding, he had put on a huge amount of weight. His face was bloated, jowls overflowing his collar. His hair had almost disappeared except for a few gray wisps over his ears. But it was definitely the same man, the malevolent eyes unchanged.

He wore a black SS officer's uniform, medals and ribbons drawing a line across his left breast to a bright red slash around his bicep. An armband, a symbol upon it.

The swastika, emblem of Nazi Germany.

The same emblem, much larger, was also on the wall behind him, the white circle around the angular black character framing his head like a halo. Eddie felt a chill. This wasn't somebody dressing up in a Nazi costume, or a thuggish modern-day imitator. The man he was looking at was the genuine article, an actual wanted war criminal.

And he had escaped not only justice, but also the ravages of time. Kroll should have been almost a hundred years old, but he appeared only half that, not even his grotesque corpulence adding any age to his features. Was Nina's discovery in Alexandria really true, then? Had the escaped Nazis found water from the Spring of Immortality?

Zane stiffened, face tight with anger. Eddie could fully sympathize. To the Englishman, the Nazis were an aggressive, powerful war machine that had tried to crush his country; to the young Jewish man, they were figures of pure evil who had attempted to exterminate every last one of his people. Kroll was a demon made flesh, emerging from the past to threaten them once more.

The demon spoke, his voice like bubbles slowly working their way up through black tar. "Good day to you all," said Kroll in heavily accented English.

Leitz's guests responded with something approaching awe. Eddie felt slightly sick when he realized why. To him and Zane, the Nazi was a monster; to those below, he was an *icon*. His earlier comment about the hand grenade had been joking, but now he wanted to do it for real.

"As Herr Leitz has told you," Kroll continued, "during the war we obtained a supply of an incredible substance, a water that slowed the process of aging. For those who drink it regularly, each five years that pass are like only a single one. We have been in hiding for almost seventy years, but our bodies have aged only about fifteen."

"I still want to see scientific proof of this," said Holmes, drawing disapproving looks from some of his companions.

Kroll scowled. "You have already been shown as much proof as we are able to provide without compromising our security. If you did not believe it, why are you here?" Holmes shifted uncomfortably, forced to concede the point. "But we had only a limited amount of the water. This meant that only select members of our group were permitted to use it." His eyes became more intense. "The situation has now changed. Our raid on the tomb of Alexander the Great in Egypt has given us the means to locate the water's original source."

That prompted intrigued mutterings from the guests. Eddie, meanwhile, had a whispered comment of his own. "What? They didn't get anything. *We* took the statue." Zane shushed him.

"Gentlemen," said Kroll impatiently. The susurration ceased. "I asked Herr Leitz to assemble you here so that I can present to you a great opportunity. You are all wealthy men, in positions of power and influence in your countries. Influence that you are willing to use to promote the ideals of history's greatest leader . . . Adolf Hitler."

One of the men jumped to his feet, right arm stiffly raised with his palm turned downward. *"Heil Hitler!"*

In moments, the others had all stood to deliver identical salutes. *"Heil Hitler! Heil Hitler!"* The bloated figure on the screen looked on with approval.

"Jesus Christ," Eddie gasped, appalled. Zane appeared ready to kill.

Kroll waited for the awful chorus to die down. "Thank you. It is very good to know that others outside the Enklave"—something about the way he said the word made Eddie realize he was using it as a proper noun—"believe as we do. And the tide of history is turning back toward us. More people join our cause every day across Europe and other parts of the world, disgusted by the failures of the supposed democracies and the pollution of their nations by inferiors. The time to act is now! All of you have enough influence to bring the masses in your countries to our way of thinking—through your newspapers, television stations, the Internet, your friends and puppets in government. If you all push together, our way will be seen as the *only* way, now and forever—and with what I am offering, you will all be able to see the work through."

The hard sell was coming, Eddie realized. Kroll had had decades to work on his sales pitch—and his audience seemed to be willing buyers.

The Nazi spoke again. "As I told you, we have obtained the means to find the source of the water. However, it will require considerable resources to secure it—and considerable amounts of money. But I can assure you that it will be worth it. Your payments now will guarantee you a supply for the rest of your lives. Which will be *very* long." He leaned back, watching his audience's response intently.

Leitz stepped forward. "You have heard Herr Kroll's proposal, and he has authorized me to act as his agent. The price for entry is . . . ten million US dollars."

That caused a flurry of consternation from the guests.

While they had come with the intention of doing business, clearly few had expected the cost to be so high. "And Leitz takes his twenty percent of it all," whispered Zane.

"Gentlemen," said Kroll, more loudly. His raised voice brought all eyes back to his image. "Ten million dollars may seem like a large sum, but you should consider it an investment—in your futures. The water from the Spring of Immortality will make the rest of your lives *five times longer,* or more. Think of what you can accomplish with those extra years. And it will be *you* who is doing it; not your heirs, not your trusts or companies. *You* will see your plans through to completion. *You* will see the final victory of the New Reich. Is that not worth the price I ask?"

Discussions began, but it was evident to the observers in the gallery that Kroll's words had made an impression. Before long, the men below gravitated to Leitz; from his smiles in response, they had decided to accept the war criminal's offer.

All but one. Holmes, the American, was still dubious. "Herr Kroll, you know that I'm a committed supporter of your goals—the world needs to be taken under firm control. But I also follow the news, and I don't just mean Fox. The raid in Alexandria yesterday . . . it wasn't successful, was it? Several of your men were killed, and I know from my sources that you didn't get what you were after. The Egyptians and the International Heritage Agency recovered the statue."

Some of the other guests regarded the challenger with surprise and even mistrust. Kroll's eyes for a moment betrayed fury . . . then control returned. "Your sources are not quite up to date, Mr. Holmes," he said. "Yes, the statue was taken from us. But we have already retaliated. This morning, my men attacked the convoy transporting it to Cairo—and their mission to recover it was a success."

Eddie flinched in shock. *Nina!* She had been with the convoy—

A hand squeezed his arm, hard. He snapped his head

around to find Zane staring at him with a grim but determined expression. "There's nothing you can do," whispered the Israeli.

"But Nina—"

"There's *nothing* you can do," he repeated. "Not now."

Stomach churning with rage and fear, Eddie looked back at the scene below. Holmes was talking with Leitz, apparently convinced. The middleman nodded, then addressed the group. "Everyone is in agreement? Then payments must be made within the next twenty-four hours, via secure electronic transfer. I will provide each of you with the necessary details."

"It's a lot of money," said Hertsmore, "but God, it'll be worth every penny."

"It will indeed," said Kroll. "Now, gentlemen, I hope that soon it will be safe for me to come out of exile and meet you all in person. Until that day, we must all work tirelessly to build the New Reich. *Heil Hitler!*"

"*Heil Hitler!*" The chant echoed around the library as Kroll's image disappeared.

"Computer, close application," said Leitz to the television. The videoconferencing program was replaced by the desktop. "Here is the account information," he said, handing out business cards. "Burn the card after you have transferred the money. The transfers will be encrypted and will pass through many proxy accounts, but it is still best to be safe."

"That fat *fucker*," Eddie snarled as Leitz showed the group to the exit. "If anything's happened to Nina—"

"Stay calm," Zane interrupted. "Wait for the others to leave. We need to interrogate Leitz."

Though still furious, Eddie recognized a change in the Israeli's attitude. "I thought you were going to hack his computer?"

"The situation's changed. If you want to know what's happened to your wife, this will be the quickest way."

"And what about Leitz? If he tells that Nazi arsehole that he had a visit from Mossad, he'll go underground again!"

Zane gave him a humorless smile. "Accidents happen. It's a long drop from that balcony . . ."

"Don't fuckin' kill him until we know what's happened to Nina." Eddie watched as the library emptied, then moved back to the door. Leitz's visitors were crossing the hall below, the white-suited man going with them. "Okay, let's have a little chat . . ."

17

It took Leitz over thirty minutes to see all of his guests out; with men this rich and powerful, pleasantries were expected. But eventually only his security detail remained as company. The extra guards he had brought in to ensure privacy could now be dismissed, but he decided to do that once he had concluded the day's business.

He went upstairs to his office. A cool breeze blew from the balcony through the elegant room as he entered—

The door slammed shut behind him.

Leitz instantly knew from its speed and force that something more than a stray gust had closed it. Without even a glance back, he lunged for his desk, right hand darting underneath it to find—

Nothing.

"You after this?" said a voice from the balcony.

Eddie stepped into view, holding a gleaming chrome automatic. "Nice little gun," he told the frozen Leitz. "Sphinx 3000, innit? Don't see many of these."

"Don't move," Zane said from behind the middleman, thumbing the hammer of his Barak.

Leitz took the click as intended: a warning. He slowly

raised his hands. "What do you want?" he said in a level but cautious voice.

"Information. Move away from the desk, to your right."

Leitz cautiously stepped sideways. Zane patted him down, finding that he was unarmed. "All right," said the Yorkshireman as he entered the room, aiming the Sphinx at its owner's chest, "since you're dressed as the Man from Del Monte, you'd better fucking say 'Yes!' to everything. Okay?"

"I should say yes, I suppose," Leitz replied, regarding him icily.

"Good lad. Now, first things first: What the fuck has that fat Nazi bastard done with Nina?"

"He means Dr. Nina Wilde, in Alexandria," said Zane, seeing the broker's incomprehension. "Your client Erich Kroll said he took the statue from her—the statue that tells you how to find the Spring of Immortality."

Leitz narrowed his eyes. "You heard our discussion? That is unfortunate."

"Yeah, for you," said Eddie. "Where is she?"

No answer was immediately forthcoming. Zane stepped closer to the white-suited man. "If you don't talk, he'll kill you for personal reasons. Or I'll kill you for *professional* reasons. Either way, you'll be dead, and we'll still get what we need from your computer."

"Your accent," said Leitz, eyeing him. "Israeli. You are with the Mossad?" For the first time, there was unease beneath his even tone.

"Not me," said Eddie firmly. "I'm just a concerned citizen."

"Answer the question," Zane ordered.

"Very well." Leitz turned back to Eddie, though he kept Zane in his peripheral vision. "Yes, Kroll's men took back the statue earlier today."

"And what'd they do with Nina?" Eddie demanded.

The answer emerged with reluctance. "Dr. Wilde and two others, a man and a woman, are still alive. I know this because I was asked to arrange transport for them."

Relief flooded through the Englishman. "Thank God," he said, glancing at Zane. "And the other woman must be Macy. They're okay!"

"For now," the Mossad agent replied. "But the only reason they're still alive is that Kroll wants something from them. Once he gets it . . ."

The fear for Nina's safety returned. "Okay, where are they going?" Eddie demanded, rounding the desk to face off against the broker. "You arranged transport—to where?"

Leitz's expression hardened. He ignored Eddie, instead addressing Zane. "If you are with the Mossad, and you are here, now . . . then you are a member of the Criminal Sanctions Unit, are you not?"

"Answer him," Zane ordered.

"I believe that Benjamin Falk was in charge of the CSU." For the first time, Leitz's expression revealed something other than cold restraint: a small, sneering smile. "Until recently. Very recently."

Zane advanced another step, raising his gun at the other man's face. "You shut your mouth."

The smile coiled more tightly. "It is a shame. All those years of faithful service, only to die on the streets of Egypt. Very sad, very sad indeed—"

Zane lashed out with the Barak, striking Leitz's head and knocking off his glasses. The broker staggered. "I told you to shut up!"

"Get a grip," Eddie warned. "He's still got guards hanging around, remember?"

Zane glared at him, but made a visible effort to calm himself. He grabbed Leitz by his lapel, shoving the gun hard against his chest. "Where is Erich Kroll? Where is he taking Dr. Wilde? Tell us, now! Or I'll kill you."

Leitz seemed to acquiesce. "Okay, okay! Everything you need is over there." He gestured at the desk. Eddie and Zane instinctively glanced toward it. "On my . . . computer." The unexpected pause instantly put Eddie on alert, but he didn't know why—

He found out a moment later. "*Alarm!*" said Leitz—

and a piercing siren shrieked as the computer's voice recognition obeyed the command.

Eddie flinched at the aural assault, as did Zane—

Leitz moved with shocking speed, one hand slicing up to seize Zane's gun and force it away from his own chest—toward the Englishman.

Eddie threw himself out of the line of fire, only for the toe of Leitz's shoe to meet his kneecap as the broker whipped around to deliver a fierce kick. He reeled, crashing against a bookshelf. The Sphinx clattered to the floor.

The other gun was now at the heart of a battle for possession—which Leitz was winning. As the pair spun around, he shoved Zane backward. The younger man's momentary loss of balance gave his opponent the opening he needed to grip the weapon with both hands and twist it through a forceful half turn—trapping the Israeli's index finger inside the trigger guard.

Zane gasped in pain as the motion almost snapped the bone. He had no choice but to yank his hand back, skinning his finger against the metal as he pulled free.

But now Leitz had the gun. He flipped it around, his own finger closing on the trigger—

Eddie hurled a swath of ledgers across the office. Volumes pounded Leitz's arm, knocking the gun away from Zane—who responded with a kick of his own, spinning into a Krav Maga move that smashed a heel into the white-haired man's stomach.

Leitz stumbled backward against the table, knocking the laser printer to the floor, and tripped over the chair. It collapsed, sending him sprawling. The Barak skidded across the marble floor. Zane ran after it, bending to scoop it up—

A blizzard slashed at his eyes as Leitz snatched the paper from the printer's tray and flung the sheaf into his face. Blinded, Zane groped for the gun, but his fingers found nothing but cold polished stone. He swatted away the last of the fluttering sheets—and was hit by the back of the broken chair as Leitz jumped up and threw it at him. He fell heavily near the balcony door.

Eddie recovered the fallen Sphinx. He turned to find Leitz standing over the Mossad agent, one foot drawn back to kick him in the face—

He snapped up the gun—but the white-suited man caught the movement, instantly abandoning his attack and launching himself at the balcony. Eddie tracked him, about to fire . . .

Leitz dived over the railing.

"Holy *shit*!" Eddie cried as his target plunged out of sight. Zane was equally shocked. The Englishman helped him up. "Did he just fucking *kill himself* so he wouldn't talk?"

They rushed outside and looked down. The cliff they had ascended dropped away below . . . to a small cove at the foot of the near-vertical chimney beneath the balcony, at the center of which was an almost perfectly circular splash. As they watched, a white figure rose from beneath the surging waves and surfaced. "He made it!" said Zane in disbelief. "He actually made it!"

Eddie stared at Leitz as he swam for the jetty. "He's either the luckiest bastard on the planet—or the best prepared. Diving about a hundred feet, into that? Jesus!" He looked back at Zane, only to find that the younger man had already returned to the desk. "What're you doing? He's set off the alarm, we've got to get out of here!"

Zane grabbed the mouse. "I can find Kroll."

Eddie hurried to him. "How?"

"The IP address of the videoconference—it'll tell me where he's located," he said as he brought up a window and rapidly tapped at the keyboard. "Okay, I've already bypassed his encryption, so I just need to . . ." More typing. "There!" He pointed at a string of hexadecimal characters, eight blocks of four, separated by colons. "IPv6, harder to remember, but . . ." He stared at it for a moment, then closed the window and jumped up. "Got it—let's go."

"You remembered all that?" Eddie asked in surprise.

"What, you didn't? Come on!"

The Israeli recovered his gun and ran to the door. Eddie followed. There was nobody on the landing. "Okay, so how are we gonna get out of here?"

Zane went to the staircase. "You're supposed to be great at improvising—I'm sure you'll think of something."

"Is that what my Mossad file says?" the Englishman asked as they clattered down the stairs. "We'll need a car, unless you want to run back to Amalfi."

"We'll take one of Leitz's. I saw aerial photos of the villa; he has a garage." They reached the hall, the Israeli pointing to a door in one corner. "That must be it."

"You sure? If it's his laundry room, we won't get far in a pair of his underpants!"

Zane yanked the door open, Eddie covering him. Glossy metal gleamed in the dimly lit space beyond: Leitz's BMW parked alongside a second vehicle. "I'm sure," the agent announced with satisfaction.

"All right, smug-boots." They rushed in, Eddie finding the light switch beside the door. "We need the key."

"Here," said Zane, spotting a nearby set of hooks bearing fobs. He picked one marked with a BMW logo, but Eddie reached past him to snag another. "What are you doing?"

The Yorkshireman grinned. "Take a look." Zane turned—and saw that beside the black 7 Series was something considerably more impressive. The second car in the garage was a bright red Ferrari 458 Spider, the roof retracted to turn it into a two-seater convertible. "Just what we need for a quick getaway."

He started to round the BMW, but Zane half jumped, half slid over the bonnet of the 7 Series to land by the Ferrari, snatching the key from Eddie's hand and vaulting into the driver's seat without a pause. "I'm driving."

"Like fuck you are," Eddie protested. "You ever driven anything like this?"

Zane started the engine, the Ferrari's V8 howling to life. "I've been trained by the Mossad! I can drive anything." He pointed at a control panel on the wall. "Open the door, and the main gate. Quick!"

Annoyed, Eddie slapped both buttons and hopped into the Ferrari's passenger seat. The outer door began to rise. Over the rattle of the mechanism and the 458's engine burble, he heard shouting from the hall. "They're coming," he warned, bringing up his gun to cover the entrance.

Zane glared at the garage door as it ambled upward. "Why are these things always so *slow*? Come on!"

"*Sav'lanut,*" Eddie said with a half smile. The glare was turned upon him. "Okay, soon as you can fit this thing under—"

Movement in the hall—a man with a gun.

"*Ici!*" yelled the guard, raising his weapon. Another man sprinted across the hall toward the doorway—

Eddie fired a single shot to deter them, hitting the door frame at eye level and sending a blinding spray of splintered wood and plaster across the opening. Both men jerked back. A glance at the garage door; it still wasn't quite high enough to let the car through . . .

Zane floored the accelerator anyway. The 458 shot forward, throwing Eddie back into his seat. He ducked as the top of the windshield's frame clipped the door— and the glass instantly crazed, the view ahead reduced to a cobwebbed haze.

Brilliant sunlight forced both men to screw up their eyes. Eddie squinted back at the house, glimpsing figures running into the garage. "Down!"

Bullets tore after them. One thunked against the raised bodywork behind Eddie's headrest. Zane yanked at the steering wheel. The Ferrari swept past two more guards standing beside another BMW outside the villa and made a tight, skidding turn around an ornamental fountain before tearing up the steep drive. More shots followed it, but they smacked harmlessly into the cliff face behind the car.

Eddie leaned out to look around the damaged windshield. "Might have known a kid like you'd suffer from premature acceleration," he sniped. The barrier at the top of the drive was rolling open—but not quickly enough. "Slow down or we'll hit the gate!"

"We'll make it," said Zane, staring intently through the spiderwebbed glass.

"No we won't!"

"We will!" He adjusted the wheel, lining up the car's nose with the slowly widening opening.

Widening—then it stopped.

"Shit!" cried Eddie. "They've pushed the bloody button to close it!"

Zane's response was to jam the accelerator down harder. The Ferrari surged forward. "We can fit—"

The gate reversed direction.

"No we can't!" Eddie cringed as the 458's front wheels cleared the shrinking gap with a hairbreadth to spare—

A shrill crunch of tearing metal—and both men were flung forward as the closing gate sheared away bodywork before smashing against the rear wheels.

In a contest between rubber and steel, the result was inevitable. Both tires exploded, one of the wheel rims being wrenched from the axle. The Ferrari careered out onto the road at the head of a comet tail of mangled wreckage, barely missing a car heading toward Amalfi, only to hit a Fiat in the westbound lane. Both vehicles slammed into the base of the towering cliff.

The Ferrari's air bags had fired, cushioning the impact. Eddie straightened groggily. "Told you. You okay?"

The younger man grimaced. "My head hurts, but . . . yeah, I think so." He clambered from the car. "At least I fulfilled an ambition."

Eddie climbed over the passenger door. "Which one?"

"To drive a Ferrari. Even if it was only for twenty seconds."

"We need to find something else to drive, fast." The gate was opening again. A shrill of tires told him that Leitz's bodyguards were coming after them in the BMWs.

He looked around. The Fiat's driver was uninjured, already gesticulating furiously through his battered car's window. A small truck behind it had skidded as it braked to avoid the wrecked Ferrari, blocking both lanes. Horns blasted as more vehicles joined the jam.

No way back to Amalfi, then—they would have to go west. Eddie checked the first few cars in the other lane. Fiat, Lancia, Fiat: Any would do, but they would need to make a U-turn to escape, which in the confined space would take time he didn't have. He needed a bike, or . . .

"Here!" he shouted, running to the fourth vehicle in the line.

Zane hurried after him—only to stop in disbelief. "We can't use that!"

"We don't have a choice!" Eddie's intended getaway vehicle was a three-wheeled Piaggio Ape, the little green pickup's rear bed loaded with gardening equipment. Its driver, a slovenly old man with a cigarette dangling from his mouth, watched Eddie approach with surprise, then fear as he saw his gun. "*Scusi, signore,* but we need-o your *auto.*"

The Mossad agent hesitated, but the roar of approaching engines convinced him. He ran to the Ape, elbowing Eddie aside before yanking the driver out of the single-seat cab. "I'll drive."

"After what you did to the last car?" the Yorkshireman hooted.

"Just get in the back!" Zane shoved the driver away and dropped into his seat.

"*Scusate,*" Eddie said apologetically to the bewildered Italian as he jumped into the pickup bed.

The Ape's little engine revved hard, sounding like bees trapped in a tin can, then the vehicle jerked into motion. The Piaggio had handlebars rather than a steering wheel; Zane jammed them to the left to pull the vehicle out from the line of traffic. With a turning circle of just twelve feet, it had no difficulty coming about even on the narrow road—although the alarming amount of body roll warned the occupants that the vehicle's stability did not match its maneuverability.

Eddie grabbed the cab's rear and leaned over to help counterbalance the Ape as the first of the black BMWs powered out of the driveway. It barged wreckage aside and swung after the Piaggio as the second 7 Series emerged behind it. "Here they come!"

Zane twisted the throttle to its limit, sending the Ape zipping along the winding cliff road as the two larger—and vastly more powerful—cars roared in pursuit.

18

Eddie crouched, bracing himself against the cab. The line of stalled eastbound traffic whipped past on the Ape's left, parked cars and wheelie bins hemming it on the right. The lead BMW closed with frightening speed.

There were two men in the car. The passenger had a gun, but the 7 Series itself was the weapon, about to ram the flimsy Ape off the road—

Eddie snapped up Leitz's Sphinx and fired. The combination of the Piaggio's rough ride and Zane's evasive driving threw off his aim, but the bullet still ricocheted off the BMW's hood. Alarmed, the driver pulled back.

But the threat was far from over. The other man lowered his window, leaning out . . .

"Hold on!" Zane shouted. Eddie grabbed the pickup's side as the Ape snaked among three young men riding scooters. Shrilling horns and angry shouts followed in the little truck's wake. The BMW braked hard to avoid hitting the riders, the driver blasting his own horn. Various rude Italian hand gestures came in response.

The passenger made a gesture of his own—with his gun. Suddenly rather less macho, the trio hurriedly pulled aside. The BMW accelerated, its twin following.

The delay had given the two men in the Ape a respite,

however brief—its top speed was only around forty miles per hour. Eddie checked the back for potential weapons. Some large plastic sacks of soil, several spades and rakes held upright against the cab by a length of bungee cord hooked into a hole in the roof, a rust-specked set of shears, a grimy plastic box containing small tools and packets of flower seeds. Not the most promising selection, but if he ran out of bullets, they would be all he had.

The black cars were gaining quickly even on the narrow road. The gunman leaned out of the lead vehicle's window, his counterpart in the second BMW following his example.

Eddie tensed, awaiting the inevitable attack. The pickup bed's low sides were thin pressed aluminum. He would be almost completely exposed to their pursuers' fire, and there was no room for him in the cab . . .

Inspiration came to him. He grabbed one of the heavy soil bags and dropped it on its edge against the tailgate. Two more joined it, wedged diagonally against each side wall—and now he had a bunker of sorts, the sacks of earth acting as sandbags.

The Ape tipped again as Zane brought it around another bend. The gap between the three-wheeler and Leitz's men shrank with alarming speed—

Muzzle flash from the lead BMW—and Eddie heard the supersonic crack of a bullet tearing past.

He dropped behind his makeshift barricade. The next shot hit a soil bag. There was a flat *whap!* and he felt the sack kick hard against him—but the round didn't penetrate, the dense, damp earth absorbing the impact.

A sharp clang and a second *thump*. Another bullet, this one punching through the tailgate before burying itself in the packed soil. He had a chance—

He readied his gun, lifting his head a fraction to spot the lead car's roof—then fired two shots at its driver.

His awkward position behind his improvised cover affected his aim, but he still hit the front of the 7 Series. The driver reacted with fright, the car swerving before he recovered.

The gunman returned fire. Most of the shots from the weaving BMW went wide, but one still smacked into the soil bags. Eddie waited for a moment, then popped up again for another attack—

To see the 7 Series charging at him.

The car rammed into the Piaggio. Even with two men aboard, the little three-wheeler was swatted like an insect. Its back end slewed sideways as the BMW pushed it along, rear tires rasping over the asphalt. Only Zane's lightning reactions saved it from overturning as he slammed the handlebars to turn the front wheel into the skid.

The impact almost hurled Eddie over the tailgate. The stacked soil bags saved him—but he lost the gun as he clung on, the Sphinx spinning away onto the road. The BMW's driver angled to smash the pinned Ape against the towering cliff wall . . .

A left turn ahead—and the man's determined expression suddenly changed to fear as he realized he was going too fast to make it around. He braked, the BMW dropping away sharply, and the Piaggio leapt back upright as Zane jerked the handlebars to straighten out. The Israeli had to lean out of the cabin to act as a counterweight as the tiny truck again threatened to overturn through the bend. One end of the bungee cord jarred loose, sending tools clattering into the pickup bed.

Eddie kicked away a shovel and moved back behind his cover. He heard the BMW closing as it exited the sharp corner. The road ahead curved right along the cliff edge. Another hit and the 7 Series would bowl the Ape over the low wall.

No gun, so how to stop it . . .

Improvise.

He grabbed one of the sacks and lifted it in front of his face and chest. Two bullets hit like punches, dark loam spraying from ragged tears in the plastic, but he took the blows—then flung the ripped bag over the tailgate.

It thumped down on the BMW's nose, spewing earth over the windshield. The gunman was blinded by the cascade. He pulled back into the cabin, coughing and spitting. Vision blocked, the driver was forced to slow, drawing an angry hoot from the second pursuing vehicle right behind him.

Houses ahead on the inside of the bend. Eddie snatched up a rake from the scattered tools and swung it, hooking the handle of a large metal wheelie bin. Pain seared through his arms as he pulled—then the rake slipped from his grip. But the bin spun into the road behind the Piaggio.

The lead driver used the windshield wipers to clear the soil—and saw the obstacle. Hemmed in on the narrow road, he had nowhere to go. Brakes shrieked, but too late—

The 7 Series plowed into the bin with an explosion of garbage. The collision threw the car off course. It veered to the right and smashed into a parked car. The passenger was launched through the windshield like a missile.

"What just happened?" Zane shouted.

"He soiled himself and binned it!" Eddie replied.

One BMW down—but the second was still a threat. It swerved around its wrecked twin and powered after the Ape.

Another gunman leaned out. Eddie dropped behind the remaining soil bags as bullets lanced across the rapidly diminishing gap between the two vehicles. One struck the cab with a piercing clang. The Piaggio reeled, the engine note dropping. Eddie thought Zane had been hit, but then the young man recovered, the sputtering two-stroke shrilling back to full power.

The road widened, and the BMW pulled alongside the Ape. Eddie raised his head. The gunman was just feet away, aiming at the Israeli—

Eddie snatched up the shears by one handle and swung them at the man's arm. Centrifugal force clacked the blades open. The metal was rusty, but the edge was still keen—and it hacked deep into the gunman's wrist. He screamed, yanking his bloodied limb back into the car. The gun dropped to the road and was lost behind them.

The BMW's driver responded by jerking the wheel. The 7 Series sideswiped the Ape, sending the smaller vehicle into the oncoming lane. Zane swerved back to avoid a head-on collision, but the other man attacked again, harder.

Eddie rose, about to stab the shears through the open window—

Zane pointed his Barak backward from the cab and fired blind. One lucky shot shattered the BMW's windshield, the others missing—but they passed close enough to the startled Englishman that he reflexively jerked back . . .

The car rammed against the Ape's side.

The little truck was again thrown into the oncoming lane—and Eddie lost his balance, tripping over the spilled tools. Arms flailing, he stumbled backward and toppled over the side—

One hand caught the dangling bungee cord.

It arrested his fall—for an instant, before the tough elastic stretched under his weight.

"Shiiiiit!" he screamed as he dropped toward the road—

The straining cord reached its limit, arresting his fall with his ankles on the pickup's side and his head just two feet above the ground . . .

Now only *one* foot.

The massively unbalanced Ape tipped onto two wheels. Zane looked at Eddie in shock as the vehicle tilted beneath him, then hurriedly leaned from the cab's right side to counterbalance the Englishman. The Piaggio wobbled, teetering on a knife-edge—but Zane couldn't stretch any farther without letting go of the controls.

The BMW's driver suppressed a laugh at the sight of the two men dangling from their vehicle like a clown car. Grinning, he brought the 7 Series back into contact—only a nudge this time, but still enough to send the Ape at the wall.

Eddie saw it rushing at him—

Muscles straining, he wound the bungee cord around his fist to raise himself a little higher, clearing the top of the low stone barrier by an inch. But he still didn't have enough leverage to haul himself back into the truck.

A telephone pole loomed ahead, waiting to slice him in two—

Zane saw it—and let go of the handlebars, almost rolling out of the cab before catching the throttle with his left hand.

The sudden shift in weight jerked the Piaggio back down onto all three wheels, practically catapulting the Yorkshireman into the cargo bed as the pole sliced through the air behind him.

But now the Israeli was trapped in the same situation that Eddie had just escaped, unable to pull himself upright. The Ape swung back across the road, Zane hearing the roar of the BMW's engine coming up fast from behind.

He twisted his head to see the twin radiator grilles rushing at him—

Eddie grabbed a heavy gardening fork from the box and hurled it through the onrushing car's shattered windshield. *"Fork off!"*

The three prongs thunked deep into the driver's throat with a spurt of blood. He spasmed, thrashing in his seat. The BMW's charge stopped inches short of Zane as the man's foot came off the accelerator, then it veered left and bumped the Ape's flank.

The blow gave the Mossad agent the extra impetus he needed to drag himself back into the cab. He stamped on the brake pedal as the 7 Series swerved past, smashing through the wall and hurtling over the cliff. It arced down toward the sea a hundred feet below, disappearing in an explosion of spray.

The Ape rattled to a halt beside the new opening. Oncoming cars stopped, their occupants regarding the scene with alarm. Shaking, Eddie climbed out of the pickup and went to check on Zane. "You okay?"

"I'm fine," said the wide-eyed young man, repeating the words as if trying to convince himself.

"You've been hit."

Zane looked at a bloodstain on his sleeve. "Flesh wound," he said, flexing the limb. "It's okay."

Eddie shook his head. "I know what flesh wounds are

like—and they fucking hurt. Are you sure you're all right?"

"Yes, yes," the younger man insisted. "What about you?"

"Not dead, still got all my bits, so . . . fine. We need to get out of here before the *polizia* show up, though. We'd better dump this thing too—it's a bit recognizable."

Zane clambered from the battle-damaged Ape and started running along the road. "Come on."

He had covered almost fifty yards before he heard Eddie shout: "Oi! You going to *run* back to Amalfi, or take the easy way?" Stopping, he saw that the Englishman had gone to the third car in the line of traffic—which happened to be a taxi.

Eddie grinned as the younger man hurried back. "That's something you learn as you get older; you don't have to do every fucking thing the hard way." The pair got in. "All right, let's go." His expression hardened. "I've got to find out what's happened to Nina."

* * *

Half an hour later, the pair were back at their car in Amalfi, the taxi driver having taken a winding alternative route to bypass the chaos along the cliff—and also to minimize the chances of the police or anyone connected with Leitz spotting them.

Eddie used the journey to try to call Nina, without success. That didn't bode well, nor did the fact that he couldn't reach Macy either. Not having contact information for anyone else in Egypt, he finally resorted to calling the IHA in New York and was put through to Seretse . . . only to have his worst fears confirmed.

After bandaging his arm, Zane had stayed outside the Lancia to make a call of his own. Seeing Eddie's grim expression as he got out, he ended it. "What is it?"

"Leitz was telling the truth," Eddie said, trying to control the cold sickness he felt. "Nina's convoy was attacked on the way to Cairo. They took her, Macy, and the head archaeologist, Banna—and killed everyone else."

"What about the statue?"

That Zane didn't know about the bronze fish told Eddie that the Mossad wasn't as omnipotent as it liked others to believe, but that gave him little comfort. "They got that too. Fuck knows where they are now. Probably on their way to wherever that fat bastard Kroll's hiding." He banged a fist in sudden anger against the car's roof. "*Fuck!* I should have been with her! I could have—"

"You could have *what*?" Zane cut in. "You just said they killed everyone else, and they had an armed escort. You wouldn't even have had a gun."

"But I could have done something—*anything*!"

"You would have *died*, Eddie." The use of his first name caught the Englishman by surprise. "They only took the archaeologists with them, and killed the rest. That means they need them for something. There's still a chance to find them."

Eddie turned away in frustration. He knew Zane was right, but that didn't make him feel any less helpless. "How, though? They could be fucking anywhere."

"I know where."

He spun sharply back to the Israeli. "What?"

"I just spoke to my people. Remember that IP address I got from Leitz's computer? They traced it."

Hope surged in Eddie's heart. "To where?"

"Argentina."

"Argentina's pretty bloody big. You'd better narrow it down a bit."

A sigh. "We have . . . mostly. But we could only pinpoint it to a small town in the southwest of the country. Everything there goes through a satellite hub, but not even the telecom company knows the physical locations of the computers linked to it. Kroll and his people might be in the town, or just outside it . . . or ten miles away."

"But Mossad'll search now they know roughly where they are, right?"

Zane looked uncomfortable. "Yes—but they still have to recall agents from other assignments back to CSU."

"How long will that take?"

"Since we haven't got absolute confirmation of the Nazis' location . . . two or three days."

"Nina and the others might be *dead* in two or three days," Eddie growled. "We should get the UN or Interpol involved."

"They'll take even longer! They won't act without proof. That's why I already arranged a flight—for both of us." For the second time in minutes, Eddie was surprised by the young agent. "We can try to locate Kroll's base ourselves. If we find it—"

"We'll find it. We're not fucking leaving until we do."

"*When* we find it, the Mossad can take action. Interpol too—if there's anything left for them." He gave Eddie a dark look. "We both have personal reasons for taking out these bastards."

"Rescuing Nina and the others takes priority, though. Even over revenge."

Hesitation, then: "Agreed," said Zane.

"Okay." The Yorkshireman extended his hand; Zane regarded it for a moment, then shook it firmly. "So it's not the Boys from Brazil—it's the Arseholes from Argentina. Let's go and wipe 'em out."

19

Argentina

The first thing Nina heard as she struggled back to wakefulness was the crackle of gunfire.

The sound sent a shock of fear through her system, driving away the fug. She was in a moving vehicle, lying on a dirty metal floor with her hands tied behind her back. Panic rose. Where was she? What had happened—

"*Sie wacht auf,*" said a man behind her.

Nina twisted to see the huge form of Walther sitting on a narrow bench. He stared back with contempt. The rumbling truck had a canvas cover over its cargo bed, gray daylight picking out the truck's other occupants.

Macy was unconscious on the floor, Banna beside her. Both were bound. Two men sat behind them, submachine guns on their laps.

Memory returned. She'd been drugged! The Nazis had hauled the survivors of the desert ambush into their van—and forcibly injected them.

How long had she been unconscious? The light outside suggested it was late afternoon . . . but her gnawing hunger told her that more than a few hours had passed. She pushed herself up to look over the tailgate—and realized she was not in Egypt anymore.

They had climbed up a hill from a vast plain, the vegetation more brown than green. A lake was visible several miles away; a small town stood amid desiccated farmland near it.

There was something else about the scene, something *wrong*, but she couldn't pin down what . . . until a shiver gave her the answer. It was *cold*. Not merely a high-altitude chill, but a deeper frigidity, seeping into her bones. It was winter. In June.

That meant she was in the Southern Hemisphere, below the tropics. Too cold to be Australia or southern Africa, too dry for New Zealand. Which left . . . South America. Almost certainly Argentina, then; narrow, mountainous Chile was lacking in great grassy plains.

"Shoulda guessed," she mumbled. She didn't need to be a Mossad agent to know that the country had been a magnet for escaped Nazi war criminals.

"What was that, Dr. Wilde?" She turned to see Rasche through an opening in the back of the truck's cab.

"Argentina," she told him. "It makes sense that you'd have found yourselves a little rat-hole here. Lots of your buddies hid out in Argentina after the war, didn't they? Mengele, Eichmann—Juan Perón really laid out the welcome mat for you."

"How do you know where we are?" Walther demanded.

Rasche gave him a sneering smile. "Because she is as clever as her reputation told us. I hope for your sake, Dr. Wilde, that you will use that mind of yours to give us what we want. And for the sake of your friends," he added, glancing at the two sleeping figures.

Another burst of gunfire, closer. Nina squirmed to the bench opposite Walther and with an effort levered herself up to sit upon it. The big German shot her a warning scowl, but did not kick her back down. She peered through the opening.

The truck was crossing a large plateau that gradually rose toward a distant range of snowcapped peaks. Stands of trees dotted the landscape between empty fields. A rusty narrow-gauge railroad track ran parallel to the

dirt road, heading for a cluster of buildings at the heart
of the upland plain.

The escaped Nazis had not spent the past seven decades hiding in a hole.

It was more than a mere farm; they had constructed
an entire *colony*. Several large houses stood at the center,
with ranks of long, low structures resembling military
barracks lined up nearby. There were also barn-like
storage structures, garages and workshops, even a water
tower.

More shots caught her attention. Off to one side was
a military training ground, an obstacle course alongside
a target range. A group of young men were firing rifles.

The chill returned, but this time Nina felt more than
just the winter cold. The youths all wore black uniforms—
and even from a distance she could make out the symbols on their red armbands. *Swastikas*.

Rasche saw her appalled expression. "The New Reich,"
he said with an oily smile of pride as the truck made its
way into the compound.

Sidings split off the railroad, an old and rust-streaked
steam locomotive on one spur with a small train of covered wooden wagons. A passenger carriage and a caboose waited on another, behind them a string of carts
that had once carried some mined mineral. None had
been used for some time; as in the wider world, rail had
given way to road, several large trucks were parked by
the workshop buildings. These too were battered and
elderly.

They turned at a junction and headed away from the
railroad to pull up outside one of the ranch houses. Walther gave a command to the two men, who dropped the
tailgate with a bang before picking up Banna and Macy.
"Move," the hulking Nazi told Nina.

She jumped down. As Walther lumbered after her,
she looked up at the house. It was distinctly Germanic,
white-painted walls divided by black timber crossbeams
with a high, steeply sloping roof. The other houses nearby
were similar in style, though smaller.

Rasche headed to the front door. Walther pushed Nina

ahead of him, her companions being carried behind. The newcomers' arrival had attracted interest, a group of young men marching along a side path looking on as they passed—

Nina's eyes locked on to one of the observers as his gaze snapped to her. Simultaneous recognition—but for her, the feeling was joined by shock. She was looking at a dead man.

It was Volker Koenig, the youth who had sought her out in Los Angeles, only to be gunned down by Maximilian Jaekel.

But that was impossible. This had to be a twin. Did he know what had happened to his brother?

The doppelgänger's group marched out of sight as she arrived at the house. A man standing on the porch snapped to attention, one arm raised in a ramrod-straight Nazi salute. Rasche returned it somewhat more casually. The guard opened the door for them.

The first thing that hit Nina was the smell: The interior stank, a pervasive miasma of cigarette smoke, coffee grounds, and stale sweat soaked into the woodwork. The group went down a long hall. Rasche knocked on an ornate dark oak door. *"Hereinkommen,"* said a voice. They entered.

Nina froze at the sight waiting for her. The room was a large study, the wooden walls and furniture all carved in an elaborate Gothic style, eagles and other motifs of the Third Reich featuring prominently. But two symbols overpowered all others. The first was a huge Nazi flag hanging on the wall behind a large desk.

The other was above the fireplace, a portrait of one of the most evil men in history.

Adolf Hitler.

Nina stared at the painting, almost refusing to accept that such a thing could still exist. It was the *twenty-first century*! How could anyone still believe in the hate-filled rantings of this madman?

Her eyes then went to the room's occupants, and she had her answer.

These men were not neo-Nazis, appropriating the basest elements of Hitler's twisted philosophy to cover their own fears and failures and inadequacies. Like Rasche and Walther, they had personally been a part of the horrors of Nazism, true believers from the start.

She knew their faces from the mug shots at the United Nations. Herman Schneider, squat and toad-like, little eyes lighting up with a predatory glee at the sight of the two captive women. Bren Gausmann, thin-faced and with a cold, dead stare that told her he would feel no more remorse at killing a human being than he would a fly.

And the leader of the group, behind the desk. Erich Kroll, bald and bloated almost beyond recognition—if not for the malignancy in his gaze. It was a look that had been the last thing countless victims ever saw.

And now it turned upon her. "Dr. Nina Wilde. Welcome to the Enklave." His voice was deep and heavy with smoker's phlegm.

Nina tried not to show her fear. "Erich Kroll. I can't say that I'm pleased to meet you."

One fleshy eyebrow twitched upward. "You know who I am."

"You're famous. Well, infamous."

"As are you." Kroll gestured at Macy and Banna. "*Wachen sie auf,*" he said. The two men carrying them deposited them far from gently on chairs against the wall—then slapped their faces.

"Hey!" Nina protested. "Leave them alone!"

Walther pounded a fist down on her upper back and knocked her to the floor. It felt as if a tree had fallen on her. "Shut up!" he barked. "You do not give orders here."

"Sturmmann," said Kroll in mild reproach. "Get up, Dr. Wilde."

Nina stood painfully. By now, the other prisoners had been forced back to consciousness. "Nina?" said Macy, confused, before fright took hold. "Oh my God! They—they killed the others, they—"

"Macy, Macy!" Nina cut in, trying to calm her. "It's

okay, we'll be okay. They want something from us—they won't do anything to us until they get it."

"The fish," croaked Banna. "Where is the Andreas relic?"

Kroll turned expectantly toward Rasche, who called back into the hall. Another man brought in the case containing the bronze artifact. The lid was raised to reveal the prize within.

Gausmann and Schneider stepped closer with greedy eyes, while Kroll leaned forward in his seat, almost willing the metal piece toward him. "*Haben wir es endlich . . . ,*" the Nazi leader whispered.

Nina didn't need to understand his words to know his meaning. "Yeah, you've got it," she said. "So why do you need us?"

"Because you will help us to use it," Kroll replied. He rose, both hands flat on the oak desktop to push his bulk out of the chair. Despite being grossly obese, he was a threatening, dangerous figure, tall and overbearing. He stood before his prisoners. "It will lead us to the Spring of Immortality."

"The Spring of Immortality?" Banna echoed. "But that is just a myth—a fantasy from the *Alexander Romance.*"

Kroll chuckled, a thoroughly humorless sound. "It is no fantasy, Dr. Banna."

"Yeah, I think that's proven by the fact that you're all standing here and not rotting in your graves," said Nina. "So how did you find out about the statue of Bucephalus? You knew it was inside Alexander's tomb even before the tomb was discovered—how?"

"I will show you." Kroll returned to his desk. Rather than sit, though, he went to the huge hanging swastika behind.

Rasche spoke in German; the words were said with a degree of deference, but were still clearly critical, even challenging. The bald man shot him an irritated look. "It is my decision, and mine alone, Rasche." That he was replying in English told Nina that he was speaking for the benefit of the three visitors, letting them know who was in charge. "The more information they have, the faster they will be able to locate the spring."

His subordinate was displeased at the dressing-down, but nodded. *"Mein Führer."*

Kroll tugged a cord at one side of the banner, drawing the swastika aside like a curtain. Behind it was revealed a large metal door with a keyhole and combination dial: a safe.

The Nazi leader pushed his fingertips under the folds of his jowls and into his collar, pulling out a key on a gold chain. He inserted it into the keyhole and turned it, then—after a wary glance at the others in the room— moved in front of the dial to enter a combination. A dull click, and he pulled at a recessed handle. The heavy door slowly swung open.

Nina's eyes widened in amazement as she took in what lay behind. It was no mere safe, but a *vault*. The metal-walled space was about twelve feet by twelve.

And packed with treasure.

Gold and silver glinted in the stark light of an overhead bulb. She saw coins, statues, even pieces of armor—all stored in open wooden crates stenciled with the eagle and swastika of the Third Reich. But it was clear what the former SS men considered the greatest treasure of all. In pride of place was a very large pottery jar inscribed with Greek text. A set of wooden steps was positioned by the pithos to give easier access to its silver-rimmed neck.

Kroll stepped into the vault. "Bring them," he ordered. The guards gestured with their guns. Nina and her companions hesitantly followed the overweight man into the confined space.

"A family of Greek farmers had been protecting a shrine to Andreas beneath their house for centuries," explained Kroll. "They had kept his secret for all that time—until we discovered it."

"And stole it," Nina said, unable to contain her caustic disgust.

"It was the property of the Reich."

"And after the Reich was destroyed, it just happened to stay in your hands, right?"

The Nazi's eyes blazed with fury. "*We* are the Reich! As long as we persist, it will never be destroyed." With a visible effort, he calmed himself. "And it is because of this that we have persisted. It has kept us young for seventy years."

"I'm guessing that it's not full of Metamucil."

Kroll had apparently never heard of the dietary supplement; he ignored her and continued. "It contains water from the Spring of Immortality. I knew of the legend—Alexander had always been a hero of mine," he said in brief reverie, "but it was hard to believe that it could be true. The moment I drank it, however, I *knew*. It had a strange glow, an almost electric charge—it was more than ordinary water. It would bring everlasting life to those who drank it—and when I read the text on the jar, I realized that the spring was still out there, waiting to be found."

"So you took it for yourself. And everything else in the shrine as well."

"It was needed." He gestured at the riches. "There was more to begin with—much more. But we had to use it. First to buy our freedom from the Allies after the war, then to pay for our escape to South America—and even more to buy the Enklave, to ensure our privacy as we worked to build the New Reich. Survival is an expensive business."

Nina glanced back at Walther, remembering what he had said in Alexander's tomb. "And I suppose after all this time, you're running out of gold."

"We will soon no longer need gold," Kroll replied. "All the money we could ever require will be ours—after we locate the spring. When the Egyptians announced the discovery of the tomb of Alexander the Great, I knew that was our chance to find it. But first we had to obtain the statue of Bucephalus. So we made plans to take it."

"How did you know about the statue?" asked Banna.

"It was not mentioned in any of the existing sources describing the tomb."

The Nazi indicated the text upon the pithos. "From this." He turned to an old wood-and-metal box. "And this—the original text of the *Alexander Romance*, written by Andreas himself."

Despite the situation, Nina couldn't help but feel excitement. "You have the original?"

Kroll nodded. "There is far more to it than any of the later versions. But the text on the pithos told us the true meaning of what Andreas wrote. He hid the truth inside the fantasy . . . and also told us which parts *were* the truth. The spring is real. And Andreas returned to it, after Alexander's death in 323 BC."

"Where is it?" Macy asked.

"If we knew that, you would not be here," the Nazi told her.

"If they knew that, we'd be *dead*," Nina added. Macy blanched.

"According to these, the spring lies somewhere along Alexander's route to India," said Kroll, turning back to the inscriptions upon the pithos. "They also say that the statue of Bucephalus that Andreas placed inside Alexander's tomb will reveal its location, but only to those who prove themselves as wise as Alexander by completing his tests. I believe you solved the first of these."

"Yeah, the riddle of the Gordian Knot," said Nina. "Use brute force to cut through the problem. I'm sure you would have come up with that answer quickly enough. It seems to be your solution to everything."

"That is because it works," Rasche said from outside the vault.

"But now that you have found the relic, the next part of the text makes sense," Kroll continued. "It says that once the riddle of the statue is solved, it will lead you from Alexander's tomb to the Kingdom of Darkness, and the spring itself." He looked back at the ancient artifact in its case. "The fish confirms a theory I have long held, but have never been able to share with the world. Do you recognize this?"

Nina examined the device he picked up, a collection of interlocking bronze cogs sandwiched between rectangular metal plates. It was a complex machine—even more so than the fish. "It looks like . . ." Surprise as her memory produced a match. "The Antikythera mechanism? A working copy?" Banna was equally astonished.

Kroll nodded. "It is an astrolabe, made by Andreas himself—as was the duplicate found in the shipwreck. When I first saw this one in Greece, I thought it was a much later addition to the shrine. It was not until I learned about the work in the 1970s to date the Antikythera mechanism that I realized its true age."

"Andreas built it?" asked the Egyptian.

"Yes. He lived for a very long time, and he learned a great deal during his life. He became an extremely clever man. Clever enough to hide his greatest discovery in a way that only those of equal brilliance could find."

"You mean the Spring of Immortality," said Nina.

"I do. Now," said Kroll, returning the device to its place, "I am learned in ancient Greek, and also in the history of Alexander himself. Given time, I will find the spring. But with three archaeologists to assist me, I am sure I will do so much sooner." He smiled, the expression conveying only menace.

"What's the rush?" said Macy. "I mean, you've kept hidden for seventy years. Why do you need it right now?"

"Because they're running out of water," Nina said, understanding. She looked at Kroll. "That's why you've taken such a huge risk by coming out into the open, isn't it? A place this big, you must have a lot of thirsty guys running around."

"The water of life is reserved for the Oberkommando!" barked one of the guards.

Nina gave him a disbelieving glance, then addressed Kroll again. "Oh, I get it. The water's only for the *elite*. The Hitler Youth turn into the Hitler Oldth, but you live forever, right?"

"When our time comes, all members of the New Reich will share the water of life," replied Kroll. The line sounded as if it had been spouted often enough to become a platitude. The guards seemed to believe it, however. "But yes, even rationing our supply, there is little left."

"You'll be able to stretch it out longer without your buddy who died in Los Angeles, I guess." The Nazi gave her a sharp look; Jaekel's death was clearly still a touchy subject. That realization triggered another, Nina's mind going back to the FBI briefing in New York. "There were eight of you originally. What happened to the other two?"

"Oster was killed before we escaped Europe. After we reached Argentina and built the Enclave, we realized that Henkel did not share our views. He was purged."

"For the good of the New Reich, right?" she said sarcastically.

"I . . . I do not understand," said Banna. "You say the water has kept you young for seventy years? How is that possible?"

"It's the carbon-60, isn't it?" Nina said to Kroll. "The buckyballs in the water? They capture the impurities in the body that encourage the aging process."

The Nazi was surprised. "You are very well informed, Dr. Wilde."

"You can thank the FBI for that. They analyzed Jaekel's flask of water."

Schneider spoke; all Nina understood was Jaekel's name, but the remark was definitely pointed. "Jaekel *failed*," Kroll replied angrily. "If he had killed Koenig before he gave the stolen papers to Dr. Wilde, the Egyptians would not have been warned of our operation, and we would not have lost so many men."

"Why did he try to kill Nina?" Macy asked hesitantly.

"Believe it or not, Dr. Wilde," said Kroll, turning to the redhead, "when we learned about the discovery of Alexander's tomb, we considered asking you to help us obtain the statue of Bucephalus."

Nina was startled. "Me? Why the hell would you think I'd do that?"

"There are certain elites—business, political, religious—who would oppose our return to power because it would threaten their own. You have been quite adept at eliminating their members." The empty smile briefly returned. "But it did not require much research to see that you do not share our vision for the world. So when Jaekel encountered you in Los Angeles, he tried to remove a potential threat after eliminating his primary target."

"You mean Volker Koenig?"

Kroll gestured at the vault door. The two guards stepped back, signaling for the archaeologists to return to the study. "Volker was a disruptive influence," said the leader as he followed them out. "A renegade and a traitor. He deliberately sought degenerate outside influences that turned him against us. But we did not realize the true extent of his treachery until he broke into my office one night. He stole the plans for our operation in Egypt—and also read all the information that had been compiled on you, Dr. Wilde." The Nazi indicated a modern laptop computer on his desk, incongruous in the Gothic surroundings. "He thought that as the world's most famous archaeologist, and the director of the International Heritage Agency, you were the best person to stop us—he did not know that you had resigned from the IHA. Nor did we. So we sent Jaekel after him . . . and you."

"How the hell did Jaekel even get into the country?" demanded Nina. "He was a wanted war criminal, and his fingerprints were instantly flagged after he died. So how did he get through immigration?"

"We have been readying ourselves for our return to the world. Every man in the Enklave has multiple passports: Argentine, German—and American. Holders of American passports are not subjected to biometric fingerprinting on arrival in the United States."

"Good to know that all that money we spend on Homeland Security's worth every penny." Kroll's phrasing prompted another question. "Wait, you said every *man* in the Enklave? What about women? I haven't seen a single woman since we got here."

Something resembling a giggle came from Schneider.

"Women have their place in the New Reich," he said, with a creepy little smile. "Where they belong." His gaze wandered lustfully over Macy's body. The young American shrank back behind Nina, suddenly very conscious of her light summer clothing.

"We are building a fighting force," announced Kroll. "For that, we need men. Females are needed to grow our numbers, but we keep them to the minimum necessary. They can be a . . . distraction." He gave the leering Schneider a disapproving look.

It took a moment for the repellent implications to sink in. "I guess when you've got no socialists, trade unionists, or Jews to come for, all that's left are women," said Nina, sickened.

"Do not test my patience, Dr. Wilde." Kroll closed the vault door, then moved the banner back to conceal it. "Now. The relic contains the location of the Spring of Immortality. You will find it for us."

"No, I won't."

The bluntness of her response surprised the Nazis. Walther moved as if to hit her again, but Kroll waved him back. "You *will*. Or we will kill you."

Nina somehow managed to conceal her fear as she stared back at the obese monster. "Kill me, and you get nothing. I don't think you're smart enough to find the spring on your own—and without it, you're just a group of thugs who are running out of money, and running out of *time*." Anger rose in the room, but she pressed on. "And that's assuming the Mossad doesn't track you down first. They know you're still alive—how long do you think it'll take them to find your little kingdom?"

"If the Mossad come, we will deal with them," Kroll growled. He took a pistol from his desk. Nina didn't need her husband's knowledge of firearms to recognize it as a Luger, the standard-issue sidearm of both the Nazi military and the SS. "As we will deal with all who oppose us—including you." He pointed the gun at the American. "Are you really willing to die to stop us from finding the spring?"

It was harder than ever for Nina to hold firm, but she

did so. "Yes," she said. Kroll's fat index finger curled more tightly around the Luger's trigger . . .

Then eased. "It would seem that you are," he said, his voice unexpectedly calm, almost curious. His malevolent eyes bored into hers for several chilling seconds—then the gun swung away.

Locking on to Macy.

The young woman gasped in fright. "You may be willing to die, Dr. Wilde," said Kroll. "But what about your friends?"

Nina sidestepped to put herself between Macy and the Luger. "Don't you even—"

This time Kroll did not wave Walther off. The huge man smashed Nina to the floor. Macy shrieked, Banna jumping back in horrified shock.

Nina groaned, her shoulder searing as if it had been hit by a baseball bat. She forced out words. "Fuck . . . you, you . . . Nazi bastard." Walther kicked her savagely in the side.

"If she is not going to help us, we should kill her," said Rasche. His eyes developed a manic gleam. "I will do it myself."

Kroll shook his head. A command, and Walther reluctantly stepped back. "Dr. Wilde, you *will* help us, or I shall have your friends tortured. To death, if necessary." He turned to Macy and Banna. "The same applies to you. Cooperate, or you will be responsible for the suffering of the others. Do you understand?"

Macy nodded in silence. "Yes, yes," whispered Banna, trembling.

"They're gonna kill us anyway," Nina warned.

"That is up to you," said Kroll. His expression of curiosity returned. "You *are* willing to die to protect the secret. Why is that? Why do you care?"

She managed a thin, sardonic smile. "Gee, why would I want to stop a gang of Nazi war criminals who're trying to build a whole new army from getting hold of the secret of eternal life? Plus you tried to kill me in Los Angeles. That's why I came back to help the IHA. You made it personal."

The SS leader was about to respond when a sudden thought stopped him. "You came *back* to the IHA," he said, calculating, "but you had kept it a secret that you had even left." He moved to stand over her. "Why *did* you leave?"

"Because I'd had enough of all the bureaucratic bullshit," Nina said, though she couldn't help a slight hesitation.

Kroll picked up on it. "I do not believe you."

"It's the truth. If you'd ever dealt with the UN, you'd know."

He shook his head, jowls rippling over his collar. "You forget, Dr. Wilde, I am an officer of the Schutzstaffel. I am trained in interrogation, and I know when someone is lying. As you are now. That tells me the matter is very important to you. So I will ask you again: Why did you resign?"

She sighed, feigning defeat. "Okay, okay. I had a half-million-dollar offer to write my autobiography and I needed time to work on it. It was a mercenary thing to do, and I'm not all that proud of it, but half a million bucks is a lot of money."

"That was not a lie," Kroll said after a moment. "But . . . it was not the whole truth, either. There is something more. Why did you resign?"

"Who am I, Patrick McGoohan? I told you the reason. Half a million reasons, actually."

Kroll's stare remained locked on to her. "Rasche," he said, "shoot one of the others in the knee. The girl or the *Araber,* I do not care which."

Rasche's face lit up. "*Jawohl, mein Führer!*" He drew his gun and pointed it at Macy's leg—

"No!" Nina cried.

Kroll raised a hand. "*Halten.*" Rasche froze, angry disappointment upon his face. "Well, Dr. Wilde? The truth—or I will command him to fire."

Nina looked helplessly up at her friend. This time, her expression of defeat was not faked. "I resigned because . . . I'm ill. Terminally ill. I'm dying."

Kroll regarded her closely, also noting Macy's dismay

at the admission. "The truth at last. Of what are you dying?"

"I was poisoned. By something the Soviets discovered in the Cold War, an organic toxin. I don't know how long I've got left, but probably not long. And *that's* why I came back to the IHA," she admitted. "So I could make one last discovery, by opening Alexander's tomb. And stopping you from raiding it." She sat up, pressing a hand to the new bruise where Walther had kicked her. Revulsion instinctively crossed her face as her fingers felt the line of tumorous bulges beneath her clothing.

Again, Kroll caught the blink-fast flicker of her expression. "What was that?"

"What was what?" Nina asked, confused.

"When you touched your side. There is something under your clothes."

"She was searched," Rasche insisted. "There is nothing hidden."

"Did you look, or did you just feel?" Kroll snapped. "Dr. Wilde, raise your shirt."

"What?" Nina protested. "What the hell for?"

"Do it!" The Nazi leader glanced at Rasche, whose gun was still aimed at Macy.

"Okay, okay! Jesus," Nina tugged up her grubby top. "There! Happy now . . ."

She had meant to say that with as much defiance as she could muster, but the words faded as she saw the growths on her skin.

In the whirlwind chaos of her visit to Egypt, she had not given them more than a cursory glance. But now she saw to her disgust and horror that even in the few days since she'd revealed them to Eddie, the loathsome excrescences had visibly grown. Worse, more had appeared, several angry red blisters extending the line of infection farther around her torso. "Jesus," she repeated, this time in a whisper.

Macy gasped. "Oh my God! Nina . . ."

Kroll bent to peer at the tumors. "They are worse than you expected." It was not a question.

"That's right," Nina said, determined not to let the

Nazi see her despair. "So you can't threaten me. I'm already dead—I just haven't stopped moving yet. And putting a bullet in my head would probably be doing me a favor."

"We still have your friends," Rasche warned.

"We may have something more." Kroll straightened, a smile slowly oozing onto his lips. "I think you *will* help us find the Spring of Immortality, Dr. Wilde. And you will do so because you *want* to."

"And why would I do that?" demanded Nina.

The smile widened, exposing crooked, nicotine-stained teeth. "In the seventy years that we have been taking the water," said Kroll, "not one of us has been ill, even for one day. Not with so much as a cold. And the water does not merely prevent sickness. It *cures* it. Schneider had pneumonia when we found the pithos; after he drank from it, the infection disappeared." Schneider nodded in confirmation. The SS commander regarded Nina with the air of someone making an offer that could not be refused. "The spring is your only hope of staying alive, Dr. Wilde. Help us find it . . . and we will share it with you."

20

Nina was speechless. Not at Kroll's offer in itself, but at what it could mean to her. She had resigned herself to the sickness spreading through her body, accepting that death was drawing ever closer . . . but now someone was offering her hope.

That someone being a murderous war criminal.

"Think about it, Dr. Wilde," Kroll went on, seeing her uncertainty. "You would not only be cured, but by drinking the water you would extend your own life. You wanted to make one last discovery—but how many more could you make with another century in which to make them? Find the spring, and I shall give you a lifetime supply of its water."

Rasche objected sharply in German. Kroll responded with a verbal explosion that made his second in command flinch. The leader stalked across the room to stand right in front of Rasche and harangued his subordinate at full volume, spittle flying from his mouth. The younger guards seemed genuinely terrified by the outburst.

Kroll finally stopped ranting—but remained in Rasche's face, nose-to-nose as if daring him to reply. Tight-lipped, jaw clenched, Rasche eventually drew himself to attention and said, *"Nein, mein Führer."* Kroll nodded in angry satisfaction and slowly stepped back, not breaking eye contact until he drew level with Nina.

"Trouble in the ranks?" she asked.

The baleful stare turned upon her. "Do not test me, Dr. Wilde. My offer is genuine—although Obersturmführer Rasche did not approve. But he is now in agreement with me. As is every other man in the Enklave." He looked to Schneider, Walther, and Gausmann, all of whom bowed their heads in deference. "Did you know that your name in German, *Wilde,* means 'a maniac,' 'a savage'? But that is not the impression I get from you. You are an intelligent and rational woman, so I will make you a proposal that only a fool could turn down. If you help us prolong our lives, I will help you save yours. I will of course let your friends go, unharmed. That is my offer. What do you say?"

Again, Nina found herself unable to answer. She didn't believe Kroll for a moment. The Nazis had only resurfaced out of desperation; even if they found their life-extending prize, they couldn't risk anyone revealing the location of their hideout. They were still on the wanted list of every international law enforcement agency—to say nothing of the blood vengeance sought by the Mossad. Letting their prisoners go would ensure their end, either in a prison cell or with a bullet to the head.

But . . .

What if the water really *could* cure her?

She knew it was unlikely. There was no proof of the water's restorative properties other than Kroll's word, which she considered absolutely worthless.

But . . .

His mere existence, decades younger than he should have been, confirmed that *part* of the legend was true. The Spring of Immortality had been found once—twice, in fact, since Andreas had returned to it after the death of Alexander the Great. Maybe it could be found again.

Maybe *she* could find it.

You're insane, she tried to tell herself. *Clutching at straws.* And she was dealing with mass murderers, ruthless members of one of the most evil organizations in history, who were now actively working to resurrect it. If the spring still existed, then helping the Nazis find it would practically be a crime in itself.

But if she could locate it and *keep it from them* . . .

The bronze relic was still in its case. The Greek text inscribed upon the ancient artifact stood out around its edge. Somewhere in the words was hidden the spring's location. She *could* find it, she was sure, just as she had found other wonders of the past.

If she made a deal with the devil . . .

"Okay," she said, looking back at Kroll. "You want me to help you locate the spring? I'll do it—if you promise you'll keep your word about letting us go."

"I promise," he replied.

Insincerity was almost painted on his face. But Nina had expected nothing else, and masked her suspicions. "All right. Then let's get started." Macy gaped at her, appalled.

"We already have maps and reference material," said Kroll. He gestured toward the door. One of the guards opened it, signaling for the prisoners to follow him down the hall.

"What are you doing?" Macy hissed to Nina as the group exited. "You actually want to *help* these people? They're Nazis!"

"Just go along with it," Nina whispered back.

Macy looked first confused, then conflicted. "Wait, you've got a plan?"

"I hope so . . ."

Further furtive discussion was cut off as they were brought into a large room. One wall was occupied by a chalkboard, smudged remnants of German visible upon it. Several maps were pinned up; Nina recognized one as a street plan of Alexandria, the others showing the Middle East at various scales.

Kroll stood before the chalkboard, the still-scowling Rasche alongside him. "Now, Dr. Wilde," he said as the artifact was removed from its case, "begin."

Nina exchanged looks with Macy and Banna, then regarded the metal fish. "Okay, based on what we learned when we examined it in Egypt, the first thing we need is a gnomon. How tall did it say it had to be?"

Banna read the text. "One *dichas*."

"Which if I remember my ancient Greek measurements was just over six inches, so fifteen-point-four centimeters." Kroll appeared surprised by her natural talent for mental arithmetic; clearly his research had not uncovered everything about her. "Okay, we need a stick exactly one hundred fifty-four millimeters tall that'll stand up vertically in this hole." She tapped the fish's eye.

"I will have one made." The Nazi issued orders, one of his men hurrying out. "What else must be done?"

Banna kept reading. "We are supposed to enter the date using the large dials, then take a reading of the angle of the sun at noon outside Alexander's tomb."

"Just like Eratosthenes," said Nina. The first person to make an accurate calculation of the earth's circumference had done so by measuring the sun's highest position in the sky over Egypt using the shadow cast by a gnomon. "Too bad you didn't know that when we were actually *in* Alexandria," she said to Kroll. "It would have saved you the cost of a flight back there."

The obese German was not amused. "The sun's position can be calculated using computers."

"I know. The IHA has a good app."

"Which you will not be using. If you log into the IHA, they will know you are alive—and where you are. I am not a fool, Dr. Wilde."

"Just a fascist," she said under her breath. "Ubayy, what next?"

"We move the pointer until it touches the shadow," said Banna. He turned the artifact over, rotating one of the dials. The little bronze marker protruding from the slot moved in synchronization. "Then we turn this small wheel"—he touched it—"which locks part of the mechanism—it becomes a base for all other calculations."

Nina read on. "Okay, then you follow Alexander's

route. Once you arrive in the Kingdom of Darkness, you dial in how many days it took you to get there from Alexandria ..." She straightened, impressed. "Wow, Andreas really was quite the gadget master. It adjusts the pointer's position to take into account the sun's precession. How much the sun moves up and down over time because of the earth's axial tilt," she added, seeing varying degrees of incomprehension on the watching Nazis' faces.

"I know what it is!" snapped Kroll. "Have you located the spring?"

"Have you located the gnomon?" she replied. "We can't do anything until we can start taking measurements."

The Nazi reddened with anger, while Rasche seemed amused that his superior had been made to look foolish. Kroll shouted more orders. Another man rushed out, coming back with the laptop from the study. A couple of minutes later, the first soldier returned, bearing a dowel. Kroll snatched it from him and thrust it at Nina.

The length of wood fit neatly into the fish's eye. "Okay," Nina said, "now we'll need a protractor, a long ruler—and a website that can tell us the sun's angle in a specific location on a specific day."

The required tools were quickly procured. Nina held the protractor against the artifact. "Find the longitude and latitude of Alexander's tomb. Then use them to calculate the sun's position at noon." As Kroll began to search for the results on the computer, she took a closer look at the parts of the mechanism visible through the slot. "You know ..."

"What is it?" Macy asked.

"I just realized that we can work out the spring's latitude right away! Based on Alexander's historical route and what's written in the *Romance*, it's most likely somewhere in northern Iran. Which"—she regarded one of the maps of the Middle East—"was a long trek in Alexander's day—weeks, or even months—but today you could fly there in a couple of hours. So if we don't advance the date dial at all, the same result is still valid . . ." She faced Banna. "How do you find out if you're at the spring?"

The Egyptian rechecked the Greek text. "Once you reach the Kingdom of Darkness, you enter the number of days you have traveled, then take another reading of the sun at noon." He indicated the series of small notches inscribed along the slot's edge. "Wherever the pointer is, if the shadow of the gnomon falls exactly five marks from it, then you are the correct distance north of the tomb. You then search for landmarks; the spring is in the shadow of a mountain peak, through the arch of Alexander."

"On the north face, I guess that means," said Macy. "If the sun's behind it at noon."

"So if the travel time between the tomb and the spring is less than one day," Nina said, almost to herself as calculations took on form in her mind, "five of these marks must be equal to however many degrees of latitude there are between the two places. Right?"

Macy blinked. "Ah . . . if you say so."

"They are. Trust me. Five ticks represent how many degrees north you have to go from Alexandria." She glanced back toward Kroll. "Do you have those figures yet?"

The SS commander was displeased at being on the receiving end of a demand, but he continued to tap on the keyboard until he had a result. "Alexander's tomb is at approximately thirty-one degrees and eleven minutes north, twenty-nine degrees and fifty-three minutes east."

"Okay, enter that into the solar altitude calculator. Set the date for tomorrow, and get the figure for twelve noon, local time."

Still bristling, Kroll did so. "The sun's position at midday is eighty-three-point-five degrees above the horizon."

"Eighty-three-point-five," Nina echoed. She used the protractor and ruler to find where the tip of a shadow cast by the gnomon would fall along the slot if the sun were at that height. "Okay, now we need to work out where the sun would be five ticks from that."

"The sun covers half a degree of arc," Banna pointed out. "We should take several measurements and find the average."

"Good point, but let's just get the basics for now."

Macy leaned closer, lowering her voice to the limit of audibility. "Slow it down, Nina! You're leading these jerks right to it."

Nina suddenly realized that her desire to discover the ancient artifact's secrets had indeed overcome the need to delay doing so. It was a trap she had fallen into before, but never had restraining her archaeological urges been so crucial. "Although yeah, we do need to be accurate," she added quickly. "We'll take measurements for eighty-three and eighty-four degrees as well. And we should double-check that we've got the sun's absolute highest position in the sky—it isn't always exactly at noon."

Rasche spoke to Kroll, suspicious, but the leader shook his head. "We must be precise. But," he went on, with a stern glare at the three archaeologists, "if I think you are deliberately slowing the work, you will be punished."

"Yeah, we got it," said Nina. That meant that they had some leeway to hold things up; the question was how far Kroll's patience would stretch. "Okay, let's get the other measurements."

The trio did so, Macy taking notes. Once they had an average result, Banna turned the bronze dial to move the pointer to the indicated position. "All right," Nina said, "we know from Andreas's text that the spring's latitude is five ticks from the pointer. So now we work backward; we measure the angle where the sun would have to be to cast a shadow on that point, and then"—she indicated the laptop—"we keep the same longitude, but keep entering latitude coordinates moving northward by steps until the sun's height there matches what we've got. That'll tell us how much farther north the spring is from the tomb."

Kroll nodded. "And then we retrace Alexander's route until we reach the correct area."

"Yes," said Banna. "The text describes Alexander

going north through mountains to reach a sea. Based on the historical accounts of his travels, that must be the Alborz range in Iran."

"So when his route gets to the right latitude," Nina continued, "there's the spring."

"Then find it," said Rasche, unimpressed.

Nina and Banna repeated the process of calculating the sun's position, this time placing the tip of the imaginary shadow on the fifth marker along the slot from the pointer. "The sun would be one-point-eight degrees lower in the sky than at Alexandria," she finally reported, having slowed things for as long as she could. "So now, start putting in more northerly coordinates until we get a match."

Kroll, still in charge of the laptop, began the laborious procedure. He entered a new position one degree north of the original, scrolled through the results to find the angle of the sun at midday, then recited it to the trio. The process was repeated with gradually increasing precision until eventually a match was found. "Thirty-seven degrees, thirty-seven minutes north!" Nina announced, despite everything still feeling a thrill of discovery. "That makes a difference of just over six and a half degrees of latitude between Alexander's tomb and the spring."

Kroll went to one of the maps. "Show me!"

She exchanged a concerned look with Macy. "We don't know exactly where Alexander crossed the mountain—"

"That does not matter for now," said Kroll. "Show me the general area—that will be enough to start making plans."

"Okay, then." Nina put her finger on Alexandria, at the map's bottom left. "So here's the tomb. We go north to thirty-seven degrees and thirty-seven minutes"—she moved her hand upward—"and then east until we're above the Alborz mountains." She sidestepped, sliding her fingertip over the paper. "So through Turkey, above Syria and Iraq, across northern Iran to . . . oh."

Rasche whirled to face Kroll. "I knew she was wasting our time!"

The Nazi leader's flabby jaw trembled with fury. "I

warned you what would happen if you tried to deceive us!"

"I wasn't!" Nina protested.

"Then explain *this*!" He stabbed his forefinger at the map. Her path across it had trailed to a stop in the Caspian Sea, many miles offshore.

"I can't! You saw the numbers—you read them out to us! That's the result we got."

"Then your work was wrong," said Rasche. "We do not tolerate mistakes!" He addressed Kroll again. "I should kill one of them as a warning."

The obese Nazi glared at Nina, considering his subordinate's suggestion . . . then shook his head. "No. They would not dare give us false results—it would be too easy for us to check their calculations."

"The numbers were right," Nina insisted. "Which means something else is wrong. We need to go through the Greek text on the fish again, see if there's something we missed."

"The Arab had a translation when we captured him," said Rasche.

"Bring it; it will save time," Kroll said. "No, wait. It is late—take them to the prison," he decided instead. "Dr. Banna will read the text during the night. We shall begin again in the morning."

Rasche's reply in German was disapproving. "Even prisoners need food," Kroll snapped. "Take them away."

Rasche issued orders, and the guards escorted Nina, Macy, and Banna from the room. As they left, Kroll spoke. "Dr. Wilde? I do not make empty threats. You *will* locate the Spring of Immortality . . . or you will suffer extreme consequences. Do you understand?"

"Yeah, I do," said Nina, trying to conceal her fear.

. . .

"Gross," said Macy, pushing away the metal tray containing the half-eaten remains of her meal. "This stuff tastes like it *came* from World War Two."

"At least they gave us *something*," Nina replied. She had been hungry enough to eat the whole of the unappetizing mash of boiled potatoes, shredded cabbage, and gray mystery meat.

"Yeah, it'll help us keep up our strength so we can bust out. Oh no, wait, we're in frickin' Alcatraz!" The young woman swept a hand around their cell. The door was a heavy slab of metal with a small peephole, while the only opening in the concrete walls was a ventilation slot high on one wall, too narrow to fit even an arm through. "And they're not going to let us go—whatever deal you made with them," she added sharply. "You really think they'll give you a lifelong supply of magic water? They're using you, Nina! Kroll wants you to believe you've got a chance of being cured so you'll find the spring!"

"You think I don't know that?"

Macy blinked. "Wait, you do?"

"Of course I do! I don't trust him any farther than I could throw him, and . . . well, the guy's a frickin' blimp!"

"So you do not want to find the water?" Banna asked, looking up from his translation notes.

"Are you kidding? Obviously I want to find it, if there's any chance at all that it might help me. Right now, though, I'm just trying to keep us all alive. The longer we can string them along, the more chance we have of getting out of this."

"So you weren't *really* going to cooperate with these Nazis?" Macy asked, now considerably happier. "I knew it!" Nina gave her a questioning glance. "Well, I was fairly sure. Pretty much."

"Thanks for your confidence," said the redhead with light sarcasm.

Macy blushed. "You did sound convincing."

"The hard part was trying not to convince myself. I mean, he was offering me a possible cure. I can't deny that I considered it."

The admission caught the young woman by surprise. "Oh, wow. God, yeah; it must have been hard for you. I'm sorry." She took Nina's hand in sympathy.

Nina smiled, grateful. "Thanks."

"Okay, so . . . what the hell do we do now?"

"All we can do is delay locating the spring for as long as possible and hope someone finds us."

Banna shook his head miserably. "What chance is there of that? We are not even on the same continent anymore!"

"There are some very resourceful people looking for us. The IHA, the UN—and Eddie." The mere thought of her husband gave her a surge of hope. He would move heaven and earth to rescue her—and probably destroy large chunks of both if necessary.

Banna seemed unconvinced, so she switched subjects, trying to keep the Egyptian's mind occupied. "Have you found out anything new about Alexander's route—like where he crossed the Alborz mountains?"

He flicked back through the notes. "He went east of Damavand—the tallest mountain in Iran. There is also a reference to a pass, but I am not sure which one. A map would help me identify it."

"Work out as much as you can," Nina told him. "Then try to stretch the rest out as long as possible before having to tell Kroll—"

A faint scrape of metal, then: "Dr. Wilde?"

The voice was male, whispered. Everyone turned in alarm to its source—the ventilation slot. "Shit," Nina whispered. If the spy had heard them plotting and reported them to Kroll . . .

"Dr. Wilde, are you there?" The voice was still low, and strained, as if the speaker was afraid of being overheard.

Bewildered, Nina replied: "Yeah?"

"Please, quiet! I do not want the guards to know I am here."

She stepped up onto the bed to look through the little opening. The metal cover at its other end had been lifted. A pair of blue eyes peered nervously back at her. "Who are you?" she demanded.

"You *are* Nina Wilde?"

"Who's asking?"

"Please, I must be sure!" The eyes glanced away as if checking for sentries, then back at her.

"Yeah, I'm Nina Wilde," she said, curiosity taking hold. "And you are?"

Relief was clear even on the small visible part of the man's face. He was young, Nina could tell; no older than twenty, if that. "I thought it was you when I saw you outside the Führer's house. I recognized you from your photographs on the Internet. My name is—"

"Koenig," she cut in, remembering the youth she had seen while being marched to Kroll's residence—the twin of Jaekel's victim in Los Angeles. "You're Volker Koenig's brother!"

"Yes, I am Roland." His surprise turned to hopefulness. "You have seen Volker?"

"Yeah, I saw him."

"Where is he? He told me he would find you, but . . . I did not think that you would come here."

"Right, we *came* here. That's why we're sitting in a prison cell," said Nina, her voice overflowing with sarcasm. "Your brother found me in Los Angeles. He wanted me to stop your people from raiding the tomb of Alexander the Great."

Roland's expression told her that while he knew something about his brother's intentions, he had not been aware of the whole story. "Where is he?"

As much as she hated the Nazis, she couldn't help but feel some sympathy for the youth, knowing what she was about to tell him. "Your brother, Volker . . . he's dead."

Roland flinched in shock. "*Nein*—no, no. That cannot be."

"He was gunned down in the street by one of your leaders! A guy called Jaekel—big scar on his face."

"Herr Jaekel, yes, of course. But—no, he would not have killed Volker."

"It happened right in front of me. And then Jaekel tried to kill me too."

"Then . . . where is Herr Jaekel?"

"On a slab. Dead," she clarified; Roland's English was

good, but he apparently didn't understand slang. "The police shot him."

He drew back. "I . . . I do not believe you."

"Why? Your brother came looking for me; he never came back, but I'm here as a prisoner instead. What does that tell you?"

There was no answer. The vent cover clanked into place. "No!" Macy gasped, jumping up beside Nina. "Don't go, please!"

A pause . . . then the plate rose again. Roland looked back at the cell's occupants. "Who else is there?"

"I'm Macy, Macy Sharif. This is Ubayy Banna." The Egyptian stood and moved into Roland's view. "We're all archaeologists; we were kidnapped."

Again the young man was shocked. "Kidnapped?"

"You've got to get us out of here, please!"

"I—I cannot. The front door is guarded. They will not let me in."

"Then get word to someone outside!" said Nina. "Call my husband—or the United Nations in New York. There's a man called Oswald Seretse; tell him where we are."

Roland retreated again, agitated. "Only the Oberkommando may use the telephone, it is not permitted—"

"*Screw* what's permitted! Just do it!"

"I am sorry, but—but I cannot help you . . ." He jumped down from whatever he was standing on, and the cover clanged shut.

"So, I guess he's not going to bust us out of here," said Macy, breaking the glum silence that followed.

"I guess not." Both women stepped down from the bed, the younger sitting heavily upon it. Nina, however, stalked across the cell in frustration. "Dammit! Nobody will even be looking for us here, but one frickin' phone call would fix that. If Seretse knew we'd been taken from Egypt to Argentina, he could start searching in the right place—"

She broke off as her mind suddenly found the missing piece of the puzzle. "My God," she gasped. "How the hell did we miss it?"

"Miss what?" Macy asked.

"I just realized why we can't find the spring. We've been starting *our* search from the wrong place!" Her companions looked mystified; she continued: "The text on the relic said to take a sun reading outside Alexander's tomb—but it didn't say *which* tomb. We all assumed it meant the one in Alexandria, because that's where we found the statue of Bucephalus. But that wasn't where Alexander was originally buried!"

"Memphis!" Banna exclaimed. "Of course—Ptolemy the Second moved the tomb from Memphis to Alexandria."

"Yeah—but Andreas didn't know that when he made the fish! He went back to search for the spring after Alexander's death, and evidently found it again, but the tomb was relocated while he was away. So all the clues, all the calculations you have to make using the relic to find the spring's location . . . they use the *original* tomb as their starting point."

"Wow," said Macy. "Andreas must have been pissed when he got to Memphis to put the statue inside the tomb and found it wasn't there anymore."

"Maybe not. It actually worked to his advantage—it makes locating the spring even more of a challenge."

Banna's expression became thoughtful. "But *we* know. So now we can find it."

"Yeah. How far apart are Alexandria and Memphis?"

"I do not know exactly," he said. "Memphis is south of Cairo, so . . . two hundred and fifty kilometers?"

"We'll need to work out the difference in degrees of latitude, though. And we can't do that without a map." Nina paced across the cell, frustrated. "But now we know what we've got to do tomorrow. We string the Nazis along for as long as we can with the wrong starting point . . . while we work out where the spring really is using the *right* starting point. Then *when*"—she placed deliberate emphasis on the word, to give hope to herself as much as her companions—"we get out of here? We're going to find it ourselves."

21

"This is it," said Zane as the Jeep crested a low hill.
Eddie surveyed the landscape. "Christ, looks like we're driving into a Clint Eastwood film. I should've brought a poncho." The scrubby plain rolled away to the distant Andean foothills. Winter had arrived, but for now the snowcapped peaks on the far horizon were keeping a jealous grip on their frozen moisture, everything a bleak, parched brown.

Zane checked a map. "The town's on the west side of the lake."

"What lake?" The Englishman searched for it. "That's not a lake, it's a puddle."

"Huh. It's much bigger on the map."

Surrounding the thin patch of water was an expanse of pale, flat ground. It was swathed in what Eddie at first thought was fog before closer observation revealed it as windblown dust. The lake had largely dried up, leaving behind a barren wasteland of silt. He guessed that the settlement had originally been built on the shore, but it was now at least half a mile from the water's edge. Village and lake shared the same name: Lago Amargo—Bitter Lake. "So Kroll and his arsewipes are hiding out here?"

"This is where the IP address originated, yes."

"Assuming they didn't route it through somewhere else first."

"It's possible," Zane admitted, "but this part of the world was a popular hideout for Nazis after the war. We're only about sixty kilometers from Bariloche, where there was a whole community of escapees—and there was a compound over the border in Chile, Villa Baviera, that was basically a cult founded by a Nazi. When the Chilean police raided it, they found huge caches of weapons, and even a tank."

Eddie gave him a disbelieving look. "A tank? How the fuck did they get hold of a tank?"

"These people can get hold of anything. They have the money they stole from Jews and others in the war, and middlemen like Leitz to supply it to them."

"Speaking of Leitz, he's bound to have told that fat bastard about us by now."

Zane nodded. "I spoke to the Mossad after we landed. He's already left Italy and gone off the grid. We tried to access his computer remotely, but he's stopped using it. He probably guessed it had been compromised."

They drove on. Scrub gave way to fields, but from the derelict state of most of the farm buildings, it seemed that the former inhabitants had given up on their profession. "So what do we know about this place?" Eddie asked.

"Not much. It used to be a mining town, but the mines closed decades ago, so they turned to agriculture." Zane looked out across the desolate farmland. "Without much success, I'd guess. The population's more than halved over the past twenty years. Beyond that, though, we couldn't find much more information."

"How are we going to find these Nazis, then? I doubt we'll get lucky and catch Kroll while he's buying the morning groceries."

"That would save us a lot of time," Zane said. "But we should see if we can get access to the town records." He glanced at a boxy equipment case on the rear seat. "I've used the cover story of being a photographer before; it's surprising how much people will open up to you if you tell them they have a pretty home."

"You'll have to be bloody convincing for that to work here." They entered the settlement proper, passing a faded sign bearing the village's name. More empty, crumbling buildings greeted them. They had gone a good hundred yards along the street before seeing their first sign of life: an old woman watching them warily from a doorway before retreating inside. Eddie whistled an ululating five-note tune, following it with "*Waah waah waaaahh . . .*"

"What was that?" Zane asked.

"*The Good, the Bad and the Ugly.*" The Israeli regarded him blankly. "Come on, don't tell me you haven't seen it?"

"It must have been long before my time."

"Tchah! Fucking kids." Ignoring Zane's smirk, Eddie guided the Jeep through the village. The buildings became grander, faded relics of a more prosperous era. Before long, they reached the center, a flaking white church on one side of a small square facing a hotel with a sign optimistically proclaiming it to be the Paradiso. None of the buildings looked anything less than a century old.

"There's the satellite link," said Zane. A large white dish was mounted on a mast on the hotel's roof, a couple of smaller ones flanking it. "The town's Internet hub must be in there. We might be able to track down the IP's physical location if we can access it."

The new arrivals were now drawing more attention. A couple of old men on a bench stared as the four-by-four passed, and a young woman peered with interest from one of the Paradiso's upper windows before hurrying from sight. Eddie pulled up outside the hotel. "Let me do the talking," said Zane as they got out.

"Why you?" Eddie demanded.

"For one thing, you're English, and England and Argentina have some issues." They headed for the entrance.

"What? The Falklands War was over thirty fucking years ago."

"The Second World War was *seventy* years ago, but

we're still hunting down people who fought in it. And for another, you're not exactly subtle."

"Bollocks!" Eddie protested loudly as they entered a large and dimly lit bar. He couldn't help but imagine that he'd stepped through a time portal to the Wild West, so dated were the surroundings. Even the lights were wheel-like wooden chandeliers, one of the few concessions to modernity being electric bulbs. There were half a dozen unenthused patrons, and a single mournful member of the staff behind the long counter. "I know what I'm doing." He marched to the middle of the room. "Oi! Anyone seen any Nazis?"

Zane shook his head. "Yes, that was really subtle."

"Might as well get straight to the point and not piss around." He went to the bar and addressed the elderly man behind it. "Hi. We're looking for some people who live around here. Germans, probably turned up around 1946?"

The barman gave him a look of bewilderment. "*Lo sentimos, pero no sé lo que estás diciendo.*"

"*No habló inglés?*" Eddie asked, to equal confusion.

"You told him that *you* did not speak English," said an amused female voice. A young Hispanic woman came down the stairs. She was around eighteen, and had the flustered air of someone who had just given themselves a last-minute check in the mirror before hurrying to meet a guest.

"Well, some people don't understand me even when I *am* talking English," said Eddie. "You seem pretty good at it, though."

"I learned it from satellite TV," she said with pride. "And from the Internet."

"Hopefully only the nice parts."

She giggled. "I heard you say you were looking for someone? I know everyone in town, I can help you find them."

Zane cut in before Eddie could speak. "We're photographers; we're taking pictures of the whole country. But we also want to interview people about what it's like to live here."

The young woman gave them a look that revealed considerable perception for her age. "That would be easier if you spoke Spanish, yes?"

"*I* speak Spanish," said Zane. "My assistant is only here to carry the cameras."

"Oi!" Eddie objected. "Assistant, my arse."

She ignored him, instead addressing Zane in rapid-fire Spanish. "I . . . yes?" he eventually replied.

Another giggle. "Your Spanish is not as good as you think," she said. "Unless you *really* paint your toenails pink?"

"Oh, he does," said Eddie. "You should see what he wears for a night out on the town an' all. Lots of frills."

"Will you shut up?" Zane snapped. Behind him, Eddie noticed one of the patrons heading for the exit—watching the visitors out of the corner of his eye. Suddenly wary, he surveyed the room. The remaining barflies hurriedly looked down at their drinks.

Zane picked up on Eddie's concern—as did the woman. She lowered her voice. "You are not here to take photos—did Roland's brother send you?"

"Who's Roland?" Zane asked.

"My boyfriend. His brother left here a week ago, but nobody has heard from him—and I have not seen Roland either. I am worried, I do not know what has happened to them."

A thought came to Eddie. "This brother . . . what's his name?"

"*Julieta, qué estás haciendo?*" said someone before she could answer.

The group turned to see a man emerge from a back room. He was in his late forties, with slicked-back black hair and a rakish mustache. The barman's look of deference told Eddie that the new arrival was his boss.

The girl, Julieta, replied in Spanish, drawing a good-natured shrug and a sigh. "I hope my daughter is not bothering you," he said. "Not many people visit Lago Amargo, and she likes to get fresh news from the outside world."

"It's no trouble," Zane assured him.

"Good, good. Then can I do anything for you? I am Pablo Silva, the owner of this hotel—and also the mayor." He gave them a beaming smile. "Are you going to be our guests?"

"Yes, we'll probably be here for a day or two."

"Good! If you need anything, I am at your service. This may only be a small town, but we pride ourselves on our hospitality."

"It looks a lot smaller than it used to be," said Eddie.

Silva shook his head sadly. "Yes, a lot of the people have moved away. Since the lake dried up, many of the farms failed. It is hard to grow crops when there is not enough water."

Julieta frowned and said something that clearly needled her father. "*No ahora,*" he said, waving a dismissive hand.

Or was the gesture *concern*? "What happened to the water?" Eddie asked.

"There was enough for everyone," said Julieta, before Silva could respond, "until the people in the Enklave blocked the river to keep it for themselves!"

Eddie and Zane exchanged glances. Kroll had mentioned the name in his videoconference with Leitz. "Where's this Enklave?" asked the Yorkshireman.

"It is a private estate," said Silva. "They own the land, so what they do there is their business."

"They have taken our water!" Julieta protested. "You know they have. You are the mayor, and the Enklave is part of Lago Amargo—why have you not done anything about it?"

Her father's tone became patronizing. "It is more complicated than that. *Hablaremos de esto más tarde. En privado,*" he added, glancing at the two travelers. "Now I need to find rooms for these two gentlemen."

With an angry huff, Julieta flounced up the stairs. Silva sighed again. "I apologize for my daughter."

"No problem," said Eddie. "So, this Enklave place—is it far?"

The mayor seemed unsettled by his return to the subject. "As I said, it is private property. The owners keep to themselves, but they pay their land taxes, so that is okay with me!" A small laugh, with little humor.

"But it must be upriver, right?" Eddie pressed on. "Otherwise they couldn't block off your water."

"It should be easy enough to find," agreed Zane.

Silva began to look worried. "It—it would be better for you not to go to the Enklave. The people, they do not like visitors . . ."

"That's okay, we won't bother them," said Eddie. "Unless they bother us."

"Really, there is nothing—" The hotelier broke off as the front door opened.

Eddie turned—and snapped to full alert. Someone had called the cops.

Three uniformed men entered the room, the cold and empty stares of mirrored aviator glasses sweeping over its occupants. The drinkers were suddenly fascinated by the bubbles in their beer. The trio swaggered toward the men at the bar.

Eddie assessed them. Two young men flanked the leader—whom he instantly knew was the greatest threat. The head cop was in his fifties, a big bear of a man who even though somewhat overweight was still packed with muscle. He had a thick mustache that drooped down around his mouth, one side of which was filled by the gnarled stub of a cigar. Heavy gold rings glinted on both hands . . . the right one hovering close to his holstered gun.

"Ah, Eduardo!" said Silva. He stepped forward to meet the cops. "This is Eduardo Santos," he told Zane and Eddie, "our *comandante* of police. Or El Jefe, as we sometimes call him. Heh-heh." The chuckle was strained.

"The Chief?" asked Eddie. "If you're the mayor, shouldn't that be *your* nickname?" There was no reply.

Santos turned his mirrored gaze to the two visitors. "Who are you?" he growled, rolling the cigar between his teeth. "What do you want here?"

"We're photographers," said Zane, giving the cops a friendly smile. "We're traveling through Argentina to take pictures of the landscape."

"You have come to a beautiful place, eh?" was the sarcastic reply. "There is nothing worth taking photographs of here. You should find somewhere else."

"Always thought beauty was in the eye of the beholder, myself," Eddie said. "Looks pretty nice to me."

The big man's blank stare locked on to him, hostility jumping from barely veiled to open. "You are English?"

"Yeah, that's right."

"Show me your passports. Both of you."

Zane complied, taking out the fake US passport under which he had been traveling. He opened it to show the cop his photo—and a pair of folded fifty-dollar bills poking from the page below. "I think everything's in order."

The Argentinean took it, giving it a cursory glance as the banknotes disappeared into his hand. However, to Zane's growing concern, he didn't return it, instead waiting for Eddie to follow suit. "Come on. Now."

Eddie found his own passport. "Here you go."

Santos snatched it from him, but didn't even open it, instead staring at the golden emblem on its cover: a lion and unicorn, the royal coat of arms of the United Kingdom. Finally he looked back at Eddie, taking off his sunglasses. The dark, deep-set eyes revealed beneath were anything but friendly. "You know what I did when I was young, English?"

"Pressed flowers and painted sunsets?" Eddie offered.

The cop did not smile at the joke. "I joined the army. I supported El Proceso—the junta—because I believe that to be great, a country, or a person, must have strength, power." He leaned closer, blowing cigar smoke into the Englishman's face. "The strength and the power to take what belongs to them. You know?"

"Yeah, I see where this is going," said Eddie, holding his ground—but also eyeing up exit routes. Behind Santos, the two junior officers brought their hands closer to their holstered weapons.

Zane also sensed the impending trouble. "Is there a problem, sir?" he asked, trying to defuse it.

But Eddie already knew they would not be able to talk

their way out. Santos and his men had been ready for a fight from the moment they entered. "I'm going to guess that he's a Falklands veteran," he told the Israeli, "and that he's not a bygones-be-bygones type."

"They are the *Malvinas*!" barked Santos. "They belong to Argentina, but you English stole them! And when we tried to take back what was ours, you fought like cowards, sank our ships—killed my friends!"

"Nothing to do with me, mate," said Eddie. "I was only about six years old when it all kicked off."

"You are all the same," the cop growled. He took out the cigar—and spat a thick brown-flecked glob of phlegm onto Eddie's foot.

"Don't do anything," Zane said urgently. "He's trying to provoke you. Don't give him an excuse to arrest us."

"They don't need an excuse," Eddie replied. The Argentinean wore an almost gloating expression, waiting for his response. "Even if we don't do anything, you're still going to arrest us on some bullshit charge and beat the crap out of us, aren't you?"

Santos smiled, the tip of the cigar glowing as he took another drag. "That's right, English. We don't like outsiders who—"

Eddie punched him in the face. "Thought so!"

The unexpected blow sent Santos reeling. He collided with the younger and more slender of the other cops, knocking him down. The *comandante* regained his balance, but was left choking and spitting—the crushed cigar had been driven into his mouth.

The remaining cop jumped back, startled, then fumbled for his gun—

Zane's leg swept up. His foot caught the cop's hand just as the weapon cleared the holster, sending the pistol spinning across the room. The man screeched in pain.

Silva gasped, then fled for his office. The other patrons also scrambled for cover. Eddie ignored them and ran for the main entrance. "Jared!"

But the Mossad agent was still fighting the third cop, delivering another brutal kick to his chest that sent him crashing against the bar. "Come on!" Eddie yelled.

Zane's gaze flicked between the Englishman and the dropped passports—then he ran after his companion.

The police chief spat out the remains of his cigar and drew his gun. The Israeli immediately changed course, rolling onto a table and grabbing its edge with one hand as he slid off the other side. His weight pulled it over behind him, the hefty wooden top slamming against the floor.

Santos fired twice. The bullets hit the table's underside—but didn't fully penetrate, the varnished surface cracking.

Zane flinched as splinters hit him. His impromptu shield had saved him, but now he was trapped behind it, cut off from the exit. And the cop was already moving to get a clear shot—

Santos was suddenly sent sprawling as a chair smashed on his shoulders.

Eddie had returned. "Have a seat!" The Argentinean fell to the floor, broken wood clattering around him. Zane jumped up and sprinted for the door. Eddie turned to follow—

Someone grabbed him from behind.

The youngest cop was back on his feet and trying to tackle him. He didn't have the mass or muscle to overpower the Englishman, but he was still wiry enough to hold him while his comrades recovered.

Sharp jabs to the chest from Eddie's elbows made the cop gasp, but he didn't let go. Changing tactics, Eddie pulled up his legs. The young man lurched with the shift of weight. Eddie kicked down again, twisting to ram his attacker against the counter—

The cop released him—not because he had realized what Eddie was about to do, but simply because he lacked the strength to maintain his grip. Both men hit the bar, the cop collapsing with a pained squawk beside his winded companion. Eddie grunted as he took the blow, using his momentum to roll over the countertop. Bottles went flying. The barman, who had watched the brawl with dumbstruck confusion, finally broke free of his paralysis and ran for the stairs.

Eddie stood. Harsh daylight glared through the door as Zane threw it open. "Eddie!" he shouted. "Get to the car!"

Two heads popped up on the other side of the counter. Both the young cops were now back in the fight, the beefier of the pair red-faced with anger. He clawed at his holster, only to find it empty. *"Dispárale!"* he bellowed. The thinner man fumbled for his own gun.

Santos was also recovering. He was between Eddie and the exit. If the Englishman tried to go around him, he would be tackled—or shot.

Which left—

Eddie vaulted onto the bar and ran along it—then veered toward Santos and leapt . . .

Grabbing a chandelier.

Lightbulbs flashed and popped as the jolt broke their filaments, but he ignored the sparks as he swung across the room—bringing up both feet to catch the startled police chief in the chest. Santos tumbled backward, scattering chairs as Eddie flew over him. The Yorkshireman landed with a bang on the scuffed wooden floor and raced through the door.

Zane was already in the Jeep. Eddie jumped in as he started it. "So much for subtle!" the Israeli shouted as he put the four-by-four into gear and floored the accelerator.

"Well, at least now we know we're in the right place!" Eddie turned, seeing the three cops barreling out of the hotel. "So you can call your Mossad mates and—whoa, incoming!"

The burly cop had recovered his gun, and he and Santos both aimed at the retreating Jeep. The third man protested, but a double crack of gunfire as Eddie ducked showed that his objections had been ignored. One bullet whipped past, the other striking the rear door.

Zane slammed the steering wheel hard over, hurling the Jeep into an evasive weave. Eddie was thrown against the door. "Jesus!" he yelped—before being flung the other way as the four-by-four swerved again.

More shots. The rear windshield shattered. Zane spun

the wheel again to send the jeep down a side street, out of the line of fire—

A bullet ruptured the front tire.

The Jeep slithered off course. Zane tried to pull it back in line, but the four-by-four's back end had already skidded wide.

Choking dust gushed in through the broken rear window. Coughing, the Israeli forced the wheel to full lock and applied more power to catch the skid. But the flat tire was dragging on the dirt road. By the time he compensated, it was too late—

The four-by-four pounded sidelong into the corner of a building. Plaster exploded and stone cracked, but the Jeep came off worse, the rear wheel ripping from the axle. Zane's head struck the driver's window hard enough to crack it, leaving a bloody smear on the glass.

Eddie sat up painfully. "Jared? We need to move." He squinted at his companion, who was slumped against the door. "Jared!"

For a moment it seemed he was either unconscious or dead, but then the Israeli opened an eye. "Benjamin?"

"No, it's me, Eddie." The Englishman pulled him upright, wincing when he saw the damaged window. At best, the Mossad agent would have a splitting headache; at worst, a concussion or even a subdural hematoma. "They'll be here any second—we've got to—"

A shout told him they were out of time. Santos and his two subordinates charged toward the wrecked Jeep, guns raised. Eddie thought about running, but by the time he got out of the car they would be upon him. Even if he had been able to make a break for it, he was unwilling to leave a wounded man behind.

All he could do was surrender. He raised his hands.

"Get out!" Santos bellowed, gun pointed at Eddie's head. The more aggressive of his comrades circled the crashed vehicle to cover its driver, while the third man held back, uncertain.

Eddie stepped warily from the four-by-four, facing Santos. The big man's sunglasses were back on, eyes unreadable. Was he going to kill him there and then?

"*Jefe!*" cried the youngest man with the same fear. "*No puedes matarlo!*"

The mirrored eyes remained locked on Eddie, his reflection staring back at him twice over behind the gun's muzzle . . . then the weapon twitched downward. "On the ground," Santos snarled.

Eddie reluctantly lowered himself to his knees. "Hands behind you," said Santos. "Miranda, *espósalo.*"

The young policeman took a pair of handcuffs from his belt and snapped them around Eddie's wrists. "Vargas?" called Santos. A reply came as the third cop dragged the semi-conscious Zane from the Jeep and cuffed him. The chief looked back at Eddie. "So, English. You thought you could get away? Only your friend is not a good driver."

"Yeah, he crashed a Ferrari the other day," Eddie replied, already tensing himself for what he knew was coming. "Don't think I'll let him drive again."

"I think that is a good idea." Santos glanced at Zane, lying at Vargas's feet . . . then his face twisted with anger as he drove a savage kick into the Englishman's side.

Eddie fell, writhing in agony—then another blow hit him in the stomach. Vomit burned the back of his throat and he gasped for breath.

"*Bastardo inglés!*" The Argentinean drew back his foot again—but Miranda darted in front of him, waving his hands and pleading for him to stop. Santos glowered at him, but withdrew. Miranda sighed in relief—only to reel away as the older man punched him hard in the face. "*No me digas cómo ejecutar mi ciudad!*" Santos growled. He looked around. Some of the town's inhabitants, Julieta among them, had come to investigate the commotion, but they all shrank away under the police chief's empty stare. Pablo Silva might be the mayor, Eddie realized, but there was no doubt who was really in charge of Lago Amargo.

Even so, Santos apparently still felt the need to show at least a pretense of working by the book. "You are both under arrest for attacking an officer and resisting arrest," he told the handcuffed men.

"Yeah, and possession of an English accent," Eddie gasped. "This how your Nazi bosses up at the Enklave keep their secret, is it? They pay you to beat the shit out of visitors?"

The police chief stared unreadably down at him—then his boot rushed at Eddie's face, and everything went black.

22

The sickly metallic taste of blood was the first thing Eddie registered as he clawed his way back to consciousness. It was heavy on his tongue, coating his teeth . . .

Sharp pain blazed through his nerves, shocking him awake. The tip of his tongue had found a corner missing from one of his upper incisors, exposing the sensitive dentine beneath. "Arse-cocking *fuck*!" he gasped.

A concerned face appeared before him: Zane. "Eddie! Are you okay?"

Eddie tried to come up with an answer. As well as the cracked tooth, his lips were swollen where Santos had kicked him, and a crusty blockage in one nostril suggested that his nose had been bleeding. Dull throbs from his torso were reminders of other impacts from the Argentinian's boots. "Been better," he croaked, "but my dentist'll be in a fucking good mood next time he sees me." He gave the Israeli a pained smile, the natural gap between his two front teeth now joined by a fresh one. "What about you?"

Zane showed him the side of his head. Rivulets of now dried blood had run down around his left ear from a cut under his curly hair. "It hurts," he said, "but I think I'm okay."

"Needs washing, though." Eddie took in their surroundings, finding that he was on a bench inside a bare and dirty jail cell. Thick metal bars made up one whole wall. Beyond them was a short corridor with an open door at the end, through which he could see the police station's main office. He sat up. "Oi! We need some water. *Agua, por favor!*"

A chair scraped, and heavy footsteps clomped toward the door. There was a gurgle of liquid, then Santos filled the frame, holding a plastic cup. "You want water?" he said, moving to the bars. "Here!" He tossed the cup's contents over the two prisoners.

Zane was quick enough to catch some. "Thank you," he said politely, wiping the cut.

Eddie rubbed his wet face, then ran his hand back over his short hair. "Okay, now how about some shampoo?" Santos grunted in dark humor.

"Eduardo?" called an agitated male voice. Santos responded, and after a moment Pablo Silva came into the corridor. He gave the battered prisoners a nervous look, then spoke to the police chief. Eddie couldn't pick out much of the muted Spanish discussion, but gathered that the mayor was extremely unhappy about the situation.

Santos was less concerned, chewing on a fresh cigar. He clapped a heavy hand on Silva's shoulder. "*Vamos a hablar con Kroll, eh?*" Eddie tried not to display any visible reaction to the Nazi leader's name. The two Argentineans returned to the office, closing the door.

"We're definitely in the right place," said Eddie. "You heard him mention Kroll, yeah?"

"I did," Zane replied. "If I can call in a confirmation, the Mossad will send a full team here."

"Yeah, but somehow I don't think we'll get our one phone call."

"Nor do I." Santos and Silva were talking in the office, a third man's voice echoing from a speakerphone. "I think that's Kroll!" Zane strained to listen, but the closed door was as much of a barrier to comprehension as the language. "What do you think they're saying?"

Eddie gave him a grim look. "Nothing good."

He was right.

The door opened again ten minutes later. Silva had gone, Santos was now accompanied by the two younger officers, Vargas and Miranda. "You letting us go?" said Eddie, knowing full well that was not the case. He and Zane stood, readying themselves for action.

Santos, though, was being cautious. "Turn around," he ordered, unholstering his gun. "Hands against the wall."

The two captives reluctantly complied. As Vargas also drew his weapon, Miranda unlocked the cell door. "You, the tall one," said the police chief. "Put your right hand behind your back." Zane hesitated, then did as he was instructed. Miranda entered the cell and fastened a handcuff bracelet around his wrist. "Now your left hand."

The second cuff clicked shut. Santos pushed Miranda out of the way. He gripped the handcuffs and squeezed until the metal cut into the skin. Zane flinched in pain. Santos stepped back—then struck the base of Zane's neck a vicious blow with his gun. The Israeli collapsed to his knees.

Eddie whirled, but found Vargas's pistol pointed at him. He froze, helpless, as Santos hit Zane again, following it with a kick to his abdomen. The Mossad agent curled up in agony.

Santos turned his gun on the other prisoner. "Now you, English. Right hand behind your back."

"Get fucked," Eddie growled.

The automatic did not waver. "Do it, or I shoot you." Vargas was prepared to fire; his boss was actively looking forward to doing so. Eddie had no choice. More handcuffs clamped painfully hard around his wrists.

Santos examined them, then smiled.

Even knowing the attack was coming, Eddie could do nothing to counter it. Searing pain exploded in his skull as the gun hit him. He crumpled against the wall, trying to dodge the inevitable kick.

He failed. The cop's boot slammed into his stomach. Eddie doubled up, a sickening dizziness overwhelming him as he gasped for air.

Santos indicated Zane. "Put him in my car," he told his men. "I will take him to the Enklave. The other one . . ." A cruel smile. "Take him to the cemetery."

Miranda regarded him first with confusion, then dismay. "But—but that is not what we do."

"He is not leaving town," said Santos. "Ever."

Miranda started to protest, but his words were cut off as Santos slammed him against the bars. "That is twice in one day you have challenged me! Do not do it three times, or you will join him!" His fingers closed around Miranda's windpipe. "Do you understand?"

All the terrified cop could do was nod. Santos blew smoke into his face, then released him. "Good. Now do as I say."

Vargas and the quivering Miranda dragged Zane from the cell. Santos watched them go, then took a long drag on his cigar. "Just you and me now, eh, English?"

"Fuckin' wonderful," Eddie rasped. "So this is how you treat tourists? No wonder that hotel was empty."

Santos chuckled. "We usually run visitors out of town. It is strange, we always find drugs on them, even the respectable ones! But they pay their, ah, 'fine' and go, and never come back. You, though . . ." His expression turned stony. "You came looking for the wrong people, English. When someone does not want to be found, they are willing to pay to make sure nobody *does* find them."

"You know they're fucking *Nazis*, right?" said Eddie. "Escaped war criminals?"

A dismissive huff, smoke wafting across the cell. "Perón and then El Proceso were happy for them to be here. They want the same thing—strength and power. And I believe that also. Argentina would be much better with a strong government again. Maybe we do not have that in the whole country . . . but we do have it here. Lago Amargo is *my* town, English. And I will not let you or anyone else take it from me."

Vargas reappeared and spoke to him. The corrupt cop

nodded, then addressed Eddie once more. "Time to go. Your friend wants to see the Enklave, so now he will. As for you, our graveyard is not very beautiful, but you should make the most of it. It is the last place you will see." He started for the door—then whipped back around to kick his prisoner hard in the chest. "Goodbye, English." He walked out, leaving Eddie paralyzed by pain.

Vargas and Miranda hauled the Englishman from the cell. They took him outside and shoved him into the back of an elderly Chevrolet police car. Eddie glimpsed a few onlookers before his head was pushed down, but no one moved to help him.

Miranda took the wheel, Vargas pointing his gun at Eddie. "You make trouble, I shoot you," he snarled as the car set off.

"We should not be doing this," said Miranda. "This is wrong! We have never killed anyone before."

Vargas responded in irate Spanish. "Yes, he attacked us," Miranda continued, "but we were going to arrest them for no reason! El Jefe did not even try to hide drugs on them."

The young cop's continued use of English was both confusing and angering his companion. "*Hable en español, pendejo!*" he barked. Miranda gave Eddie an apologetic glance, but caved in, the argument continuing in Spanish.

The car headed into the hills overlooking the little town. Somewhere up there was the graveyard, in which Eddie would become the latest nameless resident.

* * *

Zane was also going into the hills, but along a different route. He had been dumped in the trunk of Santos's own car, a half-decade-old Mercedes that nevertheless was probably the newest and most luxurious vehicle in the region. After several minutes of jolting along rough tracks, the car stopped. He squinted as the trunk lid opened and dust hit his eyes. "Get out," ordered Santos, dragging him onto the stony ground.

They were on what had once been the lake's shore, the water now just a shimmering line in the distance beyond a flat pan of exposed silt. Zane made out indistinct tracks on the surface—had an aircraft landed on the dry lake bed?

Closer by were the weathered remains of a jetty, the wood-and-stone structure extending out from the old shoreline. The rusted lines of a narrow-gauge railroad track ran to it. He turned his head to follow them, seeing that they led up the rising slope to a tall metal gate, high barbed-wire fences extending into the distance on each side.

The gate was open. An old jeep was parked just outside, two men walking from it toward the new arrivals.

One was a young blond man whom Zane didn't recognize. But the other was all too familiar.

Rasche.

Cruel glee crept onto the Nazi's face at the sight of the handcuffed captive. "I saw you in Egypt," he said. "You killed some of my men."

"And I suppose you're going to kill me," Zane replied, fighting to control his tension.

"In time. But only after you have told us everything we want to know."

Zane pushed out his chest in defiance. "I won't tell you anything."

Rasche smiled coldly. "Many have said that to me in the past. They were all mistaken. You will be no different, *kleiner Jude.*"

"*Lech lehizdayen.*"

The insult produced only mocking amusement. "Many have said that to me too. It is anatomically impossible, I am afraid. But we shall see what is possible with *your* anatomy. I have seen Jews turned into all sorts of useful things."

With a roar of fury, Zane jumped up—only to be pistol-whipped back down by Santos. Rasche stepped hard on the fallen man's neck until vertebrae crackled. "The Final Solution did not stop in 1945," he said. "It was only . . . *paused.* We shall start it again, soon enough. Perhaps you will even have the honor of being the first of its new victims."

Zane choked out each word. "You'll be . . . *dead* . . . before then."

The Nazi let out a muted laugh. "Not by you." He drew something from inside his coat.

Not a gun. An SS dagger, a silver skull on its hilt. He stepped back, bent down—and stabbed it into Zane's thigh. The Israeli screamed.

"Leitz told me that the man I killed in Alexandria was your friend," said Rasche, voice low and gloating. "Benjamin Falk, a Mossad Nazi-hunter." He twisted the blade, blood running down Zane's leg. "I was aiming at you, but one dead Jew is much like another." A last jab, Zane crying out again, then he withdrew the knife. "Do not worry—you will join him soon enough." He kicked the writhing man, then turned away.

His companion yanked Zane up, jamming a gun into his back and pushing him to the jeep. "What about the other man who was with him?" Rasche asked Santos.

The Argentinean savored a mouthful of cigar smoke before replying. "If he isn't dead already, he will be soon."

* * *

Miranda halted the car. Vargas got out and opened the rear door. "Move."

Eddie was pulled out to find himself on a hillside about a mile from the town. The wind had picked up, pale dust swirling up the slope from the dry lake bed.

Vargas turned him around—revealing the cemetery.

The plot was dotted with stunted, twisted trees between the graves. Far in the past, the inhabitants of Lago Amargo had had money to spare on the dead, small tombs and angelic statues standing among the gravestones. But the town's decline over time was easy to see; the markers became smaller, plainer, before stone finally gave way to simple wooden crosses.

"This is wrong!" Miranda protested. "We are not murderers!"

"Shut up," said Vargas. He pointed at a nearby mound of dirt, dusty tools lying beside it. "Get the shovel."

The young cop threw up his hands. "I want no part of this."

"*Cobarde*," muttered Vargas. "You, English. Get it."

Eddie's arms were still cuffed behind his back. "How, with my fucking mouth?"

The cop made an exasperated sound. He spoke to Miranda, but the other man shook his head. "Don't try anything," said Vargas as he poked his gun against Eddie's back and fumbled for the handcuff key. He tried to push it into the hole on the left bracelet, metal clinking on metal before it found its home. He turned it, and the cuff came loose. "Okay, you're going to dig—"

Eddie twisted at the waist, using his left elbow to slam the gun away from his body as his right arm whisked around to deliver a punch to Vargas's face. "Dig *this*!"

It wasn't as solid a blow as he had hoped, but it was enough to unbalance the Argentinean. Eddie shoulder-barged him, knocking him down.

But the cop still had his gun—and was already recovering. The Yorkshireman ran for the nearest row of gravestones. If he could get behind them, he would have at least partial cover . . .

Too slow. "*Bastardo!*" Vargas shouted as he scrambled upright and took aim—

A shot—but it went wide. Eddie glanced back as he reached the first of the markers to see that Miranda had grabbed his partner's arm. Vargas broke free—then clubbed the smaller man with his gun. Miranda fell against the car.

Eddie bent low and kept running, squinting as more gritty dust blew up the hillside. He swerved around a statue, intending to use it as a shield, but instead had to make a running jump as he almost fell into an open hole behind it, mud and a rusty shovel at the bottom of the half-dug old grave. He swore as he regained his balance on the other side, then hurried on. The next decent cover was a gnarled tree. He ran for it—

Dried bark exploded just behind the Englishman as he

reached safety. The pursuing cop fired again, but struck nothing.

Vargas was not a skilled shooter, then; the chances of hitting a small target with a handgun while running were minuscule, but he had still taken the shot, driven by anger and testosterone. He had a second magazine on his belt, though, so playing cat and mouse until he ran out of ammo wasn't an option. Eddie knew that his only hope of survival was to take the Argentinean down—but how?

He turned into the gritty wind. Lower down the slope, a small, blocky mausoleum stood about thirty yards distant. A plan came to him. Risky, and it depended on Vargas acting on instinct rather than logic, but it was all he had . . .

Eddie broke cover and ran. Grave markers blurred past. A shot, then another, lead striking stone behind him. Fifteen yards, ten—but the whipcrack of a third shot snapped past barely a foot in his wake. Vargas had got smart and stopped, gun in both hands for greater accuracy. Five yards, but Eddie knew that the next round would be on target—

He threw himself into a dive, thumping down in the dirt just short of the structure. A bullet seared above him. Vargas adjusted his aim and fired again—but hit only soil as Eddie scrambled behind the mausoleum.

Panting, the Englishman jumped up and grabbed a foot-long hunk of stone that had broken from the wall. The cop would take at most twenty seconds to reach the little tomb. Would he go around its right side, or the left? Vargas was right-handed, so coming from that side, rounding the obstacle counterclockwise, would give him the most advantageous positioning; he could lead with his gun as he circled. But doing so would also mean he was facing into the dusty wind at the first corner . . .

Eddie couldn't cover both sides of the tomb simultaneously. He had to make a choice, *now*. He heard the cop approaching, the gear on his belt rattling. Which way would he go?

The Englishman went to the left side, gambling that

the enraged Vargas would follow his natural instincts and protect his vision.

Pressing his back against the weathered wall, he held the stone like a baseball bat, ready to swing. The footsteps slowed, the Argentinean uncertain which side to take . . .

Left.

Eddie waited, arms tensed. Boots crunched on gravel. The gun's muzzle came into view, Vargas leaning forward to see what was around the corner—

The chunk of stone smashed against his head.

Vargas staggered backward. The gun went off—but the bullet hit the tomb, ricocheting away. Eddie threw the stone at the other man's chest. The Argentinean fell on his back.

Eddie was about to dive for the weapon, but instantly changed his plan when he saw it was pointing almost at him—and Vargas still had his finger on the trigger. Instead he darted for the nearest row of gravestones. These were as old as the mausoleum, moss-scabbed stone teeth giving him a degree of protection.

But not much. Vargas shrieked breathless abuse as he ran, firing a couple of wild shots from the ground.

The old tree was just ahead. Eddie swerved to put it between his back and Vargas's gun as he raced toward the car. It would keep him out of the cop's sight for a few seconds, but could he turn that to his advantage?

Yes.

Another change of course as he angled to retrace his own steps—and jumped down into the open grave.

The hole was four feet at its deepest, the edges crumbling. Eddie backed against the grave's end, holding his breath as he listened for Vargas. Angry gasping reached him as the cop lumbered up the hill . . . then slowed as he found he had lost sight of his target.

Eddie tensed. He knew he could never have reached the car before Vargas spotted him—but did *Vargas* realize that? If the cop thought the Englishman had gone for the vehicle, then he had a chance. If not . . .

Vargas set off again, the jangle of his equipment growing louder. How close was he? Eddie couldn't judge—and didn't dare raise his head to look. All he knew was that each step was bringing his adversary nearer, nearer . . .

And past.

The noise receded. Eddie cautiously peered out. Vargas had passed about twenty feet away, a large neighboring gravestone blocking the hole from his view. His back was now to the Yorkshireman as he advanced on the car—but it wouldn't be long before he realized his prey was not there.

Eddie picked up the rusty spade and climbed out, moving up behind Vargas. The Argentinean stopped, head cocked, listening. Eddie slipped closer.

The cop turned—

The shovel's rusted head came down on his hand like an ax, the dull clang of metal accompanied by a snap of bone. Vargas screamed, the gun falling from his broken fingers. Eddie swung the spade again—and blood and broken teeth sprayed from the Argentinian's mouth as the flat of the blade hit him in the face.

He dropped the shovel and forced the cop into a headlock, then dragged him to the open grave and threw him in. "You're fucking lucky I'm not burying you in there," he said, kicking loose dirt onto him. Vargas curled up in fear. The Englishman retrieved the gun, then returned to the police car.

Miranda was slumped against it. He looked up as Eddie approached. "Where—where is Vargas?"

"In a grave. Don't worry, he's not dead," Eddie added as he saw the shock on the young man's face. "He just wishes he was. He won't be causing any trouble for a while, though." He looked at the settlement below, then his gaze snapped back to Miranda. "Question is . . . what about you?"

* * *

The wind had picked up by the time Santos returned to town, dust from the dry lake billowing across the streets. Squinting even behind his mirrored sunglasses, he was about to head into the police station when the frantic bleat of a car horn reached him. He peered into the haze. It was the car in which Vargas and Miranda had taken the Englishman to the graveyard—but now only one man was inside.

The vehicle skidded to a halt. "What is it?" Santos demanded as the frightened Miranda jumped out. "Where is Vargas?"

"The—the Englishman," Miranda stammered. "He got loose and beat the crap out of Vargas! He was gonna do the same to me, but I got away. But he's coming, he's coming for you! He's got a gun—he said he's going to kill you!"

"Like hell," Santos growled. He stared toward the hills, but the dust obscured all detail. "Did you come straight from the graveyard?" Miranda nodded. "Then he can't have gotten far. We can stop him before he even reaches the edge of town."

Miranda's arrival had drawn attention, people coming out of nearby buildings. Silva emerged from the hotel and jogged to the two cops. "What's going on?" he called, worried.

"That English asshole's still causing trouble," Santos replied, before hurrying into the station. He returned carrying a rifle with a telescopic sight.

Silva's eyes widened. "What are you doing?"

"Taking care of a problem." Santos slapped a magazine into the Remington's receiver and drew back the bolt.

"But what if someone comes looking for him? What if they tell the federal police or the gendarmerie that he was here?"

"You've done well out of our town's little secret," the police chief growled. "Now it's time for you to help keep it."

Silva glanced around nervously. More people—including his daughter—were watching. "You can't just kill him!" he said in a strained whisper. "You said you were only going to kick them out of town!"

"Things have gone beyond that. Now, are you going

to help me?" Santos glared at the mayor, who shrank back. "Then get out of my way."

The police chief ran across the square, rifle in hand. One of the side streets was short, continuing as a track out of town toward the graveyard. The last building on the street was derelict. He positioned himself behind a crumbling wall to get a view of the entire hillside. There was little cover beyond the occasional tree or boulder; his target would have nowhere to hide.

And the moment he was seen . . . he was a dead man. Santos was an accomplished shot. The Remington's magazine held only three bullets, but one would be enough.

He raised the scope to his eye, checking each potential cover spot in turn. No trace of anyone. Dust prickled the back of his neck. Irritated, he wiped it, then resumed his search. The Englishman was out there somewhere . . .

A loud, echoing clang from behind. The church bell. It chimed again. He frowned. The priest was an old man, easily cowed; if this was some sort of attempt to warn away the visitor, then he would have to pay him a visit and remind him that God did not call the shots in Lago Amargo.

Clang. Clang. The bell continued its tuneless toll. Santos swept his scope over the hillside once more, then raised his head from the rifle for a wider view. Still no sign of Chase, but he caught movement at the edge of his vision. He glanced over his shoulder.

Some of the townsfolk were advancing toward him, twenty or more, Silva and his daughter leading them. "Hey!" he shouted. "Get back! This is police business. Go back to your homes or you'll answer to me."

The civilians stopped. He looked back at the hill, the dust clearing enough to reveal the road winding up to the graveyard.

Nobody was on it—or the surrounding open ground. Suddenly uneasy, he darted the sight from tree to rock to tree. Still no one. But Miranda had told him the Englishman was coming. Where was he?

He looked around again to find the young cop—and froze.

The bell clanged one last time. The townspeople, Miranda among them, parted from the center of the street, clearing a path for a ghostly figure striding out from a dense wall of dust.

Eddie Chase.

Santos started to bring up the rifle, only to freeze again as the Englishman swept open his leather jacket to reveal that he was armed. The gun was in his waistband, but his cold expression warned the police chief that the slightest move would see it drawn without hesitation . . . and fired.

"Miranda!" Santos called. "Stop him! You have your gun—shoot him!"

Miranda stared at him, conflicted . . . then silently retreated out of sight. Dismayed, Santos turned to Silva for help. "Pablo! Do something! You're in this with me—if I go down, so do you!"

The mayor breathed deeply before replying. "It . . . perhaps it's time this ended, Eduardo. It has gone too far."

Rage overtook fear. "You fucking coward!" snarled Santos. "All of you! You're cowards! This is *my* town— without me, you'd have nothing! I *protected* you!"

"Protected?" cried Julieta as the Englishman passed her, his stride relentless. "All you've ever done is threaten us!"

Santos shook with anger. "You bastards! I'll remember who refused to stand with me, you—"

Eddie stopped about thirty feet from the cop. "Oi! Arsehole! It's not them you want to worry about."

Santos switched to English. "You should not have come back. You should have run away, as fast as you could."

"Well, people keep telling me I'm not that bright." He took in the cop's rifle. "That a Remington? Decent gun. You should be able to take me down with one shot." His eyes narrowed. "If you're fast enough."

Santos hesitated, then turned to face him, keeping the rifle low. "What, you think this is a *shoot-out*? That this is the Wild West and you are a cowboy, like John Wayne?"

Eddie remained still, his dusty jacket flapping stiffly in the wind. "Was always more of a Clint Eastwood fan. But it's up to you. You can either give yourself up so the feds can deal with you, or . . . draw." He moved his right hand fractionally closer to his gun.

Santos caught the movement, his eyes darting between the weapon and Eddie's face. The Englishman's expression remained unreadable. The cop licked his lips . . . then almost imperceptibly began to bring his rifle toward the other man.

Only Eddie's eyes moved in response, momentarily regarding the Remington before fixing back upon the police chief. Now sweating despite the cold breeze, Santos again ran his tongue around his bone-dry mouth. If he was fast enough, he could get off one shot before his opponent reacted. It might not be a killing wound, but it wouldn't have to be—if it stopped him from firing, then a second round would finish him . . .

The rifle's barrel rose, millimeter by millimeter. Eddie remained statue-still. Santos struggled to control his breathing, feeling every beat of his pounding heart. Just a little more, and no matter how fast the Englishman drew his gun, it wouldn't be enough for him to get off the first shot. He could do it.

He could do it.

He could—

Santos burst into motion. The Remington whipped upward, the barrel swinging toward Eddie's chest—

Eddie was faster.

Santos was thrown back against the wall as a bullet ripped through his right shoulder, shattering bone. The rifle flew from his numbed hand and clattered to the ground. He gasped for breath as fire burned across his chest.

The Englishman closed on him, a near-silhouette against the dusty haze. He kicked the Remington away, then loomed over the fallen man, bringing up his gun. Santos felt a terror like nothing he had ever experienced before, not even when fighting in the Malvinas. "No, no!" he gasped, feebly raising his uninjured arm in a pathetic attempt to ward off the shadowy figure. "Please, don't kill me!" His bladder let go, hot urine soaking his clothing.

The gun remained fixed on his face . . . then Eddie turned away. "You people need a new sheriff," he told the townsfolk laconically as he walked back down the street, fading into the drifting dust.

Miranda ran to Santos, his own gun raised. "Eduardo Santos," he said, almost unable to believe that he was making the challenge, "you are under arrest for attempted murder . . ."

23

Eddie looked up at a knock on the door of Silva's office. Miranda entered, speaking to the mayor before addressing the Englishman. "Santos and Vargas are both in the jail. El Jefe's shoulder has been bandaged."

"What're you going to do with them?" Eddie asked.

"I will have to tell the federal police what has happened here. All of it," he added, with a mournful look at Silva.

The mayor dropped into a chair with a heavy sigh. "I was afraid this day would come."

"What, the day your town's little secret got out?" Eddie replied, scathing. "That you were hiding a bunch of Nazi war criminals?"

"It has never gone this far before, never!" Silva protested. "The cops were only supposed to scare people away. They never tried to kill anyone."

"But you didn't try too hard to talk Santos out of it after you spoke to Kroll, did you?"

"You do not understand," he said, hands jittering in agitation. "El Jefe is not a man you argue with. Even though I am the mayor, he . . . he has all the power."

"*Had* all the power," Eddie corrected. "You're in charge now. So do the right thing."

Silva put his head in his hands. "The men in the Enklave, the Germans . . . without them, there would not *be* a town. You have seen the dry lake, the farms—Lago Amargo is dying! It would be dead without their payments."

"But Julieta said they made the lake dry up in the first place. Get rid of them and you get your water back."

"I don't know. I don't know . . ."

Eddie banged a hand on the desk, making him jump. "I'll tell you what *I* know. Those bastards up in the Enklave have my wife and my friends. I'm going to get them back—and you're going to help me. Otherwise there really *won't* be a town, 'cause I'll burn the fucking place to the ground. Starting with your hotel."

Silva wearily raised his head. "What do you want from me?"

"I want you to call Kroll. Tell him I'm dead. That way, they won't expect any trouble when I go up there."

"But what if he wants to speak to Santos?"

"I don't fucking know! You're a politician; lie. But once you've done that, I need to know the best way to get up there, and what I can expect to find."

"I don't know," said Silva. "I have never been inside the Enklave. No one from the town has."

"Seriously?" Eddie said in disbelief. "So nobody knows what's up there?"

"I do," said a new voice.

All three turned to see Julieta at the door, which she had silently eased open. Silva jumped up, admonishing her in Spanish.

She responded in English. "No, Papá. I will not go to my room. I am not a child anymore! This town has been sick for a long time, and we all know it—but this man has helped us by stopping El Jefe. So now we must help him. It is the right thing to do."

Silva was clearly unhappy at being challenged by his daughter, but he seemed so drained by the day's events that he lacked the energy to argue with her. "How do you know what is in the Enklave?" he asked instead.

"I have been inside."

The mayor's eyes widened. "What?"

"Roland took me up the hill, in secret. We followed the old railroad."

"Roland? That *boy*?"

"You've met him?" Eddie asked Silva. "They come down to the town?"

"Once or twice a year. They buy supplies, tools, things like that. They grow their own food, but it must not be enough for all of them anymore."

"All of them?" echoed the Yorkshireman. "How many of these buggers are there? How big's this Enklave?"

"Their land starts at the edge of the lake, and goes all the way to the old mines in the mountains." The bases of the peaks Eddie had seen on the way into Lago Amargo were at least ten miles away; the Enklave was indeed huge. "It is . . ." Silva thought for a moment, "more than two hundred and fifty square kilometers. But I do not know how many people live there."

"Over one hundred," said Julieta. "Roland told me. Maybe one hundred and twenty."

"That's a lot of Nazis," Eddie muttered.

"Roland is not a Nazi!" she protested. "He is . . . different. He wanted to find out more about the world, so . . ." Guilt crossed her face as she glanced at the computer on Silva's desk. "So I let him use the Internet when you were not here, Papá. Volker, too. He used it even more than Roland."

"Volker Koenig?" said Eddie.

"Yes, Roland's brother."

"I met him. Briefly."

"Where is he?" she asked, excited. "Is he okay?"

He hesitated before giving her the bad news. "I'm . . . afraid not. He's dead."

Julieta stared at him, stricken. "What—what happened to him?" asked her father, equally shocked.

"He came looking for us, but a Nazi called Jaekel shot him. I'm sorry."

"He shot Volker?" she whispered. "But—but why? Why was he looking for you?"

"He wanted to give something to my wife—she's an archaeologist, Nina Wilde."

"I know that name!" she said. "She is famous, yes?" Eddie nodded. "Volker read about her on the computer. You are really married to her?"

"Yeah, hard to believe with a face like this, I know," he said with a bruised smile. "They're holding her, somewhere up there. I'm going to get her back, and the other people they've kidnapped too. You know how to get in?"

"Yes—there is a hole in the fence. Roland and Volker used it to sneak down to the town."

"Will you show me?"

"Of course. I will go with you."

"You will not," said Silva firmly.

"I have to, Papá," Julieta insisted. "I have to find Roland and make sure he is okay . . . and I must tell him his brother is dead."

Her father's face fell. "I . . . Yes, you are right. But," he went on, raising a forefinger in warning, "you are not to take any risks, you understand? These people have become dangerous."

"They always were," Eddie pointed out. The reminder did not make Silva any happier.

"What are you going to do once you are inside?" Miranda asked.

"First priority is rescuing Nina and the others. Then," he added to Julieta, "we'll try to find your boyfriend. Anything else that happens . . . well, that's up to them."

"What does that mean?" said Silva.

"It means that if anyone gets in my way, they'll wish they hadn't. But the main thing is finding Nina. Once I've done that, I'll bring her and the others out, then call in the cavalry."

Silva put his head in his hands again. "This could end everything. I do not know what to do . . ."

"Do what is right, Papá," Julieta told him softly.

A sigh, then the mayor looked up at Eddie. "Okay. I will phone Kroll. Then"—reluctance filled his voice—

"Julieta can take you into the Enklave. If you promise that you will keep her safe."

The Yorkshireman nodded. "I'll watch out for her, trust me."

"Okay. Then . . . good luck, Mr. Chase. I hope you find your wife, and your friends."

"So do I," replied Eddie. "So do I."

* * *

After retrieving his belongings from the police station, Eddie set out with Julieta. "So how far's the entrance?" he asked, looking westward toward the distant mountains. The crumpled hills rose quite steeply in places, but there was a distinct edge to the terrain that suggested a plateau higher up the slope.

"There is a big gate about two kilometers from here," said Julieta, pointing along the dry lake bed. "The railroad from the mines goes to it, but it has not been used for a long time. Planes sometimes land on the lake, though; they have marked out an airstrip. There have been a lot recently—more than usual."

"How often do they normally come?"

"Once every two or three months."

"Bringing people, or cargo?"

"Mostly cargo. I was once out at the lake when a plane landed, so I hid in the bushes to watch. It brought lots of wooden boxes, but I do not know what was in them. But one came not long ago," she added, "and some men got in and flew away. That was weird, because they do not usually leave the Enklave."

"How long ago?"

"Two weeks?"

Probably going to Egypt, Eddie thought; their entrance to Alexander's tomb would have taken some time to prepare. "So if nobody leaves, how did you meet Roland and his brother?"

"I told you, they were . . . different. It was over a year ago—I was looking for herbs when I found them both hiding behind some rocks. It was funny," she said, a faint flush of pink appearing on her cheeks as she smiled, "you would think they had never seen a girl before. Roland was so shy, he could hardly look at me! Volker was more . . . oh, I do not know the right word."

"Confident?"

"Yes, that is it! But he was more confident about everything. Volker was the real explorer—he wanted to know all he could. After I showed him the Internet, it was hard to get him off the computer."

"And Roland wasn't like that?"

"He was, but not so much." Another blushing smile. "He was more interested in me. They would both sneak out of the Enklave, and I would spend time with Roland while Volker used the Internet."

"What was he reading about?"

"Everything. In many languages, too—he was very smart. So is Roland, actually. He told me they are all taught English and Spanish as well as German. But Volker read a lot about history."

"What, like archaeology?"

"Sometimes. But most of it was recent history. The Second World War." She shook her head. "There were always rumors about the people in the Enklave, that they were Nazis, but my father told me not to think about them. He tried not to think too much about the Enklave himself—like it was a secret he wished was not there. He wanted me to stay away from them when they came into town, but . . . I did that anyway."

"Why?"

"They were not nice people. They always seemed very angry, looking at us like we had done something wrong—even though it was our town! But Roland and Volker were not like that. They were not supposed to go outside the Enklave, but they did—well, it was Volker's idea, but Roland went with him—because they wanted to see if what they had been told about the rest of the world was true."

Eddie smiled faintly. "If Roland'd never seen a girl before, I'm guessing they were pretty surprised about everything else they found."

"Volker was—and he was angry, too, at first. Like he didn't want to believe it. But he kept coming back to find out more, and . . . and he was still angry, but now at the people in the Enklave for lying to him."

"What did they lie about?"

"I don't know. I didn't ask, because I did not think I *wanted* to know. But when he left, he said he was going to stop the lies. Roland did not want him to go, but he said he had to. That . . . that was the last time I saw him." Her voice caught.

"I'm sorry," said Eddie.

"Thank you. I do not know how I am going to tell Roland, though." She wiped an eye, then changed direction, heading away from the lake bed. "Up here."

They climbed a rumpled slope dotted with scruffy vegetation. A tall barbed-wire fence stretched into the distance, enclosing a huge tract of land. "How far's the hole?" asked Eddie.

"Not far, inside some bushes. They check the fence for gaps, but this is hard to see from inside the Enklave. It is big enough to crawl through. Don't touch the fence, though," Julieta added in sudden warning.

"Is it electrified?"

"No, but there is an alarm. I do not know how it works, but men come down in a jeep if it is touched." She led him up the hillside to a stand of shrubs that was bisected by the fence, and pulled back a bush to reveal a small depression beneath the lowest barbed strand. Eddie bent for a closer look. It would be a tight squeeze, but he would fit through.

He surveyed the grounds within the fence. No sign of life, or any indication that they were being observed. Some laborious mental arithmetic during the walk— if Nina had been with him, she could have done it in moments—had told him that the Enklave's perimeter was over thirty miles long; a lot of ground for a hundred or so people to monitor, especially with so many blind spots caused by the rippled terrain.

"Okay," he said, "I'll go first, then you follow. If you're *absolutely* sure about coming."

"I am," said Julieta firmly. "I have to know that Roland is okay. There is a way up where we will not be seen—Roland took me once because I wanted to see where he lived."

"How long will it take to get there?"

"About two hours."

Eddie checked his watch. By the time they reached the top, they would be heading into darkness, but that could be to his advantage. "All right then. Let's go."

He dropped onto his back and wriggled under the barrier. There was a tense moment when the wire almost brushed his stomach, but he sucked it in and passed through without incident. On the other side, he rose to his feet and checked his surroundings.

The landscape looked little different from that outside, but it felt as if a switch had been flipped, putting him on high alert. He was about to head into the Nazi stronghold—into darkness in more ways than one. "Where Llamas Dare," he muttered, before turning as Julieta emerged. "You okay?"

"Yes."

"Good. Which way?"

"There." She pointed along a crease in the hillside. "It goes to the railroad bridge."

"Okay." He drew the gun he had taken from Vargas and pulled back the slide to chamber the first round from its reloaded magazine. "Let's get started."

24

Nina looked up from the bronze fish at a quiet "Psst" from Macy. The young woman gave the bored guard a sidelong glance to make sure he was not paying close attention, then whispered: "I don't know how much longer I can keep this up. I've worked out the same set of map coordinates six times already; they'll figure out that we're screwing them around sooner or later."

"Hopefully later," Nina replied. The archaeologists had covertly used the position of Alexander's original tomb in Memphis as a new baseline to calculate the latitude of the Spring of Immortality, and the text upon the relic describing the king's journey to narrow down its probable location to a mountainous region of northern Iran. However, the maps on the wall were of a scale too large to pinpoint the site exactly. "We've got to stretch this out for as long as we can."

"But when they realize that we have kept the spring from them, then what?" said Banna. The Egyptian was tired, despair clear in his voice. "If we give them what they want, they might let us go . . ."

"They won't," the redhead told him firmly. "The moment we're no longer useful to them, they'll kill us. If we give them the spring's real location, they'll have everything they need to kick-start their goddamn New Reich."

"Then—then we give them the wrong location!" He waved a hand at the maps. "We name a place, tell them it is there—"

"You think they won't check it first?" Macy cut in. "We can't just pick some random spot and hope they'll believe us."

"She's right," said Nina. "Kroll's computer gives them access to satellite photos, terrain maps. The text on the fish describes the area around the spring—which means that if we choose a location, it has to match that description. But *we* don't have satellite maps, so if we make some place up, we won't know if it fits—"

The guard belatedly registered the muttered discussion. "Hey! What are you talking about? Have you found what we are looking for?"

"No, we haven't," said Nina. "We were just translating this Greek text."

The guard's permanent scowl made it hard to tell if he believed her or not. "Work faster," he finally said. "And if you talk, talk loud so I can hear you."

"*Jawohl,*" she replied, loudly and sarcastically. "Okay, so maybe we need to go through the whole translation again. Start from the beginning. It'll take time, but we want to be sure we're right. Don't we?"

Banna nodded reluctantly. "We will do it your way. But if they lose their patience, then what—"

He broke off as the door opened. Rasche entered, his piercing stare locking on to Nina. "Come with me," he snapped. "All of you."

"Where are we going?" she asked.

A chilly smile. "Herr Kroll wishes you to meet an unexpected guest." He drew his sidearm and gestured for the prisoners to go ahead of him.

The trio were marched through the compound to a windowless concrete bunker. Nina spent the journey in a state of growing apprehension. Who was the "guest"? Rasche's sadistic amusement suggested that it was somebody she knew . . . which meant another friend had been captured by the Nazis.

Walther and Schneider joined them at the building, the latter giving Nina and especially Macy lecherous looks. The corpulent Nazi leader was waiting within, as was Gausmann. The latter wore a pair of heavy leather gloves, and to Nina's alarm had a set of knuckle-dusters clutched in one fist. The dull metal was spattered with blood. "Dr. Wilde," said Kroll. "Dr. Banna, Miss Sharif. I hope you are making progress."

"Not much," said Nina, trying to mask her dread. Someone lay on the floor behind Kroll and Gausmann, back to her and hands secured behind him by a plastic zip-tie. The man's head was blocked from her view by the obese German, but more spilled blood was visible in little pools around him. "All our calculations still say that the spring's latitude is six and a half degrees north of Alexander's tomb, but . . ." A groan came from the slumped figure.

"But what?" Kroll prompted, ignoring the sound. Gausmann kicked his subject.

Nina continued, mouth dry. "We've tried taking into account possible calculation errors by Andreas, but even then the results are the same—it always ends up in the Caspian."

Kroll fixed his gaze upon her. "You would not be lying to me, would you, Dr. Wilde?"

"No, I'm not lying," she insisted. "We just need more time to work it out."

He shook his head. "You are out of time. We are all out of time." He stepped aside to give Nina a clear view of the man on the floor.

She gasped in shock. It was Jared Zane.

The Israeli's ripped clothes were stained with blood, cuts and angry bruises visible through the torn fabric. He weakly turned his head, revealing the damage done to his face. One eye was swollen and purple, and a bloody lump marked where his nose had been broken. A thick line of blood and saliva oozed from his mouth.

Macy and Banna both reacted in horror at the sight,

but Kroll's full attention was on Nina. "I believe you know this man, Dr. Wilde."

There was no point denying it; Rasche had seen Zane rescuing her in Alexandria. "Yes," she whispered.

"And you know that he is an agent of the Mossad?"

She said nothing, in case it was a trap; Zane might not have confessed that fact. Rasche sneered at her. "He *is* a Mossad agent. Trying to protect him will gain you nothing."

Nina still did not reply. Rasche raised a hand as if to strike her, but Kroll waved him off. "It is of no consequence whether she admits it, or not," he said. "What *is* of consequence, Dr. Wilde, is that a Mossad agent— a member of their Criminal Sanctions Unit, the so-called Nazi-hunters—has found the Enklave. Where one comes, more will soon follow, like rats. Our secret has been discovered. So we must act quickly to protect ourselves. But our first priority is to locate the Spring of Immortality." He crossed the room to stand in front of her, close enough for her to smell the stale tobacco on his breath. "You will do that for us. And you will do it *now*."

"I can't," she said. "We need to go back to the original Greek, in case we missed something. There must be—"

"No!" Kroll barked. "I do not believe you." He stepped back and regarded each of the trio in turn. "I think you already *know* where to find the spring, and that you are keeping it from us." His gaze returned to Nina. "You *will* tell us."

A fearful silence followed—broken by a faint voice from the floor. "Nina . . . ," croaked Zane. Gausmann kicked him again. The Israeli gasped, but forced out another word. "Eddie . . ."

"Eddie?" Nina echoed. Kroll had turned to look at Zane; she ducked around him to get closer. "Jared, what about Eddie? Where is he?"

Rasche yanked her back. "Who is Eddie?"

"Her husband," said Kroll. The answer was matter-of-fact—but then realization made him whirl back to Nina. "Wait—your husband was with this man?"

A sudden fear rolled over her. "Yeah . . ."

"In Italy?"

The feeling became more intense. "Yes, he was . . ."

"Leitz said there was someone else with the Mossad agent," Rasche reminded Kroll. "He must have been the other man that Santos arrested!"

Kroll's piggy eyes widened. He addressed the others in German. Nina picked out an obscenity easily enough: *Scheiße!* Whatever had happened to Eddie, the Nazi leader was displeased about it.

Fear was replaced by hope. Zane had found the Enklave, and he had been traveling with Eddie—so her husband was here too. And judging from Kroll's reaction, he was causing as much trouble as ever. She exchanged a look with Macy, who had reached the same conclusion. There was still a chance they might get out of this.

But the other Nazis—Gausmann, Walther, Schneider—didn't appear as concerned as their commander, while Rasche merely shrugged. Then the sense of hope curdled in her stomach as she saw Schneider's face break into a nasty little smile. Something was wrong, very wrong . . .

Kroll scowled, then stood over Zane. "Tell her," he growled, nudging the Israeli's bruised side.

"Tell me what?" Nina demanded.

Zane lifted his head, coughing wetly to clear blood from his mouth. "Nina, I'm . . . I'm sorry, but . . . he's dead."

"No," she breathed. "I don't believe it." Behind her, Macy choked back a shocked sob.

"I'm sorry," Zane repeated, "but . . . it's true. Cops in the town . . . Nazis paid them to keep this place secret. They . . . arrested us, brought me here, but . . . they were told to kill Eddie."

"They *did* kill him," said Kroll, annoyed. "The mayor himself told me. Idiots!"

"What does it matter?" asked Rasche, dismissive. "He was a threat, he was eliminated."

"You are an idiot too, Rasche!" Kroll snapped. "Are you deaf? She is *his wife*." He pointed at Nina. "We could have used him to force her to tell us the location of the Spring of Immortality!"

Nina was no longer listening, the discussion receding into the distance. Eddie *couldn't* be dead! She had thought more than once in the past that she had lost him, only for him to reappear with a quip and a cheeky smile—not least right before they finally took the plunge and got married. It would happen this time too.

Wouldn't it?

But it wasn't just Kroll giving her the news. Zane had no reason to lie to her. If Eddie was still out there, potentially able to help, then his best course of action would have been to say nothing at all . . .

As if reading her thoughts, Zane spoke again. "Nina, I'm so sorry . . . I tried to help him, but—" He was cut off by Gausmann's boot to his stomach.

Kroll finally turned away from his subordinates with deep irritation. "The situation has not changed, Dr. Wilde," he said. "You will still tell me what I want to know."

Nina struggled to speak, choked by raw emotion. "If Eddie's dead, then—then you can go *fuck* yourself. All of you. Without him, I've got nothing left to live for."

"You will not die slowly," said Gausmann, almost with relish.

"Shut up," Kroll told him. "Dr. Wilde, we may not have your husband, but we have other people you care about. Your friends here." He looked first at Zane, then Banna and the tearful Macy. "Will you let them die to keep your secret?"

"There *is* no secret," Nina spat. "We followed Andreas's instructions exactly, and the results always end up in the sea. Either there's something missing from the clues, or the spring's not where he thought it was—if it even exists anymore. I don't know how to find it!"

Kroll regarded her in silence . . . then slowly smiled, a chilling sight. "I am impressed. You have almost convinced yourself that you are speaking the truth. But I know you are lying."

"She's not," said Macy. "We've been working on it flat out all this time, and we still haven't found it."

The SS commander turned to her. "You are not so convincing, I'm afraid. And as for you . . ." He moved on to Banna, who was so overcome by fear he couldn't even speak. "No. You know where to find the spring." He returned to Nina, the stink of his breath once more hitting her nostrils. "I have looked into the eyes of many people as I questioned them, so many I have lost count. I know, I *always* know, when they are telling me a lie. And you are lying."

Nina felt her heart pound. Kroll wasn't the only one who could tell what a person was thinking from their eyes; she knew that he had decided to do something terrible to force her to cooperate. "I'm not. Honest to God, we didn't get anything else from the relic. That's why we need to start again with a new translation, find out if—"

She stopped abruptly as the obese man drew his Luger. "Dr. Wilde, you have three friends in this room: a fellow archaeologist, your protégée, and a Mossad agent who saved your life. You will now make a choice—which one of them I kill."

Banna let out a terrified gasp, Macy went pale. Zane tried to speak, only to be silenced by another kick from Gausmann. "If you do not choose one," Kroll continued, "I will kill *two* of them. You have thirty seconds to decide . . . or to tell me the location of the Spring of Immortality. Your time begins now." He nodded to Rasche, who raised his watch arm.

Macy fearfully gripped Nina's hand. "Oh God! Nina, what do we do?"

Despite her own terror, Nina stood firm. "There *isn't* anything we can do, because we don't know where the spring is!"

The Nazi leader was unmoved. "Twenty," Rasche announced.

"We can't tell you what we don't know," Macy begged the watching men. "Don't hurt us, please." Nina felt a rush of pride at her friend's bravery. With her backup, they might call Kroll's bluff . . .

If it *was* a bluff. She knew from the Nazi's reputation that he had no compunction about killing. But even as she squeezed Macy's hand in reassurance, she saw that Banna looked about to vomit, his face pallid and sweating, hands trembling.

Ready to crack.

Kroll knew it too. Years of interrogation and torture had taught him how to spot a confessor as well as a liar. He went to the Egyptian, raising the gun to his chest. "Do you have something to say, Dr. Banna?"

"We don't know where it is!" cried Nina, willing Banna to hold his nerve as Rasche counted down to ten seconds. "We need more time to find it!"

Rasche spoke over her. "Three. Two. One—"

"Wait, wait!" Banna shrieked. "We know where it is, we know, *we know*! Don't kill me, please!"

"Ubayy, no . . . ," Nina gasped, defeated.

Kroll gave her a brief look of satisfaction before returning his attention to Banna. "Where is the spring?"

"I don't know exactly—but wait, wait!" he shrilled as the gun pressed against his sternum. "The tomb, Alexander's tomb; it was *moved*! Ptolemy moved it from Memphis to Alexandria!"

Kroll's eyes grew wide in realization. "Yes . . . yes, of course! They are over two hundred kilometers apart . . ."

"Andreas did not know that the tomb had been moved when he made the statue," Banna gabbled. "The spring is six and a half degrees of latitude from the tomb—but the tomb in Alexandria is over one degree farther north than the old one. That is why the results were in the sea! The spring is a long way south of where we first thought."

"And you have located it?"

Banna slumped in capitulation. "Yes. Not precisely, the maps were not detailed enough, but to within about thirty kilometers."

"And if you have a more accurate map . . . can you find it?"

"Yes. Yes, I can."

Zane reached pleadingly toward him. "No, don't give it to them . . ."

"Silence," snapped Kroll. Gausmann stamped the Israeli's hand back to the floor.

"What have you *done*?" Nina said to Banna.

"I have saved our lives!" he replied, tears streaming down his face. "He was going to kill us, Nina!"

"They're going to kill us anyway! These people are *Nazis*—they're murderers, psychopaths! And you just gave them a way to live forever!"

"You made the right choice, Dr. Banna," said Kroll. He stepped back, but did not lower the gun. "Now that you have agreed to help us, you will live. However . . ." He glanced down at Zane. ". . . I do not need all of you."

"What?" Banna said, shocked. "No! You said you would not kill us if we told you how to find the spring!"

"Yes, I did." Kroll looked back at Nina. "But I will not tolerate deception, Dr. Wilde. I must make an example of one of you."

Macy's hand tightened around Nina's as Kroll lowered the gun toward the Israeli. "Oh, Jesus," she gasped.

"If you're going to kill anyone," Nina said desperately, "kill me! I'm the one who lied to you!"

"No, I am not going to kill you, Dr. Wilde," said Kroll. "Not yet. But I *am* going to kill someone we do not need."

Zane gasped out a final defiant Hebrew curse as Kroll took aim. The Luger moved up his body, pointing at his stomach, his heart, his face . . .

Then the Nazi whirled around—and fired.

The bullet hit Macy in the upper chest. The young woman convulsed, her hand clenching painfully tightly around Nina's. She stumbled back a single step, staring at her friend with wide-eyed disbelief . . . then her fingers went limp and she crumpled to the floor.

Nina couldn't move, cold shock locking every muscle solid. For a moment her mind flatly refused to accept what she had just seen; she could still feel the warmth of Macy's touch, the pressure of her grip. She was still standing beside her, whatever lies her eyes were telling her . . .

The feeling faded, and was gone.

"*No!*" Nina screamed. "No, you motherfucker, *no!*" Paralysis was replaced by panic. She dropped to her knees beside Macy, pressing both hands over the wound. Hot blood squelched between her fingers. "Macy, no! You bastards, help her!"

Walther hauled her up, Nina struggling uselessly against the huge man's hold. Macy tried to reach after her, but her arm flopped to the floor as the bloodstain swelled. "Nina, I . . . ," she whispered, her breathing rapid and shallow. "I don't—I don't want to *die!*"

Time seemed to slow for Nina, the air turning as thick as molasses. "No, you fuckers!" she wailed, thrashing and kicking at Walther. "Please, I'll do anything you want, just help her! Don't let her die! Please, God!"

The war criminals stared back at her without pity. "You brought this upon yourself," said Kroll.

Helpless, Nina looked back at the trembling Macy. "Oh God," she said, eyes brimming. "I'm sorry, I'm sorry . . ."

A solitary tear ran down Macy's cheek. "Nina . . . ," she said, the name barely audible . . .

Her shivering stopped.

Nina tried to speak, but the only sound that emerged was a choked sob of grief, horror, fear . . . *guilt.* Her legs weakened, Walther's relentless grip alone keeping her upright.

A gesture from Kroll, and the big man let go. Nina slumped to the floor beside Macy. Vision blurred by tears, she groped for the young woman's hand. "No, no . . . oh God, no," she managed to say, her whole body shaking as she wept. "She—she was only a kid, she never hurt anyone! Why did you have to kill her?"

"I only need one archaeologist," said Kroll, unmoved. He gestured at the shell-shocked Banna. "He has proved that he is . . . cooperative. He will take us to the spring, because he knows now what will happen if he refuses. A difference of one degree of latitude would place it in northern Iran, yes?"

Banna did not reply. Rasche twisted his arm behind his back. "Answer him!"

"Yes," said the Egyptian in a weak, tremulous voice. "That is where it must be."

Kroll nodded. "Very well. You will work out the exact location, while I contact Leitz and arrange transportation." He straightened, addressing his officers. "We must be ready to move out as soon as possible. Make the preparations. The Mossad may already be on their way." He paused, glancing at Zane as if only just remembering that he was there, then continued issuing orders in German.

Walther summoned several men from outside. One was assigned to escort Nina back to her cell, another taking Banna to Kroll's residence. Two more picked up the battered Israeli, far from gently. Nina took one last despairing look back at Macy as her friend's body was wrapped in plastic sheeting, then she was forced from the bunker.

"Those *fuckers*," she hissed. "I'll kill them. I'll kill them all . . ."

Zane spat blood onto the ground. "I don't think you'll get the chance."

"Why not?"

"I speak German; I know what Kroll's planning." He drew in a pained breath. "They're going to have a big rally tonight, to psych everyone up to move out . . . by executing two enemies of the Reich."

He didn't have to say any more for Nina to know they were the Mossad agent . . . and herself.

25

Eddie surveyed the steepening hillside above. He and Julieta had intermittently crossed the narrow-gauge railway as they headed deeper into the Enklave, the line zigzagging laboriously up the slope. They were over two miles from where they had come through the fence, but the railway had covered a much greater distance in an effort to make the gradient manageable for locomotives. Anyone traveling uphill by train still had a long way to go. There were five more legs of track above their position.

A more direct route was possible on foot—once they cleared the current obstacle. "Are you sure this is safe?" he asked his guide.

Julieta nodded. "Roland and I have crossed this before. There will not be anyone watching."

"I wasn't asking if it was being watched. I meant, is the bloody thing going to collapse underneath us?"

Before them was an old wooden trestle bridge, spanning a rocky rent in the hillside about two hundred feet across and sixty deep. The railway only had a gauge of two feet, less than half that of a standard track, and the bridge itself was little wider, with no railings. The sleepers were close enough together to walk on, but had been exposed to the elements for a very long time.

"It has stood here for over a hundred years, so there is no reason why it would fall down now."

"Believe me, when I'm around, stuff falls down all the time. Or blows up." He completed his sweep of the landscape; nobody was in sight. "But if we've got to go across it . . ."

"It is the fastest way," she assured him. "If you are worried, I can go first?"

"Nah, that's okay," he said, heading for the trestle. "I'll be all right. If I think light thoughts . . . ," he added under his breath.

His concerns about the bridge's integrity turned out to be, if not unfounded, at least exaggerated, however. It did not take long to cross—though he had a few unsettling moments along the way as old wood crunched under his weight, splinters dropping into the void.

"Okay," he said with relief as he reached solid ground, Julieta following, "which way now?" He looked along the line, seeing that it looped tightly back over itself to begin the next uphill leg several hundred yards distant, where a small bridge crossed above a cutting.

"That way." She pointed up the slope. "There is a path to a little ruin. Roland took me there to see the houses in the middle of the Enklave."

"How close did you get to them?"

"A mile, maybe? He did not take me nearer because he said it would not be safe if I got caught."

"For him, or for you?"

She sucked in her lower lip. "For him, I thought. But after today, I don't know . . ."

"You don't have to get any closer with me. Once I've had a look at the place, I'll go in on my own."

"No, no," she said. "I have to find Roland, and tell him about Volker."

"Okay," Eddie said with reluctance, "but when we get up there, stay behind me and do what I tell you. I'll keep you safe."

They set off up the stony path. "So you have done this before?" Julieta asked. "Are you a soldier?"

"Used to be. I work for the United Nations now."

"What do you do? You said your wife was an archaeologist—are you one too?"

He laughed, surprising her. "Nah. Nina'd love it if I was, but once she starts going on about three-thousand-year-old winnet pickers or whatever, I tune out. My job's basically to keep her out of trouble." His mood became more somber. "Haven't done that great at it recently."

"I am sorry," Julieta said quietly.

"Don't worry about it. Right now, I just want to find her and make sure she's okay."

"And . . . if she is not?"

"Then I'm going to make someone regret it."

She was noticeably less talkative for the rest of the ascent. At one point they crossed a hairpin loop at the end of a leg of track, before leaving the railway behind as they approached the top of the hill.

"The ruin is over there," Julieta announced. "By those trees."

Eddie saw foliage against the darkening sky. "Okay. Stay low."

He dropped to a crouch as they reached the crest of the hill. The ruin, a half-collapsed stone hut, was fifty feet away. Ahead, the landscape flattened out into a plateau, gradually rising to meet the steeper foothills of the Andes. Most of it seemed to be farmland, lying empty during the winter before planting season.

"All right," he said once he was certain that the Enklave's occupants were not patrolling this part of their domain. "Follow me."

He quickly reached the derelict structure, the young Argentinean scurrying behind. A collapsed beam marked an easy route up to what remained of the flat roof; he clambered along it, then at the top dropped to a crawl and moved to get his first clear view of the heart of the Enklave.

Initially it seemed nothing special; just a large farm surrounded by fields. But closer observation told him that more went on here than growing crops. The heart of the complex, about a mile to the west, looked more like a military camp.

There was a set of binoculars in his gear; he took them out as Julieta moved alongside him. "Roland told me he lives in one of those buildings," she said, pointing.

It snapped ten times closer in Eddie's view as he brought up the binoculars. It was unmistakably a barracks: plain concrete outer walls, which he knew from his own military experience would make the interior cold and damp in winter and a sweatbox in summer. Yellow bulbs glowed behind small windows, and as he watched, a young man by the door tossed away the flaring stub of a cigarette and went inside, giving him a glimpse of metal-framed beds. "Doesn't look like he gets much privacy."

"No, he said he has to share with twenty men. The first time he told me, I laughed, because I did not believe him. Who would live like that?"

"People trying to start an army." He surveyed the other buildings. More barracks, garages and workshops, and a white-painted structure that had the look of a medical center. It was larger than he would have expected, though—for such a small community, the odds of more than a handful of people at once needing hospital treatment were slim—and the lights within suggested that it was in continuous use. What was going on inside?

He put the question to the back of his mind as he panned across a group of houses. Unlike the utilitarian barracks, these were far more luxurious and comfortable, with a distinctly Bavarian style. Kroll and his cronies obviously lived there, the war criminals who had founded the hidden community treating themselves to all the comforts of their stolen wealth while their followers were crammed into concrete boxes.

A bright light came on outside his field of vision, starkly illuminating the houses. He looked over the top of the binoculars to locate the source, then examined it through the lenses. Near the barracks was an open square that he guessed was a parade ground, a raised stage at one end. A set of powerful floodlights had just come on to illuminate it. Men carrying chairs and lengths of wood filed across the open space toward the platform. They were going to build something—but what?

"Eddie," Julieta whispered. The urgency in her voice instantly put him on alert, and he lowered the glasses. "Over there."

A vehicle had left the central compound and was crossing the farmland. Eddie tensed, but soon saw that it wasn't coming toward them, instead heading for some low mounds about half a mile northwest. Through the binoculars, it was revealed as an old US Army surplus jeep, two men in the front seats.

"Are they looking for us?" asked the nervous Argentinean.

"I don't think so, but let's not move while they're out there." He watched the jeep cross the barren fields and scrabble up a slope. Once at the top, it continued along the rise for a short way, then stopped.

Julieta squinted at the distant vehicle. "What are they doing?"

"Not sure, but the two guys in it are getting out. They're going to the back, and—"

"And what?"

He didn't answer, suddenly filled with fear. The men had just hauled something out of the four-by-four, a shape shrouded in plastic sheeting.

A corpse.

He couldn't make out any details through the wrapped layers, but he *could* tell from the overall shape that it was a woman. The pair carried the limp body away from the jeep, then tossed it without ceremony into a ditch. Their grim job done, they went to their vehicle and returned the way they had come, not once looking back.

Eddie jumped from the roof. "Come on." Julieta climbed after him and went to one side of the ruin. "No, this way."

"But the buildings are over here."

He fixed her with a stone-cold stare. "They just dumped a woman's body. If it was Nina . . . I'm going to go into that place and kill every last one of them."

The Englishman started for the mounds. Julieta hesitated, then hurried to catch up.

⋅ ⋅ ⋅

Nina curled in a tight ball in the corner of the cell, forehead pressed against her knees and eyes tightly shut. It was the nearest she could get to shrinking and shrinking until she fell through a crack in the floor and was swallowed by the earth, never to be seen again. Macy's last moments kept replaying in her mind, an endless loop of pain and horror that she would see until she died.

And right now, she wanted nothing more than for that moment to come. She had failed, utterly and completely. Her stupid, selfish desire to make one last big find had handed the Nazis the very thing they had sought . . . and in the process, she had killed her friend.

A sob escaped her mouth. She squeezed her legs harder, trying to crush herself out of existence . . .

"There was nothing you could have done."

Zane's words stirred Nina out of her numbness. "What?"

"What happened in the bunker." The Israeli was lying on the bed; he painfully sat up. "You couldn't have saved her. Kroll was going to kill all of us except Banna, no matter what; he's the only one they need to find the spring."

"I *could* have saved her," Nina whispered. "If I'd told Kroll about Alexander's tomb being moved, I—"

"Then he would have killed Banna and Macy and kept you alive. They only need one archaeologist now that they know where to look—and the second they find what they're after, they won't need any. I'm sorry about your friend, and about Eddie too. But once these bastards catch you . . ." He hung his head.

"What—what happened to Eddie?"

"There's a town near here, and the local cops and the mayor are in Kroll's pocket. It seems they usually just scare off tourists, but after Eddie marched into a bar and asked if anybody had seen any Nazis, it didn't take long for them to figure out that we were a threat."

"He's . . . not subtle, no." For a moment, her mental picture of the dying Macy was replaced by one of Eddie striding into a room and asking the blunt question in his broad Yorkshire accent . . .

She almost smiled. Almost.

But the image vanished as Zane continued: "The cops called Kroll and told him we'd been arrested. The man we went after in Italy, the Nazis' middleman—he must have told Kroll about us. They knew I was a Mossad agent, but since Eddie wasn't Israeli they didn't know who he was. Kroll told the cops to kill him."

"But . . . you didn't see them do it?" The tiniest glimmer of hope rose within her. Eddie had been believed dead before . . .

The spark was snuffed out. "No, but they told Kroll that it was done. He *gloated* about it while Gausmann was torturing me." Zane clenched a fist in anger.

The only emotion Nina now felt was despair. She drew her legs up to her body once more, sinking back into anguished misery . . .

A rattle from above.

Even in his weakened state, Zane still jumped off the bed and whirled to find the source of the noise. "What was that?"

"Quiet, quiet," came a whisper from outside the air vent. "Dr. Wilde? Are you there?"

Nina looked up. "Roland?"

"Yes. Is it safe?"

She stood. "Check the door, make sure no one's there," she told Zane in a low voice, before adding: "He's not a threat. I think."

The Mossad agent was not convinced, but nevertheless went to the cell door. He listened for several seconds, then nodded. Nina climbed onto the bed and looked through the opening.

It was now dark outside, but the single bulb cast enough light to reveal the young man's blue eyes looking back at her nervously. "What do you want?" she demanded.

"I need to know what happened to my brother," said Roland.

"I already told you. He tried to give me the plans for the raid on Alexander's tomb, but Jaekel shot him."

He hesitated before speaking again, agitated. "Herr Jaekel has not been seen for days. They say he is away on important business for the Reich, but . . ." Another pause, then: "Volker . . . he became opposed to the Reich after reading about the outside world on the Internet. He did not believe it at first, and nor did I. But the more he saw, the more he thought the Oberkommando had lied to us."

"And what did *you* think?"

The question caught him off guard. "I . . . do not know. I still do not. Jul—A friend, from outside the Enklave, has told me things that contradict what I have been told all my life, but . . . Why would our leaders lie to us?" The question was almost plaintive.

"To get you to do what they want," Nina growled. "There you go, your first lesson in politics. I suppose they told you they had to hide out here because they were unjustly persecuted when the rest of the world conspired against Hitler's Germany?"

His reaction told her that was not far from the truth. "That is not what other people say, though."

"No, it isn't. The Nazis were genocidal thugs, the most evil regime in history. Their leaders were psychopathic murderers—and they still are. They killed your brother, and they killed my—" Her words caught in her throat. "And they killed my friend!"

Even through the vent, it was impossible for Roland to miss her anguish. "What? They killed . . ."

"They killed Macy! Kroll shot her—she'd done nothing, but he murdered her!"

He drew away. "No, not Herr Kroll. He is our Führer! I do not believe—"

"But she's not here, is she?" said Nina, wanting to scream the words into his face. She leaned away from the vent. "Do you see her? *Do you?*"

Roland's eyes flicked across the cell, seeing Nina, Zane at the door . . . but nobody else. "No," he admitted.

"That's because she's *dead*! Kroll murdered her—because I wouldn't give him what he wanted!"

He shook his head. "No, the Oberkommando would not murder an innocent person . . ."

"Your brother knew they would! That's why he left here, why he came to warn me what they were doing—because he discovered how evil your precious fucking leaders are! What do you think he was reading about on the Internet? Kroll's been lying to everyone here for the last seventy years. But Volker didn't believe him, and went to find the truth out for himself. And you must at least have doubts, otherwise you wouldn't be here talking to me now."

"I just want to learn what happened to my brother—"

"I *told* you!" Nina growled. "Jaekel shot him dead—just like Kroll shot Macy. He shot her, and then they wrapped her up in plastic and hauled her away like . . . like she was garbage!" The pain of loss clenched around her chest once more, but she refused to be silenced. "They're murderers, all your leaders. They're wanted war criminals! Volker discovered that, and they killed him to protect their secret. Why won't you believe me?"

Roland stared at her in silence. She thought he was about to turn and leave, that her last tiny hope was gone—but then he spoke. "Plastic . . ."

"What?"

"You said they wrapped Macy in plastic." Uncertainty filled his voice. "I saw something wrapped in plastic being put in a jeep."

"Where were they taking it?" Zane asked.

"There is a dump in some little hills. We burn trash there sometimes. They were going there."

"Then *you* go there," said Nina through clenched teeth. "You go there, and see for yourself." He blinked, about to move but then hesitating. "Go and see!" she shouted, no longer caring if the guard heard her. "Go and see! *Go and see!*"

Roland glanced around fearfully, then dropped and ran. The vent cover clanked back into place.

"The guard's coming," Zane warned. He quickly returned to the bed as Nina stepped down.

A fist pounded on the metal door. "Silence in there! What is going on?"

"Nothing," sighed Nina. She went back to the corner, tears rolling down both cheeks. "Nothing at all."

26

It took Eddie and Julieta twenty cautious minutes to reach the mound where the jeep had stopped. Twilight was now upon them, the Andean peaks to the west indistinct silhouettes against a backdrop of brooding clouds. Off to the southwest, the heart of the Enklave was picked out by numerous lights. Even without binoculars, Eddie could tell that the parade ground was full of activity.

But his priority was discovering if his fears were justified. There was still enough daylight to show a large ditch with numerous objects at its bottom. He couldn't make them out clearly, but a stench of moldering rubbish gave him a good idea what he would find. The Nazis had been using it as a dumping ground. "Okay, I'm going for a look," he told his companion as he took out a torch. "Wait here."

He started into the pit before switching on the light to keep it hidden from any observers. The first thing he saw was charcoal and ash; the Nazis had been burning their garbage. But it was not a regular event, as more had since been thrown in, the circle of light finding broken furniture, crates and pallets, shredded tires. They were not what he was looking for, though. He reached the bottom of the hollow . . .

Plastic glistened in the beam. He froze as he made out the shape wrapped in the translucent sheeting. Definitely a human body. A woman.

"What is it?" Julieta called.

"Stay there," he ordered, breathing faster as he approached. He still couldn't pick out any detail through the plastic . . . but what he could see made him more and more reluctant to take another step.

Blood had run down the inside of the sheet, dark smears marking where it had congealed. A gunshot wound, from the amount—but who was the victim?

He reached the body and brought his torch to the head. A face was vaguely visible through the wrapped layers, although too distorted to identify. Was the hair red? The plastic made it hard to tell even that much, colors muted beneath it.

Eddie crouched beside the figure. There was only one way to know.

He propped the torch on a broken crate, then with deep foreboding began to unwrap the sheeting.

It unfurled as he pulled at it. The body shifted slightly, the head tipping back. That meant the death was recent; rigor mortis hadn't set in. He tried to keep focused on that bit of cold scientific fact rather than succumb to emotion, but he couldn't stop himself from tearing ever harder at the plastic. His heart raced as he ripped away the last piece to reveal the woman's face—

It wasn't Nina.

A flash of pure, joyous relief—instantly overwhelmed by shame and guilt for the feeling. It wasn't Nina, but he still knew her.

Macy's frightened eyes looked lifelessly up at him, her expression telling him that she had died in pain. He stumbled back.

"Eddie?" called Julieta, alarmed. "Are you okay?"

He heard her descend into the pit. "No, stay back," he warned as he forced himself to return to Macy. Jaw clenched, he gently touched her cheek. Her skin was cold. "Oh God . . ."

He brought his hand to Macy's eyes and carefully

closed them. It did not lessen her look of fear, but now she at least appeared to have found some small amount of peace. He retrieved the torch and turned his attention to her body, tugging away more bloodied plastic to reveal a single gunshot wound. Fairly large caliber, the military part of his mind noted, probably nine millimeter. Fired from very close range, judging from the traces of gunpowder. She had been looking right at her killer when he pulled the trigger . . .

His breath caught. Macy had only just started her life, choosing her own path for the first time, promise and discovery before her—and now it was over. Everything that she had been and ever would be, stolen from the world.

His vision shimmered with tears, but grief was already being forced aside by fury. The people who had done this were going to pay—

Someone touched his shoulder. He spun, raising a fist before realizing that it was Julieta. She flinched back. "Sorry," he said, but the burning rage did not subside.

She peered timorously at the body. "Is it . . . your wife?"

"No. But she's one of my friends. Her name's Macy, Macy Sharif." He looked down at the shrouded corpse again, repeating her name as if in requiem. "Macy Sharif."

Julieta whispered a Spanish prayer, making the sign of the cross—then suddenly stopped. "Someone is coming!"

Eddie snapped off the torch and crouched, pulling her behind a rusted sheet of corrugated steel. A torch beam jittered above, then angled down as its owner reached the edge of the dumping ground. Eddie watched through a hole in the metal. The light swept over the garbage, fixing upon Macy. A moment's hesitation, then the man clambered into the ditch and moved toward her.

The rage returned. Eddie started to take out his gun, but changed his mind. A shot might be heard—and he also had an irresistible urge to kill the Nazi with his bare hands, to hear bones break and feel the windpipe crush as he broke the bastard's neck . . .

The intruder reached Macy's body, stepping around it to get a clear look at the face. He was only ten feet from the Englishman, and didn't have a weapon at the ready. Eddie knew he could reach him before he had time to react. He moved out from his hiding place, crossing the few steps to his target.

The man turned as he heard a noise, but too late—

"No!" cried Julieta. "It's Roland!"

Eddie had already grabbed him, arms clamping around his head and upper chest. One sharp twist would be all it took . . .

"Please, *no*!" Her voice was a scream. "Don't hurt him!"

"He's one of them," he snarled.

"No, he isn't! I love him! Please, let him go!"

Roland squirmed helplessly in Eddie's grip, struggling to breathe. "You speak English?" His prisoner managed a terrified nod. "You do *anything* I don't like, I'll kill you. Understand?" Another feeble twitch of the head. "Okay."

Eddie released his hold and shoved Roland to the ground. He shone his torch at the panting youth's face— feeling a shock of recognition. He was the twin of Volker Koenig, indistinguishable from the man who had been gunned down in Los Angeles. His eyes were wide with fear.

Eddie felt no sympathy. Macy's had been the same. He drew the gun, making sure the young man could see it. "You're Roland Koenig?" he demanded, ignoring Julieta's frightened protests.

"Yes," gasped the blond. He peered past Eddie. "Julieta? Is that—"

"Shut up," Eddie snapped. "You're talking to me." He gestured with the torch at Macy's body. "Who did that? Who killed her?"

Roland didn't dare look away from him. "I do not know. She was taken to the Oberkommando, but—but I do not know what happened to her. I was not there."

"Then what the fuck are you doing here now?"

"I was told Macy was here. I did not believe it, but she

said I should go and see, and—and she was right. It is true . . ."

"*Who* said? Who were you talking to?"

"Dr. Wilde. She—"

"Nina?" Eddie exclaimed. "Nina Wilde?" Roland nodded. "You spoke to Nina? When?"

"Not long ago—about twenty minutes, twenty-five?"

The Englishman felt a rush of relief. Nina was alive! But the Nazis had murdered Macy; they could kill Nina too. "Where is she?"

"In the *Kerker*, the prison. There was a man with her, but I do not know who he is. The other man, the Arab, he was not there."

"The man with her now—was he young? Loads of curly hair?"

He nodded. "He was hurt. There was blood all over him."

Julieta came closer. "Please, let him go."

Roland looked up as the torchlight's spill illuminated her face. "Julieta!" Even with a gun aimed at him, he smiled. "What are you doing here?"

"I came to find you," she replied, kneeling and taking hold of his hand. "I had not seen you for days, and after what happened to Volker, I was worried."

His smile vanished. "Dr. Wilde said that . . . Volker is dead. Is it true?"

Julieta glanced at Eddie, reluctant to answer. Roland turned back toward the Englishman. "Yeah. Your brother's dead," Eddie told him.

"But—" The young man looked at Julieta again, as if hoping for a denial, but none came. "No . . ."

Eddie remembered the youth's earlier words. "Nina told you to come out here. Why?"

It took a few seconds for Roland to compose himself enough to reply. "I did not believe that Herr Kroll had killed her friend. Dr. Wilde . . . challenged me to see for myself. I thought that if she was lying about Macy, then she must also be lying about the other things she said." He turned away, downcast. "She was not lying."

"No, she wasn't. And I'm not lying either: I'm going

to get her out of there, and I'm going to kill anyone who gets in my way. Are *you* going to get in my way?"

Though afraid, Roland still found enough courage to look Eddie in the eye. "No, I am not. I do not know what to think anymore. All I want is to be sure that Julieta is safe." He faced her. "I will take you back home."

She shook her head. "No. Roland, we have to help him rescue his wife. *You* have to help him. For Volker."

He looked between them, unsure what to do. "At least show me where this prison is," said Eddie.

Julieta held Roland's hand tighter. "Please, Roland. Something bad is going on. Help him stop it."

"I . . . Very well," he said, with a deep sigh. "I will show you. But Julieta, you cannot come with me." She tried to object, but he raised a hand. "Please. I love you, and I do not want anything to happen to you. I did not think before that you would be hurt if you were caught in the Enklave, but now . . ." A grim glance at Macy's body. "Wait for me; I will find you."

She nodded reluctantly. "I will wait at the ruin. And . . . you will take care of him?" she asked the York-shireman.

Eddie was in no mood to make promises, especially concerning the people who had killed Macy, but he tipped his head slightly. "We'll see."

He lowered the gun and backed up so Roland could stand. The young couple embraced, then kissed, speaking in Spanish. Roland sounded more fluent in that language than in English; meeting Julieta had encouraged him to focus his linguistic skills. "All right, get a bloody room," muttered Eddie. The pair unwillingly separated. "Julieta, get going—but take these, and watch out for trouble." He gave her the binoculars.

"What kind of trouble?" she asked.

"Explosions, shooting, screaming, that kind of thing. If you see any, get out of here, fast. I'll watch out for your boyfriend."

The two kissed again, then Julieta said, *"Te amo,"* before making her way back out of the pit.

"*Te amo,*" Roland called to her, watching her retreat until she was lost to the shadows.

"Christ, young love," Eddie said impatiently. "Come on, then."

Roland climbed out of the ditch. Eddie gave Macy's still form one final look. "You're not going to stay here," he told her quietly. "I'll make sure you get a . . . a proper burial." He felt his throat clench again; he caught himself. "And the people who did this are going to pay. All of them."

27

The young man led the way toward the heart of the Enklave. Even though it was now dark, they used the sparse vegetation to stay concealed as much as possible. "All right," said Eddie, "I need to know this place's layout. Where's the prison?"

"It is on the far side of the compound, past the *Kinderhaus*," Roland replied.

"The what?" He knew the two parts of the compound word—*child* and *house*—but wasn't sure if it meant what he thought.

"The children's building, there." Roland pointed at a large white-painted structure beyond the barracks. "It is where I grew up. Where we all grew up."

"All the kids live in one building?"

"Yes. I was surprised when Julieta first told me she lived only with her father and mother."

"Wait, you mean you *didn't* live with your mum and dad?"

"No, I was born of one of the *Zucht-Frauen*."

"What are they?"

"There are nine at the present time, I think? Six of them are *Kindermädchen*; they look after the children and teach them useful skills, like cooking and how to make clothes."

"What about the other three?" Eddie asked, with the distinct feeling that he wouldn't like the answer.

Roland hesitated. "They are kept in a ward for . . . breeding."

The Englishman stopped. "You mean they're *prisoners*? They're, what, literally *breeding stock*? Jesus!"

"Only those who are not totally obedient to the Reich . . ." The youth trailed off under Eddie's glare.

"So women who don't do as they're told get locked up to become baby machines? What happens to men who—" He already knew. "They're just fucking executed, obviously. Like your brother."

Roland could no longer meet his gaze. "I . . . I cannot believe he is gone."

"Yeah, he's gone. He was shot in the fucking street by that scar-faced bastard Jaekel. So, is that how it was? He was the freethinking, troublemaking brother who didn't like what Kroll and the other Nazi shitehawks were doing and died trying to stop it, and you were the good little boy who always did what he was told, however fucking evil it was?"

"I never did anything evil!" the youth protested. "I just . . . never doubted what our leaders told us."

"Now'd be a good time to start. You need to pick a side, son. The people who killed your brother, and Macy, and about twenty million others—or people like me who're trying to stop history from repeating itself. Who's it gonna be?"

Roland shook his head, conflicted. "I do not know what to do . . ." He finally looked up at Eddie. "But I promised Julieta that I would help you find Dr. Wilde, and I will keep my promise."

He set off again, Eddie staring angrily after him before following. "How do I get into this prison?"

"There is only one entrance, and there is a guardroom beyond it. But you will be able to talk to Dr. Wilde from outside—there is a hole for air in the back wall." He glanced back with a half smile. "I used to sneak around and talk to Volker through it when he was in the prison for getting into trouble." The smile faded at the thought of his late brother.

"So you went outside the Enklave to hook up with Julieta, and talked to your brother in secret when he was in the slammer? You don't always follow orders, then. There's hope for you yet." Eddie was already working out possible plans of action; if he reached the prison unseen, he could get Nina to create a distraction inside her cell while he entered the building . . .

Roland stopped behind a clump of trees. "Sentries walk along this path," he explained, indicating a route circling the settlement. A barbed-wire fence ran along its outer side.

The Englishman checked in both directions. "I haven't seen anyone."

"No. That is strange, we always have a night watch. It must be because of the rally."

"What rally?"

"The Führer, Herr Kroll—he ordered everyone to attend a rally tonight. I do not know why, though. A big announcement."

Eddie regarded the floodlights. "They were building something on a parade ground with a stage at one end—is that where they're holding it?"

"Yes. I saw them taking wood to it, but I do not know what they are making."

"You said *everyone's* going to be there?" Eddie asked. Roland nodded. "So I might be able to get into this prison while it's going on?"

"Perhaps. The order was given to everybody in the Enklave." He pointed toward some bushes forty yards past the fence. "There is a trench behind them. We can use it to get closer."

"Lead on." Eddie let Roland go first, still keeping the gun at the ready. The young man had seemed genuinely devastated on learning what had happened to his twin, but he might still fall back on learned behavior and protect his leaders by betraying his new companion. For now, though, there was no indication that he meant to give away Eddie's presence. They crawled under the fence, then Roland led the way to the end of the ditch, bringing the pair to within a hundred yards of the buildings. The nearest was a large and ugly block silhouetted by lights behind. "Okay, where are we?" Eddie asked.

"That is the motor pool and the auto workshops," Roland told him. "We will have to go all the way around the compound to reach the prison from here."

The young man started to move, but Eddie held his arm. "Wait—that garage, is there a back door?"

"No, but . . . I know a way to get inside without being seen. Volker and I used to sneak in to play in the trucks when we were children." A quizzical glance. "Why do you want to go inside?"

" 'Cause when I get Nina out, I don't want a hundred pissed-off fucking Nazis chasing after me in half-tracks." He nudged Roland on.

"We only have trucks, and some jeeps. And tractors," Roland told him as they cautiously crossed the open ground.

"What about the railway? Are there any trains?"

"Yes, there is a steam engine, but it has not run for years."

They reached the rear of the garage. Eddie peered warily around its corner, ducking back as two men walked past on the building's far side. However, they were not looking in his direction. He leaned out again, seeing that they were heading toward the floodlit glare of the parade ground. More Nazis trooped by. "Looks like this rally's about to start. That'll keep 'em occupied, then. How do we get in?"

"Here." Roland moved to a pile of old tires and assorted machine parts against the side wall. He rolled a rusting truck wheel back a few feet to expose a dark hole at the bottom of the flaking planks.

Eddie bent to look through. The garage had shutters fronting each work bay, and some were open, letting in spill from the floodlights. But the interior itself was unlit. He made out vehicles lurking within, and more trucks and jeeps just outside. "Do they keep *all* their cars and stuff here?"

"Yes."

He weighed up his options. Desperate as he was to save Nina, it was unlikely that he could simply march into the prison, gun blazing, and bring her out. But if the guards were at the rally, or if only a single man was left on watch . . . "When does the rally start?"

"In twenty minutes," Roland told him.

Eddie made a decision. "Okay, wait here. I'm going to sort out these trucks." The blond man retreated, leaving him to crawl through the little opening.

The garage smelled strongly of spilled diesel and grease. This end of the building was home to racks holding tools and boxes of engine parts, as well as ranks of jerry cans and fuel drums. He crept past them to find a dented six-wheeled truck that from its dated styling appeared at least thirty years old. None of the other vehicles was any younger, so sabotaging them wouldn't be difficult.

He neared an open garage door, getting his first clear look at the floodlit parade ground—and froze.

Construction work had finished. The fruits of the Nazis' labors now stood before the stage.

A pair of gallows.

Each of the tall beams stood sixteen feet high, a noose already hanging from the crossbeam of one while a man on a ladder threaded a second rope into place on its neighbor.

Two gallows. Two prisoners. Eddie already knew who was due for the drop. A Mossad agent was an enemy the Nazis would want to get rid of as quickly as possible, and since Roland had said Banna was not in the cell, that meant Kroll had decided which archaeologist he was going to use to find the spring. And it wasn't the stroppy redhead from New York.

A flash of pride that Nina had told the obese Nazi where to go was overpowered by fear for her life. She and Zane would be the main attraction at the impending rally. The stage was backed by huge swastika banners, men already assembling before it with red armbands standing out under the glaring lights. How the hell was he going to save them from the hangman with over a hundred Nazis watching?

He slipped back into the shadows as more young men passed the garage. Their reaction to the sight of the gallows was the opposite of his: an expectant thrill. "Goose-stepping little shits," he muttered—but then he took a closer look. They were all in uniform, but none appeared armed. A hundred Nazis, but no guns . . .

A glance back at the tool shelves, and he had his plan. He returned to the hole to see Roland still outside. "Herr Chase," whispered the youth. "Have you finished?"

"Change of plan," Eddie replied. "Look, you know this place well, right? Ways to move around without being seen, hiding places, that kind of thing?"

"Yes. Ever since we were children, Volker and I explored the Enklave whenever we could."

"Good, 'cause we're gonna need 'em. Is there somewhere you can wait for me behind that stage?"

Roland looked uncomfortable. "Everyone is expected to attend the rally. I should already be in my quarters to put on my uniform—if I am late, they will search for me. And if they are searching for me, they may find you."

"They'll wish they hadn't."

"But if anyone is missed, the whole Enklave will be placed on alert, and you will never save your wife and your friends. I must go, I am sorry. But there is a red hut on the far side of the parade ground; under it, there is room to hide if you can get in without being seen. I will meet you there." Seeing the Englishman's doubting expression, he added: "I promised Julieta I would help you. I would never lie to her—so I will not lie to you."

Eddie was still dubious, but was also running out of time. "Okay then," he finally said. "You go and get ready."

"What are you going to do?"

"Fix those trucks. And get some weapons."

Roland frowned, puzzled. "But there are no weapons in there."

Eddie gave him a sardonic smile. "People always said the Nazis were unimaginative . . ."

28

Nina looked up as the cell door swung open, revealing four men waiting outside.

Four men dressed in full Waffen-SS uniforms.

Zane drew in a sharp breath at the sight, and she felt a chill of disbelieving fear. These were not costumes; they were *real*. The Nazis were supposed to be dead and gone, as much a part of history as Alexander the Great. Yet they had survived, trapdoor spiders patiently waiting in their remote hiding hole, ready to reemerge as cruel and evil as ever . . .

All carried submachine guns. The leader jabbed his weapon at the prisoners. "Stand up. Now."

"*Fick dich ins Knie,*" Zane told them with a defiant snarl. The lead Nazi's lip curled in anger—then he clubbed the Israeli with his gun. Two of his companions joined in, the fourth man pointing his weapon at Nina to deter her from interfering.

"Leave him alone, you bastards!" she yelled. They ignored her, each man getting in one final blow on the Mossad agent before he was hauled up and his hands cuffed behind his back.

"It is time," intoned the leader. "Move." He and another man dragged Zane out as the remaining pair secured Nina's hands, then took her by both arms and followed.

The concrete jail's outer door was opened—and she heard men chanting in unison as an amplified voice echoed above the noise, ranting in German.

Kroll. The Nazi leader had started his rally, working his troops into a frenzy of hatred. She felt sick. This was not a decades-old recording. This was happening *now.*

To her.

The soldiers took their prisoners through the heart of the Enklave to an open area under piercing floodlights. Ranks of uniformed men stood on each side as Nina and Zane were brought toward a stage at the opposite end.

On it sat the Nazi leaders, looking down upon their followers as if on thrones. Schneider. Gausmann. Walther. Rasche. And standing upon a rostrum at the center of the stage, his bloated body squeezed into a black SS uniform, was Kroll, one hand repeatedly stabbing the air to emphasize his words. The crowd roared a horrifying response to each proclamation: *"Sieg heil! Sieg heil! Heil Hitler!"*

Nina glanced fearfully at the audience. Faces twisted in loathing turned toward the two captives. The Nazi rank and file ranged in age from their teens to their fifties; the water in the pithos had not been shared. She saw only one hard-faced woman among the men, as caught up in the mania as her male companions. Arms stretched aloft in rigid salutes. *"Heil Hitler! Heil Hitler!"*

But the crowd was not the most terrifying aspect of the rally. Nina stiffened in fear as she was forced ever closer to the two gallows. A tall wooden stool stood before each, nooses dangling above them.

Kroll's gaze turned to the new arrivals. "And now here are the spies," he barked, switching seamlessly to English. None of the audience had any difficulty understanding him; the change was to terrorize the prisoners. "This agent of the Jewish Mossad is the reason we must act now to protect our future. Where there is one rat, more will soon follow, so we must leave before they find us—but this rat will not live to see that happen!"

"*Sieg heil! Sieg heil!*" Men on each side screamed and jeered at Zane.

"And with the Mossad agent is an American puppet of the Zionists," Kroll continued, "an official of the United Nations!" Boos and abuse came from the crowd. "She was given the chance to renounce her allegiance and serve the New Reich, but she refused—so now she will pay the price!"

Nina and Zane were taken past the front row of baying Nazis to the gallows. There they were separated and hauled to the stools. The Israeli tried to break loose, but was beaten to his knees. Kroll glowered down at them. "This is the fate of all enemies of the Reich," he intoned, his voice echoing from loudspeakers around the square. "All those who oppose us will die! *Der Henker wird nun seinen Platz einnehmen.*"

His reversion to German startled Nina, but his instruction soon became clear. Gausmann stood and descended to the twin gallows. White gloves covered his hands. He was not just the Enklave's chief torturer; he was also its executioner.

"No," gasped Nina, shrinking back. Her guards gripped harder, holding her in place. Gausmann went to Zane first, pushing the noose over his head and pulling it chokingly tight around his neck before turning to Nina. "Get back! Get the fuck back!" she yelled, kicking at him. She caught him on the shin; he flinched, then punched her in the stomach. She doubled over before being yanked upright by the soldiers. "*Schlampe,*" the German hissed as he forced the noose into place and tugged it hard.

Kroll's voice boomed from the speakers with triumphant fury, whipping the crowd into a frenzy. Gausmann checked the ropes, then signaled to the Nazi leader. "Pull them up!" Kroll ordered.

The lines were raised via pulleys, snapping taut. The noose dug deeply into Nina's throat. She tried to scream, but it was compressing her windpipe. Pain crackled through her neck as she was hauled upward. For a terrifying moment she thought her spine would snap under the unsupported weight of her own body . . . but then the two guards took her by the legs, relieving the torment.

But only slightly. She still couldn't breathe, desperately trying to draw in air as she was lifted to stand upon the high stool. The rope's pull ceased when her boots touched down on its flat top, leaving her wobbling over five feet off the ground.

Zane was raised into position beside her. The ropes were secured around hooks on the vertical poles. Nina squinted at the crowd through pain-squeezed eyes, a sea of screaming faces and armbands red as blood. *"Sieg heil! Sieg heil! Sieg heil!"* Their animalistic roar was almost physical, threatening to push her from her treacherous footing by sheer volume. She clenched her toes, trying to hold herself steady—

The most frightening realization of all struck her. The drop was not enough to kill them from the fall alone. A longer plunge would sever the spine, causing near-instant death through shock . . . but this would leave the victims conscious as they slowly strangled, kicking and writhing for the howling crowd's entertainment.

She looked across at Zane. He glanced back, jaw clenched tight in a refusal to show fear—but she could see it in his eyes.

And he could see it in hers.

Gausmann stepped behind her as the guards retreated. "The American will be the first to die," Kroll announced with relish. Every muscle in her body quivered as she fought to stay upright. The crowd blurred behind tears, becoming an amorphous mass of hatred and rage. *"Drei! Zwei! Eins!"* The awful roar briefly subsided in anticipation . . .

A flare of light and color arced in from one side of the square—

Glass smashed—and screams erupted behind Nina as a Molotov cocktail exploded between the four guards,

splashing them with liquid fire and setting their clothing
and hair aflame.

Gausmann instinctively jumped away as burning gasoline sluiced across the space between the stage and the
gallows. A second Molotov hurtled over the floodlit parade ground, bursting in the crowd's front rows. The
unity of the chant changed to discordant shrieks of pain
and fear as the audience broke ranks and scattered, trying to flee both the blaze and their flaming comrades.
The Nazi leaders stampeded for the back of the stage as
Eddie rushed into the square, gun in his right hand—
and a fire ax in his left.

One of the four men hit by his first bomb had only
been caught on the sleeve, managing to tear off his uniform jacket before raising his weapon—

The Englishman's bullet blew a bloody chunk from his
skull. The Nazi fell back into the fire. The other three
guards were wreathed in flames, agony as their skin
charred and blistered overpowering any thoughts of re-
taliation.

Eddie angled toward the gallows. Gausmann saw him
coming. With no gun of his own, the executioner turned
to run—but then lunged back at Nina to kick the stool
away—

A gunshot hit him in the chest. He fell between the two
scaffolds, one lashing foot missing the stool by barely an
inch.

Eddie ran to the gallows. He swung the ax, severing
the rope, then spun to catch his wife as she fell. "Whoa!
Got you."

"Eddie, oh my God!" Nina gasped as he dropped her
onto her feet. "I thought you were—*look out!*"

An armed Nazi barged through the panicked crowd.
His submachine gun came up—

Eddie sent the ax whirling across the gap to slam deep
into the man's rib cage. He fell backward, spewing gore.
The other Nazis around him fought even harder to get
away, trampling one another as the regimented crowd
broke up into a frantic scrum. One of the floodlight
towers toppled and fell as men were forced against it,

crushing several as it hit the ground, its bulbs exploding in showers of sparks. "You thought I was what?" he asked Nina, about to untie her hands before realizing they were handcuffed.

"I thought you were dead!"

"So did these arseholes, thank God. Where are the keys?"

Nina nodded toward the smoldering uniform jacket. "That guy's pocket."

Eddie started for it—then saw that Gausmann was not dead. The executioner's chest wound was gushing blood, but still he managed to lever himself onto his side . . .

To kick away Zane's stool.

A round from Eddie's pistol exploded from the back of Gausmann's skull—but the Israeli was already falling. He let out a strangled cry—

The rope jerked taut. The drop had been less than a foot, but it was enough to snap the noose tight. Zane's eyes bulged, and he thrashed helplessly as his throat was crushed by his own weight . . .

Eddie whipped up his gun and shot the rope.

The bullet hit the vibrating line just below the pulley. It snapped, but not fully—

Zane felt the impact. He kicked, hard, and the remaining strands broke. He dropped heavily to the ground.

Shouted orders from the crowd. Eddie saw a tall Nazi in a junior officer's uniform yelling to his underlings as he stabbed a finger over the dying flames at the Englishman. A counterattack would come at any moment . . .

Another gunshot turned the clock back by several seconds as the officer's brains splattered over the men behind him. Panic took hold of the mob once more.

Eddie snatched up the jacket, hearing a faint clink of metal. He pulled out a set of keys and ran back to Nina. "Here," he said, freeing her right wrist. He pushed the keys into her hand. "Unlock Jared."

She hurried to the slumped Israeli as Eddie used a foot to drag two Heckler & Koch MP5 submachine guns away from the burning guards. He kicked one to Zane as Nina released him, then collected the other. The weapon was hot from the fire, but not unbearably so. He fired a sweep into the crowd, sending a clutch of Nazis falling, then joined his wife. "Can you walk?" he asked Zane.

The Mossad agent grimaced as he sat up, collecting the MP5. "As long as I can shoot, I'll crawl if I have to."

"Running'd be better." The initial shock of the assault was fading; though most of the audience had fled the parade ground, he spotted Nazis now running back *into* the square—carrying weapons, metal glinting under the remaining floodlights.

Nina helped Zane stand. The Israeli had also seen the new threat and unleashed two bursts from his own weapon. Screams sounded above the hubbub as four more Nazis were cut down.

"Come on, this way." Eddie pointed toward where he had made his entrance, near the stage. "There's a place we can hide."

Nina saw another MP5 lying by one of the dead guards. "No, we need to find Banna!" she said as she snatched it up. Eddie's questioning gaze flicked between her and the gun. "If I see Kroll, I'm going to kill him," she told him. "He murdered Macy."

"I know." An exchange of grim looks, then they ran down a narrow passage between two buildings. "Where's Banna?"

"Kroll was forcing him to work at his house."

"Well, that's convenient—we can take out that fat bastard at the same time." Eddie looked around the corner. People were still running from the parade ground, but none was close by, the fires and gunshots having deterred anyone from coming in the direction of the stage. He heard the piercing shrill of whistles rising above the confusion—more junior officers trying to regroup their squads. "Where's the house?"

She pointed. "Over there."

Eddie hesitated—it would take them away from the red hut where Roland had told him to hide—but Nina was right: They had to find Banna. "Okay, come on."

They hurried through the settlement. Away from the

floodlights, the Enklave was not well lit. Keeping to the shadows, they made their way toward the houses. More whistles screeched behind them. "It won't be long before they come after us," Zane warned.

"Then we'd better be quick," Eddie replied as they crossed the railroad. "Which house?"

Nina pointed at Kroll's residence. "That one."

Lights were on inside. "I'm guessing that Banna'll be guarded." She nodded. "Be careful, then. Jared, you ready?"

The battered Israeli held up his MP5. "Yeah."

Eddie was first to the door. He waved for Nina to take cover to one side as Zane readied his weapon, then pushed it open, snapping up his own gun. Nobody was in the hall. "Okay, where?" he whispered.

"Second door on the left," Nina replied.

They entered. Eddie went to the door, about to kick it open . . . when he had another idea and rapped on the wood.

"What are you doing?" Zane whispered.

"Being polite."

"But—"

Eddie waved him to silence as a voice came from inside the room. *"Ja? Wer ist da?"*

"Das Flugzeug ist bereit! Es kann beladen werden," the Englishman replied, to mystification from his companions.

The guard inside the room was equally bewildered. *"Was?"* A creak of floorboards from the other side of the door, then it opened—

Eddie punched the surprised soldier hard in the face, sending him to the floor. A kick to the head knocked the Nazi out cold. *"Dummkopf,"* he told the unconscious man as he moved inside. No other guards—but Banna looked up in shock. Several maps of the Middle East and Iran were spread across the table, along with translations of the Greek texts and numerous notes.

"I didn't know you spoke German!" said Nina.

Her husband gave a wry smile. "I don't. One of the

Nazis says it in *Raiders of the Lost Ark*. No idea what it means, but I always thought it sounded cool."

Zane took up position to guard the entrance. "It means 'The plane is ready—'"

"Don't tell me!" Eddie protested. "It'll spoil it."

Banna hurried to Nina, shocked and relieved. "I— I thought they had killed you!"

"I'm okay," she said, greeting him with a brief embrace. "But we've got to get out of here." Though Banna was keen to leave, his face warned her that he had bad news. "What's wrong?"

"I . . . I located the spring. And I told Kroll where it is." The young man looked miserably at the floor. "I had no choice. I am sorry."

"Shit." Nina regarded the Egyptian's work in dismay. "What if we take all this? Can he find the spring without it?"

"I am afraid so. I showed him the location—here." He pointed at a spot on one of the more detailed maps. As the archaeologists had deduced earlier, it was in the Alborz mountains, below the Caspian coastline. "But . . ." His expression showed a flicker of hope.

"What?"

"The text on the relic—it said that after you pass through the Gate of Alexander, if you do what Andreas did, the fish will show you the spring."

"What does that mean?" asked Eddie.

Nina shook her head. "I don't know, but if Kroll doesn't have the fish, maybe he won't get to the spring either." There was no sign of the bronze artifact. "Where is it?"

"In his vault," Banna told her.

"Then we'd better get it." She hurried back to the door. "Eddie, this way. Kroll's got the Andreas relic in a safe."

"But he has the key," objected Banna.

"We can't let him take it." She went to the Nazi leader's study and opened the door.

"We could just kill the bastard," Eddie suggested as the others followed her—then froze when he saw the room's interior. "Fucking hell," he said in disgust, staring at the portrait of Hitler. "Definitely kill the bastard."

Nina pulled aside the swastika banner to reveal the vault door. "It's in here—and so's their supply of the water from the Spring of Immortality. Without it, they've got nothing."

"So how do we get it open?" asked Zane.

"I was kinda hoping Eddie had brought about half a ton of explosives with him."

Eddie shrugged apologetically. "Sorry, love. What you see is what you get."

"Yeah, I accepted that when I married you. But we've got to—"

A sound from the hall—someone entering the house. "Get back," Eddie whispered. Everyone moved to the study's periphery as he quietly closed the door.

Someone spoke in German: Kroll. The Nazi leader was angry, barking orders. *"Ja, mein Führer,"* said a subordinate, hurrying back outside.

Eddie brought up his gun—as did Zane, then Nina. The floorboards creaked as Kroll came toward the study. The Englishman gave Zane a look: Nobody had closed the door to the map room, and the unconscious soldier was lying in plain sight . . .

But Kroll walked past without pause. The door opened—

Eddie was about to greet him with his gun, but Nina beat him to it. "Don't fucking move," she snarled, pointing her MP5 at his head.

Kroll froze. "Dr. Wilde!"

"Yeah, that's right. And I'm sure you remember Jared."

Zane advanced on the obese Nazi. "I remember *you*," he said in a menacing tone.

"Go to the vault," Nina ordered. Kroll raised his hands and stepped into the room.

Eddie shut the door. "Ay up. So you're the leader of the master race, eh? Master bators, more like." He nodded at the portrait. "You'll need a wider frame than Shitler there to fit your gut in the picture."

"Who are you?" Kroll demanded.

"Eddie Chase. Nina's husband."

"But I was told you were . . . Of course. Did you kill Santos? Silva would never have dared betray me if he was alive."

"Shut up," Nina snapped. "I ought to kill *you* for what you did to Macy." The image of her friend's last moments came unbidden to her mind.

The dark glare turned upon her. "Then why do you not, Dr. Wilde?"

"Don't tempt me." She could—and she *should,* the desire for vengeance rising within her. All she had to do was pull the trigger . . .

"They'll hear the shots," Eddie warned, but that wasn't what stopped her. The Nazi leader was unarmed, defenseless. Just like his victims—but that would make her no better than him. Her face twisted with anger, but her forefinger did not move.

"I knew you could not," said Kroll smugly. "You are a product of your *modern* and *civilized* democracy." The words oozed sarcasm. "America and the United Nations are both the same—weak, degenerate, cowardly. Too squeamish to do what must be done."

Zane pressed his own gun against Kroll's head. "She may be. I am not. You know that I came here to kill you."

"No, you came here to *find* me, boy," the Nazi sneered. "To bring me to your so-called justice. You still *fear* us, don't you? Even after all this time. The Mossad does not hesitate to assassinate Arabs, Muslims, even Canadians—but Nazis, no, you dare not just murder us."

"You're right," said Zane, after a moment. "We don't murder Nazis. We make *examples* of them." He tilted his head to show the red ligature mark around his throat. "The last person to be executed in Israel was Adolf Eichmann. He was hanged. I've felt the rope around my neck—and I'll be there when you feel it too. Only you'll have no friends to rescue you."

"One man, in over fifty years," was Kroll's disdainful response. "The Mossad fears us more than we fear you—"

"Oh, bollocks to this," snapped Eddie. "This vault—how does it open?"

"There's a combination lock," Nina told him, "but he's also got a key. Around his neck."

Eddie reached under the folds of fat overflowing Kroll's collar to pull out the chain holding the key. A sharp tug, and it snapped. He put the key in the lock and turned it. A faint *clunk* came from the metal door, but it did not open. "All right, Das Bloat, what's the combination?"

"I will not tell you," said the Nazi.

The Englishman shrugged. "Okay, then I'll shoot you."

"And you will never open the vault." He gave the others a look of contempt. "The New Reich will still rise, even without me. You cannot change the course of history!"

"Oh, I don't know about that," Nina fired back. "I'm getting quite good at it—I've had a lot of practice. You still need Andreas's fish to find the Spring of Immortality—so if we take it and the last of your water, then even if you get to Iran, you're left with nothing."

"Except ulcers from worrying about Mossad catching you before Interpol does," added Eddie.

The Nazi leader was still defiant. "But you cannot open the vault. Even if you kill me, my men will soon come looking for me—you will have to leave here or die, and once you are gone, they will open the vault and find the spring."

Nina stared hard into the repulsive man's eyes, just as his gaze had once drilled into hers to seek hidden truths . . . and this time, it was she who caught a flicker of fear. "No," she said quietly, remembering something from her first visit to his study. "No, they won't."

"I assure you that they will!"

"I don't think so. You're the only one who knows the vault's combination, aren't you? You hid it from the others when you opened it before." Kroll tried to maintain his angry mask, but now the others saw the worry behind it. "That's how you keep your power, isn't it? You're the only one who can give them the water, so they *have* to follow your orders or they start getting older, just like everyone else. And you've all gotten so used to staying young, you can't bear the idea of aging."

"Even without me, they will open the vault soon enough," he growled.

"But only to get the water. Rasche and the others aren't as convinced by the legend as you, are they? Now that your hiding place has been exposed, they'll just take what they can and run. Your dream will die with you."

Kroll's silence spoke for him. Eddie pushed his gun against the German's head. "Okay, unless you think your magic water'll cure a bullet in the brain, you'd better open that fucking door in the next five seconds. *Fünf, vier, drei . . .*"

"*Englisch Schwein!*" the Nazi hissed—but he still reached to turn the combination dial. Eddie waited until he heard a click, then shoved Kroll away and pulled the handle.

The steel door swung open, revealing the treasures inside. "Not a bad collection," said the Englishman, seeing the glint of gold and jewels. "Alexander's was better, though."

"And Alexander's wasn't stolen," Nina added. Banna moved alongside her to gaze in wonderment at the relics. The metal fish was not in sight. "Okay, where is it?" Kroll said nothing. "Eddie, see that big jar at the back? Can you smash it?"

Eddie grinned. "Love to." He raised his gun.

"No, wait!" Kroll gasped. "I will get it."

"I'll watch him," said Zane. He pushed Kroll forward with his own weapon.

Nina and Banna moved to let the Nazi into the vault. Zane stood at the door, MP5 locked on to the obese man. Kroll licked his lips as he glanced back at the Israeli, then he lifted the twin of the Antikythera mechanism off a case and opened it to reveal the Andreas relic. "It is here," he croaked.

"Great," said Nina. "Bring it out."

He reached for the bronze fish—

"Herr Kroll!" called a voice from the hallway. "*Wir haben noch sie nicht gef—*"

The door opened, a harried man in his forties rushing in—only to stop in alarm at the sight of the intruders as they whirled to face him. He shouted a warning and groped for his holstered gun.

Eddie pushed Nina aside and fired. The new arrival fell backward in a spray of blood. Zane turned back to cover Kroll—

The astrolabe smacked hard against the Israeli's head. He stumbled away from the entrance. Eddie also spun, but Kroll had already dropped the mechanism and pulled the startled Banna to him as a human shield. The Nazi retreated into the vault, grabbing the door's inner handle and using his considerable weight to haul upon it.

Eddie took aim through the rapidly narrowing gap, but he couldn't shoot without hitting Banna. The last he saw of Kroll was a snarling half smile, then the door closed with a heavy bang.

Nina ran to the vault, hearing a rattle as the combination tumblers were reset from within. "Dammit! We've got to get it open!"

"There's no time," Zane said. Shouts came from outside the building as the Nazis reacted to the gunfire. "We need to get out of here!"

Eddie grabbed a chair and hurled it through the window. Wood and glass disintegrated. "Quick route," he said.

"But what about Ubayy?" said Nina, with a helpless look at the closed vault.

Zane ushered her to the new exit. "We can't help him."

Eddie knocked out the remaining daggers of glass, then climbed through to a lawn behind the house. Nina followed. "They've still got the relic!" she said. "They'll be able to use it to find the spring—"

"Herr Chase!" A strained whisper from nearby.

Eddie searched for the source, spotting movement behind a bush. "Roland?" he called.

The young man emerged from the shadows. He had changed into a Nazi uniform since the Englishman last saw him. "Yes! I went to the red hut, but when I saw you were not there, I thought you had either run for the ruins or come here after Herr Kroll." He regarded Nina grimly. "Dr. Wilde, what you told me, about Macy—it was true." A glance at his left arm—then he tore off the swastika armband and threw it aside.

"Yeah, it was," she replied as Zane landed behind her, "but we don't have time to talk about it." A crash from inside as the front door was kicked open.

"Follow me," said Roland, running down the lawn. The others hurried after him, Zane limping from his leg wound. "I know another hiding place."

A wooden fence surrounded the garden, but it was quickly vaulted. Eddie glanced toward the center of the compound, seeing men heading for the house. The Nazis had regrouped and were now out for vengeance. "Where do we go?"

"This way." The young blond led the way to the rear of a barn. The ground sloped away into a drainage ditch, exposing part of the structure's foundations. Roland went to a particular section of planking and pulled at it. The boards came away to reveal a dark space behind. "Under here."

Nina entered first, the men following her. Eddie went last, pulling the wood back into position. He crouched beside it, gun at the ready. Before long, he heard voices outside. Pale torchlight flashed through the cracks in the wall. He tensed as someone came closer . . . and passed, calling out in German before moving away.

"They did not see us," whispered Roland in relief. "I used to hide in here with Volker when we were children. No one ever found us."

"So now what?" asked Nina. "They'll still be looking for us, however long we wait."

"No—they are going to leave. Herr Kroll—*Kroll*," he corrected, pointedly removing the honorific, "told us at the rally that the Mossad has found the Enklave. Some wanted to stay to defend it, but he has ordered that we are to fly to the Middle East to find the Spring of Immortality. There will be airplanes at the dry lake in the morning."

"But the spring's in Iran," Nina objected. "How are they going to get to it? The Iranians won't exactly welcome a battalion of Nazis at Tehran airport with open arms."

"They won't be going to Tehran," said Zane. "Leitz—Kroll's broker—has the connections to get them into the country without anyone asking questions. He just has to pay off the right people—and with almost a hundred million dollars in the bank, Kroll can afford it."

"That's if they actually get to the planes," said Eddie, as a truck engine started to turn over. Even in the darkness, Nina could tell that he was smiling.

"What do you—" the Israeli began, only to be cut off by the flat *whump* of a fire suddenly igniting. Someone yelled in fear—then the cry was drowned out by an explosion that shook the barn's timbers. A moment later, the blast was followed by several more. Screams and cries echoed around the Enklave above the thunder of a fearsome blaze.

Nina jumped. "What was *that*?"

"Vehicle maintenance, SAS-style," Eddie replied, with distinct glee. "Amazing what you can do with some rewiring and a few cans of petrol."

"It will not stop them, though," said Roland. "They will get to the lake even if they have to march."

"They can't take much with them, though," said Nina.

Eddie had an unwelcome thought. "Unless they let the train take the strain . . ."

* * *

"*Mein Führer,*" said Rasche. The Nazi leader had opened the vault from inside, and two of his men were helping him out. "You are still alive. I am relieved."

"Yes, of course you are," Kroll growled, catching his subordinate's greedy glance over his shoulder at the pithos. He gestured at Banna. "Secure the Arab; I want him under constant guard. Have you caught them?"

"Not yet. Walther is leading the search, but there has been no sign of them in the compound. They must be making a run for the outer perimeter."

"They'll head for the town. Send men to intercept them."

Rasche looked pained. "The jeeps have been . . . sabotaged. So have the trucks."

"Sabotaged? How?"

"They exploded."

Kroll responded in much the same way. *"Exploded?"*

"Yes. The man who attacked the rally, Wilde's husband—he rigged them to detonate when the engines were started. We lost ten men in the fire. We can reach the airstrip on foot, of course, but we won't be able to take anything large or heavy." Another look at the vault's contents, this time with concern. "The jar—even with most of the water gone, it still weighs almost ninety kilos. And then there is the remaining gold—"

"We don't need it anymore. We have millions of dollars."

"*Leitz* has millions of dollars. Do you trust him that much?" The bald man's lack of an immediate answer spoke volumes. "Until the money is secure in our own accounts, we still need the gold. Perhaps we should divide our forces? You lead a contingent to Iran to search for the spring, while I evacuate a small group with the treasure and the water—"

"We stay together, Rasche," said Kroll, threat clear in his voice. "This is a key moment for the New Reich. If we falter now, we will fail—so we will continue exactly as planned. We will travel to Iran, find the Spring of Immortality—and take it for ourselves!"

Rasche tried to contain his frustration. "But how will we transport everything we need?"

"The train," Kroll snapped. "We'll use the train."

"But it hasn't run for, what, two years now? It might not be safe."

"Put the men, and as much equipment as will fit, aboard the train. Fire it up." When Rasche did not respond at once, he bellowed: "That is an order! Obey it, *now!*"

Rasche brought up his arm in an angry salute. "Yes, *mein Führer.*" He stalked from the room.

Kroll glared after him, then turned. Banna had been watching the German discussion in fearful incomprehension. "Now, Dr. Banna," the SS leader said in English, "you will take us to the Spring of Immortality."

29

Nina woke with a start. She had not imagined that she could fall asleep, her body still churning with fearful adrenaline, but in the darkness beneath the barn it had come upon her with surprising swiftness. It had been anything but restful, though, a swirl of nightmarish images. "What—" she gasped, before remembering the need for quiet. "What's happening?" she whispered. "How long was I asleep?"

"A few hours," said Eddie. She was lying against him, his arms around her. "Seemed like you needed it."

"I guess I did." She put her hands over his and turned her head so their cheeks touched. "I'm sorry."

"For what?"

"For not telling you how much I loved you when you left Egypt."

"Well, we *had* just had a fight."

"I know, but . . . When Kroll told me you were dead, I thought the last thing we'd ever said to each other was some stupid argument."

"Hey, I'm the one who should be apologizing," he replied. "I acted like a complete knob. *I'm* sorry." He shifted position to kiss her. "I'm just glad you're okay."

"I'm glad you came to find me."

"I always will, love."

Nothing more needed to be said for each to know how deeply the other felt. Another kiss, then she looked around at a hissing noise. "What's going on outside?"

"It's a steam train," he told her. "They're going to use it to take everyone out of here."

"Yeah, I saw it," she said, remembering the rust-covered tank engine from her arrival in the Enklave. "It didn't look like it had been used for years, though."

"They've been shunting stuff about, so it's still got a bit of life left in it. Mind you, they only have to get to the bottom of the hill and then they're done with it. So long as the brakes work, they could just bloody free-wheel it down there."

"We can't let them escape. They've got Ubayy, and the Andreas relic—they'll be able to find the spring."

Zane was looking through a crack between the planks. "I agree, but it's too dangerous to move right now. There are men everywhere. They're clearing the place out—right now they're taking things from Kroll's house."

"Probably everything from the vault," said Nina. She gently loosened Eddie's arms and shuffled across the low space to see for herself.

The view through the narrow gap was limited, but enough to show dawn breaking on the eastern horizon. Beyond the main dirt track running through the compound, the locomotive was now at the head of a train. A single passenger carriage was connected behind it, followed by a line of six wooden freight wagons. Men were loading the first and last of the trucks: assorted crates into the latter, boxed treasures and large metal drums into the former. The barrels were empty, but a flash from the top of one of them told her their purpose. The *Alexander Romance* described Andreas using a silver container, and the pithos in the vault had been lined with the precious metal; Kroll intended to store his new supply the same way.

She spotted the corpulent leader heading for the train. Instead of his SS uniform, he was now wearing an anonymous dark suit and overcoat. Most of his forces had likewise donned pale-brown fatigues lacking any kind of military insignia. "Looks like they're going to leave the country incognito."

"Well, marching through the airport in full Nazi regalia might be a bit noticeable," said Eddie, joining her.

An item of cargo caught Nina's attention. Unlike the others, this had not been crated up for transport. "It's the pithos," she said as two men carried the container across the road. "I knew that fat son of a bitch wouldn't leave it behind." Kroll stood beside the first freight wagon, watching as it was lifted inside and secured with ropes.

Eddie was more concerned with what was being put aboard the last truck. "Ay up," he muttered, nudging Zane. "They're ready for trouble." The Israeli whispered a curse as several long dark green wooden cases were loaded.

"What are they?" Nina asked.

"RPG-7s," her husband told her. "Rocket launchers. As well as machine guns, explosives, a shitload of ammo . . ."

"Oh, great. As if they didn't have enough firepower." The soldiers were all armed with MP5s. "Wait, there's Rasche."

The tall Nazi joined his commander as a man brought a case from the house. Kroll summoned him over; he opened it. Morning sunlight glinted off bronze within. "They've got the fish," she said.

"And Banna," Eddie added. Two soldiers escorted the archaeologist to the train. The Egyptian's head was low, his attitude of utter defeat clear even at a distance. The Nazis pushed him inside the lead carriage before following their prisoner aboard. "They must be about to move out."

Kroll gestured, and the soldier closed the case and loaded it onto the treasure wagon. Walther rounded a building, a large group of men following him. They assembled beside the train while the hulking German joined Rasche and Kroll. The latter began to shout commands.

"Ah, Scheiße!" gasped Roland. The young man scurried over to stare through the gap in the wood. Zane simultaneously reacted with alarm at the Nazi commander's words.

"What is it?" Nina asked.

"He's ordering them to burn the place down!" Zane replied. He listened as Kroll continued. " 'Leave nothing for the Argentine vultures and the rats of the Mossad . . .' They're taking the guns and the gold, and destroying everything else."

"They're not hanging about, either," said Eddie. The soldiers were already dispersing. They had been prepared for Kroll's order, igniting rags in the necks of Molotov cocktails. "Shit! I think it's time to move!"

He had barely finished speaking before a soldier ran to the barn above their hiding place and hurled a blazing bottle inside. It smashed against the rear wall, flames spraying outward. Light from above suddenly flooded the foundations. Burning fuel dripped through holes in the wooden floor.

More shattering glass and sounds of leaping fire came from outside as the Nazis spread out to obliterate what had been their home. "They will see us if we go out there," warned Roland.

"They'll *smell* us if we stay in here—we'll be a fucking barbecue," Eddie shot back. He scrambled to the entrance and forced the panel aside. Nobody was in sight. "Everyone out!"

The Yorkshireman exited first, then helped Nina through. Roland came next, holding in a yelp as a burning ember dropped onto his neck. Zane was last to leave, bringing up his MP5 as he got to his feet. "Where do we go?"

"Into the garden," said Eddie, gesturing at Kroll's residence. It was already ablaze, flames rising from the ground floor, and the houses of the other Nazi leaders were going the same way. "They won't go back to somewhere they've already set alight, and if we stay behind the fence, nobody'll see us." They hurried along the rear of the barn. "Plus we can keep an eye on the train from there."

Roland stared in disbelief as they got a wider view of

the Enklave. "They are really burning it down," he said, dismayed. "Everything . . ."

"Good riddance," said Eddie as he helped Nina into the garden. Zane and Roland climbed after them. "I just wish those bastards were still inside."

Zane moved into the bushes, cautiously peering over the fence at the railway. "Eddie, look at this."

Eddie took in the scene. Against a hellish backdrop of flames and smoke, the Nazi soldiers were returning to the waiting train. Kroll clambered into the first carriage, the elderly vehicle rocking on its twin bogies as his weight unbalanced it. Walther entered after him, leaving Rasche to oversee the troops.

It was the remaining Nazi leader, Schneider, who caught his attention, though. "What's that slimy bastard doing?" The round-faced SS man was talking to a small group of women—some of whom, Eddie saw, were pregnant. "Roland, c'mere. Are they who you told me about?"

The young man joined him. "Yes. But I cannot hear what he is saying to them."

"Whatever it is, they don't like it." Some of the women reacted with shock and even tears to Schneider's words, one running to him with her hands clasped together. The oldest of the group, pinch-faced, with her graying hair drawn into a severe bun above her SS uniform, yanked her back, then slapped her across the face. "Jesus!"

"That is Dagmar Metzger—she is the head of the *Kindermädchen*," said Roland.

"You don't sound surprised that she's smacking a pregnant woman around."

"She is in charge of discipline in the *Kinderhaus*. All the children fear her." He gave Eddie a somewhat shamefaced look. "So do the men who grew up under her."

The Englishman frowned as Schneider spoke to the now weeping young woman, patting her shoulder . . . then slipping his fingers through her hair and caressing it. "Creepy little shit," he muttered.

"Herr Schneider takes . . . personal care of all the women in the Enklave," said Roland, his dawning dismay suggesting that he had never thought to consider that anything but normal until now.

"Yeah, I bet he does," said the disgusted Nina. Metzger exchanged words with Schneider, then gave him a Nazi salute and snapped orders to the five younger women. All were now crying, the one who had been slapped close to hysteria. The leader of the *Kindermädchen* ignored their tears, pointing across the Enklave, and they set off with deep reluctance, Metzger practically dragging the weeping woman. "Where are they going?"

Roland stared after them. "The *Kinderhaus* is in that direction . . ." The sudden horror in his voice drew all eyes to him. "No, they would not. They would not!"

"They wouldn't what?" Nina asked.

"The children—they must still be in the *Kinderhaus*!"

"Jesus Christ, they're going to burn the fucking place down with the kids inside it!" Eddie realized. "That's why that girl was crying—they've just been told to kill their babies!"

Nina stared after the departed women in shock. "Oh my God! We've got to stop them!"

"No, Kroll and the others are about to leave," protested Zane. The Nazis had now organized themselves into groups of around twenty beside each of the four empty wooden wagons. Schneider joined Rasche as the soldiers began to climb aboard. "We have to go after them."

"They're still watching out for us," Eddie warned. Several men were guarding the train. "We won't get close—and there must be ninety of them against four of us."

"I know, but—" The Israeli stopped as the locomotive's whistle echoed across the compound. All the men bar the guards had now squeezed into the trucks. Rasche and Schneider boarded the carriage. The train edged forward, the wagons clattering against one another. The sentries kept pace, first walking before starting to jog as the huffing old locomotive gradually picked up speed. "We can't let them escape!"

"They can't go that fast," said Eddie, fighting his own urge to pursue the Nazis. "I saw the track on the way up—the hairpins are so tight, they'll have to slow right down to get around them." He turned to Roland. "Can we get to this house without being seen?" The blond man nodded. "Okay, let's do it." He started down the garden, Roland and Nina following.

Zane didn't move. "Dammit, Eddie!"

"We can still catch up," the Englishman insisted.

"These are kids we're talking about, Jared!" said Nina. "We can't let them burn them alive!" The Mossad agent clenched his jaw, aggrieved, then hurried after them.

They vaulted the fence, giving the barn a wide berth as its roof collapsed. Eddie checked the dirt road bisecting the compound for stragglers. There were none, and as he glanced along the railway, he saw the last guards being pulled aboard the train. "Okay, we're clear. Roland?"

The young man pointed past the fire-racked barracks. "That way."

They rounded the inferno, the white-painted block of the *Kinderhaus* coming into view ahead. "Shit, we're too late!" Nina gasped. Smoke was already rising from within.

The women were outside the main entrance, which was being secured by Metzger, closing a padlock on a length of chain. One of the younger women desperately tried to push her away, but was thrown to the ground. Another rushed at her—only to stumble back as Metzger drew a Luger and shouted at her, daring the others to advance.

A scream from inside, the cry of a frightened child. More rose behind it. "God, they're dying in there!" said Nina. "We've got to do something!"

Zane snapped up his MP5 and fired. Metzger fell backward as a bullet hole burst open in her chest. "Done."

"Okay, straight to the point," said Eddie as he and Roland ran to the building.

The remaining women regarded the pair with shock and fear. Roland spoke urgently to them in German. "There are twelve children and three of the *Zucht-Fr—*

the other three women trapped inside," he told Eddie as Zane and Nina caught up.

"Get 'em back," the Yorkshireman replied, raising his pistol. A single shot, and the chain snapped. He kicked the doors open. Smoke gushed out—followed by several panicked children, ranging in age from around five to eleven. He did a rapid head count. "Okay, that's eight! Where are the rest?"

"They are too young to get out on their own!" shouted Roland. He ran inside.

Eddie raced after him, holding a hand to his mouth and nose. The smoke was getting thicker, weaving lines of flame on the floor where fuel had been poured. "What about the other women?"

"Down there!" A side passage led off the main corridor. Roland went to a door opposite. "The children are in here!"

"You get them, I'll get the women." Eddie hopped over a track of fire and went down the passage. There was a door at the end with a small barred window. He looked through to see a dimly lit cross between hospital ward and prison cell. Three beds occupied it. Each held a woman, wrists and ankles buckled to the metal frame. Two were visibly pregnant. The one nearest the door turned her head to regard him blankly, the others not responding to his appearance or the chaos outside. Drugged.

He unbolted the door. "Jared! I need some help here!"

The Israeli ran in as he started to unfasten the first woman. "The fire's getting worse," Zane warned. "If we stay in here much longer, we won't get out."

"Then bloody hurry up and help me!" The buckles came free. Eddie pulled the woman upright, getting only a vacant stare in response. "Shit, she can't even walk. We'll have to carry 'em."

"There are three of them and only two of us," Zane pointed out as he released the second prisoner.

"Yeah, I *can* count!" He lifted the limp woman over his shoulder and headed out as quickly as he could.

Roland emerged from the nursery ahead of him, a crying baby in each arm. A blond girl of about three followed, only to cower fearfully back from the flames. "Get them outside!" Eddie ordered as the young man hesitated, about to return for her. The Englishman altered course, hopping over the fire to scoop the child up with his free arm. Holding his breath as more smoke swirled around him, he jumped back, now passing through rather than over the growing blaze. "You said there were four kids! Where's the other one?"

Roland coughed violently before replying. "Still inside— I could not carry them all!"

Nina ran down the corridor. "I'll get it!" she cried.

"No, it's too dangerous!" Eddie shouted, but she was already past him. "For fuck's—I mean, flip's sake," he said as the little girl gawped at him. Roland reached the doors; Eddie hurried after him, emerging to find the five *Kindermädchen* waiting. They took the babies with tears of joy and relief. He deposited the girl on the ground, then put the pregnant woman down.

Roland was still coughing, bent almost double. Whatever he had inhaled, Nina had just run straight into it. Eddie took several deep lungfuls of clean air before charging back inside.

The flames were spreading across the passage. Zane came around the corner, carrying the second captive woman. "I freed the last one for you!" the Israeli said as they passed.

Eddie didn't reply, pausing to squint through the darkening cloud at the nursery door. He heard a baby screaming, but the smoke blocked his view of everything inside—except the shimmering glow of flames. "Nina! Get out of there!"

Nina wanted to do exactly that. The nursery was full of acrid black smoke; something made of plastic had caught light. But the baby's terrified cries forced her deeper into the miasma. Almost blinded, she held her breath and felt her way toward the source of the noise, bumping against cribs before reaching the last occupied one.

The baby squirmed as she picked it up. It weighed at

least twenty pounds, probably close to a year old. "Okay, I got you," she cooed, trying to calm the child as she turned—

A loud crunch of breaking wood—and she jumped back as a flame-wreathed ceiling beam smashed down in front of her. "Jesus!"

One end of it had landed on a piece of furniture. The burning beam lay at an angle, too high to climb over and too low to crawl under.

She was trapped—

A shape appeared through the haze behind the barrier— Eddie, carrying another pregnant woman. "Nina, get back!"

She jumped away as he kicked the bed supporting the blazing joist. Already damaged by the falling timber, its legs collapsed under the blow. The beam pounded to the floor, spraying out cinders.

But the way out was now clear, if only for a moment as the flames thrashed and wafted in the displaced air. She summoned up her courage, then made a running jump over the obstacle. The fire lashed back up behind her as if realizing it was about to lose its prey, scorching her legs, but too late.

"Come on!" Eddie gasped. He waited for Nina to pass, then followed her out.

The fire in the corridor had risen higher. Nina shrieked as she jumped through it, flames licking at her bare arms. The rectangle of daylight ahead was almost totally obscured by smoke. She bent down, trying to hold her breath as she raced for the exit. Floorboards cracked underfoot as the blaze ate through them. She almost stumbled, barely staying upright as she sprinted the last few yards—

She burst into the open, choking smoke suddenly replaced by clear air. Eddie was right with her. A moment later, ash and sparks erupted behind them as the ceiling crashed down.

Zane and Roland were waiting with the women at a safe distance. "Eddie!" shouted the Israeli. "Are you okay?"

"Fine—if I was a charcoal briquette," Eddie replied, coughing. "Did we get 'em all out?"

"We did," said Roland with relief.

The Englishman looked at his wife, and the baby she was holding. "You know, that suits you." Nina gave him a soot-smudged smile.

One of the women ran to her. She took the baby and clutched it tightly. *"Danke,"* she cried, in tears. "Thank you!"

"I'd say *my pleasure,* but, well," Nina replied breathlessly, before going to her husband. He put down the last rescuee, the others hurrying to check that she was all right. "Eddie! Thank God."

"You okay?" he asked.

"I'm gonna need a couple of gallons of witch hazel," she said, her arms reddened and sore. "And now I know what it's like to be a sixty-a-day smoker. But yeah, it won't be smoke inhalation that kills me." She touched her side, feeling the eitr infection through her grubby clothing.

"We can't waste any more time," said Zane. "We've got to stop the Nazis."

"How are we gonna catch them?" Nina asked wearily. "Eddie blew up all their trucks."

"I've got an idea," Eddie said. "Roland, will this lot be okay?"

"Yes, I think so," the youth replied.

"Good. You need to go down to the town—there's a cop called Miranda, tell him what's happened and get him to bring in the feds, and Interpol. They'll want to go through this place."

"What's left of it," said Nina, taking in the burning buildings.

Roland nodded. "What are you going to do?"

Eddie gave him a tired grin. "Catch a train. Nina, Jared, come on."

"Where are we going?" Nina asked as they started back through the Enklave.

"The railway. There was a brake van on one of the sidings—a caboose, I think you call 'em. They'd use it to slow down the train when they took whatever they mined here down the hill. Hopefully it'll still slow *us* down if we can get it moving."

They reached the tracks, passing the line of rusting ore trucks to find the little wagon standing alone on a spur. It was barely more than a wooden box on wheels, short verandas overhanging each end. The glass in the windows had long since broken, leaving it largely open to the elements. Eddie hopped up to find that the interior was as functional as the outside, a bench beside a corroded iron pedestal. A large metal wheel was mounted flat at its top. "Okay, I'm guessing this is the brake," he said, straining to turn it. There was a shrill of metal, and the van shuddered as long-locked brake shoes were released.

Zane regarded him dubiously. "What *exactly* are you planning, Eddie?"

The Englishman looked down the track. "The plain's on a slope. Once we get this thing rolling, it should freewheel after the train—all we've got to do is slow it down on the curves so it doesn't fly off the track." He saw the Israeli's increasingly skeptical expression. "It's either that or *run* after the fucking train. And from the way you were limping, that's probably not what you want to do."

Nina was equally uncertain. "Are you sure this'll work?"

"It's our only chance of rescuing Banna and getting that fish." He jumped back down and went to the van's rear. "We need to push it."

He leaned against the chassis beside the coupler and braced his feet against a sleeper. A metallic groan came from the wheels. "It probably hasn't been moved in years," said Nina as she joined him.

"Shame we don't have a bucket of WD-40," he replied. "Okay, get ready—and *push*!"

She added her weight to his. Another moan as rusty parts scraped against each other, but this time the van shifted, inching down the narrow track. "That's it!" Eddie grunted. "Jared, give us a hand!"

Zane reluctantly took up position beside them. With all three of them driving it on, the brake van gradually picked up speed. The noise from the axles faded as the surface layer of rust on the wheel bearings was ground away. Eddie glanced around the side of the wagon. "Points coming up," he warned as it trundled toward an intersection. "Once we're through 'em, it should be clear to go."

The van rocked alarmingly, wheels screeching as it crossed onto the main line. Nina cringed at the noise, but kept pushing. "Whoa, it's rolling!" she said as she realized her effort was now more about keeping up with the caboose than forcing it onward.

"Get on, quick!" Eddie hopped aboard, then pulled Nina onto the rear veranda.

Zane swung himself up. "Will it go fast enough to catch them?"

"It'd better," Eddie replied as the brake van rumbled down the line. "'Cause after everything they've done, I'm not letting those bastards get away."

30

Nina looked ahead. The train was out of sight, but a drifting line of smoke revealed its position over the crest of the hill. "They must be a mile ahead of us by now. We'll never catch up!"

"We will," said Eddie. Expansion gaps between each section of the old rails made a loud *ka-clack!* as the brake van's wheels passed over them—and the time between each noise was gradually shrinking. The truck was already at running pace. "I doubt that train gets much above twenty on the straights, and it'll have to slow down even more on the curves."

"And what about when *we* go around the curves?" Zane asked, eyeing the brake wheel.

"Well, we'll figure that out at the first one, won't we?" He joined Nina, looking down the line.

"So when we catch up with them—assuming we even stay on the track—then what?" she asked.

"If we can match speeds without being seen, this thing should automatically hook onto the back of the train." He pointed at the coupler. "Then I can climb aboard and go along the roof to get Banna and that fish."

"And if they see us?"

"Plan B."

"Which is?"

"Buggered if I know. But it'll probably involve shooting." He watched the empty farmland roll past. "Ay up. We're definitely getting faster." Twenty miles per hour, he estimated, and the wheels' metallic chatter was becoming more frantic.

The track curved away to the right, heading for the first hairpin at the top of the long descent to the plain. The Nazis' train was indeed only crawling, the stem of the wafting smoke plume moving slowly across the plateau's edge to their left. Eddie thought back to his ascent with Julieta. "You know something? If they're going that slow, we can get *ahead* of them."

"How?" Zane asked.

"They're still only on the first leg of the track. If someone jumps off, they can run down the hill and get in front of them on the second one. Maybe chuck a big rock on the track and try to derail them."

"By 'someone,' you mean you, right?" Nina said dubiously.

"Jared's leg's pretty knackered, so yeah. Unless you want to?"

"That would be a big no, but I don't want you to do it either."

"We've got to stop that train somehow."

Zane limped to the front of the wagon. "He's right. And even if he can't do it at the first turn, he can still go down to one below and try again. Better decide soon, though," he added. The van was still gaining speed, the first hairpin coming into view ahead.

"Slow us down," Eddie decided, pointing at the wheel. "I'll jump as we go around the corner. Soon as you're clear, take off the brake and let it freewheel until you come to the next turn. You should catch up with the train pretty fast." He checked his MP5, finding it almost empty. "Jared, top up with this," he said, tossing the magazine to the Israeli. Dropping the empty submachine gun, he secured his pistol inside his jacket and took up position, ready to leap off.

"Eddie, this is crazy," Nina protested.

"No change there, then." The brake van was now doing over twenty-five miles per hour, the ground blurring below. "Okay, Jared, you ready?"

The Mossad agent finished reloading and went to the brake. "When you are."

"All right, start slowing us down. Not too much, though—you need enough speed when you come out of the bend to keep going."

Nina went to her husband. "Eddie."

"What?"

"Don't die. Please. I can't lose anyone else."

He turned away from the approaching curve to meet her eyes, then kissed her. "You're stuck with me until the end," he promised.

"I'd better be," she replied, managing a faint smile.

"We're almost there—get ready," Zane warned. Nina withdrew, holding a handrail as Eddie prepared to jump. "Okay . . . I'm slowing us down." He turned the brake wheel.

Nothing happened.

Nina looked at him with concern. "Anytime you like. Although preferably now."

He spun it through another two turns. "It's not working!"

The wagon went faster as the slope steepened. "Shit!" Eddie cried. "We're *all* gonna have to jump—"

"No, wait!" The Israeli kept spinning the wheel—and finally felt resistance. The van juddered as the rusty brake shoes scraped the wheel rims.

Eddie flinched as sparks sprayed out below him—then cringed at an earsplitting screech of metal. "Jesus Christ!"

Nina braced herself against the side wall so she could clap both hands to her ears. "So much for the element of surprise!"

Gripping the brake with both hands, Zane had no way to muffle the noise. All he could do was grimace as he pulled harder. The van didn't slow, but the noise became even louder.

"Too fast, too fast!" Eddie shouted over the piercing

cacophony. "It'll fly off the track!" The first turn was approaching, the ground beyond falling away.

Zane hauled on the wheel with his full weight. The corroded brakes finally bit—and he staggered as the wagon abruptly slowed. Nina shrieked as the deceleration threw her forward. Eddie clung on, more sparks spitting at his boots.

Centrifugal force suddenly caught everyone as the van swung around the hairpin bend—too fast—and started to tip over, top-heavy on the narrow track . . .

Zane kept up the pressure. The brakes clamped more tightly—and the caboose jolted back upright as it sloughed off more speed around the turn. Nina could see the back end of the train in the distance as it rounded the second reverse.

Eddie jumped—

He landed on his feet—and immediately wished he hadn't.

The hillside below the track was much steeper than he had expected. "Whoa, shit, *shit*!" he yelped as he ran headlong down it. If he tried to stop, he would fall and tumble down the hillside, with a good chance of seriously injuring himself by smacking into a rock or tree. He had to find a shallower gradient to slow down safely . . .

But the slope only got steeper. The railway's next leg came into view below—and he realized with horror that it had been cut into the hillside. He was approaching a near-vertical drop of around fifteen feet. Whether he ran or rolled, he would hurtle right over it—

A small stand of shrubs and trees off to the left overhung the cutting. Eddie angled toward them, boots skidding on the gritty topsoil as he fought to stay upright. The bushes might be strong enough to catch him.

Might be. But he was out of options.

He careered toward the vegetation. Get ready, and *drop*—

He deliberately fell onto his left side. Even prepared, the impact still hurt as he bounced off the ground and was pitched down the slope like a barrel. Through the crazy blur of his vision he saw the bushes rushing at him.

Eddie closed his eyes, arms up to shield his head—

He hit the first bush—and it disintegrated in an explosion of dry wood, not slowing him in the slightest.

The one below it fared no better, ripping from the ground as he grabbed at it, but it did at least arrest his roll. He slithered downhill on his back, the cutting looming below as he whipped under a tree at its edge . . .

He stamped both feet down as hard as he could—and launched himself into the air as the ground fell away.

Branches lashed at him. A thicker bough hit his chest; winded, he clutched his arms tightly around it. A moment's dizziness as he was whiplashed back and forth, then he came to rest, entangled in the foliage with broken twigs digging painfully into his flesh. The railway line was directly below his precarious position.

He clung on, catching his breath—then looked up in alarm at the sound of gunfire.

. . .

The shriek of brakes had drawn the attention of everyone in the lead carriage. "What was that?" Kroll demanded, looking back up the hillside.

"There," snapped Rasche, pointing. The train had just negotiated the second hairpin—but the Nazis saw the loose wagon coming down the first long leg of track above them.

"It'll crash into us!" said Schneider as the brake van picked up speed.

"No," said Kroll. "Someone's aboard it." He turned to Banna, who was seated between his guards at the front of the compartment. "Your friends are trying to rescue you," he said in English. The Egyptian's momentary relief vanished as he added: "They won't reach us. Walther!"

"Sir!" said the huge man.

"Tell the men to shoot at that wagon as it goes past. I want everyone aboard it *dead*!"

* * *

"Jared, they know we're here," Nina warned. The train had exited the loop and was now coming back down the leg of track below—and she saw Walther lean from the first coach to bellow orders at those in the wagons behind him. Men with submachine guns appeared in the open doors. "Shit, they're going to shoot at us!"

"Get behind the brake wheel and stay low," ordered Zane, hurrying to the front. "They're aiming up at us— the floor should give you some protection."

She took his advice. "So what are you doing?"

"Shooting first!" He lined up his weapon on the approaching train—and opened fire, sending a sweeping spray of bullets along its side.

Windows in the carriage shattered, splinters flying from the flanks of the wooden wagons behind it. One Nazi was hit in the chest and fell backward among his fellows, another toppling out with a scream. The steep slope threw him back under the wheels, spraying the two rearmost trucks with blood.

Zane kept firing as the train passed below, a third man falling as a wound burst open in his abdomen—but then a hollow clack came from his MP5 as the magazine ran dry. "Down!"

Nina dropped flat, the Israeli hunching beside her as automatic weapons opened up. Bullets ripped through the old wooden walls, flinders stabbing at the pair. The heavy steel chassis clanged as rounds struck it hammer blows from below. Then the gunfire tapered off, a few final shots hitting the rear of the van before it rolled beyond the Nazis' firing angle.

Nina's relief was short-lived as Zane saw the turn coming up ahead. "*Harah!*" he gasped. "The brake!"

They both leapt up and grabbed the wheel, forcing it around. Another hideous shriek assaulted their ears. The van slowed as it reached the tight bend, but barely enough. Even braced, Zane still struggled to stay standing, while Nina would have been thrown against the wall if not for her white-knuckled grip on the brake as the wagon hurtled around the hairpin.

A harsh clatter over the metallic squeal—then a loud bang as something hit the van's underside before bouncing away down the hillside. "That was one of the brakes," said Zane, still holding the wheel in place.

Nina tried to push it back. "Let go—we've got to catch up!" They had come around onto the second leg of the descent, the train pulling away from them farther down the track.

A disbelieving look. "We might not be able to stop."

"The brakes are still working!" That she had to shout over the shrill was proof enough. "Come on, speed us up!"

Zane reluctantly released the wheel. The noise stopped, and the brake van ran freely once more. The Israeli swapped his empty MP5 for Nina's, while she went to the front, watching as the distance to the train began to shrink.

. . .

Eddie finally extricated himself from the tangle of branches. He checked that he still had his gun, then prepared to drop. The shooting had stopped; all he could hear now was the clank and huff of the train.

Which was getting louder, and louder—

He looked up the track—and saw the locomotive coming right at him.

If he stayed in the tree, he would be blasted by superheated steam. But if he fell to the track, he wouldn't have time to scramble clear before the train mowed him down . . .

He kept hold for a couple more seconds, then dropped—

He landed with a heavy clang on the front footplate, just above the cowcatcher. He grabbed the boiler for support, immediately regretting it as the hot metal scalded his hands. Yelping, he let go and twisted to grip the footplate's edge.

The heat radiating from the smokebox was almost unbearable. He leaned over until he could peer around the blocky water tank on the boiler's side. The line's gentle curve revealed the single passenger carriage and six wagons trailing the engine.

Some distance behind, he saw the brake van rolling in pursuit. But the Nazis had also spotted it. Walther shouted orders from the carriage, the commands relayed back along each wagon until they reached the second-to-last car. A man in its open door waved to signal understanding, then he and another Nazi started to clamber back along the side of the truck.

Eddie realized what they were doing. The last wagon contained heavy equipment—and heavy *weapons*.

He tugged a sleeve over his palm before taking hold of the edge of the smokebox and reaching with his other hand for the water tank. Grimacing at the heat, he maneuvered himself around the front of the boiler.

The footplate above the wheels was narrow, the overhanging tank making it all the harder for him to maintain a toehold as he shuffled sideways. Machinery pounded beneath him, jets of steam hissing from the cylinder and the valve gear slicing back and forth just below his feet. The poor condition of the track amplified the locomotive's rocking motion—a particularly severe jolt made him slip, the toe of one boot skipping off a wheel before he jerked it away. One second later, and the connecting rod would have sliced his foot off.

Heart pounding, he continued onward. Movement through the grubby round window in the cab's face—the fireman's head swinging repeatedly in and out of view as he shoveled coal into the furnace.

The two Nazis reached the ammo wagon, one hanging from a railing as he fumbled to release the door's catch. The brake van was still steadily closing. Eddie glimpsed a pale face inside it: Nina.

The threat to her life spurred him on. He changed tack, pressing both hands flat on the top of the tank and taking all his weight on his arms as he swung himself along the footplate. Walther leaned from the first carriage again, barely twenty feet away, but he was looking rearward. The ammo truck's door finally opened. The first Nazi ducked inside, his companion clambering along the wagon's flank to follow him.

Open an RPG-7's crate, prep the launcher, load the round, take aim, fire; Eddie knew from experience that it was neither a complicated nor a time-consuming process. He moved even faster, at last reaching the cab. Grabbing a handrail, he hauled himself into its open side.

The fireman's back was to him—but the driver reacted to the intruder with alarm. He reached for an overhanging chain to sound the whistle in warning—

Eddie didn't have time to get his gun. Instead, he shoulder-barged the fireman. The man squawked, dropping his shovel as he collided with the driver. They caught the throttle lever, pulling it open. More steam rushed into the cylinders, and the locomotive lurched and gained speed.

The Englishman drew his weapon—but the driver pushed the fireman back at him. The impact knocked the pistol from Eddie's hand. It landed among the spilled coals at their feet.

Eddie drove the fireman back across the cab in a third volley of human Ping-Pong. This time, the Nazi staggered in front of the firebox—and a tongue of flame from the open hatch caught his leg.

Even with fireproof clothing, the heat made the man scream. He jumped away—only to be hammered into unconsciousness as Eddie snatched up the shovel and smacked the blade against the back of his head. The fireman crumpled, his head landing in the mouth of the furnace and instantly being swallowed by a ball of greasy flames.

The driver recoiled in horror—then made another lunge for the chain. Eddie whipped the shovel at him, catching the other man a solid blow, but too late. The whistle shrilled.

He hit the Nazi again, sending him spinning against the firebox, then threw the shovel down to grapple him. "Woo-woo, fuckface!" he growled, repeatedly pounding the man's head against the unyielding metal of the controls. Blood spouted on the third strike; he let go, and the driver collapsed beside the burning fireman.

The engine shuddered. Eddie glanced through a port-hole to see the hairpin approaching with alarming speed. He was tempted to leave the throttle wide open and send the whole train flying off the track with all the Nazis aboard, but then remembered that Banna was still a prisoner. With a muttered curse, he pushed the lever back to roughly its original position; stopping the train would be suicide, as he would be swarmed by soldiers.

It was still moving too fast for the turn, though. The wheels screamed as the engine entered the hairpin, coal skittering across the footplate. Eddie grabbed his gun before it followed the black chunks out of the cab's open side. Behind, the carriage shimmied on its twin bogies, throwing its occupants around in their seats. The four-wheeled wagons were affected even more as the vibrations snaked along the length of the train. One man was flung from an open door, cartwheeling down the hill before a boulder brought him to a skull-cracking stop.

The locomotive slowed, the sheer weight of iron and steel holding it on the track. Eddie looked across the hairpin at the rest of the train. The soldiers who had entered the ammo car came back into view at its open door. One held an RPG-7 launcher, hoisting the metal tube onto his shoulder and leaning out, his companion holding on to him as he prepared to fire.

He took aim, forefinger finding the trigger . . .

Eddie's own finger was faster.

Most of his shots from the rocking locomotive hit only wood—but one found its target, sending a spurt of red over the launcher as the Nazi's cheek blew apart.

The man fell back into the wagon—reflexively pulling the trigger.

The RPG-7 round burst from its tube, propelled by its initial booster charge. It hit the stacked crates in the ammo truck, bouncing off—then the main rocket fired. The wagon's interior filled with flames as the warhead ricocheted in the confined space.

The second man dropped and shielded his face as the grenade whirled past and wedged between two crates, fire spewing from its tail. The warhead was impact-detonated, but it had hit the boxes before arming itself.

The Nazi realized what had happened. He scrambled over and grabbed the squirming projectile by its conical warhead, struggling against the rocket's force to hurl it through the open door—

The motor burned out—and its self-destruct activated.

The warhead exploded in his hand, ripping the wagon open. Planks and panels scattered along the track. Part of a wall fell outward, only a buckled metal support keeping it attached as it dragged along the ground.

Wind fanned the flames. Cracks and thumps came from burning boxes as the ammunition inside cooked off and exploded. A flaming case fell from the open side, rolling to a stop inside the hairpin. Bullets ripped through the wood and thudded against the train. One man was hit in the stomach and collapsed with a scream.

Walther, however, was only concerned about the rounds from a much closer source. He looked toward the locomotive. *"Es ist die Englander!"*

Eddie fired again, but the huge Nazi jerked back into the carriage, the bullet blasting a chunk from the window frame. "Shit!"

"Scheiße!" gasped Walther, staring at the broken wood where his head had just been. "He's in the engine—he must have killed the drivers!"

Kroll glared at him. "So kill *him*!"

"What about the others behind us?" Rasche demanded. The brake van came back into view on the leg of track above them as the train exited the hairpin.

"Tell the men to keep shooting—no, wait!" The obese Nazi twisted in his seat, glimpsing the wrecked and burning ammo truck before it was blocked from his view by the rest of the train. "Detach the rear car! It's dragging on the ground; they'll crash into it!"

Rasche shouted the order to the men behind, while Walther brought up his gun.

* * *

"Don't shoot, don't shoot!" Nina cried as Zane prepared to strafe the train again. "You might hit Eddie!"

"Where is he?"

"Where do you think?" She pointed at the locomotive. A familiar stocky, balding figure stood in the cab.

The Israeli made a *tsk!* sound, then redirected his aim at the Nazis in the wagons. "Is it okay if I shoot *them*?"

"Go right ahead—wait, what're they doing?" A command had been passed down the train, and now a man was being hoisted from the door of the second-to-last truck by the others inside. He clambered onto the roof, then hurried along it to climb down into the gap in front of the ammo car. "Shit! They're going to uncouple it!" A moment later, the burning wagon separated from the train, rapidly falling behind as the smashed bodywork scraped along the track bed like an anchor.

Zane fired, the climber falling and being run over by the ammo truck, then darted to the brake wheel. "We've got to stop! If we hit it—"

"I'm not leaving Eddie!" said Nina.

Her determined, anguished face told the Mossad agent that the only way she would abandon her husband would be if she were unconscious, or dead. Unwilling to put her into either state, he nevertheless took hold of the brake control. "If we don't, we'll never make it around the next bend."

Nina took in the track below. "Slow us down—but don't stop," she told Zane as she moved to the compartment's left side to act as a counterweight. "I've got an idea."

He turned the wheel. The remaining brake shoes closed, sparks flying again. "What?" he shouted over the noise.

"If we're still moving fast enough when we catch up with that truck, we'll ram it right off the track!"

"Or *we* might go right off the track—or it could blow up and take us with it!"

"Just do it," she ordered. Zane gave her a somewhat sarcastic *yes, ma'am* look.

The van entered the tight left hairpin—faster than before. Both its passengers had to strain to stay upright. Stray rounds from the burning ammo box struck wood, Zane flinching as one seared past his head.

The wheels on the inside of the bend skipped along the rail as the van tipped. The Israeli turned beseechingly toward Nina, wanting to brake harder, but she shook her head. "Keep going! We're almost—"

The vehicle lurched as the rusted track buckled under the stress. Nina shrieked and lost her footing. Both inside wheels left the ground, the wagon starting to overturn—

Zane let go of the brake and threw himself at the inside wall. The impact and shift in weight arrested the van's roll . . . then it fell back down, kicking up a huge burst of sparks as the wheels hit the rail, and flew out of the curve like a slingshot stone. Nina and Zane exchanged relieved glances—which vanished as they remembered what was waiting for them.

He jumped up to look ahead—and immediately dived back to the floor. Nina took his hint and did the same—

The brake van rammed the trundling ammo truck, the latter's dragging bodywork tearing away as the collision propelled it forward. The two couplers locked together—and the wagons raced down the hill after the train with ever-increasing speed.

Nina raised her head to see the less-than-ideal result of her plan. "Buggeration and fuckery!"

* * *

Eddie saw the brake van almost overturn on the loop, but then his view was blocked by the passenger carriage. A glance from the cab reassured him that Nina and Zane had made it around—but his brief appearance drew fire from Walther. The German bellowed more orders.

The Englishman could guess what they were: Walther was telling his men to climb out and move along the train to retake the engine. He couldn't cover both sides at once; sooner or later they would overpower him.

He would have to take the fight to them first.

The next right-hand hairpin was approaching. Eddie thought for a moment, then pulled the throttle lever open. The locomotive's huffing exertion increased. He scrambled on top of the coal bunker behind the cab, then jumped onto the first carriage's roof—and ran.

Its occupants heard him. *"Tötet ihn! Tötet die Engländer!"* Kroll yelled. Bullets punched up through the metal behind Eddie's feet. He yelled, jumping over the gap behind the passenger coach to land on the first of the goods wagons.

The loot truck. The Nazis' most precious possessions were under guard inside.

Not for long.

Handrails ran above the doors on each side. Eddie shoved the gun into his jacket as he angled right—and jumped, twisting in midair to grab the railing as he fell.

The train swept into the turn at dangerous speed. Eddie swung through the open door at the two Nazi guards—

The nearest took the Englishman's feet to his stomach. He flew backward and disappeared with a shriek through the other doorway.

Eddie landed and drew his gun—but the second guard dived at him. Both men fell against the pithos, tearing loose one of the ropes holding it. The Nazi pinned Eddie down, driving a knee into his stomach before swiping the pistol from his hand.

The Yorkshireman pounded a retaliatory fist into the Nazi's side. The other man yelled. Eddie twisted, trying to throw him off—but the soldier's hands clamped around his throat and squeezed with vise-like force.

31

Flames from the ammo truck whipped back at the brake van, more bullets cooking off like deadly firecrackers. "This thing could blow any second," Zane warned. "Great plan!"

"I'm an archaeologist, not Casey Jones!" Nina shouted back. "We've got to disconnect it!"

"By 'we,' you mean . . . ," the Israeli muttered as he went to the front veranda, arms raised to protect his face from the heat. Nina took the brake as he leaned over the barrier and groped for the coupler's release handle.

It was just out of reach. He pushed himself farther, toes leaving the floor as his fingertips rubbed the rust-scabbed metal—

A grenade explosion shook both wagons. The lurch sent the Mossad agent over the wooden wall. He kicked his legs back to counterbalance himself, but too late.

He dropped—

His right hand clamped around the coupler handle—and he forced his arm straight, taking all his weight on his wrist and locked elbow. But he couldn't hold himself upright. He slowly slid sideways, about to fall under the brake van's whirling wheels . . .

Nina grabbed his legs. "I've got you!" Zane gasped in breathless relief, then tugged the lever.

It didn't move.

He tried again, harder. It shifted, but the couplers remained locked. The collision had buckled the metal.

More ordnance detonated, flinging out shrapnel. Nina ducked, then strained to haul the Israeli back into the caboose. Her plan had failed, and now they faced a choice between being blown up or flung off the track—

"Wait, wait!" he yelled. "It's moving, I've got—"

A harsh clank—and Nina fell backward, dragging Zane with her. The coupler opened, separating the two wagons . . . but they were still rolling downhill at matching speeds, racing toward the next hairpin. "Get the brake!" he yelled.

She scrambled to the pillar and twisted the wheel. The brake van shuddered, slowing—and the other wagon suddenly raced away as if propelled by a rocket. Zane joined her, tightening the brakes' grip.

Trailing smoke, the ammunition truck reached the bend and whipped around it. For one impossible moment, it seemed as if the runaway wagon would make it through the turn . . . then its front wheels jolted off the track. It bounded over the sleepers and careered down the hillside, crashing into a clump of scrawny trees and coming to a precarious halt not far above a lower leg of the track.

The brake van followed it around the hairpin, again on the verge of overturning . . . before steadying and coming out of the turn. "How many more of these goddamn reverses are there?" Nina complained rhetorically. The train was drawing away from them. "Take off the brakes, we need to catch up."

Zane complied. Gravity took hold again, the van regaining speed. They had lost ground on the Nazis, but she calculated that they would be able to keep pace, and she felt a small surge of hope as she saw that there was no sign of Eddie on the ground beside the line. He was still aboard the train . . .

. . .

He was—and fighting for his life.

Eddie struggled to break the Nazi's grip on his neck, but the young man's tendons felt like coiled steel. He switched tactics, driving punches at the soldier's face with as much force as he could muster from his awkward position. The man recoiled from the first blow, and the second, spitting blood, but if anything the attacks only made him squeeze harder. Another punch, but the Englishman was weakening . . .

Something moved through the edge of his vision. The loose rope from the earthenware jar, swinging back and forth as the train rocked—

He grabbed it—and whipped it into a loop around the Nazi's neck.

The man's triumphant snarl abruptly changed to a rictus of alarm as Eddie yanked the rope tight. He released one hand to pull at it—

Eddie took full advantage, again driving his fist at the other man's jaw—this time without the Nazi's arm obstructing the strike.

There was a sharp crack as the soldier's front teeth snapped. The man screamed as exposed nerves were rasped by broken enamel. He jerked back—allowing Eddie to slam a knee into his side. The soldier hit the floor.

Eddie gripped the rope with both hands and pulled as hard as he could, at the same time twisting on his side to deliver a two-footed kick. The Nazi rolled away—and out of the door. He was dragged along by the train for a moment before his neck broke with a horrible crack.

Eddie released the line. The end snapped away, then fluttered limply in the wind as the body fell beside the track.

Wheezing, he got up. He needed to find the Andreas relic—but found himself facing the pithos. "Pith off," he said, managing a smile.

* * *

Kroll stared back at the burning ammunition truck, before remembering that there were much closer dangers. "Walther! Is the Englander dead?"

"The men are climbing along both sides of the train," Walther replied. "They'll get him."

The Nazi leader leaned over to look down the train's length. "They'd bet—"

Sudden horror choked off his words as he saw something emerge from the wagon behind. Something as tall as a man, engraved with ancient Greek text and topped with silver . . . "The jar!" he managed to cry. "The water jar!"

The other Nazi leaders rushed to see—as the pithos was kicked out of the truck. It barreled away down the slope, rolling faster and faster . . . until it hit a rock. The great jar exploded into a billion fragments, its precious contents splashing over the bleak hillside.

Rasche shook with anger. "The water . . ." He rounded on Kroll. "That was *all* the fucking water! What the hell are we supposed to do now?"

Kroll struggled to control his own fury. "We carry on with the plan," he told the others, before adding to Rasche alone: "I think we're committed to it now."

Rasche glared at him, then went to a window to scream at the men clambering along the train's side. "He's in the treasure wagon! Kill that bastard! Come on, *move!*"

* * *

Eddie heard the enraged yelling even over the locomotive's huff. He was about to have visitors.

Where was the relic? He had seen it being loaded, but one wooden box looked much like another. It had been among the last of the treasures put aboard, though, so it would be near the doors. Considering its importance, it would also have been put somewhere safe—or at least, he realized as he glanced at the ropes that had held the pithos, secure.

Only one crate was tied down. He was about to yank at the knots when more shouts prompted him to check outside. He peered out of the left-hand door—to see soldiers clambering along the train, holding the railings and guttering at the edge of the roof. A man reached across from the wagon behind to get a grip on the loot truck—

Eddie shot him in the stomach. The Nazi hit the ground with a crunch of bones. Another round took out the man behind him. The others following tried desperately to find cover, but by now the Yorkshireman had darted to the other side of the wagon to take out a third man less than two feet from the open door. The corpse flailed away down the hillside.

He darted back to the crate and released the ties. The lid had been nailed shut, but dashing the box apart on the floor took care of that. Crumpled paper spilled out—and amid it, the dull gleam of bronze.

Eddie picked up the relic. It was too large to fit into any of his pockets. He still needed both hands, so he hoisted up the back of his leather jacket and shoved the artifact headfirst inside the waistband of his jeans, flat against his buttocks. "Can't believe putting a fish in my pants is the *least* insane thing I've done today," he muttered. It was far from comfortable, and risked limiting his movements, but he shrugged the jacket back down over its protruding tail and went to the left-hand door.

Their comrades' deaths had dissuaded the other soldiers from advancing along the train's side. They could still come from above, though. If he was going to rescue Banna, he had to get on the roof before them.

He looked ahead—to see the driverless locomotive lurching into the next hairpin. "Oh, *shite*!"

The snaking effect was more violent as it rippled back along the train. Eddie grabbed the door frame to save himself from being thrown out. A truncated scream came from behind; he twisted to see a soldier—or rather, *half* a soldier—being spat out by the grinding wheels.

The Nazi had taken cover between two of the trucks, only to be shaken loose onto the track.

Eddie clung on. If the train derailed here, the terrain was steep enough to kill everyone aboard when the wagons rolled over. He braced himself, ready to dive out and take his chances if the engine came off the tracks . . .

Somehow, all its wheels stayed on the rails. The rocking subsided as the locomotive clanked on to the next leg of the descent.

Eddie recognized what lay at its end—the extremely tight spiral loop that he had passed with Julieta on his way into the Enklave. There was no way the train would make it around at its current speed.

He pulled himself onto the roof. Smoke rose ahead where the burning ammo truck was wedged among the trees. Cracks and bangs warned him that bullets were still cooking off.

The brake van was freewheeling down the line above. He glimpsed Nina inside the bullet-pocked wagon. A wave to assure her that he was okay, then he narrowed his eyes against the hot smoke from the locomotive's chimney and moved forward, wondering how the hell he was going to get Banna out of a carriage full of armed and angry Nazis.

* * *

"He's alive, Eddie's alive!" Nina cried, seeing her husband on the roof.

Zane pointed behind the Englishman. "So are they!" The soldiers climbing along the train resumed their pursuit. "Get the brake!"

He brought up his submachine gun as Nina took the wheel. Zane aimed, waiting until he was sure that Eddie was beyond the MP5's spread of fire—then pulled the trigger.

Bullets sprayed the train. A man on top of one wagon was hit in the leg and fell over the edge, another Nazi clambering along the side taking an explosion of splinters to his eyes from a near-hit and losing his grip in shock. He was dragged under the wheels and vanished in a wet burst of red.

The other men on the roof dropped flat—but Zane's magazine was now empty, and he had no replacement. The silence told the Nazis all they needed to know. Guns came up—

"Down!" Zane yelled. Nina dropped as more bullets ripped into the brake van. Planks cracked and split, showering them with broken wood. There was a sharp bang as a supporting beam gave way—and a whole section of the curved metal roof crashed down into the rear of the compartment, pieces of the van's side scattering onto the hillside behind it.

The front half of the wagon remained intact, but was far from undamaged, more rounds striking home. Nina buried her head in her arms as a bullet hit the brake wheel's column with a shrieking clang. Zane crawled across the floor as another plank blew apart behind him. Then the onslaught died down as the caboose and train passed each other, heading in opposite directions.

The Mossad agent risked a look through the ragged hole. "*Harah.*" His attack had delayed the Nazis but not deterred them; the men on the roof were already getting back up. "They're still going after him."

Nina rose to see—but her own life took priority as the battered brake van rumbled toward the next hairpin. "Oh, crap!" she gasped, grabbing the wheel.

Zane sprang up to help her. The brakes shrieked in protest again. This time, something was wrong: there was a new noise, a grating rasp accompanied by a harsh judder. "That doesn't sound good!"

"Let's hope it works better than it sounds!" Nina maintained her hold. The wagon slowed, but the noise and vibration only grew worse.

Another lurch as the van swept into the hairpin. This time, they had shed enough speed to get around without teetering on the very edge of disaster—but as they eased the wheel back open, a clamor of disintegrating metal gave notice that another set of brake shoes had failed. Catastrophe was still waiting in the wings.

* * *

Schneider peered nervously at the track ahead. "We're going too fast! We'll never make it around the loop."

"Somebody has to climb into the engine and slow us down," said Kroll, his gaze fixed upon Rasche.

His second in command was not pleased. "What the hell do I know about driving a train?" He addressed the men guarding Banna. "You two! Does either of you know how it works?"

"I once rode in the cab when I was a boy . . . ," one offered hesitantly.

"That's good enough. Get out there and stop this thing!"

The soldier gave his companion a worried look, then saluted and went to the door. He was about to open it when a thump came from the roof at the rear of the carriage.

Walther's face crunched into a snarl. "It's the Englander!"

Kroll glowered at the huge man. "What are you waiting for? *Kill him!*"

* * *

Eddie hunched down, feet wide apart for stability on the rocking coach. The smoke was thicker this close to the locomotive, cinders searing his exposed skin. He shielded his face, trying to come up with a plan to save Banna that didn't involve simply swinging through a window and hoping for the best—

He flinched at a gunshot, fearing that the men in the carriage were firing through the roof again. But the crack had come from one side. The train was passing the ammunition truck. The trees around it were ablaze, the wooden wagon an inferno. Forget bullets; the risk now was from explosives. He turned his head to watch it go by, trying to judge when he would be out of danger . . .

A different threat came into sight—soldiers on the roof, coming after him.

He crouched as low as he could as he drew the gun.
But he didn't have enough bullets left to kill them all.

That didn't stop him from trying.

The leading Nazi was hit in the shoulder, losing his
balance. The crack of bone as he landed headfirst was
audible even over the engine's din. The other soldiers
dropped to their bellies, bringing up their MP5s to shoot
along the roof—

A huge explosion came from the hillside.

The ammo wagon blew apart in a massive fireball—
disintegrating the trees. Unsupported, the truck's blazing remains jolted loose and hurtled onward down the
hillside, the mangled front end of the chassis biting hard
into the ground and sending the entire wreck flipping
end-over-end at the train—

It hit the two rear wagons. Both were bowled off the
line, almost dragging the truck ahead after them before
the coupler snapped. The jolt threw Eddie's pursuers
from the roof and into the carnage below. Nazis were
flung shrieking from the open doors and crushed under
the wrecks as they rolled down the slope. The fiery remnants of the ammunition wagon bounded through the
chaos, flames swallowing soldiers and exploding grenades ripping bodies into bloody pieces.

Eddie clung to the roof as the remainder of the train
shuddered. The two destroyed wagons had contained
half the Nazi troops—and all the other deaths meant
that Kroll's forces were now seriously depleted. But even
with those losses, he still had another two truckloads
of soldiers, plus however many were in the passenger
carriage—

A slam from below. Eddie twisted, catching sight of a
man's head; someone had come out of a door and was
climbing along the side of the coach toward the engine.

One fewer to deal with inside, then. He looked back
to check that there were no Nazis coming after him,
then rose and moved to get a clear shot at the man heading for the locomotive—

A hand clamped around his ankle like a bear trap.

Walther had leaned out of the coach to grab the Englishman, pulling hard on his leg from behind. Eddie tried to bring his gun to bear, but the hulking Nazi had already thrown him off balance. He fell, landing mere inches from the edge of the roof. The choice was between keeping hold of the gun and stopping himself from going over—he took the latter, the pistol skittering along the weather-scoured metal before clunking to a stop in the gutter.

The German tugged harder, trying to drag him over the side. Eddie kicked, catching Walther's fingers. A satisfying roar of pain came from below. The hand withdrew. The Yorkshireman rolled away from the edge, the bronze fish's tail digging into his back, and scrambled for his gun.

A hefty thud came from behind as Walther clambered onto the roof. Eddie lunged for the weapon—but the Nazi hurled himself onto him, his sheer weight pounding the breath from the Englishman. Before Eddie could recover, the SS man hauled him up and turned to sling him off the back of the coach onto the track below—

The train lurched violently as it clattered over the little bridge at the top of the loop.

Alarmed, Walther dropped his opponent and fell to his knees, gripping a protruding ventilator cover to steady himself. Then tension turned to triumph as he saw something an arm's length away.

Eddie searched for the gun—only to see the Nazi snatch it up with his free hand. Murderous glee flashed in Walther's eyes as he took aim—

The soldier reached the cab and pulled the brake lever.

The train staggered as the remaining wagons concertinaed against one another. It skidded along the track, wheels locked—then swung into the loop. Everyone inside was hurled sideways as it screeched around the tight descending turn.

Those above were no better off. Eddie slid helplessly across the roof—

His back scraped over another ventilator, the squat

metal cone ripping through his leather jacket—and snagging on it. He jerked to a stop, both legs flailing over the side of the train.

Walther was forced to release the gun to hold the vent with both hands. It banged back into the gutter. He swore, then saw Eddie's plight and dropped flat, gripping the roof's edge to pull himself closer to the Yorkshireman as the train continued its squealing turn. "Pig!" the huge Nazi spat. "You have spilled our water—so now I will spill your *blood*!"

Eddie tried to move, but his jacket was still snared on the vent cover. Face red with rage, Walther reached out, thick fingers grasping at the Englishman's neck . . . and squeezing.

The choking Eddie had received from the guard in the treasure wagon had been a light tickle by comparison. Walther's grip felt as if it could crush steel. He realized he had no hope of prying open the Nazi's fingers—so instead he attacked. With his other hand holding on to the carriage, the German couldn't defend his face. Eddie stabbed at his eyes—

Walther simply raised his head, his longer reach putting him beyond the other man's strikes. All Eddie could catch was his chin, but even that was too far away for him to do more than bruise it. "Now you will die!" the SS thug snarled. "Die, you English bastard, *die*!"

Eddie thrashed and kicked, but couldn't break free. Never mind suffocation; Walther was about to snap his neck. He made one last hopeless swing at the Nazi's jaw as something loomed behind it . . .

The punch was abandoned mid-throw as he saw what it was—the bridge, the train looping back around to pass beneath it. Instead he braced both hands palms up under Walther's chin, forcing his head back. The Nazi grinned malevolently at the futility of this final action—

The back of Walther's skull burst apart as it smacked into the unyielding end of a rusty girder.

The big man instantly went limp, collapsing on top of Eddie before sliding off the roof. His body bounced off the side of the cutting and fell under the train's wheels, mangled pieces being dragged along before the gory mush was finally spewed out over the side of the track.

Eddie kept his head down until the train was clear. "Like a bridge over troubled Walther," he wheezed, even a bad joke feeling necessary to celebrate his survival.

A metallic squeal from above. He looked back to see the brake van pass over the crossing and start around the loop. With the train still slowing, Nina and Zane were quickly catching up.

Too quickly. If the train stopped, the van would smash right into it . . .

The Nazi leaders had realized the same thing. Kroll screamed *"Schnell! Schnell!"*—and the man in the cab released the brakes, the carriage shuddering as the train rolled freely once more. A moment later, a bellowing huff of smoke burst from the chimney as the soldier opened the throttle. The wheels spun wildly before finding traction, and the locomotive lurched forward.

The jolt of acceleration kicked Eddie backward. Fabric ripped. He struggled, finally pulling free and exhaustedly standing. As the locomotive came out of the bottom of the loop, the brake van screeched around the tighter upper section, descending to pass under the bridge. Even with the train picking up speed, it would catch it in seconds.

He retrieved the gun. A moment of indecision—then with deep reluctance he turned and ran back down the train, vaulting over the gaps between the cars. He felt disgusted at himself for abandoning Banna, but he knew that climbing into the carriage to rescue him would result only in his death. Also, without the relic, the Nazis needed the young Egyptian to find the spring. They would keep him alive . . . until he was no longer needed.

The train emerged onto the next leg of the track. The brake van rounded the loop behind it. He jumped onto the last remaining wagon and pounded along its roof. Shouted German came from below—then geysers of bullets erupted behind him as the enraged Nazis opened fire. The brake van was thirty feet behind the train, twenty, Nina and Zane urging him on . . .

Eddie reached the rear of the wagon, shots bursting up at his heels—

He didn't stop.

The track blurred below as he made a running jump off the back of the train, the brake van rushing at him.

Falling short—

He threw out both arms—and hit the veranda with an agonizing bang. But he couldn't get a firm hold. He clawed at the wood—then fell toward the track . . .

Hands grabbed his wrists.

"Got you!" Zane grunted. Eddie swung his feet before finding the coupler and using it to push himself upward.

Behind the Israeli, he saw Nina standing at the brake. "You got him?" she shouted.

"Yeah!" Zane replied, hauling Eddie over the barrier.

"Great—'cause we need to *duck*!" She twisted the wheel and dropped, the two men hurriedly doing the same—

Bullets hammered against planks as the Nazis opened fire. But the train was pulling away. The fusillade died down, a few last rounds smacking home before the gunmen were carried out of range.

Eddie shook off broken wood and looked at Nina. "Are you okay?"

"Yeah," she replied. "Jesus, what about you?"

He realized he was covered with Walther's blood. "Don't worry, it's not mine. Well, most of it." He noticed a lump of gray matter stuck to his jacket. "Looks like I finally got some brains," he said as he flicked it away.

Nina made a disgusted face. "Gross. What about Ubayy?"

"I couldn't get to him. I'm sorry. But," he added on seeing her dismay, "they'll need to keep him alive for now."

"Why?" asked Zane as he went to the brake column.

"'Cause I've got the fish." He proudly produced it from his trousers, to his wife's amusement. "So they need him to find the spring."

"That's assuming we let them get away," Zane said, determination returning to his voice. He released the brakes.

"How're we going to stop 'em?" Eddie said. "There's three of us, and a gun with"—he slid out the magazine to count—"two bullets. They've still got two trucks full of arseholes with automatic weapons."

"I don't know how! But we can't let them escape."

"Not after what they did to Macy," said Nina. Her voice was quiet, but the anger behind it was clear.

Eddie shook his head wearily, then rose. The train was still drawing away as it headed for the trestle bridge. He glimpsed Rasche shouting orders from the carriage.

Wait—*what* orders? The brake van was now beyond an MP5's effective range, and all the heavy weapons had been in the destroyed ammunition truck. But the soldiers in the last wagon were leaning from both doors as if preparing to attack . . .

His gaze snapped past the train. It was almost at the crossing—

"Shit!" he gasped. "Put the brakes back on, quick!"

"What's happening?" Nina asked in sudden concern.

"They're going to blow up the fucking bridge!" The soldiers were being passed objects by their fellows inside the wagon: *grenades*.

Zane hurriedly spun the wheel back the other way. The brakes wailed again. "We'll never stop in time!"

"We'd bloody well better!" Eddie tossed the relic to Nina, then joined the Israeli and added his weight. The stench of burning reached them as flying sparks set light to splintered wood.

The train crossed the bridge—too quickly, parts of the track bed shaking loose as it thundered over the ravine. The men leaning from the rear wagon stretched out farther, others inside holding them steady . . .

Arms swung in synchrony, tossing grenades onto the line.

The train continued. Seconds passed, two, three—

The explosions came so close together that they seemed like one single blast. Sleepers flew like scattered toothpicks, the central section of the bridge rocking wildly before support beams broke and a full third of the old structure collapsed into the canyon. The train was already safely across, carrying on down the hill.

Eddie and Zane watched the disintegration in horror. *"Benzonah!"* exclaimed the Israeli.

"That, and fuckery!" Eddie added as they both hauled harder on the wheel. The piercing screech of the brakes grew even louder—

Then abruptly stopped at a crack of shearing metal. The wagon picked up speed again.

Zane gave the wheel a last useless spin. "We'll have to jump!"

"We'll be killed!" Nina protested. The ground was littered with rocks.

"It's our only chance!"

"We're going too fast," Eddie said. He looked back, but jumping from the van's wrecked rear onto the track would make little difference—

The roof. The piece that had fallen into the cabin was curved metal, somewhat wider than the track, and about five feet long . . .

He ran to it. "Give me a hand!" he yelled as he strained to lift the roof section.

"What are you doing?" Zane demanded.

"You ever been surfing?" The steel plate shifted; Nina joined her husband to help turn it over, the concave underside now facing upward. There was a chain with a hook at one end amid the debris. Eddie made sure it was firmly attached to the chassis, then fixed it to the roof's cross-brace.

The Mossad agent watched in disbelief. "Are you *crazy?"*

"After six years with Eddie, this is normal!" Nina assured him. She helped her husband to push the roof piece off the rear veranda. As it slammed down on the track, the chain jerked taut, and the steel plate lashed from side to side before stabilizing, dragging along behind the runaway wagon with a nerve-shredding shrill.

"Climb onto it," Eddie told his wife. He held her hand as she cautiously stepped down. The horrible noise worsened as she put her weight on the roof, the chain straining—but holding. "Jared, come on!"

Zane looked between the rapidly approaching bridge and the makeshift sled, then shrugged. "You've stayed alive this long, old man," he said. "I guess you know what you're doing!"

"Oh, fuck no," said Eddie as the Israeli clambered down beside Nina. "I'm still making this shit up as I go." A small grin as he readied his gun and followed Zane onto the roof, which shimmied under the extra load before straightening out. "It's worked so far, but"— he took aim at the chain—"there's always a last time!"

He fired—

Sparks flew—but the bullet glanced off the chain without breaking it. "And this might be it," he added with considerably less humor. "Okay, and—now!"

The final shot—and the chain snapped.

Friction instantly snatched at the improvised sledge, almost pitching Eddie off before Zane caught him. The brake van raced away onto the bridge. The broken structure shook beneath it—then the wagon sailed off the end of the track, arcing down across the ravine to carve through the trestlework on the far side like a wrecking ball. What was left of the other half of the crossing came down on top of it.

"We're not stopping!" Nina cried as the skidding roof section reached the bridge.

"*Jump!*" Eddie yelled. They all flung themselves off the back of the sled—

Even after losing most of their speed, the landing on unforgiving wood and steel was punishing. Nina, the lightest, was the first to roll to a halt, still clutching the bronze relic.

But Zane and Eddie tumbled onward, the sledge flying into the void ahead of them as they reached the end of the line . . .

The Englishman splayed himself flat, the wooden sleepers scraping painfully against his back—but the extra drag stopped him. Zane bowled past, screaming as he went over the drop—

Eddie caught his leg. The Mossad agent's wail was abruptly cut off as he swung back and hit the trestle-work below the broken track. He hung upside down for a moment before the realization sank in that he was not falling to his death, and he twisted to take hold of the wooden beams. "You okay?" Eddie gasped, straining to hold him.

"Yeah," came the breathless reply, "but get me up, quick! This thing's going to collapse!" A sonorous creak as the bridge swayed queasily emphasized his point.

Bloodied and bruised, Nina nevertheless limped to aid them. They dragged Zane onto the bridge, then helped him up. "Come on!" she cried, running back along the shuddering span. Sleepers dropped away in her wake, forcing Eddie and Zane to vault over the gaps.

A loud crack—then a sound like the clatter of giant dominoes falling. Eddie glanced back to see the entire track bed disappearing plank by plank into the ravine after them. "Shit! *Leg it!*"

Nina reached solid ground. The two men hurled themselves into dives to land beside her as the bridge cascaded into the canyon in a huge cloud of dust and flying debris.

Eddie stared at the destruction, then looked up at the now distant train as it continued down the hill toward the dry lake—where he saw movement. "Over there!" he said, pointing.

An aircraft, a large twin-prop cargo plane, was coming in to land on the desiccated lake bed. A second aircraft followed it a few miles distant. "Leitz's transport," Zane muttered. He shakily pushed himself upright, then slammed a frustrated fist into his palm. "Dammit! We'll never catch them now. They'll be long gone by the time we get to the lake."

"We know where they're going, though," said Nina as she helped Eddie up. "Northern Iran."

"That doesn't help us! They'll have a head start—and we don't know exactly where they're headed. But they've still got Banna, and he can take them to the spring."

"We can locate it too," Nina reminded him. She held

up the relic. "I can make the same calculations that he did. But first we need to contact the Argentinean authorities, the IHA—and the Mossad too. If we act fast enough, we might be able to catch them before they leave the country."

Zane did not seem confident of success. "Maybe. But I think Leitz will have arranged something special for them."

"Leitz was the guy you went after in Italy, wasn't he?" Nina said. "What happened there?"

"Long story," said Eddie. He looked toward the distant town. "I'll tell you all about it on the way down."

32

The Caspian Sea

A day later, Nina was on the opposite side of the globe. She *thought* it was a day later, at least. Exhaustion and emotion had screwed up her body clock even without factoring in the confusion of multiple time zones. But one thing she was sure of was that while it might help her physically, she had no desire to sleep. Every time her eyelids closed, she glimpsed the horrors she had witnessed in the Enklave. Macy's murder, Zane's torture, the burning building with terrified children trapped inside . . . and the crowd of frenzied Nazis baying for her death as the noose tightened around her throat—

Nina drew in a sharp breath. For a moment, she had felt the rope's strands cutting into her skin. She touched her neck to reassure herself that there was nothing there.

She tried to force the jumble of memories following the escape from the Nazi compound into a coherent time line. On arriving in Lago Amargo, Eddie had gotten a policeman named Miranda to call the Argentinean federal police, who arrived in force a few hours later. Not long after that, the survivors from the Enklave were secured, Roland and Julieta having a joyful reunion. Julieta's father, the mayor, had turned himself in to the *federales* over some connection with Kroll and his people; two badly beaten local cops were taken into custody far less willingly.

By then, Nina had contacted Oswald Seretse in New York. That in turn led to a conference call with the FBI and Interpol in which Zane's fears were confirmed: The surviving Nazis had indeed left Argentina undetected. "How the fucking hell do thirty Aryan shitheads with guns stroll through customs without being spotted?" had been Eddie's incredulous contribution to the discussion, and Nina's own response had been scarcely less restrained.

But she knew where they were going. Iran.

She recalled from her time as the IHA's director that the Iranian government would not cooperate with the agency, considering it too closely tied to the United States, and it was barely more willing to work with international law enforcement. Seretse relayed the news that the Iranians had been warned about the Nazis, for which Interpol was thanked and assured that the elite Revolutionary Guard would detain them. Zane, silently sitting in on the call, responded only with a sardonic shake of his head. "Leitz will already have paid off the local Revolutionary Guard commander to act as their escort," he said when it concluded. "The Guard like to parade themselves as the moral guardians of the Islamic revolution, but they're corrupt from bottom to top. Especially the top."

So now, instead of returning to New York as she had told Seretse, she was in a fishing boat that had set out from Astara at the southern tip of Azerbaijan, heading southeast across the Caspian Sea.

Eddie entered the small cabin. "I wouldn't bother getting up," he told his wife as she sat up on the narrow bed. "It's dark, and it's pissing down." He wiped a hand over his damp hair and took off his ravaged leather jacket.

"How long before we get there?"

He perched beside her. "A few hours yet. This isn't exactly a speedboat."

"Unlike those things the Mossad brought." Zane was aboard the old trawler with them—along with a small squad of young and determined-looking Israeli agents.

"Yeah. I'm still not Mossad's number one fan, but they've got some pretty cool gear." He smiled, then rested a gentle hand on her stomach. "How are you faring?"

"Fine. A little Dramamine works wonders."

Another smile, but his eyes were serious. "I didn't mean seasickness. I meant . . . everything else."

"I'm trying not to think about it," she said. "It's . . . it's too much to process right now. Especially . . ."

"Macy?"

She nodded. "Seretse will have told her parents by now, but . . . I'll have to talk to them when this is over. I'll *have* to. But what am I going to say? *I'm sorry for your loss—oh, and by the way, it was all my fault your daughter was murdered?*"

"No." Eddie's hand moved firmly to her shoulder as he looked deep into her eyes. "No. It *wasn't* your fault, and I'm not going to let you blame yourself for it. Okay? I know what you're going through; I had to tell Mitzi's parents what happened after she got shot in Austria. I blamed myself at the time, and God knows her mum and dad blamed me too. But now . . ." He paused, the incident still emotional even after several years. "Just because she was with me didn't make it my fault. It took a long time, but eventually I realized that. That punk-haired Russian bitch killed her, not me. And it was Kroll who killed Macy, not you. I know you *want* to blame yourself, but you can't. I won't let you blame yourself for the rest . . ." He trailed off.

"Of my life?" Nina finished.

A grim nod. "It's not fair. It's not fucking *fair*!" he said with sudden anguish. "Everything we've been through, everything we've survived—but you've still got *that* growing inside you." He jabbed his other hand toward her side. "Has anything changed?"

"Yeah, but . . . not in any good way." She tugged up

her shirt. Even over the short time since she had last examined them closely, when Kroll made his Faustian offer, the growths had become more malign.

The sight made Eddie sag. "Christ. It just gets worse."

"I know. I know." She wrapped both hands around his. "Don't look at it. Don't even think about it. I'm trying not to. I've got more than enough worries as it is."

"Me too. Although at the moment, one of the biggest is that we're about to sneak into Iran with a bloody Mossad strike team. If we get caught . . ."

"Thanks for reminding me; I've been trying not to think about that either!" They both managed to smile. Nina pulled his hand to her lips and kissed it. "Thank you."

"For what?"

"For being with me."

"Where else would I be?" he said, with a mock shrug. "Like I said, you're stuck with me to the end."

She grinned, squeezing his hand. "I'm glad." Another kiss, then she regarded his bruised face. "God, you look tired. When did you last get any sleep?"

"I had a bit on the flight from Argentina, but not much. It took ages to get hold of Hafez." Nina had long been impressed by Eddie's extensive list of friends around the globe; Hafez was an Iranian whom she had met on her very first adventure with the man who would later become her husband. "You can't just ring up someone in Iran and say, *We're coming in with a bunch of Mossad blokes, can you meet us?* There's a lot of buggering around with code words and satphones. Before that? I dunno, probably when I went over to Argentina in the first place."

"So you're planning to sneak into a hostile country on an hour's sleep? Bad idea. If we've got a few hours, you should make the most of them. Come on, lie down with me."

He seemed oddly reluctant. "I'm not sure there's room for both of us. And you need it more."

"No, I don't." Sleep was the last thing she wanted,

knowing what visions waited behind her eyes. "Edward J. Chase, take off your clothes and get into bed, right now!"

The order was given with humor, and he smiled in response, but he was still reticent even as he peeled off his clothing. She soon realized why. He was covered in angry bruises and cuts. "Oh my God!" she cried. "When did you get all those?"

"Remember those Argie cops?" he said as he unfastened his belt. "One of them was a Falklands veteran. He had a chip on his shoulder about Brits. So he tried to knock a chip *off* my shoulder. Took one out of my tooth too." He slid his jeans down to reveal more afterimages of a beating. "Also, jumping off a moving train while fighting Nazis *really fucking hurts.*"

"But you came through it." Nina regarded him with loving sympathy as she pulled back the sheets. "And you saved me."

Now naked, he stood before her, all the accumulated injuries to his muscular body exposed—not merely the most recent, but old scars too. He looked back in silence for a long moment, then spoke. "Get undressed. I want to be with you."

There was no jokiness behind his words, just a heartfelt desire for closeness, intimacy, that he knew she shared. She said nothing as she slipped off her top. Her own wounds were revealed, but neither looked anywhere but into the other's eyes.

Eddie climbed into the cramped bunk, tugging the covers over them. "Seems like forever since we were last like this."

"I know." Nina nuzzled against his chest as he wrapped his arms around her, feeling his warmth. "Too long."

"I hope that bloody door locks," he said. "Don't want a load of salty seamen coming in here."

"I might," she said with a grin that was more than merely suggestive.

He laughed as he reached up to switch out the light.

"Now I *know* I can't let you go," he said, running his hands down her body. "I've made you as bad as me!"

* * *

A knock on the cabin door forced the couple back to wakefulness. Nina raised her head, realizing with surprise that she couldn't remember falling asleep—or having any dreams, good or bad. "What?" she called as Eddie sat up.

"It's almost time," said Zane from outside.

"This is it, then," Eddie told Nina, groping for the light switch.

She kicked away the sheets and swung her feet down to the deck. "Did you sleep?"

"Yeah. I think that was what I needed."

"And by 'that,' you mean . . ."

"Yeah. *That*." He grinned.

"Me too."

"We didn't use any protection," he noted. "What changed your mind? After all that time not wanting to take any risks?"

"For one thing, I decided to trust the doctors' opinion that the eitr infection isn't transmissible. For another . . ." She touched his cheek. "I couldn't live what's left of my life without being so close to you again."

He smiled lovingly, then kissed her. "You know, I'm really glad I married you."

"So am I." She started to dress. "Hmm. I could use a shower, but I doubt this boat's got much of a bathroom."

"What, doing a King of the World on the bow and hoping the waves splash you isn't enough?" He retrieved his clothing, giving the tumors on her side a mournful glance. "This *is* it, isn't it?"

"What do you mean?"

"After this, once we're done, *if* we're done . . . it's only going to be you and me, right? No more little operations to help out the IHA? Just the two of us, together. To the end."

Nina nodded. "Yeah. To the end."

"Promise?"

"I promise." A moment as they exchanged looks, then kissed again.

"Thanks," said Eddie as they finished dressing. "Okay, so before that . . . let's go and invade a hostile country."

Zane was waiting for them on the old trawler's darkened bridge. "Did you sleep well?" he asked, with a hint of a knowing smile.

"Best I have for ages," Eddie replied. "What's the sitrep?"

The Israeli directed his attention to a GPS screen. "We're twenty-five miles off the Iranian coast. Captain Aslanov"—he nodded toward the bearded middle-aged Azerbaijani at the controls—"says that going any closer will definitely draw attention from their patrol boats. They sometimes investigate ships even farther out, so he's taking a risk just being here."

"Well, yeah, with a hold full of Mossad spooks. How long will your little toys take to get us ashore?"

"Not long. We've used them to infiltrate the country before."

"Are you sure they won't be seen?" asked Nina. The trawler's hold contained a pair of small, odd-looking speedboats. "Don't the Iranians have radar?"

"They do, but"—a grin—"our boats don't need to worry about it. Your *head* has a bigger radar cross section than they do. Well, Eddie's does, definitely."

"You saying I've got a big head?" the Englishman faux-protested.

"I never even thought about it. Okay, we're ready to go. Our radar says the nearest other ship is three miles to the southeast, and Captain Aslanov thinks it's probably a patrol boat. So he'll raise his nets and use them for cover while we drop our boats, then we'll let him get clear before we move off." He checked his watch. "It's three thirty-six. Sunrise is at about five fifty, so that gives us just enough time before dawn to get to shore, hide the boats, and meet your friend. If he's there," he added.

"He'll be there," Eddie assured him.

"Good. So are you ready?"

"As I'll ever be," Nina said, with a sigh.

They headed to the trawler's deck. To Eddie's relief, the rain had stopped. Aslanov whistled to his crew, who raised the nets on the starboard side like a curtain, blocking everything behind them from potential observers aboard the Iranian patrol vessel. The Mossad agents brought their boats out of the hold and moved them to the port side.

The vessels, slender launches with angular, faceted prows made from a textured material resembling carbon fiber, were quickly lowered into the sea. "With me," said Zane, climbing into the lead boat after the pilot. His leg was still stiff from Rasche's stab wound, but it had been stitched up and treated as best it could be. He helped first Nina, then Eddie down. Another agent joined them, the five remaining men boarding the other craft.

"Bit nippy," said the Englishman as a stiff breeze blew across the water. Nina had donned a black parka, but he had chosen to stay with his torn jacket.

"Why didn't you wear something else?" she asked. "That's not just ruined, it's covered in . . . I don't even want to *know* what it's covered in."

"Dead Nazis, mostly. Which is why I'm keeping it on."

"To remind you who we're up against?" asked Zane.

"No. To remind me to finish the job. There's still plenty of 'em left."

The boats were pushed clear of the trawler. Engines revved, and the old vessel wallowed away. "Okay, keep down," said Zane. The launch's seats were set very low inside the hull, the passengers leaning back almost horizontally as if in a racing car.

"Isn't it kinda hard for the driver to see?" Nina asked. The view ahead was mostly obscured by a raised lip above the top of the dashboard, into which was set a softly glowing GPS display.

"We're on open water, so we won't run into anything—I hope!" The Israeli watched the trawler until it was well clear of the two bobbing stealth boats. A command, and the pilot started the engine, a muffled rumble coming from the rear of the vessel. Another growl from astern told them that the second boat had followed suit.

The pilot slowly opened the throttle to bring the vessel around toward the coast, a flashing green diamond marking a waypoint on the GPS, then increased power. Both boats surged across the water, their shallow keels and ducted propellers barely raising a wake.

Nina was very glad of her motion-sickness remedy. Even though the huge inland sea was quite calm, the same low profile that made the vessel nearly invisible to radar also meant that it was very sensitive to even small waves, each new crest thumping up through the hull into her spine. But she could tell from the speed at which spray was whipping past that the boats were fast.

Zane occasionally raised his head to look for more Iranian patrols, but the sea held only darkness. "How much longer?" Eddie shouted to him over the smack of the waves.

"Fifteen minutes! You're sure your contact will be there?"

"He was sneaking me and my mates into Iran while you were still playing with fucking Lego," Eddie replied with faint impatience. "Yes, I'm sure."

"Just checking." In the screen's glow, Nina saw Zane's mouth curl into a smirk. "So, you operated in Iran when you were young? What was it like there when the Shah was still in power?"

Eddie kicked Zane's seat. "Fuck off, you cheeky little bastard." Nina laughed.

The two boats continued onward. After another ten jolting minutes, the pilot reduced power. The GPS display showed they were approaching the shore. Nina saw with disquiet that there were lights along a good swath of the coastline. "Jeez, are you sure we'll be able to land without being seen? And how are we going to hide the boats?"

Zane produced night-vision goggles and surveyed what lay ahead. "That's a forest," he said, pointing out a gap over a mile long in the line of lights. "The Sisangan National Park. We've used it as an entry point before. And I doubt anyone will be on the beach this early in the morning."

"I dunno," said Eddie. "You'd be surprised how many people in New York are out jogging at the crack of sparrowfart."

"Iran isn't exactly the world's jogging capital," the Israeli replied. He surveyed the shoreline again, then issued an order. The boats angled for the forest's eastern end, reducing power to glide up to the empty beach.

To Nina's alarm, headlights were intermittently visible through the trees behind the shore. "I thought nobody would be around?"

"It's a highway," Zane replied, unconcerned. "No one driving along it will be able to see us." The pilot brought them in until breaking waves began to rock them, at which point Zane and another Mossad operative jumped out, dragging the craft ashore. The second boat came in alongside. The other occupants disembarked, and the agents picked up the empty vessels and carried them across the sand into the trees. Grubby tarpaulins were draped over them, the coverings weighed down with rocks.

"*That's* how you're hiding them?" Nina asked. "What if someone looks under the tarps and finds two super-high-tech stealth boats?"

"Trust me, nobody will look," said Zane, scooping up a handful of dirt and tossing it over one of the tarpaulins. The other got the same treatment. "Tourists who come here either walk on the beach or go into the forest on the far side of the highway. Even if they see these, they just look like ordinary boats when they're covered—nothing worth paying attention to. I told you, we've done this before."

"Yeah, hiding something in plain sight by making it look really boring does actually work," Eddie told his wife. "Did it a few times in the SAS: We'd park up in a rusty old van to bag someone and nobody'd give us a second look. Well, except that time some little scrote opened the back door to see if there was anything he could nick. Blew the op, but it was worth it for the look on his face when he saw us all pointing guns at him. I think he genuinely shat himself."

"Lovely," she said, still unconvinced. But the Israelis were satisfied by the boats' new low-tech camouflage and set off through the woods.

It did not take long for the group to reach a dirt track cutting through the strip of forest between the beach and the highway. A van lurked in the darkness. Two of the Mossad agents drew their weapons and moved into the trees to cover it.

"Is that Hafez's?" Nina whispered.

Zane regarded it through the goggles. "I can't tell if there's anyone inside."

"I can," said Eddie. Before anyone could object, he advanced on the van, whistling loudly and tunelessly.

The Israeli made an aggrieved noise. "He's being subtle again. That worked out so well last time!"

The driver's door opened, a cloud of smoke wafting out. The lurking Israelis' guns snapped on to the bearded man who emerged. "Oi, Hafez!" Eddie called. "You really ought to stop smoking—it gives away that you're in there when it leaks out of the windows."

Hafez Marradejan took a long, mocking drag on his cigarette. "You used to smoke too, Eddie!" he rasped.

"Yeah, but that was a long time ago. I've sorted myself out since then." He embraced the older man. "Glad to see you again."

"And you. Six years, I think it has been?"

"About that, yeah. Did you have any trouble getting here?"

"Only from my wife! She was not pleased when I told her I was going to drive across half the country to see an old friend." A cackle, which turned into a cough, then Hafez peered past the Englishman. "So, where are the others?"

"In the woods." Eddie turned and waved. "It's okay, come on out."

Nina was first to leave the trees, Zane and most of the other Mossad operatives following more cautiously. The two men keeping watch remained in the shadows, wary of deception or ambush.

But there was neither. "Hafez!" said Nina. "Hi, remember me?"

"Yes, of course!" he replied, clasping her hand and shaking it. "You have become famous since then, no?"

"Or infamous. And married too." She took hold of Eddie's arm.

The Iranian grinned. "Ah, so he did not sort *himself* out. I thought so!"

"Are you okay? The last time I saw you, you'd been shot in the leg."

"An old wound now," he said dismissively, before giving the other men a quizzical look. "And these are . . . ?"

"Jared Zane," said Eddie, introducing the Israeli, "and his . . . associates. Probably best that you don't ask where they're from."

Hafez finished his cigarette and ground it under his foot. "Pfft. I know Israeli special forces when I see them. Or Mossad, but the two are almost one these days." Ignoring Zane's surprise, he went on: "You have vouched for them, Eddie, so that is good enough for me. And from what you told me, their business here is not with the people of Iran."

"No," Zane said. "At least not today."

Eddie sighed as Hafez narrowed his eyes. "He doesn't like the Iranian government any more than you do," he told the younger man, "so don't even *start* waving your cock around."

Hafez opened the rear doors. "It is big enough for all of you. Including the two men in the trees." Again Zane was caught by surprise; the Iranian gave him a yellow-toothed grin.

"I keep telling this kid how useful experience is, but he won't bloody listen," said Eddie, smirking. Zane shook his head, then signaled for the pair to join the others.

"So, I am taking you into the Alborz mountains?" asked Hafez as the Israelis clambered into the van.

"Yeah," replied Nina. "The only problem is, I don't

know exactly where. I've narrowed it down to a fairly small area near one of the passes, but we'll still have to search when we get there."

"I will get you as close as I can." With all the Mossad agents now squeezed inside, he closed the doors. "Oh, even though I will take the back roads, you will still need to wear a head scarf," he told Nina apologetically. "Red hair, it stands out—and with a truck full of spies, I do not want to attract attention!"

"That's okay," she said, touching her bedraggled pony-tail. "The state my hair's in, I'm happy to keep it under wraps."

Hafez smiled. "There is one in the front. Okay, now we can go." He opened the passenger door for her and Eddie, then returned to the driver's seat. There was a packet of Winston cigarettes on the dashboard; he flicked out one of the white cylinders with an almost automatic movement and put it in his mouth, then hesitated. "You think I smoke too much?" Eddie nodded. "If you can give up, then bah, so can I." He returned the unlit cigarette to its home. "For one day, at least."

Nina fastened a black scarf around her head as the Iranian started the engine. "You don't appreciate your health until you lose it," she told him, with a sad look at her husband.

* * *

The target area was only some sixty miles from the land-ing site as the crow flies, but the journey was consider-ably more circuitous. Hafez was being extra cautious, avoiding major settlements and not wanting to draw the slightest interest from anyone they passed, be they civil-ian, police, or military. By the time they left the coastal plain and began to ascend into the long east–west range of the Alborz, it was after eleven o'clock.

Nina's prior visit to Iran had taken her to its dry and dusty western region, so the landscape came as a sur-prise. The mountains trapped clouds rolling in from the Caspian, resulting in a thick verdant carpet of forest covering the entire northern flank of the peaks. "Beautiful, yes?" said Hafez as the van cruised up a tree-lined road winding deeper into the wilderness.

"It is," she agreed. "But finding what we're looking for in these woods might be harder than I thought."

"Hopefully Kroll and his lot'll have the same problem," said Eddie.

"Guess we'll find out soon." There was a satnav on the dash; it showed that they were only a few miles from their destination—or at least the start of their search.

Minutes passed, the Iranian swinging the van around a series of hairpin bends as the potholed road ascended the pass. The clouds thickened the higher they climbed, casting a gloomy pall over both the scenery and Nina's mood. She had barely escaped with her life from the Nazis . . . but now she was likely to face them again.

She *had* to do it, though. Kroll and the others had been trying to escape the world's notice. But if they found the spring and shared it with their wealthy backers, they would regain influence around the globe.

She couldn't let that happen. If she did, Macy and many others would have died for nothing . . .

"This is it," said Hafez, bringing her back to immediate concerns. A muddy track to one side headed into the thick forest.

Eddie was immediately on alert. "Someone's been up there recently," he said, spotting tire marks in the wet earth. "Hafez, pull over."

The back doors were flung open even before the van fully halted. Zane and the other Israelis jumped out and dispersed rapidly into the trees, guns readied. Eddie drew his own weapon, a nine-millimeter BUL Cherokee pistol provided by the Mossad agent. He examined the tracks. "A jeep, plus . . . three trucks," he reported. "Pretty heavily loaded an' all. They've gone into the woods— but they haven't come out."

"I suppose it's too much to hope that they were full of lumberjacks?" said Nina.

Zane joined the Englishman. "Four-by-fours, big ones," he said. "Most likely Neynava troop trucks. Three of them would be enough to carry Kroll's forces. The jeep was probably a Safir—the Revolutionary Guard commander's ride." He saw Eddie's impressed expression. "I might not be as experienced as you, but my intel's right up to date."

"So now what?" Nina asked.

"We can't risk taking the van any farther," Eddie replied. "They might hear it."

"I do not want to leave you behind," Hafez protested from his vehicle.

"I'm not saying you should go back home. But you'll need to get out of sight. There was another track about a mile down the hill; use that." He surveyed the cloud-shrouded peaks to the south. "Nina, how far are we from the spring?"

Nina checked a map. "Four miles, at least." She had marked the search area; it was higher up the slopes. "That way," she said, pointing. "The tallest mountain could be the one from Andreas's text."

"They won't get trucks up there," Zane noted. "They'll have to go on foot."

Eddie went to the van. "Hafez, we'll go on from here. Wait for us where I said."

The Iranian reluctantly agreed. "For how long?"

"Fucked if I know, mate. Jared, you got any walkie-talkies?" Zane nodded. "Okay, give one to Hafez." He turned back to the older man. "We'll give you a squawk when we come back. *If* we come back."

"You do not sound confident."

"There's ten of us, and about thirty of them. And they've got one of our friends hostage. I've had *worse* odds, but . . ."

Hafez got out and embraced him. "Allah be with you, my friend. And you too, Nina," he added over Eddie's shoulder. "I will wait for you. Well, until I run out of cigarettes!"

"Go on, bugger off," Eddie told him with a grin. The Iranian detached himself, accepting a radio from Zane and climbing into the van. A quick U-turn, and the vehicle headed back downhill.

Nina took off her head scarf. "I just hope we won't need to get out of here in a hurry . . ."

"Yeah, me too." Eddie gazed back at the mountains. The tallest peak was well over half a mile high, the uppermost section of its southern face a near-vertical wall dropping down to the steep forest below. "Okay, we'd better get started. We should stay clear of this track, though. Just in case someone comes back along it."

"Definitely," Zane agreed. "Which way?"

Eddie checked Nina's map before indicating a rise about a mile distant. "Over there. We can go along that ridge. It'll be a hell of a lot easier than climbing straight up its side."

The Israeli nodded, then told his men to move into the trees. "You ready for this?" Eddie asked his wife.

"Not really," she said, "but . . . I'm doing it anyway."

He smiled, then kissed her. "Come on, then."

Hand in hand, they followed the others into the dense, damp forest.

* * *

The going soon became harder than expected. Not because the terrain was particularly difficult, though it was quite steep in places. What was wearing the party down wasn't physical. Under the thick, obscuring canopy of the trees, the atmosphere was oppressive, the very air thick and cloying. With clouds blotting out the sun, there were not even shafts of light through the trees to relieve the twilight gloom.

"What was this place called in the *Alexander Romance*?" Eddie asked as they trudged up the slope.

"Alexander first knew it as the Land of the Blessed," Nina replied. "But once he was inside, he started calling it the Land of Darkness—or the Region or Kingdom, depending on the translation. Andreas called it the Kingdom of Darkness on the relic. It's an accurate description, whichever way. There's a passage in the *Romance* where it got so dark even in daytime that Alexander and his men couldn't go any deeper without risking getting lost."

"So how did they get through?"

She smiled. "Wisdom. There was an old man in Alexander's army who told him they should only ride mares who had foals. They left the foals behind, so when they eventually returned after exploring, the mares led them back to their children. Alexander was so impressed that he gave the old man ten pounds of gold as a reward."

"See, Jared?" Eddie called to the Israeli, who was a short distance ahead. "Age and experience win again." He turned back to Nina and asked more quietly: "Would that actually work?"

"I haven't a clue. I'm not a horse expert. But it was while they were exploring that Andreas found the Spring of Immortality, so if it still exists . . ." She let the words hang in the stifling air.

Zane slowed to let them draw level. "What did it say about the spring in the *Alexander Romance*? What exactly are we looking for?"

"There wasn't much description in the *Romance* itself," Nina told him. "Alexander and his men had a choice of paths; the left one turned out to be impassable, so they went right even though it was darker—actually, Alexander later left a message for travelers that to get through the Land of the Blessed, they should always take the right-hand path. They eventually found a place where the water 'flashed like lightning,' which Andreas discovered to be the Spring of Immortality. As for what Andreas said on the inscriptions on the fish"—she glanced over her shoulder at her backpack, which contained the bronze artifact among her other gear—"the spring is through the Gate of Alexander, which is in the shadow of the area's tallest peak. The mountain we're heading for seems to fit the bill, but beyond that, all I can hope is that we'll know it when we see it. *If* we see it."

"And if we're not too late to get to it," Eddie said with a sudden urgency as he saw the men ahead react to something. "Get down."

They crouched behind a tree. "What is it?" Nina asked.

"I can hear an engine," Zane whispered. "It must be

on the track." He produced a pair of compact binoculars and peered downhill.

The sound of a vehicle jolting along rough ground reached them. But nothing was visible for several seconds . . . until a flicker of movement appeared between the trees, heading toward the road.

"It's the jeep," said Zane, tracking it. "A Safir; I was right," he added with a little smugness directed at the Englishman. "Looks like an officer in the passenger seat . . . Revolutionary Guard."

"What about the other trucks?" Eddie asked.

"I can only hear the jeep." They waited in silence until the vehicle passed and its engine note died away. "I think that was the local Guard commander going home rather than sit around in a damp forest. Leitz paid him to get Kroll and his men to where they want to go, but now that he's fulfilled his part of the deal, he's leaving."

"I can't blame him," said Nina. "But I guess that means they've already started their search." She looked up the slope, but nothing was visible through the tree cover. "And we've still got two or three miles to go."

"We'd better keep moving, then," said Zane.

The team continued through the woods, eventually reaching the ridge. The trees thinned out as they climbed, enough of the sky visible to let Nina get a GPS fix. "Okay, this is where we are," she said, showing the others their position on the map. "So it's about another two miles to the search area. I would have tried to use the fish to confirm we're at the right latitude, but it's kinda cloudy." Muted amusement from the others.

"It'll take a while to check the whole thing," said Eddie. The zone she had marked covered close to half a square mile. "And that's assuming it's not already crawling with Nazis."

"We know roughly what we're looking for, though." She produced the bronze fish from her rucksack, running a fingertip along one of the lines of Greek text. "The Gate of Alexander seems from the context to be a physical structure. It might still be standing."

Zane examined the map. "Won't it be lower down

than that? Surely a spring can't start too high up a mountain; where would the water come from?"

"Actually, there are springs recorded practically on mountain summits. The reservoir can be miles underground—the weight of the rock forces the water up through fissures." She folded the map, returning it and the artifact to her pack. "But according to Andreas, the Gate of Alexander is in the shadow of the tallest peak, so I'm guessing—I'm *hoping*—that it's not right at the top."

"She's usually pretty good at this, don't worry," Eddie told the Israeli. "Okay, crack on!"

They set off again, tromping back into the darkness of the forest. The ground became steeper, slowing their progress. It took well over an hour before they reached the edge of the target area, the sheer-sided peak looming over them to the south, and nearly another hour after that before their search found anything.

What they discovered was not a spring, or any kind of gateway.

"Shit!" Eddie hissed, waving the others to a halt. "Get into cover!"

"What is it?" Nina asked as she scurried behind a tree.

"Footprints. They're already here!"

The forest floor was covered in a thick layer of fallen foliage, absorbing the group's individual tracks, but not even the carpet of mulch could hide the passage of dozens of men. A churned trail of boot prints angled up the shadowed hillside.

Zane glared up the slope. "They might have found the spring already."

"Maybe, but they haven't come back down yet," Nina said. "We've still got a chance to stop them."

"We're outnumbered at least three to one!"

"Thought that was what Mossad were into," said Eddie with a half smile. "Surrounded by your enemies, never backing down, all that?"

The Israeli was not amused. "This isn't exactly our homeland. But no, I wasn't planning to back down. Not when we're this close."

The team moved parallel to the Nazis' trail, leaving a gap of about a hundred feet. They headed higher, alert to the slightest activity. But all they heard was glum birdsong. The climb continued, five minutes passing without incident, ten—

One of the Mossad agents raised a hand. Everyone immediately stopped and crouched. Nina saw nothing ahead. She tried to pick out any sounds over the sudden drum of her heart . . .

Faint voices reached her, along with a rhythmic thumping and scraping. Looking uphill, she saw that the slope eased not far above, a broad shelf running across the forested hillside. The noises were coming from higher and to the right. "Sounds like they're digging."

"Back up," ordered Zane. "We'll go around them and get a view from above."

"Keep well clear," Eddie warned. "They might have posted sentries."

The group made a wide circle around the hub of activity, looping in toward it from higher up. The digging was taking place a few hundred feet above the shelf, not far from the base of the peak's southern face. Eddie dropped to a crawl, stopping behind a fungus-covered log. The Mossad agents spread out nearby, Zane and Nina joining the Englishman to look through the trees at what lay below.

"Oh God," Nina whispered. "We're too late . . ."

33

Kroll surveyed his men's work with satisfaction—and growing anticipation. "You should feel proud, Banna!" he said to the cowed Egyptian. "You brought us here, and we've found exactly what Andreas described. The Gate of Alexander."

The Nazi troops were excavating what they had discovered protruding from the slope. Whether it had been deliberately buried or the soil had simply built up over time, Kroll neither knew nor cared; what mattered was that the way to the spring was almost clear. The Gate of Alexander was a stone arch four yards high and three wide, at the end of a passage cut into the hillside. Behind it was a stone slab, clearly covering an entrance; another few minutes of work would see enough dirt cleared away for it to be pulled open.

"If that's really what this is." Rasche sat on a tree stump nearby, watching with impatience. The silver-lined water barrels were lined up behind him.

"What else could it be?" Kroll strode to the arch and pointed at the Greek text carved into it. " 'This gate marks Alexander's journey into the Land of the Blessed. Heed his words, and you will have nothing to fear.' This *is* the place—the spring is here."

"Where, though?" The question came from a figure wearing white, his clothing incongruous among the soldiers' pale brown fatigues. Frederic Leitz had joined them on their arrival in Iran, large sums of money smoothly changing hands to ensure that their presence in the country would go without official notice, and also to provide them with an escort to their destination. The Revolutionary Guard had now gone, but left trucks below to take the Nazis—and the thousands of gallons of life-prolonging liquid they hoped to be carrying—back to their chartered plane. "If there is a spring here, then where's the water?"

"Inside there." Kroll jabbed a fat finger at the stone slab. "Andreas built a shrine to hide it, so only those equal to Alexander would ever be able to find it. We've proved ourselves worthy."

The entrance was now clear. Ropes were hooked to the top of the slab, then under Schneider's direction the soldiers formed into lines and heaved upon them. Loose soil dropped around the great block, the lines drawn taut as guitar strings . . . then its upper edge crunched away from the surrounding rock.

"Keep pulling!" Kroll bellowed. "Get it open! Pull, pull!"

Schneider took up the shout, turning it into a chant. The soldiers hauled in unison. The slab tilted outward, little by little—then suddenly broke free and slammed to the ground.

Kroll pushed through his men. There was indeed a passage hidden behind the slab. "It's here!" he shouted. "Bring the lights—we've found it!"

* * *

The triumph in Kroll's voice told Nina that he had reached his goal. "What do we do?"

"Attack now, while they're still off guard," said Zane, checking his Uzi submachine gun. "We'll cut most of them down before they can react."

"And you'll cut down Ubayy too." Rasche was pushing the young Egyptian after the Nazi leader.

"It's a price we'll have to pay." He signaled to the other Mossad agents.

"It won't work," Eddie told him urgently. "We're too far off, and there's too many trees in the way. You won't even get half of them before they regroup."

"We can still take out the leaders, though." Weapon ready, Zane started to move out from his hiding place.

Eddie pulled him back. "Jared," he said, fixing the angry young man with a firm stare, "trust me. It *won't work*."

Zane glared at him, the other operatives watching intently. Then he muttered a curse. "So what *do* we do?" he demanded.

"Nothing we can do; not yet, anyway. We need to get a better position, for a start."

"But we've got the higher ground here—*and* surprise."

"Which means sod-all if you don't have decent line of sight."

Zane clenched his jaw in frustration, but finally nodded. "Okay. We'll wait." Another signal, telling his men to hold. "But we can't let them get away with the water. If they start to pull out, then we attack—whether we're in a good position or not."

"We might not need to," said Nina as furious shouting arose from below. "I don't think they've found what they expected . . ."

*   *   *

Kroll eagerly led the way through the entrance. Schneider, Leitz, and Rasche followed, the latter bringing Banna with him. The Nazi leader shone his torch around the underground space, the beam finding . . .

Very little. The short passage from the surface opened into a small chamber, the walls lined with murals and Greek text. A stone basin was set into a side wall. Kroll's eye was instantly caught by the glint of silver. He hurried to it, finding the elongated oval bowl lined with the precious metal. It was filled with water—but only a small amount, the shallow receptacle not much larger than the size of two cupped hands. A thin silver spout projected from the wall just above it. Glistening at the tip of the metal pipe was a water droplet. He watched it intently, but it showed no signs of growing larger.

"Is that it?" asked Leitz.

"Is that *it*?" echoed Rasche, with scathing disappointment instead of curiosity. "I could *spit* more than that! That much water wouldn't even last us a month!"

"Shut up," Kroll snapped, dipping a fingertip into the liquid. He felt the same electric tingle as he had over seventy years earlier, the very first time he touched the water hidden beneath the farmhouse.

"Have we found it?" said Schneider. "Is it the spring?"

"It is," Kroll replied, feeling relief . . . and a rising anger. Rasche was right: The amount of water in the brimming basin was only a tiny fraction of what they needed. "But—"

Rasche completed his thought. "But not enough. There isn't enough!" he erupted. "We would have been better off if we'd stayed in the Enklave and never even gone to Egypt!"

The Nazi leader turned upon him. "Are you questioning me?"

"You're damn right I am! We've lost our base, we've lost over half our men, we've lost what little water we had left—and you've taken money from a lot of very powerful people with the promise of a share of—of this *piss-puddle*!" He stabbed a finger at the basin.

Schneider glanced toward the soldiers staring through the entrance. "Not in front of the men. We can't afford to seem divided."

"Don't tell me what to do, you degenerate little shit!" Rasche shouted, before glaring at the white-clad man. "And I doubt even if we refund them that Leitz will return his percentage."

The Luxembourger raised his hands in feigned apology. "All transactions are final. That has always been our deal."

"There won't be any refunds," growled Kroll. "This is an all-or-nothing mission. And I'm not willing to accept nothing."

Rasche made a disgusted sound, then stalked out. "We've thrown it all away!" he fired back over his shoulder.

Kroll scowled after him before rounding on Banna, who had been watching with fearful incomprehension. "Dr. Banna!" he barked, reverting to English. "We followed *your* instructions to this place. But this is not a spring; it is not even a trickle." The droplet of water on the spout's tip had still not swelled enough to drip into the basin. "Where is the spring? Tell me!"

"I—I do not know!" Banna cried. "This is what Andreas described—we came through the Gate of Alexander, just as the text said."

"And what else did it say? If you're hiding something—"

"You still have pictures of the relic!" Banna interrupted, finding some small cinder of defiance. "You read the Greek text yourself—and you did what it said to do! It brought us here." He gestured at the bowl. "That is the spring, where Andreas said it was hidden. I am sorry it is not all you hoped for, but there it is."

Kroll's hand moved as if to draw his holstered Luger, but then withdrew. "I will bring the photographs. Read the text again, and make sure you have not missed anything." He glowered at the young archaeologist. "If you cannot find the spring, you are of no use to me—just like the American girl. Remember that. Schneider, watch him," he ordered as he left the chamber. Leitz followed, leaving Schneider to hold his prisoner at gunpoint.

The soldiers looked on uncertainly as he emerged. "Well?" demanded Rasche. "Now what do we do?"

"We wait for the Arab to read the Greek text again," Kroll replied. He ordered an underling to give a folder of photos to Banna, then mopped his damp brow. "We'll make camp in the meantime. On the flat ground, down there. I've had enough of hills."

"And what if the Arab doesn't come up with anything?"

"Then I'll tear this mountain apart until we find the spring." The obese SS officer stared at his subordinate, daring him to make a challenge; when none was forth-coming, he began to waddle down the slope.

· · ·

"Are they leaving?" Nina asked, partly in hope and partly disbelief, as the Nazis filed away after Kroll. From the team's position above the dig site she had been un-able to see what was inside, but even at a distance it was clear from Rasche's body language alone that it had not lived up to expectations.

"No, Kroll said something about making camp," Zane told her.

"Must be going back to that flat bit to do it," Eddie said. He had taken a rough head count; there were be-tween twenty-five and thirty Nazis, and nearly all were now on the move. "Fat bastard can't handle steep ground."

Nina thought back to their circuitous ascent. "That's, what? A hundred yards down the hill?"

"At least. Why, what're you thinking?"

"If they leave the site unguarded, we can walk right down to it!"

Zane surveyed the scene below. "I see four men stand-ing watch—and Schneider went into whatever's down there and hasn't come out."

"Five against ten," said Eddie. "I like those odds a lot better."

"We still have to save Ubayy, though," Nina reminded him. "They might kill him rather than give him up."

"They won't get the chance," said Zane, with under-stated menace. "Okay, once the rest of them are clear, we'll move closer. We won't do anything until we're sure we can secure Banna," he assured Nina.

They waited for some time. The main group of sol-diers was now out of sight farther down the hill, though occasional sounds of activity as they set up camp reached the observers. The four men guarding the entrance were initially alert, but quickly settled into what Eddie knew from experience was an occupational hazard for any soldier: boredom. They were not expecting trouble . . . so neither were they prepared for it.

"Safe to move?" Zane asked the Englishman, who nodded. "Then let's go."

The little group began its cautious descent toward the arch. They were not wearing camouflage gear, but their dark clothing provided adequate concealment in the pervading gloom beneath the trees. Moving as stealthily as they could, they closed on the Nazis below.

They were about fifty feet from the dig when one of the guards turned. Everyone froze, but he looked into the tunnel, not up the hill. After a moment, Schneider emerged. He spoke briefly to the sentries, one of whom went into the shrine to replace him, then headed downhill.

"I like the odds even better now," Eddie whispered to Zane.

"So do I," said the Israeli. He gestured for his comrades to stop, and mimed attaching a silencer to a gun.

Eddie shook his head as the men fitted suppressors. "It's too risky. The shots'll still be heard."

"Not by anyone in the camp. They're too far away."

"Maybe, but what about the bloke in the cave? If he hears the noise and looks outside to see his mates all keeling over dead, then he'll scream for help—and Kroll and his goons'll hear *that*."

"What do we do, then?"

"Keep it old-school. You brought knives, didn't you?"

"We did." A small, grim smile.

Zane issued new orders, then he and two of his men, Arens and Galitz, dropped to their bellies and slithered down the hill. Eddie and the others hung back, silenced weapons ready in case anything went wrong. But the three sentries were oblivious to their approach, two of them chatting off to one side of the opening. The third was farther away, looking longingly toward the encampment.

The latter was the danger, Eddie realized. Despite his clear desire to join the rest of the group, he still occasionally glanced back at the arch. If he caught movement in his peripheral vision, everything would go to hell . . .

Galitz and Arens reached a position ten feet from the pair of guards and stopped, silently rising into crouches. Zane continued toward the third man, going around the other side of the archway to keep himself hidden from the two sentries. Timing was everything; it would be almost impossible to eliminate both men without making some noise, giving him only a couple of seconds to reach the third.

He shifted the hefty combat knife in his hand, the matte-black blade barely more than a shadow. The guard was still gazing downhill. Zane nodded to his comrades. They started across the last few feet to their targets, their leader readying himself to strike the moment they reached them . . .

The lone guard turned his head.

It was just a glance back at the entrance—but it snapped into a double-take as he saw the pair of dark figures descending upon his fellows. He opened his mouth to scream a warning—

Zane was still eight feet away—but his knife crossed the distance in a fraction of a second. It stabbed deep into the sentry's neck, rupturing his windpipe with a spurt of blood.

The other Mossad operatives darted forward to grab both their targets simultaneously, yanking their heads back and slashing their throats. But the danger wasn't over. Zane's victim was still alive, clawed hands pulling at the knife as he staggered in front of the arch. If the man inside saw him . . .

The Israeli ran to drag him back—but heard a startled sound from the entrance. He spun to see both Banna and his guard staring at him.

The Nazi whipped up his gun—

The Egyptian leapt at him, slamming him against the tunnel wall. The Nazi staggered, but retaliated by smashing his weapon against Banna's stomach.

The young archaeologist fell with a winded gasp. His attacker recovered, bringing his gun to bear—

Three bullets ripped into his chest. The Nazi collapsed

as the muted thumps of Zane's gunshots echoed through the trees.

• • •

Eddie watched with dismay. "Shit!" he said, raising his Cherokee and looking down the slope. Only in Hollywood did a suppressor reduce a weapon's discharge to a soft sneeze; three shots from a silenced gun still sounded like three shots, just quieter. He had heard them clearly from his vantage point—but had the Nazis down the hill?

Zane and his companions dragged the twitching bodies behind nearby trees, then took up positions to cover the slope below. The other agents moved to back them up. Everyone waited, senses straining to detect the first sign of danger . . .

Noises came from down the hillside—but not shouts of alarm or screamed orders. Instead they were almost comically innocuous, faint laughter from some shared joke. A scent of cooking food reached them. "Must be their lunch break," said Eddie, lowering his gun.

"Are we safe?" Nina asked.

"For now, but we can't hang about." He jogged down the slope, his wife following.

Zane met them at the entrance. The young Israeli was breathing quickly. "Are you okay?" Nina asked.

"Yeah," he replied. "That was close, though."

"What about Ubayy?" She looked through the arch. Banna got to his feet, surprise and relief on his face as he saw her. "Oh, thank God. Ubayy! Are you all right?"

"Yes, yes, I am okay," he replied, emerging shakily. "What about you? You came after me on the train, but then I heard an explosion—and Kroll told me the bridge had been destroyed . . ."

"We jumped off," Nina told him, before embracing him. He was quivering with the release of tension. "Then we followed Andreas's instructions on the relic to get here—but I see you did too."

"Yes, I am sorry," he said, stepping back with a hangdog expression.

"Don't worry about it." She looked up at the arch, taking in the Greek text upon it, then past Banna into the tunnel. "What did you find in there? I'm guessing from Rasche's reaction that it wasn't what they'd hoped for."

Banna managed a faint smile. "No, it was not." He led her into the dark little shrine.

Her husband and Zane came with them, the other Mossad operatives keeping watch outside. "Is that the spring?" said Eddie, seeing the basin. "Just that?"

The Egyptian nodded. "There is only a tiny amount of water. Kroll and Rasche argued about it. I do not know what they said, but Rasche was very angry."

"I'm not surprised," said Nina. "They came here thinking they'd find enough water to last decades, and all they got was this? It wouldn't even make a decent cup of coffee."

"That doesn't matter," said Zane. "What does is that we can stop them from getting it. Permanently. If we blow up this room, they'll have nothing."

"That's pretty much all they've got now," Eddie noted as the Israeli headed back outside.

Nina used a flashlight to examine the walls. "Yeah, I know. But . . ."

"But what?"

"It doesn't feel right. This place was obviously built by Andreas and his followers—his name's here, and here." She darted her light across the Greek text. "But it's just a room—and that little puddle's not the big prize we've been led to expect."

"I had thought that also," said Banna, collecting the photographs. "Kroll ordered me to read the text again to see if I had missed something. There was a line about the fish . . . but it came *after* the clues that led us here, once we were through the arch."

"Yeah, I remember. Something about doing what Andreas did with the fish. But why would you need the fish to find the spring when you're already *at* the spring?" She turned back to the basin. "Unless . . . this *isn't* the spring."

Eddie dipped a finger into the water. "Ow!" he said, in surprise rather than pain. "I just got zapped."

"That fits what Kroll said about the water he found in Greece—and the FBI analysis of that flask in LA." She thought for a moment, then switched off the flashlight.

The basin was plunged into shadow. Banna joined them, drawing in a startled breath. "It is alight!"

A faint shimmering glow came from the water, reflecting off the precious metal lining the basin. "Just like the *Alexander Romance* described it," said Nina. "It looks like it's flashing like lightning, don't you think?" She hesitantly put her fingers into the bowl. The initial electrical tingle made her flinch, but she held firm, lowering them into the water until she touched the silver containing it.

It was mostly smooth . . . but as she slid her fingertips around, she felt faint impressions in the surface. "There's something here."

Eddie leaned closer. "I don't see anything."

"Hold on." She switched the flashlight back on and directed it at the basin, but the reflected glare obliterated any detail. "Ubayy, hold this, but don't point it at the water. Aim it over there." She indicated the far wall.

Banna did so. The light was now more diffuse—providing just enough relief for her to pick out shapes imprinted into metal. "Here, look," she said, running a finger over one of the oval bowl's long sides. "There's a little ledge here, just under the surface—and another opposite, like something's meant to rest on top of it." A probe uncovered a third at the narrow end beneath the spout, but this was different: a tiny metal protrusion, square in cross section, set between two indentations. "And this looks like it fits into something . . ."

Zane returned, an agent called Haber following. "I've got the explosives," he announced, three blocks of yellowish C-4 in the crook of one arm. The other man put down a pack and took out several more. "We don't have time to plan a proper demolition, so we'll have to collapse the ceiling." He set down his cargo and took out a string of detonators.

"Wait, not yet," said Nina, alarmed. "I've found something—I think it's part of Andreas's challenge."

"I don't care," Zane replied as he pushed the detonators into the soft bricks. "Making sure the Nazis don't get the water is all that matters now."

"But this might not be the only source," she protested. "The text said that once you reach this place, the fish will show you the spring—*the fish*!" she cried in sudden realization.

"Christ, what about it?" Eddie demanded. "Only way I'd get that excited about a fish is if it came with chips."

Nina pulled the artifact from her rucksack. "Ubayy, the light!" The excitement in her voice captured even Zane's attention.

"What is it?" Banna asked as he redirected the beam at the basin.

"Look at the bowl—the shape and size of it. It's a hell of a lot like this!" She held the bronze relic above the water, revealing that they were a very close match in dimensions. "The upper and lower fins should fit perfectly on these little notches along the long sides—and as for the mouth . . ."

She carefully aligned the twin curves of the fish's lips with the carved recess beneath the spout. They were a perfect fit—and the metal nub slotted neatly into its mouth. "The fish goes into the basin," Nina explained as she prepared to seat the relic upon the other indentations. "Do what Andreas did, put it in the water, and . . ."

She lowered it into place—and jumped away in shock as it *moved*.

"What the *fuck*?" Eddie said. The fish's tail had started flapping the moment it was laid fully flat in the water, kicking up little splashes. "How's it doing that?"

"I don't know," said Nina, watching in amazement. "Something to do with the charge in the water, I guess. Maybe some kind of primitive motor?"

"A motor?" said Zane, incredulous. "I thought this thing was two thousand years old! They didn't have motors back then."

"All you need to make the simplest kind of motor is a wire and an electrostatic charge—that's been known for centuries. And there have been plenty of cases where relatively advanced technology and ideas were lost or forgotten for long periods before being rediscovered. Andreas was well traveled and lived for hundreds of years, thanks to this water—that was plenty of time for him to combine different pieces of knowledge." She looked more closely. Glimpses of a moving mechanism were visible inside the slot along the relic's back. "He had a sense of humor too. According to the *Romance*, he discovered the spring when he dipped a preserved fish into it and it jumped back to life. Probably galvanic response, the electrical charge making the fish's muscles twitch, but by making this fish do the same, it brings everything full circle—"

The flapping abruptly stopped. Simultaneously, a deep *clunk* came from the chamber's rear. Zane snatched up his Uzi. "What was that?"

Nina took the flashlight from Banna. "Something just released . . ." She directed the beam into the shadowed corner.

Where one of the reliefs had previously been flush with its neighbor, there was now a small gap, a line of blackness an inch wide separating them. Nina scurried to investigate. "There's a passage back here!" she announced.

Banna lifted the fish, which gave one final jerk of its tail before falling still. "Nina!" he said, feeling the protrusion under the spout with his little finger. "Something was turning in its mouth. This spike must have fit into it like a key."

"The fish unlocked it when it moved . . . and showed us the Spring of Immortality. Just like Andreas said," said Nina, going to the crack. "It's still here—inside the mountain. Give me a hand."

Eddie and, after a moment of reluctance, Zane helped her to pull open the secret door. The flashlight revealed a narrow passage beyond, angling steeply upward. Banna joined them, and they stared into the darkness.

"So are we going up it?" Eddie asked, breaking the silence.

"Are you kidding?" replied Nina, starting through the opening.

"Wait, wait!" snapped Zane. "What about the Nazis? If they come back while we're in there, we'll be trapped—and we'll have led them right to the spring! We've got to destroy this."

Nina stopped and rounded on him. "After everything we've been through, we're right on the doorstep of something amazing—and you want to blow it up?"

"He's got a point," said Eddie. "If those bastards leave here with a tanker truck full of magic water, then they've won. And everyone they killed will have died for nothing," he added, with considerable meaning.

Nina regarded them both for a moment. "Then blow it up," she finally said. "But I'm still going inside. No matter what."

"No you're not," her husband said firmly.

"Then why am I even here? Eddie, I told you: This is more than just what I do—it's who I *am*. You of all people should know that by now. I might be dying, but I'm still not going to give up a foot from the finish." She turned to Zane. "Even if you blow up this room, the Nazis'll just dig it out again—having the Mossad destroy it will prove to them that the spring's really here. But if you destroy the *source* of the spring . . ."

"We brought cyanide—a contingency plan," the Israeli admitted. "If we poison the water, it might kill the Nazis *and* their backers . . ."

Eddie was now faced with options he disliked from both sides. "You're not going up there," he told Nina, "and *you*," he said to Zane, "you're not poisoning Iran's water supply with fucking cyanide—that kind of thing counts as an act of war! Just blow this place up and let's get out of here." He looked back at Nina. "Please?"

"Eddie, she's right," Zane was forced to admit. "Andreas and his followers dug all this out by hand—even if we destroy this room, it won't take long to clear it with power tools and explosives. We'll only delay the Nazis, not stop them. And if we leave here, we'll lose track of them."

"So now you want to go in there too? A minute ago, you couldn't wait to blow everything up!"

"I know, but Nina's made me realize there's a better alternative. I don't just want to *stop* these Nazis," he said, with sudden vehemence. "I want to *kill* them. I want them to pay for everything they've done. Not just what they did to me"—he brought a hand to his bruised face—"but for what they did to my people—and your friends. Surely you can't disagree with that."

"No, I can't," Eddie replied grudgingly. "I owe them for Macy, at the very least."

"And Dr. Assad," said Nina. "And Bill, and Dina, and everyone else they murdered to find this place. We can't let them control the Spring of Immortality. No matter what. You remember how I said I wanted to leave a legacy? Well, stopping Kroll and the other Nazis would be better than any book."

Eddie rubbed his forehead, conflicted and exasperated. "All right. We make sure they don't get the spring—we poison it, blow it up, whatever. But we need to be quick, okay? It won't be long before someone wonders why those guards haven't come down for their bratwurst."

"Agreed," said Zane. "Haber, you bring the explosives and detonators," he told the other Mossad operative. "I'll tell Behr and Arens to keep watch—the others will come with us. The more men we have, the quicker we can set the C-4 if we need to," he explained to Nina before hurrying back outside.

"You absolutely sure about this?" Eddie asked his wife. " 'Cause if we go in there, we probably won't come back out."

"I've been on a one-way trip from the moment I was infected by the eitr," Nina insisted. "If I'm going to die . . . then I want to die *for* something, not *of* something. And I know you've always thought the same way. Fight to the end, as you say."

"Fight to the end," he echoed, almost automatically,

before adding: "Buggeration and fuckery. I've made you *way* too much like me."

"You're a bad influence, Eddie Chase," she said, smiling. "But I love you all the same." She kissed him. He pulled her close and returned it, with passion. Banna blushed, finding a new fascination with the stone basin.

The moment was broken as Zane returned with five of his men. "The Nazis are still in their camp, but I don't know how long they'll stay there. Haber, are you ready?"

The agent picked up the pack of explosives. "Yes."

"Good. Nina? You should lead the way—this is your find."

"And Ubayy's," said Nina.

The Egyptian shook his head. "It is an incredible discovery, but . . . the credit is yours. I wish I had not found it."

She gave him a sympathetic look, then faced the darkness beyond the secret door. "Okay, then. Let's end this."

Steeling herself, she entered the passageway, Eddie and the others following.

34

They made their way up the steep tunnel. The last man, Krebs, tried to pull the door shut behind them, but was forced to leave it slightly ajar as the gap closed on his fingers. The passage was only wide enough for the group to proceed in single file, Nina's caution—and archaeological urge to examine her surroundings—soon bottling up the others behind her. "Come on, love, shift it," Eddie complained. "We're on the clock."

"I know, but look at this." Dust covered the stone floor, undisturbed for millennia—and visible in her flashlight's beam were faint imprints, the sandaled feet of the last person to exit before the place was sealed. "Who knows how old these are?"

"Nobody, and I doubt anyone but you cares either."

"All right, jeez! Can't a dying woman make her last discovery without being hassled?" But she increased her pace.

Zane shone his own light past the couple. "How long is the tunnel?"

"I think I can see the top," Nina reported. "It opens out."

"Sounds echoey," said Eddie as they neared the summit. "Must be a fairly big space."

Nina reached it—and stopped in surprise, the others bumping together behind her. "Ah . . . yeah. You could say that."

They had emerged onto a ledge overlooking a deep vertical shaft, a ragged rift at least a hundred feet across that dropped away into the heart of the mountain. "So," said Eddie, peering over the edge, "finding the spring's going to take a bit longer than we thought."

Nina shone her torch downward. The powerful beam was reduced to a dim pinprick on the bottom far below. "Damn, that's deep." She brought the light back up, seeing pathways carved into the walls of the shaft. They had been paved with stone slabs, but many were uneven or missing entirely, exposing the raw rock beneath.

"There's a way down here," said Zane, moving left along the ledge to illuminate the top of a steep path that descended clockwise around the shaft.

"And here," added Eddie, finding a second route to the right. This one spiraled counterclockwise into the darkness below.

"Which do we take?" Banna asked.

Nina tried to track one, but sections were blocked from view by the folds of the craggy walls. "I don't know. It looks like there are junctions lower down, but I can't see how they connect."

"We should split up," said Zane. "One group takes the left path, the other the right. We'll divide the explosives— that way, whoever gets—"

"No, no!" she interrupted, disparate pieces suddenly slotting together. "We take the right path. We *always* take the right path!"

"What do you mean?" Eddie asked.

"It was written on the arch—'Heed Alexander's words, and you will have nothing to fear.' It's what he said in the *Romance*, remember? Once you go through the arch, you always take the right-hand path or else you'll become lost. 'Lost' in this case meaning falling two hundred feet onto solid rock. This whole thing is part of Andreas's challenge; I wouldn't be surprised if the left path's booby-trapped somehow."

Banna surveyed the chasm nervously. "We still might fall, whichever path we take. It does not look safe."

"He's right," said Eddie. "Nina, it'll take ages to get to the bottom—if we even can. We should just rig the tunnel with C-4 and get out of here."

"I don't think we'll get the chance," Zane said, whirling at the sound of someone running up the passage. He hefted his Uzi, but lowered it as he saw the two rear-guard Mossad agents. "What's happening?"

"They're coming," Arens reported breathlessly.

"How many?"

"All of them," the other agent told him. "We could never have stopped them, so we came to warn you."

"Shit," muttered Zane. "We won't have enough time to set the explosives."

"We could hold them off here," suggested Behr. "They can only come up that tunnel one by one."

"They'll make it eventually," Eddie warned.

Zane considered his options, then: "Okay, Arens and Behr, hold them for as long as you can, then follow us down." He looked back at Nina as he went to the counterclockwise path. "I hope you're right about going right."

"So do I!" she replied. "I'll go first—just in çase I'm not." She started down the ledge.

"Going into the depths of the bloody earth after some ancient legend?" grumbled Eddie as he followed. "Been doing that a *lot* lately . . ."

* * *

"Sir! Over here!" yelled a soldier. Kroll looked toward the source of the shout as he strained up the hill. The man was pulling a bloodied corpse out from behind a tree.

"Here's another one!" a second soldier reported.

"It can't have been the Egyptian," snarled Rasche, striding ahead of the Nazi leader. "Someone else is here." He glared back at Leitz. "Your Iranian friends, perhaps?"

"It's not them," panted Kroll. "It's *Wilde*. She survived the bridge explosion, then followed the clues on the fish, just like us. And she brought the Mossad with her."

"So where are they?" asked Schneider, eyes darting nervously across the forest.

Kroll reached the arch, pausing to catch his breath as he pointed at the opening. "In there. Secure it," he ordered. "Quickly!" Several soldiers ran into the shrine.

"But there was nothing inside," said Rasche.

"Nothing that *we* saw. But there must have been more to it."

"Then Banna lied to us. I'll kill him when I find him!"

"We'll kill them all," Kroll growled. One of the soldiers hurried back out and saluted him. "What have you found?"

"There's a tunnel, *mein Führer*!" the man said excitedly. "It wasn't there before."

"Obviously it wasn't there before, idiot," snapped Rasche. "Where does it go?"

"Up into the mountain, sir. We couldn't see the end."

"That's where they've gone," said Kroll. "To find the spring—before we do."

Schneider regarded the opening with alarm. "To take the water for themselves?"

"No. To stop *us* taking it!" He called out to his troops. "We are going to make an assault on the spring! Everyone ready weapons!"

"How big is this tunnel?" Rasche asked the soldier.

"Only wide enough for one man at once, sir."

The SS officer turned back to his commander. "We won't stand a chance. Two or three men could hold off an entire *Zugtrupp*."

"Not necessarily," Kroll replied. "Leitz! The equipment you supplied; did you bring a thermal sight?"

"If you asked for it, it's here," Leitz replied.

"Good. Then fit it to a rifle—if anyone puts their head around the end of that tunnel, blow it off!"

* * *

Nina made her way carefully down the ledge. It was just wide enough for her to walk normally, but she still kept her back against the wall, sidestepping as quickly as she dared. Her flashlight picked out the path ahead—but she paused as someone else's light briefly flicked across the chasm.

Eddie stopped behind her. "Hang on, everyone," he called. "What is it?"

"I saw something, over there." She redirected her torch. "On the other path . . ."

She fell silent as she saw it. As did the others.

"What is *that*?" Zane exclaimed, adding his own beam to Nina's. Others followed suit to illuminate the entire object.

"That," said Banna, astonished, "is a Phytoi."

The lights danced over a statue carved from the rock face, a humanoid male over thirty feet tall. It was naked, but appeared entwined in vines and leaves. The sculpture had been hidden from their initial vantage point on the ledge by a fold in the cavern wall. The other route downward crossed right in front of its chest, the great figure's arms spread wide along the ledge. Bizarrely, instead of hands it had what resembled curved saw blades extending from its forearms.

Nina remembered the name. "It's a creature from the *Alexander Romance*, isn't it?"

"Yes; plant men or forest men, according to different translations," Banna confirmed. "Alexander fought a tribe of them after conquering the Achaemenid Empire. They killed a hundred of his soldiers."

"Something to avoid, then," said Eddie. "Those arms—they look like they might swing out."

"You're right," Nina said as she directed her light along one of the jagged limbs. "Could be a booby trap."

"Then you were right about taking this path," said Zane.

"I hope so. It doesn't mean we won't run into something ourselves, though."

"Find out soon," the Yorkshireman said, with a note of impatience. "We can't stand around when there's a bunch of Nazis coming after us."

"Okay, okay," she said, turning the light back to their route. "How long do you think we'll have before—"

Gunfire erupted above.

"About *that* long," said Eddie. "Arse!"

Nina turned unwillingly to hurry on down the narrow path. The unyielding stone wall brushed her right arm, nothing but darkness waiting below to her left.

The firing continued, the Mossad agents' shots interspersed with more distant retorts and the whine of rounds ricocheting off stone—then a much louder *boom* made both Eddie and Zane look up in alarm. A cry came from one of the Israelis, followed by the sound of something crashing over the lip of the precipice. Zane snapped up his torch just in time to see one of his men flash through its beam. He plunged out of sight. A few seconds later, a faint *thump* reached the group.

The remaining man above shouted in Hebrew. "They've got a sniper rifle," Zane told Eddie, tight with anger.

"They must have thermal sights," said the Englishman. "Get your other guy out of there." Zane yelled an order, then hurried after Nina and Eddie as they set off, even faster than before.

The American made her way around another crease in the rock—then slowed. "Careful, there's a junction," she warned as Eddie came up behind her. The path split, the right-hand route continuing on around the chasm while the other doubled back, beginning a clockwise descent.

"Which way?" he asked. "Right again?"

"What if it's a trick?" said Zane.

"I don't think so," Nina said, with what she hoped wasn't misplaced confidence. "Alexander said always to follow the right path." She set off down it.

Zane looked up as the rest of the team descended after her. A light above told him that Arens was making rapid progress. But a rising tramp of boots also warned that the Nazis were closing. He shone his torch past Eddie and Nina at the route ahead. "There's no cover—they'll be able to snipe us from the top ledge."

Nina traced the path with her own light. The Israeli

was right: Anyone at the entrance would have clear line of sight, unless . . . "No, keep going!" she said. "We couldn't see the statue until we were partway around, so if we go far enough, the wall will block us too!"

"Unless they follow us," Eddie pointed out. "Maybe we should've gone the other way at that junction." He directed his torch along the alternative route. "Or maybe not!"

Nina looked across the chasm to see what he had found. Another section of the towering wall bore carvings, these of trees, rising sinuously up along the other ledge. Ominous holes dotted among them suggested that the petrified forest held secrets. "I definitely think we came the right way."

Shouting in German. She looked up. They hadn't yet gone far enough around the shaft for the upper ledge to be blocked from sight; lights flickered from it as the Nazis exited the tunnel. "They're here," Zane warned. "Come on, faster!"

"*Sie sind hier unten!*" someone yelled. Torch beams swept from the high ledge, finding Arens as he scurried down the path, locking on—

Muzzle flashes erupted among the shafts of light. The chasm rang with the shrill crack of bullets hitting rock—then a scream as the Mossad agent was hit. He fell into the darkness below.

Galitz yelled an obscenity. He stopped to fire back up the shaft—forcing Haber behind him to halt as well. "No, keep moving!" Eddie shouted. He, Nina, and Banna were almost at the point where the towering fold in the cliff face would shield them.

Zane hesitated, caught between the desire for revenge and the need to reach safety. He chose the latter. "Come on!" he cried, hurrying after the trio. "Get into cover!"

The next three men followed their leader as Haber yelled for Galitz to move. He turned, starting after his companions—

A boom from above—and a high-velocity bullet ripped through his back and exploded out of his abdomen, the impact throwing him against the wall.

Haber jerked away in shock before recovering. He started to step over the fallen body—

A second round blew his skull apart.

* * *

"Got him!" the sniper reported, staring intently through the thermal imaging scope attached to his MSG-1 rifle. There had been no time to check that the sight was correctly aligned after its hurried fitting, but at a range of less than a hundred yards, it made little difference.

"Shoot the others, quick!" Kroll ordered. More lights were scuttling along the ledge ahead of the two dead men—heading for cover behind part of the cavern wall. The first three torches disappeared from view, the others racing to catch up.

The sniper swung the rifle to track them. Bright shapes appeared in the electronic haze of his sights. He zeroed in on the leader. Taking out the first man would trap the others behind him, making them easy prey. The luminous red crosshairs found the running figure . . .

He fired—just as the ghostly shape disappeared as if it had darted behind a curtain. A flash as the bullet struck rock. The cavern's walls were a uniform temperature, a featureless gray in the thermal scope, rendering the obstructing outcrop invisible. The sniper whipped back to find a new target and fired again, but in his haste the round hit only stone between two of the fleeing men. Before he could reacquire, they too had vanished.

"Dammit, you missed them!" Rasche snarled.

"Go after them," Kroll ordered. "Schneider, take the lead."

"With me," Schneider told the sniper, before calling several other soldiers to join him. He fixed his torch upon the left-hand path. "Down here! We'll go around that rock formation and pick them off from above." He led the descent, heading clockwise around the chasm's inner wall.

"I'll go the other way," said Rasche. "We'll catch them in a pincer." He summoned more men, then addressed Kroll once more. "Will you follow us down?"

"Of course," the obese German shot back, not liking his mocking undertone. "I want to see the spring for myself."

"I understand. It's just that these ledges look rather . . . narrow." Rasche couldn't quite contain a smile.

Kroll's anger flared. "Shut up and get after them!"

"Yes, *mein Führer*!" The second in command snapped an overly enthusiastic salute, then ordered his group down the right-hand path.

* * *

"Is everyone okay?" Nina asked as the Israelis caught their breath.

"We are—but we lost Galitz and Haber," said Zane, grim. "And the explosives too. That only leaves us the poison—if we can even reach the spring to use it."

"Can't exactly go back now," Eddie pointed out. He heard voices above. "Shit, they're coming after us. If they get past that statue, they'll have a clear shot." He directed his torch up at the imposing figure of the Phytoi. "How far down are we?"

Nina briefly redirected her flashlight downward. "Nearly halfway, I'd guess."

"Not far enough!" Eddie saw spears of light stab out from the ledge leading past the statue. The Nazis were fifty feet higher, about to round the great fold of rock to get a direct line of sight upon their quarry. "Keep going—if we can get under 'em, it'll make it harder for them to target us."

But even as he followed Nina down the winding ledge, he knew they wouldn't make it. The first man's light came into view, another appearing behind it a moment later.

Someone shouted in German. Nina recognized the reedy voice: Schneider. The creepy little Nazi was leading their pursuers, running past the statue to reach the perfect firing position—

An echoing *crunch*—and the shouts from above turned into screams.

Everyone on the lower ledge whipped their torches up to see the Phytoi's outspread arms swing out from the

wall—swatting the entire column of Nazis off the path.
Those not sent flying into nothingness were impaled on
the spikes, while Schneider's shriek was cut off as he was
pulped between the two stone limbs when they smashed
together.

"We *definitely* took the right path," Nina gasped.

* * *

Kroll stared down the shaft. "Rasche!" he bellowed.
"What happened?"

Rasche hurriedly ordered his team to hold position.
Lights shone across the chasm. "There's . . . it's a giant
statue," he called back in disbelief. "Its arms swung out
and knocked everyone off. It's a booby trap." Fury rose
in his voice. "This whole place—you've brought us into
a fucking *booby trap*!"

"Stay calm, Rasche!" Kroll shouted, less concerned
about his increasingly unreliable subordinate than the mo-
rale of the men with him. He needed everyone to focus
on their task. "It's part of Andreas's test. Only those
who are Alexander's equal can pass it."

"Then I guess Schneider wasn't up to the challenge!"
A pause, then: "Which isn't really a surprise, the per-
verted little turd. But we still have to get down there."

"Can you see any more statues?"

"Not from here."

"Then keep going! I'll follow you down. We've got to
stop them from reaching the spring, no matter what!"

* * *

Nina arrived at another split in the pathway. Again a
new leg peeled left, running clockwise around the shaft,
while the original continued in the opposite direction.
Keep to the right, she told herself.

Eddie followed her. "Hope Andreas wasn't taking the
piss with that part of the story." He looked up, following their course back around the chasm—and saw torch
beams above. A large group was coming down the spiral
ledge after them, approaching the first junction. "Go on,
go left, you bastards!"

• • •

Rasche's team arrived at the fork. "Which way?" one man asked.

"Split up," Rasche decided. "Everyone ahead of me goes right, everyone behind goes left. And if you come around a corner and find a huge statue, *stop*!" He followed the first group of soldiers down the right-hand path, the rest peeling away behind him.

"Sir!" someone called before long. "I see them, over there!"

"Hold here!" ordered Rasche. Off to the left, the other half of his group was making steady progress downward, but his gaze was fixed on something more distant. Lights were visible on the far side of the great fissure, some thirty yards lower.

The SS man smiled. Wilde and her companions were far enough away to make the shot difficult with a submachine gun . . . but several submachine guns firing on full auto would spray enough bullets to ensure they hit *something*. "Ready weapons! Take aim—"

A sound like rushing wind—then the cracking of dozens of mighty whips echoed around the shaft, followed by shrieks of pain and panic.

Rasche spun to see the second squad's torches plummeting down the abyss, their screaming owners falling with them. "What in hell—"

His own unit hurriedly aimed their lights at the clockwise path. The other group had passed in front of tall carvings of trees . . . but now only one man remained, hanging from the ledge and desperately clawing for a grip with both feet.

He found it, pulling himself up—only to be blown backward as a fearsome gust of dusty air exploded from a hole in the wall, lashing him with something resembling switch-like lengths of branches. The luckless soldier plunged after his comrades with a howl of terror that was abruptly cut off by a wet bursting noise.

Rasche glared back across the shaft at the fugitives.

"Shoot them! Fire, *fire*!" Weapons burst into life—but the distant figures were already hidden behind another rock formation.

. . .

Eddie pushed Nina against the cliff wall, Banna and the Israelis huddling for cover behind them as bullets cracked off stone. But the Nazis had lost their line of sight. He squeezed past his wife to take the lead. "What the bloody hell was that? Sounded like Indiana Jones and Catwoman having a whip fight."

"I think I know," said the panting Banna. "There is a story in the *Romance* of Alexander finding trees with a sap like myrrh; when his men tried to collect it, they were ferociously whipped by invisible spirits. The carvings we saw could have been those trees, but I do not know how they killed the Nazis."

"Probably a bellows system blowing out leather strips or ropes from the holes," said Nina. "The trigger would have been under one of the paving slabs, so when someone stepped on it . . . What?" she added, aware that her suggestion was being treated with skepticism. "I've seen this kind of stuff before! This isn't my first ancient booby trap."

"They do all sort of blend together after a while," Eddie admitted.

"So Andreas based the traps on the *Romance*?" asked Zane.

Nina nodded. "He wrote it, so he got to cherry-pick his favorite parts. It fits with the whole idea that finding the spring is a challenge based on Alexander's adventures, though. If you read the *Romance*, it gives you clues about the dangers."

"So what's the next one?"

"Who knows?" said Banna. "Huge fleas, men without heads, birds with human faces—it is full of incredible creatures."

"Giant crab," said Eddie, looking at something below.

"Yes, there is a giant crab in the story too."

"No, I mean—an *actual* giant crab. Down there."

"What?" said Nina, stopping to see for herself. To her amazement, she found exactly what her husband had described. Beneath them was the bronze statue of a crustacean, the body a disk about three feet across with a pair of much larger claws extending ahead of it. The metal creature faced up a steep slope descending from another junction ahead, a slot along the center of the paved path looking suspiciously like a track. "Okay, so again, we definitely go right," she said. "I don't know what that thing'll do to us, but I'm pretty sure it'll involve big-ass claws."

"Look—there are spears," said Banna. Several long bronze shafts with sharp tips were propped at the fork.

"Were there spears in the story?" Eddie asked.

"Yes, but they were all broken by its claws."

"Then why are they there?" Nina wondered aloud. "Another part of the challenge?"

Eddie was first to the junction. "Doesn't matter, since we're not going down there." He directed his light over the right-hand route, which curved around a crease in the cliff. It was devoid of mythical creatures. "Okay, this way looks safe. We need—"

Flashes of fire from higher across the shaft—and bullets smacked against the rock face in front of him.

He retreated, but the barrage followed as the Nazis hurried along their own path to bring him back into sight. It finally ceased as he pressed his back against the wall near the spears, protected by a slim overhang, but they would reach a clear vantage point in seconds. "Shit! We can't go that way."

Nina assessed the other route. It was steep enough to shield them from the Nazis if they stayed low . . . but it had its own dangers. "We'll have to go down there."

"What, and catch crabs?" Eddie protested.

"More like the crab catches us—but we don't have a choice!"

"I'll cover you," said Zane. "Latner, stay with me. The rest of you, go!" He went to the outer edge of the intersection, turning off his flashlight and fixing his sights on the chasm's far side. Another Mossad agent took up position with him as Banna and two other men, Taubman and Krebs, moved to join Eddie and Nina.

The Yorkshireman aimed his torch down the new path. The bronze monster lurked at its foot, claws poised as if ready to snap into motion at any moment. "Caught between a Reich and a hard case . . . ," he muttered. "Okay, Nina, stay behind me—and keep your head down!"

He hunched low and scuttled down the new path. Nina followed—just as the Nazis came into sight and attacked again. Zane and Latner retaliated, Banna shrieking and covering his ears as he was forced to duck under their fire to reach the junction. The two other Israelis went after him.

The descent was so steep that Eddie had to turn sideways to find purchase on the slick slabs with the edges of his soles. Another look ahead. He didn't know when the crab would start moving, but he was certain that it would . . .

More rounds rained down. Zane crouched to present as small a target as possible, searching for their source. He flicked his Uzi's selector to single-shot, took careful aim at one of the muzzle flashes, and fired. The man lurched backward, rebounding off the wall and falling screaming into the blackness below.

The other Nazis intensified their assault. Zane scrambled onto the slope, dropping flat on his stomach to shoot back over its top. Latner tried to follow—but was hit in the leg. The Mossad commander grabbed at him as he fell, but his fingers only brushed the other man's clothing. Latner went over the side, a brief cry sharply truncated as he hit an outcrop below.

Zane could only spare his comrade an anguished glance. "What's happening down there?" he shouted.

"Nothing—yet!" Eddie replied. He was halfway toward the waiting crustacean, tension rising with every step. The ancient mechanism's trigger might be jammed or broken, but based on past experience, it was far more likely that it would activate once he reached the point of no return.

Three-quarters of the way, and the bronze beast still

had not moved. Given the steepness of the slope, with a few steps of run-up he could jump right over it . . .

Footfall on another paving slab—which shifted under his weight. "Aw, crab!"

With a shrill of metal against stone, the monster jerked into motion.

"Get back!" Eddie shouted, retreating. The crab jolted after him. Its claws swept from side to side, intermittently jerking upward to deter anyone from vaulting over it. He glimpsed a metal post protruding up through the slot into a hole on its underbelly; the mechanism was under the path itself, clanging chains hauling it along its track.

"To where?" Nina protested, bumping into Banna. The Nazis were still shooting, the crack of splintering stone above her almost as loud as Zane's return fire.

Krebs sidestepped to the edge of the path and raised his Uzi. "Out of the way!" he shouted.

Those lower down hurriedly moved against the wall as he fired. Bullets clanged off bronze, the noise like the tolling of a dozen discordant bells. But the crab continued inexorably toward them, the rounds barely denting the metal. "Stop, stop!" Nina cried as a ricochet struck the rock just above her head.

The Israeli ceased fire—then rose, judging the timing of the claws' sweeps. "I'll jump over it!"

"No, you won't make it!" Eddie warned—but Krebs had already rushed past him. He ran at the crab, making a flying leap—

One claw lashed upward as if the creature had seen him coming. Krebs's foot clipped it, pitching him forward. He threw out both hands to catch himself, but his right arm buckled as he landed hard on the unyielding stone—and he rolled over the edge. The Mossad operative's terrified wail lasted only two seconds before he hit the bottom of the shaft eighty feet below.

The crab continued its remorseless advance. "What do we do?" said Nina in rising panic.

Eddie desperately searched for any weak spot in the metal monster. Disabling even one claw would give them enough space to jump over it . . . but whatever moved the pincers was buried inside the shell. The only visible part of the workings was the support pole through the track—

The sight stirred an unexpected memory. "Jared!" he yelled. "Those spears—I need one of 'em!"

Zane broke off from his defense to shout back. "What? If bullets don't stop it, what's a spear going to do?"

"Just do it, quick!" The crab was now more than half-way up its path, squeezing those trapped above into an ever-smaller space.

Zane fired a burst at the Nazis—then sprang up and ran for the spears. Bullets hit the pathway behind him. He thumped against the wall, then grabbed one of the bronze shafts and tossed it base-first down the slope. It clanged on the stone flags, skittering downhill until Taubman snatched it up. "Here!" He passed it forward.

"Nina, give me some light!" Eddie said as he grabbed the ancient weapon and flipped its point toward the approaching crab. She shone her flashlight at the bronze behemoth. "All right, you shellfish bastard," he said, raising the spear . . .

He lunged, stabbing it down—not at the crab itself, but under it. The tip caught against one of the cracks between the stone slabs. Eddie crouched, keeping the weapon pressed into place as he lowered it almost flat against the slope. The crab ground over the shaft—and he pulled it up.

The monster's weight almost wrenched the spear from his hands. He held on, straining to lift it. The metal shaft bent—but the crab tipped upward as the chains dragging it uphill forced it onto the makeshift ramp.

The claws swung at the Englishman. He tried to dodge, but couldn't move without releasing the spear. The tip of a bronze pincer slashed through his sleeve, tearing leather—and skin. He yelled in pain, but held his ground.

Another claw stabbed at him, its sharp point racing toward his chest—

The crab suddenly lurched as the spear lifted it up—

and came loose from the post beneath. With nothing to support it, the metal creature skidded back downhill with a horrific screech, claws flailing, and flew off the precipice. No longer carrying a ton of bronze, the counterweighted pole shot past the startled group and hit the slab at the end of the track with enough force to split it in two. A moment later, the crab slammed into the ground with a boom that reverberated through the entire chasm.

Eddie dropped the bent spear, wasting no time worrying about his wound as he ran down the path. "We're clear—come on!" The others rushed after him.

Zane darted from his cover and raced pell-mell down the slope. "What did you do?" he called to Eddie.

"Ramped it out of the slot," the Englishman replied as he reached the foot of the steep section. "I remembered how I used to make racing cars do *Dukes of Hazzard* jumps when I was a kid by putting lolly sticks on the track." The lack of any immediate response made him add: "What, you don't have Scalextric in Israel?"

"No, all we have to play with are dreidels," the younger man said sarcastically.

"You were a weird kid, Eddie," Nina told her husband. "Although it explains a lot: You spent your childhood wrecking toys, and now you do it for real."

"Tchah!" The path ahead continued its descent around the chasm wall. "Okay," Eddie said, surveying it, "this goes all the way to the bottom."

Nina's own flashlight revealed a rubble-strewn rock floor below. But something in her peripheral vision caught her attention. At first she thought it was a fallen torch that had fared better than its owner, but when she looked directly at it, it disappeared. She glanced away and the faint glow returned—revealing itself to be coming not from the chasm, but another chamber entirely. "There's a way out over there," she said, her light finding an arched opening, clearly man-made, at the base of the cliff.

"Must be what we're looking for," said Eddie. "This fucking spring'd better be in here after all this!"

Nina followed him down. Banna and Taubman were

right behind her, Zane bringing up the rear. A shout came from above, followed by another fusillade of gunfire, but the incoming bullets hit only stone.

They reached the ground. "Turn off the lights!" the Englishman ordered as he ran for the passage. He could see a shimmering luminescence from beyond the opening, low but still enough to show that the way ahead was clear.

Torches clicked off. The Nazis fired a few more shots, but their targets were now lost in the darkness. Some way above Rasche's group, Kroll shouted a command for them to speed their descent.

Eddie reached the entrance. The passage was almost ten feet high, turning a corner ahead. The soft light rippling over the walls grew brighter. "What the hell is that?" he asked.

"Water flashing like lightning," Nina replied. They rounded the corner, catching their first sight of what lay beyond . . . and stopping in amazement. The others stumbled to a halt, equally awed.

They had reached the Spring of Immortality.

35

"Bloody hell," said Eddie as he took in the sight. "Andreas was a busy boy."

They had entered a large subterranean chamber. The high ceiling was raw and natural, but everything beneath the level of the entrance had been worked upon by hand over a long period of time, the walls smooth and vertical. The stone was streaked with veins of silver, gleaming in the eerie light.

The source of the illumination was a pool of water fifty feet below. The glow came from within the water itself, foxfire coursing gently through its unreadable depths.

Incredible as the sight was, it was not what had reduced the visitors to gawkers. The walls were not the only man-made feature. A stone viaduct led from the entrance across to the far side. Two thirds of the way over was a low structure: a tomb. On top of the little mausoleum was the statue of a kneeling man, his back to them—facing a much bigger figure sculpted from the opposite wall.

Nina recognized it, as did Banna. "It is Alexander!" the Egyptian exclaimed.

"You're right," she said, amazed. The handsome yet cruel features were the same as those she had seen in the tomb in Alexandria, though on a far greater scale. This Alexander was not merely larger than life, but an actual giant, towering over everything else. Even in the half-light from the pool, his haughty, almost sneering expression was clear, the king regarding everyone beneath him with disdain.

"What's he holding?" Eddie asked. Both Alexander's hands were raised to his chest, something made from polished metal cupped in them. A set of stone steps led up to it.

"It looks like a bowl," said Nina. "Come on, we need to see!" She started across the viaduct, Banna following eagerly.

"No, we need to poison the spring," countered Zane. He gestured for Taubman to cover the entrance, then set down his pack and took out a white plastic container.

Eddie, torn between going with his wife and preparing for the inevitable attack, looked over the viaduct's wall-less side. The glowing pool was large, the far wall over a hundred feet away, and it was impossible to tell how deep it was. "How much have you got? A pound? I know cyanide's lethal even in small doses, but there's a *lot* of water down there."

"It'll be enough," the Israeli insisted.

Nina paused beside the tomb, Banna continuing ahead. "I don't even know if that's the spring down there—the water isn't flowing," she said. "It might just be a storage pond. If you poison that but don't take out the actual source, you've wasted your time."

"Then what do you suggest?" asked Zane with a flash of anger.

"There are Greek inscriptions by the statue of Alexander—"

"And on this tomb also," Banna reported.

"They might help us find the spring itself, or at least confirm that that's the source down there."

"And help you make another big discovery," said Zane, cynicism now joining displeasure. "That's not why we're here."

"It's why *I'm* here! You've got your mission—and I've

got mine. It'll be my last one, but I knew that going in. Do what you have to, but I'm going to see what we've actually found." Ignoring his glare, she rounded the tomb after Banna.

"Eddie!" Zane protested.

The Englishman gave him a shrug. "We're here now, might as well look. And she does have a track record with this sort of thing, so . . ." With that, he followed her. Zane muttered in annoyance, but went after him.

Nina joined Banna, who had shone a light over the huge statue before turning to examine the tomb. The little structure was actually set into the viaduct, steps leading down below floor level to its entrance. "This is the tomb of Andreas!" the Egyptian proclaimed in excitement as he read the text inscribed above the opening. "If these dates are correct, then he died in 22 BCE—over three hundred years after Alexander!"

The American aimed her own flashlight at the figure atop the mausoleum. It was an old man, face gaunt, kneeling in supplication to the mighty figure facing him. "So that's what a three-hundred-year-old bloke looks like?" said Eddie. "He doesn't seem a day over two hundred."

Even Zane was impressed, however reluctantly. "He must have worked for every day of it to have built all this."

"He did not build it alone," Banna told him. "He had followers. They protected the secret of the spring after he died."

"*Long* after he died," said Nina, reading more of the ancient text. "This place wasn't sealed until the first century CE. And the Greek farmers Kroll stole the pithos from were still guarding it in the 1940s."

"Talk about loyalty to the cause," Eddie said.

"Andreas really *did* want to make finding this place a challenge worthy of Alexander."

"Well, we found it—does that make me Eddie the Great?"

"Only in your head," she replied with a smile, illuminating the entrance. A stone sarcophagus was visible within. She descended the steps to enter the tomb.

The plain surroundings of his last resting place suggested that Andreas, a simple cook in life—at least to begin with—had remained uncomplicated until death. A scuffed and dented silver jug, a traditional Greek amphora with a single handle on its long neck, rested on top of the sarcophagus. "A silver vessel . . ."

"What about it?" Eddie asked as he and Banna entered.

"The *Romance* said Andreas first took the spring's water in 'a silver vessel.' Maybe that's it. He kept it his whole life."

"There is something else," said Banna, indicating a plaque upon the coffin lid. Words were carved into the polished marble.

Nina leaned closer to read them. " 'Here lies Andreas, friend and betrayer and protector of Alexander the Great,' " she recited. "Interesting phrasing . . . 'Humble in death as in life, as should all men be who compare themselves to the king of Macedon. Remember this if you seek to take what I had denied him, and if you do not, then go in peace and live your life as it should be.' " She stared at the plaque, thinking.

A warning shout from outside. "Taubman just saw the Nazis," warned Zane. "They've almost reached the bottom of the shaft. Nina, I need to know, *now:* Is the water below us the spring?" He held up the cyanide.

"I do not think it is," Banna told him. "Look, here." He backed out and aimed his light at the giant statue of Alexander. Greek text was carved into the wall level with the great figure's cupped hands. "It says, 'He who believes himself equal to Alexander, step up and receive your reward.' The silver bowl—the spring must be there."

More beams fixed upon the gleaming basin, revealing a feature carved into Alexander's breast just above his hands. Silver glinted within a small opening in the stone. "The water must come out through that hole," said

Eddie. "Jared, *that's* where you need to stick your poison." He drew his gun. "Nina, you and Ubayy—"

He broke off as he saw his wife's expression. It was one he had seen before, deep thought turning to realization . . . or revelation. "What?"

"Mixed messages," she said, almost distractedly, as she looked between the two stone figures: the great proud Alexander and his weary servant. "The statue of Bucephalus, the bronze fish, and now Andreas's tomb all said one thing, but Alexander himself says another . . ." Another moment of musing—then her eyes widened. "Oh my God."

"What?" Eddie demanded. The other two men also gave her questioning looks.

"Andreas's challenge—it's not what we thought! I'll explain later—*if* we stay alive. Right now, though, we're all in agreement that no matter what, the Nazis can't be allowed to leave here with the water, yes?"

"Yes, absolutely," said Zane, with no hesitation.

"Definitely," Eddie agreed. Banna also gave a frightened nod.

"Good." Nina steeled herself before continuing. "Okay, so here's what we have to do. *Surrender.*"

Her husband and the Mossad agent reacted as if she had spoken in Swahili. "You *what*?" said Eddie.

"No!" protested Zane. "We'll be handing them the spring!"

"I know—which is why we've got to do it. Jared, tell Taubman to hold fire. It's our only chance."

"I'm not giving myself up!" the Israeli insisted. "We have to kill as many of them as we can. Eddie, you're with me, aren't you?"

Eddie hesitated, then stood with Nina. "Sorry, but no. I'm with her. To the end. Which," he added in a spiky tone, "might be very soon." Nina nevertheless gave him a loving smile.

Zane regarded them both with angry disbelief. "If you're not going to fight, then I am!" He called out to his comrade. "Taubman! Get ready to—"

"No!" Nina cried, breaking away from the group and

running past the tomb toward the entrance. "Don't shoot, hold your fire!"

"Hey! Get back here!" Zane shouted. "What's that stupid woman doing?"

"Oi!" snapped Eddie. "Watch your mouth."

Zane looked stung. "Eddie, she's giving up our only chance to stop them! Why are you going along with her?"

"Because she's my wife—and because I trust her. And so should you." The Israeli had no reply.

Nina reached the end of the viaduct and entered the passage. Taubman turned in surprise as she ran up behind him. "What are you doing?" he asked.

"Keeping us alive—I hope. Go and wait with Jared." Before he could stop her, she rushed past.

Fear rising, aware that the only greeting she might get was a burst of bullets, Nina left the tunnel. She saw the lights of Rasche's team approaching the foot of the spiral path. Higher up was a larger group; Kroll and Leitz were following them down. She summoned her full resolve as the nearer Nazis reacted to her appearance ... and raised her hands, waving her flashlight above her head. "Don't shoot, don't shoot! We surrender!"

Torch beams locked on to her. "Do not move! Where are the others?" Rasche shouted.

"Through the tunnel. We're surrendering—there are only five of us left, and we've got nowhere to go."

The Nazis reached the chasm floor. Some came to her, while others held back, weapons raised. "If you are lying, you will die!" Rasche growled.

"I'm not lying. We're giving up."

One soldier roughly pulled her arms behind her back as another searched her. Finding nothing, he shouted to Rasche, who issued an order. The rest of the advance party hurried over, keeping their guns fixed on the tunnel. Kroll called down from above. Rasche replied, then faced Nina. "What is through there?" he demanded, pointing at the archway.

"Andreas's tomb—and the Spring of Immortality," she replied.

Suspicion was clear on the SS man's face. "And you are willingly giving it to us? I do not believe you. You are trying to delay us while the Jews sabotage the spring!"

"No, I'm not. I'm surrendering because . . . because there's nothing else we can do."

Rasche frowned, then barked commands. His men ran toward the opening, two remaining to guard their prisoner. He shone his torch at her. "You have already been sentenced to death," he said, seeing the red marks still visible on her neck. "We *will* carry out your sentence."

Nina felt a chill as a ghostly echo of the rope pulled around her throat. "All I ask is that you let me see the spring flowing first. That's my only condition."

"You are in no position to make demands!" the Nazi snapped. "I should kill you right here." He started to raise his gun, but a shout from the next chamber caught his attention. A brief exchange, then: "Your companions are also surrendering. You said there were five of you; if we see anyone else—"

"There's nobody else," Nina told him. "You have my word."

"Your word is worth nothing, American." But the moment of imminent threat had passed. "Move!"

He pushed her into the tunnel. As they rounded the corner, Nina saw that Taubman had joined the others— all of whom were now kneeling before the tomb with their hands behind their heads, surrounded by Nazi soldiers.

Not even the sight of his captured enemies could prevent Rasche from being amazed by the chamber, however. He stared up at the towering statue as they crossed the viaduct. "So it was real all along . . ."

"You didn't believe it?" Nina asked. "Even though the water kept you young?"

"I do not believe in myths as Kroll does. But . . . he was right." Rasche shook his head as if astonished at making the admission, then called to the other men. A reply came in the affirmative, one soldier indicating a small pile of weapons and equipment. "Stand with them," Rasche ordered Nina.

"You okay?" Eddie asked as she joined the prisoners.

"Yeah," she answered. "I just hope I've done the right thing."

"So do I," said Zane, not concealing his bitterness.

"Silence," barked Rasche. He looked the prisoners over, ending with Zane. "You too were sentenced to death, *Jude*," he said with a sadistic smile. "I will enjoy ending what we started."

The Israeli stared coldly back at him. "It doesn't matter how long you live. The Mossad will find you."

"I will live longer than you," Rasche scoffed.

The rhythmic tramp of marching feet echoed down the passage. The rest of the Nazis arrived, some bearing the empty water barrels. Kroll was at their head.

The Nazi leader was visibly struggling not to show his breathlessness from the effort of the descent. But his physical weakness did not make him any less threatening. He took in the spirit-lit wonders of the cavern with triumphant awe, then fixed his gaze gloatingly on the redhead. "Dr. Wilde. Thank you for leading us to the Spring of Immortality. It will give us life . . . but for you, it will bring only death."

36

The obese Nazi laughed at his own joke, his men joining in obsequiously. Eddie was unamused. "Christ, and I thought *my* one-liners were shit."

A soldier clubbed him across the back. "Shut up," said Rasche.

Kroll gave the moment of violence only the briefest glance. "Where is the spring?" he asked Nina.

"There," she said, pointing at the huge statue. "It's waiting for you to take it."

Rasche spoke to his leader, mistrust clear in every word. Kroll nodded. "He is right," he told her. "Why should we believe that you would hand over the spring now, after all you have done to keep it from us?"

"Because . . . there's nothing we can do to stop you," she replied. "We couldn't have held you back for more than a few minutes."

"And that?" Kroll gestured at the plastic container among the weapons on the floor; a soldier presented it to him. He shook it; it was full. "Potassium cyanide," he said, reading the label. "You were going to poison the water? Why did you not do so?"

"There wouldn't have been any point. The water down

there isn't the spring, it's only an overflow. The statue is the source."

He stared past her at the stern figure of Alexander. "Show me."

Nina helped Eddie up. Rasche spoke sharply, and one of the Yorkshireman's guards pointed his gun at them. She gave Kroll a scathing look. "If you don't mind?"

"Let them stand," the German ordered. "But at the first sign of treachery, kill them."

"Why wait?" said Rasche as the group started for the statue. "We are going to kill them anyway."

"I'll tell you why," Nina said to Kroll. "Maybe none of the others are, but *you're* a scholar. You studied the history of Alexander the Great—and because of that, you realized the importance of the water you found in Greece when anyone else would have just stolen the treasure. There's more to this for you than money, or securing the water. This is a *confirmation* of what you've always thought: By beating Andreas the cook, you've proved you're Alexander's equal."

Kroll's already ample chest swelled still further in pride. "That is true. And it is only the beginning. Once we have control of the water, we will lead the world into a new age. And we will have you to thank for opening the door."

"Which is why I'd like to make a last request." He stopped to listen, everyone else following suit. "I know I'm not going to leave here alive, but I want to ask you, one scholar to another, if I can watch you draw the first water from the spring. To prove that *I* was right." Nina's voice became pleading. "I got involved in all of this because I wanted to find one last great secret from history before I die. Will you let me see it through to the end? Please?"

Rasche let out an impatient snort. "No. No more quests and riddles; just *kill* them, Kroll."

Kroll flushed with anger. "You do not give orders to me, Rasche! Dr. Wilde is right—this place is a part of history. And today, we shall *make* history." He addressed his men. "The New Reich was born in exile, building its strength in secret. But today, we shall use the Spring of Immortality to retake our rightful place in the world!" What began as a speech became a rant, as spittle-flecked as an address by Hitler himself. "Our victory is inevitable! We came to this place as soldiers—but we shall leave it as conquerors!" He pointed at the towering statue. "And I shall lead you to glories that not even Alexander the Great could imagine!"

"*Sieg heil! Sieg heil!*" his men chanted, arms snapping into salutes. Even Rasche joined in.

Leitz had remained slightly apart from the Nazis, keeping a gun on the prisoners. "So where is this spring?" he asked. "I would like to see what is worth so much money."

"Dr. Wilde, show us," Kroll ordered.

Nina led the way to the far end of the bridge. "It's up there," she said, pointing at the statue's hands. "You can see the Greek text: 'He who believes himself equal to Alexander, step up and receive your reward.'"

Kroll swept his light over the carved words. "Then I shall. The secret of eternal life . . . and it belongs to me!"

"It belongs to *us,*" Rasche said pointedly.

Kroll ignored him, starting up the steps. "We've *given* it to them," Zane said in disgust.

"It's not over yet," Nina replied under her breath.

Eddie instantly picked up on her undertone of anticipation. "Wait, what's going to happen?"

"I'm not sure—but Kroll might get more than he expects." Her husband became more alert, poised to react. Zane also prepared himself for action.

The SS officer reached the top of the stone flight, standing fifteen feet above the viaduct. He shone his light first over the polished basin in Alexander's cupped palms, then at the chest of the great figure just above it. A silver tube six inches across protruded from the stone. The precious metal was clearly an intrinsic part of the water's strange properties, Nina realized; the dense veins in the rock must have played some part in its creation, and Andreas and his followers had contained it in the same material to keep it active. The Nazis were similarly taking no chances, their own silver-lined containers standing ready to be filled.

Kroll made an impassioned proclamation in German to his men, rousing cheers, then sneered down at Nina and her companions. "Now you will have your last request, Dr. Wilde. You will see me draw the water from the spring . . . and then you will die." The men holding them raised their guns.

"What about *my* last request?" Eddie complained. "A cheese-and-Marmite sandwich?"

Kroll looked irritated, but turned back to the statue. He took hold of the silver bowl to lift it from Alexander's hands . . .

It didn't move.

Impatient, he tried again, harder. Resistance for a moment, then it came free—with a sudden rattle like a chain being released—

Water flowed from the spout. But it was no mere trickle.

A jet blasted out of the metal pipe, hitting Kroll square in the chest and bowling him down the steps. As he fell, the geyser passed over him and into those below like a water cannon. Men were knocked to the floor, others scattering to dodge the powerful surge—

Eddie and Zane were already moving. The Englishman smashed an elbow into a soldier's face before twisting to wrest the gun from his hands. He pulled the trigger as he spun, sending a swath of bullets into the crowd. Nazis fell screaming.

The Israeli, however, had a single specific target. He lunged at Rasche. The German snapped up his gun, but Zane kicked it from his hands and over the edge of the viaduct before whirling into a Krav Maga leg sweep to slice Rasche's feet out from under him. The Nazi slammed down on his back. Before he could recover, the younger man leapt on him and pounded a fist into his face.

Nina grabbed the bewildered Banna as chaos erupted around them. "Behind the tomb!" she cried, pushing him through the mob. They had only seconds to get clear—

A new noise warned her that even that was optimistic. The high-pressure roar was joined by echoing cracks of splintering rock. The statue's chest was splitting, jagged rents radiating outward from the silver nozzle. "Eddie!" she cried. "It's gonna collapse!"

* * *

Kroll had landed at the base of the steps. He looked up in horror as one of the great hands broke off and smashed on the floor. The whole viaduct trembled as the thunder grew louder. He scrambled away, slipping on the wet surface—

The statue exploded as the pent-up water burst free.

A tsunami crashed onto the bridge. Kroll was snatched up by the churning flood and hurled along the viaduct. He plowed into the panicked soldiers, knocking several down like skittles before they too were swept away. The silver-lined barrels were sent flying by the water they had been meant to hold.

Eddie saw the wave rushing at him. He immediately ceased fire and ran, making a flying leap to climb up on top of the tomb. Zane abandoned his attack on Rasche, using one of the dead men as a springboard to jump after the Yorkshireman.

Others were not so quick to react—and it cost them their lives. Taubman had hesitated for a critical moment after Kroll was blown from the steps, and was now trapped among a crush of Nazis as they tried to flee. The surging water hit the men like a train, hurling them into the inescapable pit below.

Banna was luckier, the water sweeping him past the low structure. He slithered spread-eagled along the flagstones, catching himself at the edge.

Nina, though, was slammed against the tomb. She tried to cry out, but couldn't draw a breath as frothing water hit her face. She clawed at the stone wall, fighting to hold on against the relentless current—

Something rushed at her. She only had a fraction of a second to recognize it as Kroll—then the Nazi leader collided with her, knocking her down. The torrent swirled them down the steps into the crypt below.

Nina hit the sarcophagus shoulder-first, the inrushing wave bowling her over it and sending the battered silver jar into the water. She fell after the amphora, sound suddenly muffling as she was submerged.

Her skin tingled, an electric charge running over her body. But she wasn't thinking about the spring's strange properties, trying only to get her head above the surface. One arm felt dead, numbed by the impact. She groped with the other to push herself up. A gasp as she took in air—

Then she choked as Kroll shoved her back underwater.

She managed to twist onto her back just before he pinned her to the floor, but couldn't move any farther against his great weight. One of his hands clamped over her mouth and nose, the other pushing down on her neck. "You American bitch!" he shouted, voice distorted through the rising water. "You really are *wilde*, a maniac! You have killed us all—but first I will kill *you*!"

* * *

Eddie and Zane clung to the statue of Andreas as spray washed over them. A Nazi tried to scramble onto the tomb's roof to escape the surging water—only to take the Englishman's boot to his face. He tumbled off the bridge with a scream.

But the wave's power was rapidly dissipating as it sluiced over the sides of the viaduct. Several Nazis had survived the flood—Rasche among them. Without so much as a glance back at his troops, he sprinted past the mausoleum toward the cavern's entrance.

"I'm going after him!" Zane shouted. He jumped down, wincing at a sharp pain in his injured leg, then snatched up a dropped flashlight and ran after his nemesis.

The soldiers spotted him. Guns swung at the Mossad agent—

Eddie's own gun barked on full auto as he swept its fire across the clutch of Nazis. Blood fountained from bullet wounds—but then the MP5 fell silent, its magazine empty.

A flash of white. He whirled—to see Leitz below him. The middleman was bringing his gun to bear on the Yorkshireman—

Eddie hurled his own useless weapon at him. Leitz whipped up his left arm in defense. The MP5 cracked against his elbow—then spun over it and hit his head, knocking him off balance.

Before he could recover, Eddie jumped off the tomb to deliver a flying kick to his chest. "Leitz out!"

The Luxembourger flew backward—over the viaduct's edge. The white figure plunged toward the pool . . . then twisted in midair, bringing his arms down to vanish under the water in a swan dive. "Bollocks!" said the Englishman, reluctantly impressed as Leitz resurfaced. "Got to give him at least a seven-point-five for that—"

A crackling boom echoed around the chamber as a six-foot hunk of stone broke from the statue. It rolled down the steps, driven by the jet of water, before falling over the side and arcing down at Leitz.

He looked up—and screamed—

The boulder hit him, kicking up a plume of pink spray. "Okay, *that's* worth a perfect ten," said Eddie. He turned to locate his wife, only to find with alarm that she was nowhere in sight. "Nina!"

* * *

Nina tried to blow water from her mouth and nostrils, but the Nazi's palm blocked her airways. A surge of primal terror: She was going to drown! She swallowed, gulping down as much liquid as she could to keep it from her lungs, but there was no air to replace it.

Kroll's hand twisted to get a firm grip on her throat. Nina tried to pull his blunt fingers open, but his hold was too strong. The numbness in her other arm had passed, replaced by a dull pain—she brought it up, but still couldn't prise him off.

The Nazi leaned closer, his face just above the surface

of the rising water. She glimpsed his snarling mouth, his eyes—

She lashed her hand up, trying to blind him—but the water slowed her movement. He jerked away, yelling in German, then spread his hand over her face like some huge loathsome spider and shoved her head down hard against the stone flags.

All Nina could do was squirm as what was left of her breath knotted in her chest. She groped uselessly for his face, then her hand dropped back into the water as her strength faded. A terrible pressure rose within her, a balloon swelling inside her skull with each pounding heartbeat—

Her fingers touched something. Not stone, but metal, a rounded shape on the floor . . .

The silver jar.

The vessel with which Andreas had first taken the water from the Spring of Immortality. The start of everything—and now her final hope to end it—

Her hand closed around the handle—and she used her last dregs of energy to swing it at Kroll's head.

Brimming with springwater, the metal jug weighed almost three pounds. There was a flat *clunk* as it struck his skull. The Nazi fell against the sarcophagus.

Nina broke his hold and pushed herself out from beneath him. She dragged herself up, expecting to breach the surface—but the water had risen higher. Panic hit her, a fear that the entire chamber had flooded—

She burst from the water. It was at stomach height, and climbing rapidly as the torrent cascaded down the steps. The new air burned in her tortured lungs. She gasped, still feeling as if Kroll's hand was clenched around her throat . . .

It was.

The SS commander grabbed her again, bellowing in German as he tried to drag her back underwater—

The entire bridge shook—and Andreas's sarcophagus broke apart. The lid slid off and slammed down on Kroll's leg like a guillotine.

The Nazi leader screamed as the heavy stone block

snapped his shinbones and crushed his foot. He fell back into the churning pool, chin only just clearing the surface—but the water was still rising. *"Hilfe!"* he cried between breaths. "Help me!"

Nina forced her way through the deluge to the steps, then looked back. The water reached Kroll's mouth. He spat, desperately straining to raise his head higher, but the stone slab was an immovable anchor. "Dr. Wilde! Please!"

"You brought this upon yourself," she replied in a cold echo of his own words when she had begged him to save Macy. "You wanted the water? It's all yours. Drink up."

"No! *No!* You—" His yells became an unintelligible gargle as the flood rose over his face. Nina watched as he flailed and squirmed, bubbles belching from his mouth . . . then he went still.

Still gripping the jug, she clambered up the steps. The viaduct trembled again, deep splashes echoing through the cavern as stones broke away and fell into the pool below. She stumbled, the onrushing water threatening to throw her back into Kroll's sunken tomb . . .

A hand clamped around her wrist.

She looked up in fear—which became relief as she saw Eddie. "Nina!" he said. "Thank God! Are you okay?"

"Yeah" was all she could say.

"Where's Kroll?"

"Drinking his fill."

He helped her up, starting toward the tunnel. Somehow she forced her leaden legs into motion. Ahead, Banna waited anxiously at the end of the corpse-strewn bridge. "Where's Jared? Did he make it?"

"Yeah, he went after Rasche—" Eddie broke off as the viaduct shook as if hit by an earthquake. Booms and cracks erupted behind them as the section beneath the steps disintegrated. "Oh *shit*! Déjà fuckin' vu! Run!"

Fearful adrenaline gave Nina a new surge of energy. They sprinted along the bridge as it crumbled behind them. What was left of the statue of Alexander sheared from the cavern wall, the smaller figure of Andreas briefly watching it disappear before falling too as the tomb shattered beneath it. The pair raced toward the exit, the wave of destruction following them. "Run, *run*!" shrieked Banna.

"I bloody *am*!" Eddie gasped.

They kept running, thirty feet to go, twenty—

The viaduct bucked underfoot—then fell away.

Nina and Eddie both screamed and flung themselves into a last desperate leap for safety. They landed hard on the final few intact feet of the bridge, tripping and rolling as the rest of the structure dropped into the frothing pool below. Banna dragged them clear as the thunderous cacophony subsided.

"Thanks," Eddie wheezed. "Fuck me! That was bloody close." He crawled to his wife. "Are you all right?"

She opened her eyes, surprised that they were still alive. Her hand was clamped tightly around the silver jug. "Yeah, I . . . I think so." Falling debris had disturbed whatever caused the springwater's sparkling glow, but there was still enough light to see that the bridge and the great statue had been obliterated, only rubble remaining. "What about the Nazis? Did we get them all?"

"No, one got away," said Banna. "The Israeli went after him."

"It was Rasche," said Eddie. He stood. "I'm not letting him escape."

"Nor am I," Nina said, determined.

They hurried into the huge chasm. Eddie saw two torch beams flicking along the rising path above. "There!"

* * *

Zane pounded after Rasche. The pain from the stab wound was like red-hot iron burning into his leg, but his desire to catch Benjamin Falk's killer seared even hotter, driving him onward.

Rasche was now only twenty yards away, slowed by a treacherous section of pathway. The German shone his light downward, picking his way along step by step.

Zane swept his own torch beam ahead, taking in the missing slabs in a flash, and kept running.

The other man's light flicked back at him. *"Scheiße!"* Rasche hissed. He increased his pace, caution overcome by fear.

Zane raced in pursuit. He glimpsed lights in his peripheral vision: Eddie and Nina starting up the ledge below. He gained on the Nazi, jumping over a gap without even looking. Rasche glanced back—

And stumbled on a loose stone.

The SS man let out a sharp gasp of fright. He clutched at the wall to stabilize himself—

The Israeli tackled him.

They fell, Zane landing on top—and then both went over the edge.

The Nazi shrieked, fingers scrabbling at the cliff before catching a ragged outcropping just beneath the path. Zane slithered past him, jerking to a stop as he grabbed Rasche's jacket with one hand. Threads in the seams popped and snapped, but the fabric held . . . just.

Rasche tried to shake him loose. The Mossad agent tightened his hold—then clenched his free hand into a rock-solid ball and plowed it into the other man's stomach.

The impact made Rasche convulse. "No!" he gasped. "What are—" Another brutal blow left him breathless. Zane pulled himself higher, gripping the Nazi's shoulder, then drew his fist back again. *"Verrückte!* If I fall, we both die!"

"Then we die," Zane snarled. "But I'll take the last Nazi with me!"

He smashed a knuckle-splitting punch into Rasche's face. "This is for Benjamin!" he cried as the German howled, blood gushing from his nose. A second blow brought a dull snap of enamel from inside the war criminal's mouth. "And every Jew you've ever killed!" The Israeli wound up for a final attack—

Rasche lost his grip with one hand, lurching as the other took the full weight of both men. His jacket slipped around his shoulder—and a seam ripped. Zane dropped several inches, only the garment's silk lining holding it together. He flailed, fingertips scraping the rock face in a fruitless search for support.

Even straining to keep his hold on the cliff, Rasche saw a chance for survival—and revenge. He reached down to snatch his SS dagger from its sheath.

The blade stabbed at the young man's throat—

Zane's hand snapped to intercept it, clapping around the Nazi's wrist.

But he had only halted the knife, lacking the leverage to force it away. Rasche's face contorted into a furious grimace as the shuddering dagger crept toward Zane's neck. "You think you can kill me, little *Jude*?" he snarled. "The Allies couldn't in the war. The Mossad couldn't *after* the war . . ." The point pressed against the Israeli's skin—then sank into it. "And you will not now!"

A choked grunt of pain and fear escaped Zane's mouth. Blood ran down his neck, at first only an ooze, but within a couple of heartbeats it became a thicker, faster flow. Rasche growled with sadistic glee—

"*Jared!*"

Eddie's voice echoed around the chasm. A torch beam locked on to the two men. The Nazi flinched, momentarily dazzled—

The instant of distraction was enough. Zane pushed the knife away with rage-fueled strength. More blood ran out, but he ignored the wound as he twisted Rasche's hand up—bringing the blade toward the war criminal's chest.

Rasche tried to resist, but the quivering dagger edged ever closer. "*Nein!*" the Nazi shrieked. "Don't do it!"

"You've killed your last Jew," snarled the Israeli. The trembling dagger's tip slowly penetrated Rasche's shirt—then sank through flesh, between ribs. The arrogance and hatred that had defined the Nazi's expression vanished, replaced by a single emotion: raw terror. "Now you know what they felt."

Rasche opened his mouth to scream—as Zane thrust the dagger into his heart.

The cry died in the Nazi's throat, only a choked gurgle

emerging. He shuddered . . . then his hold on the cliff weakened, and released—

Eddie dived and grabbed Zane's arm as the two men fell.

Rasche clawed at the Mossad agent, making one last attempt to drag the other man down with him, but his grip was too weak. He plunged into the darkness. The scream finally came, only to be cut off by the wet crunch of breaking bones and rupturing organs as he smashed on the rocks a hundred feet below.

The Englishman lay on his front, upper body over the edge as he gripped Zane's arm. "Nina, give me a hand!" he gasped. She and Banna helped him haul the Israeli up. "Jared! You okay?"

Zane slumped against the wall, exhausted. "Actually, yes," he gasped, pressing a hand to his bloodied throat. "Mission accomplished."

"Great," said Nina. "Then let's get the hell out of here."

* * *

The climb back to the surface was considerably slower than the descent. But eventually they reached the entrance, even the gray daylight of the forest dazzling. The group staggered out through the archway and collapsed on the damp ground. "Hope Hafez hasn't buggered off," said Eddie, looking downhill. "It's a bloody long walk back to the boats."

Zane's gaze turned to the shrine's entrance. He spoke softly in Hebrew. "A Kaddish," he told the others. "For those we have lost. All of them," he added to Nina.

She nodded. "Thank you." Banna closed his eyes and bowed his head.

Eddie left a moment of respectful silence, then took the battered silver jug from his wife. Most of its contents had been spilled during the escape, but there was still a small amount of water inside. "They all died because of what's in here. We should pour the bloody stuff away and be done with it."

"Maybe," said Nina. "But . . . it's the last surviving

relic of Andreas, the only proof that the *Alexander Romance* was true. It should be preserved just for that—even if we're the only ones who know the full story."

"Yeah, 'cause we're the only ones who got out of there alive." A pause, then he regarded her questioningly. "How did you know the statue was a trap? Where was the real spring?"

"That *was* the real spring," she replied. "The whole place was a trap—Andreas never meant *anyone* to get it."

"Then why have a bloody treasure hunt with clues telling you how to find it?" Eddie demanded.

"It was a test. The whole thing, not just the clues leading to it." She gestured at the arch. "When he first found the spring, Andreas thought he'd made a mistake by not immediately telling Alexander what he'd discovered. But that was when he was a young man—and also just a humble cook serving the greatest king in the known world. He was overawed by Alexander, full of hero worship. But as he got older, and wiser . . ."

"He figured out the truth about Alexander," said the Yorkshireman, realizing where she was leading. "He was just as big an arsehole as any of the kings he defeated. Maybe even more so. He actually *tried* to take over the world."

"And came as close to succeeding as anyone ever has," Banna pointed out.

Nina nodded. "Andreas started out thinking that he should have given the Spring of Immortality to Alexander. After he died, his empire very quickly fell apart—but imagine what he could have accomplished if he'd lived for another thirty, sixty, a hundred years! As Andreas used the water to live longer *himself*, though, and saw other rulers continuing the same old cycles of conquest and all the pointless death and destruction that came with them, he changed his mind. If Alexander had been given essentially eternal life, he would have become the world's greatest *tyrant*. Imagine if Hitler had ruled unchallenged for a century. Or Stalin, or Mao."

"Or the men who paid Kroll millions of dollars for the water," said Zane. "They want to stay in control of their *business* empires, but the reason's the same: They never want to give up their power."

"That's right. Death's the great equalizer; it doesn't matter how much you've achieved, or how big your kingdom is—you lose it all when you die. But if you can *delay* death, then you'll keep accumulating more and more power and wealth."

"Compound interest's great if you're already a rich bastard, innit?" said Eddie. "I still don't get why he didn't just brick up the spring and be done with it, though. Why did he make it into a test?"

Banna's eyes widened. "Because it is a test that you do not *want* to pass!"

Nina grinned. "Yeah. If you fail the test at any stage, then you're not Alexander's equal—so not a threat to the world. If you don't realize that you have to sacrifice the statue of Bucephalus to get the artifact hidden inside it, if you can't figure out how to use the fish to locate the spring, and if you can't tell the fake spring behind that arch from the real one, you've wasted a lot of time and effort . . . but at least you stay alive. Anyone smart and resourceful enough, and therefore *dangerous* enough, to get all the way to Andreas's tomb, though . . ."

"You go to fill up the bowl, like Kroll did, and *bam!*" crowed Eddie. "You get a Nazi surprise."

She sighed at the pun. "Although Andreas still gave you one last chance to turn around and leave. All along he kept saying that only Alexander's equal is worthy of immortality . . . but also that nobody *is* Alexander's equal. Even his own coffin had a clue. It said that Andreas was humble, and so was everyone else compared to Alexander."

Banna nodded. " 'Remember this if you seek to take what I had denied him.' He meant the water from the spring."

"But the statue itself basically said, 'If you think you're as great as Alexander, then step right up and claim your prize.' It contradicted everything Andreas had said before. And *that's* when I realized it was a trap," Nina told them. "You have to be smart and resourceful and dangerous to reach the spring—and then *arrogant* enough to ignore what Andreas said over and over by claiming it. That proves you're as much a potential tyrant as an immortal Alexander would have been. And it gets you killed."

"There was still a load of water in the pool, though," Eddie pointed out. "Andreas was taking a gamble that someone wouldn't just drop buckets on ropes."

"The whole place was designed to channel people right to the statue," Nina countered. "Even if I hadn't pointed Kroll there, he would have gone to it anyway. How could he resist? And like I said, it targeted arrogance, hubris. No self-respecting Alexander wannabe would waste time lowering buckets when they can literally wrest control of the Spring of Immortality from his hands. And Andreas knew that." She looked up at the arch. "For good or bad, there's only one man of Alexander the Great's stature in all of history—and Andreas wanted to make sure that remained the case. He and his followers built the whole place to honor him and his achievements ... while at the same time eliminating anyone who might become the *next* Alexander."

"The question is," Zane said, "what do we do now? About the spring, I mean. The cave has collapsed, but the water's still down there. We stopped the Nazis from getting it, but I don't want the Iranians to have it either."

"We leave it down there," Nina said firmly. "Close the secret door and bury it. If anyone finds it again, they won't realize its significance—it'll just be an archaeological curiosity."

"But what if somebody comes looking for the Nazis?" asked Banna.

"Like who?" hooted Eddie. "The Revolutionary Guard won't give a crap what happened to them. They took their money and left. If they think about 'em at all, it'll be like they disappeared in the Bermuda Triangle."

"A new legend—thirty men come into the forest searching for the Spring of Immortality, and are never seen again," said Nina. "The Last Nazis. I quite like the sound of that."

Zane gave her an approving smile. "It has a nice finality to it. Hopefully it'll be the CSU's last-ever operation."

Eddie stood and went to the entrance. "Come on, then. We've got some digging to do."

They dragged the bodies of the Nazi sentries into the inner tunnel, then pushed the hidden door closed and shoveled soil back into the excavated opening. When the arch was finally covered again, they set off down the hill, leaving behind the secret of the Kingdom of Darkness.

Miami, Florida

Seventeen Days Later

"I'm not sure I can do this," Nina whispered.

"You'll be okay," Eddie assured her as they approached the casket following the service. The line of mourners in the chapel was long; Macy had been a popular and sociable young woman, while her parents were wealthy and well connected in Miami and beyond. "I'm sure the funeral people made her look . . . good."

"No, I don't mean seeing her in—in the coffin." Grief clenched Nina's throat at the thought of saying her last good-bye. "I meant . . . her mom and dad." She glanced ahead, to where Amir and Isabel Sharif were waiting. "How can I face them after this? After what I—"

"You *didn't* do it," he said, gently but firmly. "They know that. They've been told what happened."

"But what if they blame me? What if they think I got their daughter killed?"

"Then they're wrong." But he had no more advice to offer, his own heart as heavy as hers.

They reached the casket. It took all of Nina's will to raise her gaze to the figure inside it. Macy lay with her eyes closed as if in a serene sleep. Eddie had been right about the work of the funeral directors: They had made her as beautiful as she had been in life. "I'm so sorry," she whispered, eyes filling with tears. "Oh God, I'm sorry . . ."

Her husband stood by her in stoical silence, though his own shimmering eyes revealed his true feelings. Both looked at their friend for the last time, then reluctantly moved on.

Nina took Eddie's hand and squeezed it tightly as they approached Macy's parents. Isabel regarded them uncertainly before recognition sparked in her eyes. "You're Nina, aren't you? Nina Wilde?"

"Yes, I am," Nina replied. "I am so, so sorry about Macy. She was . . . she had so much energy, she helped me see things in new ways. She was—she was my friend. I'm sorry," she repeated, bracing herself for the worst; despite Eddie's attempts to convince her otherwise, she still felt responsible. Macy's mother and father could well blame her too . . .

But there was no explosion of fury or outrage. "Macy told me so much about you. She . . . she idolized you," Isabel said, her emotions clear despite her soft, controlled voice. "She said you helped her decide what she wanted to do with her life."

Amir was more open with his feelings, anger underlying his grief. "A man from the United Nations, Oswald Seretse, gave us the official report on what happened to Macy," he said. "But that didn't tell us what we wanted—what we *needed* to know." He fixed Nina with an intense gaze. "Our daughter—did she . . . suffer?"

Nina was silent for a long moment. "No," she finally said, shaking her head. "No, it was very quick. I don't think she did." She closed her eyes, seeing Macy's fear-filled face looking back at her, and tried not to sob.

The reply was what the Sharifs had wanted to hear, though. "Thank you," whispered Amir. Isabel clutched his hand, tears rolling down her cheeks. "Thank you."

"If there's anything we can do . . . ," said Nina.

"That's very kind, but . . . no, thank you." He put his arms around his wife and held her close.

"I'm so sorry for your loss," Eddie told them. The line of mourners was building up behind; as much as he wanted to say more, he did not want to monopolize Macy's parents. He accepted their silent thanks and ushered Nina on.

Many of those who had already paid their respects were still milling in the chapel, talking quietly. One visitor, however, had drawn attention even from those who didn't know him personally; for once, Grant Thorn was uncomfortable with that situation. He appeared almost relieved to see Eddie and Nina, and gestured them to join him and his companion, Marvin Bronze. The Hollywood star wore a black silk suit, his normally gelled hair for once combed flat. "Grant, hi," Nina said, giving him a brief embrace. "Are you okay?"

"Yeah," he replied, tight-lipped, then: "No. Not really. This is all . . . you know? Too much."

Eddie nodded. "I'm sorry."

"Me too, man. It's . . . it's not fair." He sighed. "She coulda been a star, you know? She really had something. The first time I met her, when I helped you with that thing in New York? I thought she was just some—" He glanced toward Macy's parents, then lowered his voice. "Just some bimbo. But she wasn't. She was way more than that." He sniffed. "We had so much fun together. And now she's—she's gone . . ."

Marvin patted his shoulder. "It's okay. You're okay."

The reply was little more than a whisper. "I don't know if I am." Grant wiped his eyes, then turned back to the couple. "This might not be the best place to talk business, but . . . buying the movie rights to your book, Nina? I don't think we'll be doing that. Not right now, it's . . . it's too soon. You were right: Real people get hurt doing what you do." He looked at the coffin, then lowered his head, unable to bear the sight. "It's not just fun and games anymore."

"It never was," she said sadly.

"Maybe I'll see you around sometime," he said. "I've still got a place in New York, so . . . who knows, huh?" An attempt at a smile, as convincing as any of his other acting, then he put his arms around Eddie and hugged him. The Englishman returned the gesture. "The people who did this to her . . . you got them, right?"

"I got them," Eddie replied. "All of 'em."

"Thanks, dude. Thank you." He released Eddie and shook his hand.

"I'm sure you two want some time to yourselves," Marvin said. "Grant, let's leave all these good people in peace, huh? Macy's family have enough pain without having to deal with the paparazzi."

Nina remembered seeing a couple of photographers outside the funeral home, but had not made the connection with Grant until now. "They're waiting for you?"

"Yeah," said the star with a glum nod. "They've been tailing me ever since I arrived in Miami."

"Vultures," growled Marvin. "Even at a funeral they won't leave him alone."

Eddie looked toward the door. "You want me to beat 'em up for you? Be just like old times."

Grant gave his former bodyguard a tired smile. "That'd be cool, but . . . I guess I've got to deal with this myself. Come on, Marv." He and his business partner said their farewells and departed, camera flashes from outside surprising some of the mourners before the doors swung shut.

"We should go too," said Eddie.

"Yeah, but . . . let's wait a minute," Nina replied. "I'm kind of a celebrity too—if Grant draws them away, hopefully none of them will pay attention to me. I don't think I could cope with it. Not today."

"If anyone hassles you, they'll get a zoom-lens enema." She almost smiled.

By the time they stepped outside, to Nina's relief the photographers had followed their prey. Someone else was waiting for them, however. "Ay up," said Eddie, seeing a familiar face in the shade of a nearby tree.

"Jared?" said Nina as the couple approached the Mossad agent. "What are you doing here?"

"I'm in Florida on business," said Zane. "But when I heard about the funeral, I thought I should pay my respects. I didn't know Macy, but . . . I know how close she was to you."

Nina dabbed away a tear. "Thank you."

Eddie had other concerns. "What kind of business?" He eyed a newspaper the Israeli was holding, recognizing the masthead as that of a British publication. "Why've you got a copy of the *Times*?"

"I bought it in London before flying here," Zane replied. "For you, actually. I thought you might want to read it." He passed him the paper. "The story on the fourth page, top right."

Eddie opened the newspaper. He recognized the man in the picture accompanying the article at once. " 'Baron Winderhithe dies in fall at home,' " he read—before looking back at Zane with sudden understanding.

"Who's Baron Winderhithe?" Nina asked.

"Some toff twat—who was also one of the bastards bankrolling Kroll. Died in a fall, did he?"

Zane's face betrayed the tiniest hint of satisfaction. "A tragic accident. He tripped on the marble staircase at his house and broke his neck. It took him a couple of minutes to die."

Nina was speed-reading the article. "It doesn't say anything about marble stairs here . . ." Now it was her turn to realize the truth. "Wait, did *you*—"

"Better not to ask," said Eddie. "So what about the others who were at Leitz's place? Did they have tragic accidents too?"

The Israeli nodded. "It's strange how many rich men have slippery floors, or crash their cars, or hit their heads when they dive into their swimming pools. All that money, and they still can't buy safety."

"Yeah, funny, that." A quizzical look. "That Yank, Thomson Holmes—didn't you say he was from Florida?"

"I did. I told you, I'm here on business." A faint smile, with considerable darkness behind it.

"What kind of accident did he have?" Nina asked.

"I haven't decided yet. But I'm sure it'll be in tomorrow's news."

"I . . . don't want to know," she said. "I've seen too much death lately."

"We all have." For a moment Zane was lost in thought. "Anyway, I have to go. But it's good to see that you're okay, Nina—and so are you, *alter kocker*."

"Fuck off, kid," Eddie replied, but with humor. The younger man grinned, then turned away toward his car.

"What does that mean?" Nina asked.

"Private joke." Eddie checked his watch. "We've got to go too, if we want to catch our flight back to New York."

"Yeah." She gave the chapel a last sad look. "It's time we went home."

. . .

Night had fallen by the time they returned to their building. Despite her tiredness, Nina still thought to collect the mail from their box, opening it as they ascended in the elevator. "Junk, junk, bill, junk . . ."

"Shouldn't there be a big check in there by now?" Eddie asked. "I thought you were supposed to get an advance when you signed up to write your book."

"I guess publishing works on archaeological time-scales . . ." She trailed off as she glanced at another letter.

"Big check?" Eddie asked.

"No, it's from my doctor." She gazed at the page.

Worry filled his voice. "Bad news?"

"Unexpected" was the distracted reply. Before Eddie could say anything more, the doors opened at their floor. "Can you take our stuff in? I need to use the bathroom."

"Human cart horse, reporting for duty," he grumbled as he picked up their bags and followed her to the apartment. She immediately went into the bathroom and closed the door.

Eddie took the luggage into the bedroom, then got a drink from the kitchen before slumping on the sofa, exhausted physically and emotionally. In his weary state, it took a while before he belatedly registered that Nina had not yet emerged. "Everything all right?" he called.

No reply. Wondering if she had fallen asleep, he went

to the bathroom. The door was not locked. He peered inside, finding Nina sitting on the toilet, with the lid closed. "You okay?"

Nina blinked. "Hmm? Oh, yeah, yeah. I'm fine." An odd look came over her face. "I'm actually . . . I don't know, to be honest."

He crouched before her, concerned. "What's wrong? Is something the matter?"

"There's something, yeah—well, two things. But I'm not sure if *wrong*'s the right word."

"You're worrying me a bit, love—you're not making a lot of sense." He sniffed the air. "You haven't been smoking anything funny, have you?"

"Yeah, right," she scoffed, the ludicrous accusation helping to bring her mind back down to earth.

"So what are these two things?"

"One of them is . . . well, it's easier if I just show you." She lifted her top to reveal the skin beneath. The swollen lumps of the eitr infection were still there . . . but they had shrunk considerably, the smallest ones having already disappeared and scabbed over. "I first noticed the change a few days after we got back to the States, but I didn't tell you because . . . well, I was afraid I might jinx it. So I went to the doctor for some tests." She held up the letter. "These are the results."

"And?"

"And . . ." She paused, still not quite able to believe it herself. "As far as they can tell, the infection is in remission. The tumors are shrinking—the cancerous cells are dying."

He cocked his head, wary of false hope. "So what does that mean?"

"It means that maybe . . . Kroll was telling the truth. The water from the Spring of Immortality really does cure diseases."

He glanced back through the door. The silver jug currently resided in a cupboard, having been sealed until they could decide what to do with it; revealing its existence would only risk sparking a new search for the spring. "But you didn't drink any of it."

"Not from Andreas's jar, no—but I swallowed about half a gallon when Kroll tried to drown me. It didn't even occur to me at the time, but now . . ."

"The stuff actually *worked*?"

"I can't think of any other explanation. The doctor wants to do more tests, but based on what he's found so far, I really am getting better. There's another thing too. I had some, ah . . . symptoms of something else. I just checked to see if I was right. And . . . I was."

"About what?"

She hesitated, then took a pen-sized plastic object from the shelf above the washbasin. Eddie did a double-take as he first identified it—then saw the two dark lines in the testing kit's little window. "Is that—"

"Yeah, it is. I'm pregnant."

He stared at her, unsure if he had heard her correctly—then broke into his first smile of the day.

Don't miss the eleventh explosive
Nina Wilde and Eddie Chase adventure

THE
REVELATION
CODE

Continue reading for a sneak peek

Coming soon from Bantam Books

PROLOGUE
Southern Iraq, 2002

The half moon cast a feeble light over the desolate, sand-swept plain. The region had been marshland not long ago, but war changed that. Not directly; the islands spattering the expanse between the great rivers of the Tigris and Euphrates were not destroyed by shells and explosives. Instead, spite had drained them, the dictator Saddam Hussein taking his revenge upon the Ma'dan people for daring to rise against him following the Gulf War. Dams and spillways reduced the wetlands to a dust bowl, forcing its inhabitants to leave in order to survive.

That destruction was, ironically, making the mission of the trio of CIA operatives crossing the bleak landscape considerably easier. Had the marshes not been drained, they would have been forced to make a circuitous journey by boat from their parachute landing point on the Euphrates' northern bank. Instead, they had driven the battered Toyota 4x4 waiting for them almost in a straight line across the new desert.

"Not far now," said the team's leader, Michael Rosemont, as he checked a hand-held GPS unit. "Two miles." Their destination was the isolated Umm Al Binni lake, where they were to meet with a rebel group of Marsh Arabs.

The driver, Gabe Arnold, peered ahead through his night-vision goggles. He was driving without headlights to keep them hidden from potential observers. "I can see the lake."

"Any sign of Kerim and his people?"

"Yeah—they've lit a fire. But . . . I can see something else. I think it's a building, some ruins."

Rosemont looked ahead, but all he could see in the darkness was a tiny point of orange. "There wasn't anything marked on the maps."

"It's in the water. Musta been exposed when the lake dried up."

"Are Kerim and his people there?"

"No, they're maybe two hundred yards away."

"It's not our problem, then. Let's go meet them." Rosemont clicked off the safety of the M4 carbine on his lap. The third man, Ezekiel Cross, did the same with his own weapon. They might have been meeting friendlies, but those at the sharp end of intelligence work in the CIA's Special Activities Division preferred to be ready for any eventuality.

Arnold brought the Toyota closer. The orange light was revealed as a small campfire, figures standing around the dancing flames. All were armed, the fire's glow also reflecting dully off assorted Kalashnikov rifles. To Rosemont's relief, they were lowered, none pointed at the approaching vehicle.

Yet.

Arnold halted the 4x4. The men around the fire watched intently, waiting for its occupants to make the first move. "All right," said Rosemont. "I'll go and meet them."

He opened the door and stepped out. The action brought a response; some of the Ma'dan raised their guns. The CIA commander took a deep breath. "Kerim!

Is Kerim here?" Mutterings in Arabic, then a man stepped forward. "I am Kerim. You are Michael?"

"Yes."

Kerim waved him closer. The Ma'dan leader was in his early thirties, but a hard life in the marshes had added a decade of wear to his face. "Michael, hello," he said, before embracing the American and kissing him on both cheeks.

"Call me Mike," Rosemont said with a smile.

The Arab returned it. "It is very good to see you . . . Mike. We have waited a long time for this day. When you come to kill Saddam," a spitting sound, echoed by the others as they heard the hated dictator's name, "we will fight beside you. But his soldiers, they have tanks, helicopters. These are no good." He held up his dented AK-47. "You have brought new weapons?"

"We have." Rosemont signaled to the two men in the Toyota.

"Show 'em their toys!"

His companions each brought a crate to the group. "This fire'll be visible for miles," Cross complained as he arrived. "Stupid making it out in the open, real stupid."

Kerim bristled.

Rosemont shot Cross an irritated look, but was forced to admit that he had a point. "You can put this out now," he told the Ma'dan leader. Kerim gave an order, and one of his men kicked dirt over the little pyre. "Why didn't you set up by those ruins over there? You could have waited for us in cover."

The suggestion unsettled his contact. "That is . . . not a good place," Kerim said, glancing almost nervously at the waterlogged structure. "We would not have chosen to meet you here."

"Why not?" asked Arnold, setting down his case.

"It is a place of death. Even before the water fell, all the tribes in this part of the marsh stayed away from it. It is said that . . ." He hesitated, as if summoning up the courage to continue. "That the end of the world will begin there. Allah, praise be unto him, will send out His angels to burn the earth. It is a place we fear."

With the fire extinguished, the ruins were now discernible in the moon's pallid light. The squat structure was not large, and the other buildings and walls surrounding it had crumbled, but it seemed to Rosemont that its central core had remained intact over—how long had it been submerged beneath the lake? Centuries, millennia? There was something indefinably ancient about it.

Not that it mattered. His only concerns were of the present.

"Well, here's something that'll make Saddam fear *you*," he said, switching on a small flashlight and opening one of the crates.

The sight of its contents produced sounds of awe and excitement from the Ma'dan, who congregated more closely for a better look. Rosemont lifted out an olive-drab tube. "This is an M72 LAW rocket. We'll show you how to use them—but if you can fire a rifle, you can fire one of these. We've also brought a couple thousand rounds of ammunition for your AKs."

"That is good. That is very good!" Kerim beamed at the CIA agent, then passed on what he had just been told to the other Ma'dan.

"I guess they're happy," said Arnold on seeing the reaction.

"Guess so," Rosemont replied. "Okay, Kerim. We need to get your intel on Saddam's local troops before—"

A cry of alarm made everyone whirl. The Marsh Arabs whipped up their rifles, scattering to crouch in the nearby patches of dried-up reeds. "What's going on?" Cross demanded, raising his own gun.

"Down, down!" Kerim called. "The light, turn it off!"

Rosemont snapped off the torch and ducked. "What is it?"

"Listen!" He pointed across the lake. "A helicopter!"

The CIA operatives fell silent. Over the faint sigh of the wind, a new sound became audible: a deep percussive rumble. The chop of heavy-duty rotor blades.

Growing louder.

"Dammit, it's a Hind!" said Arnold, recognizing the distinctive thrum of a Soviet-made Mil Mi-24 gunship. 'Is it coming this way?"

"Can't tell. Get the NVGs from the truck—shit!" Rosemont jumped up as a horrible realization hit home. "The truck, we've got to move it! If they see it—"

"On it!" cried Arnold, already sprinting for the Toyota. "I'll try to hide it behind the ruins."

"They might still see its tracks," warned Cross.

"We'll have to chance it," Rosemont told him. "Kerim! Get your men into cover over there." He pointed toward the remains of the building.

The Ma'dan did not take well to being given orders. "No! We will not go into that place!"

"Superstition might get you killed!"

"The helicopter will not see us if we stay in the reeds," Kerim insisted.

"Let them stay if they want to," said Cross dismissively. "We need to move."

"Agreed," said Rosemont, putting the LAW back into its case. The Toyota's engine started with a growl, then sand kicked up from its tyres as Arnold swung it toward the ruins. "Come on."

They ran after the 4x4, leaving the Marsh Arabs behind. It took almost half a minute over the uneven ground to reach the outer edge of the ruins and find cover among the tumbledown walls. By now, Arnold had stopped the Toyota beside the remains of the main structure, its wheels in the water. He jumped out.

"Where's the chopper?"

Rosemont looked over a wall across the lake—catching his first glimpse of the Hind. He couldn't see the helicopter itself, but instead saw the flash of one of its navigation lights. A reflection told him that it was less than fifty feet above the water. A couple of seconds later, the light flared again . . . revealing that while the Hind wasn't heading straight at them, it would make landfall at most a couple of hundred yards beyond Kerim's position.

"If it's got its nav lights on, then they don't know we're here," said Cross. "They'd go dark if they were on an attack run."

"Yeah, but they gotta be using night vision to fly that low without a spotlight," Arnold warned. "They might still see us."

"Let's hope not." Rosemont kept watching as the helicopter neared the shore, the roar of its engines getting louder.

Tension rose among the three men. The Hind appeared to be traveling in a straight line—if it suddenly slowed or altered course, they would know that they had been spotted . . .

The gunship's thunder reached a crescendo—

And passed. It crossed the shore and continued onward across the barren plain, a gritty whirlwind rising in its wake.

Arnold blew out a relieved whistle. "God damn. That was close."

Rosemont kept watching the retreating strobes. "Let's give it a minute to make sure it's gone—Cross, what the hell? Turn that light out!"

Cross had brought out his flashlight, shining its beam over the ruined structure. "I want to see this."

"Yeah, and the guys in that chopper might see you!"

"They won't. Look, there's a way in." A dark opening was revealed in the dirty stone; not the jagged gash of a collapsed wall, but an arched entrance. He waded into the lake, the water rising up his shins as he approached the passage. "There's something written above it." Characters carved into the stonework stood out in his light.

"What does it say?" asked Arnold, moving to the water's edge.

Rosemont reluctantly joined him. "I don't know what language that is," he said, indicating lines of angular runes running across the top of the opening, "but the letters above it? I think they're Hebrew. No idea what they say, though."

"We should find out." Cross aimed his light into the entrance, revealing a short tunnel beyond, then stepped deeper into the water.

"Cross, get back—God damn it," Rosemont growled as the other man ducked through the arch. He exchanged a look of bewildered exasperation with Arnold, then started after him.

"Wait here and watch for the chopper. I'll get him."

He splashed into the lake. Cross had by now disappeared from sight inside the ruined structure, spill from his flashlight washing back up the tunnel. "Cross! Get out of there. We've got a job to do."

There was no reply. Annoyed, Rosemont sluiced through the opening and made his way into the building's heart, turning on his own flashlight. The water rose to his knees. "Hey! When I give you an order, you—'

He stopped in amazement.

The room was not large, only a few yards along each wall. But it had clearly been a place of great importance to whomever had constructed it. Stone columns coated in flaked gilding supported each corner of the ceiling, bands of pure gold and silver around them inset with numerous gemstones. Not even the grime left by their long submersion in the lake could diminish their splendor. The walls themselves were covered in the skeletal ancient text he had seen outside. There were more passages in Hebrew too, but the other language occupied so much space that these were relegated to separate tablets laid out around the room's waterlogged perimeter.

It was obvious what the temple had been built to contain. The wall opposite the entrance contained a niche a little over a foot high, more gold lining it. Carvings resembling the sun's rays directed his eyes to its contents.

A strange stone figure filled the nook, the body human—but the head was that of a lion. Wrapped tightly around the statuette's torso, shrouding it like wings, were several metal sheets embossed with a pattern resembling eyes.

Cross stood at the alcove, his flashlight just inches

from the artifact as he examined it. "Do you see it?" he gasped. "Do you *see* it?"

"Yeah, I see it," Rosemont replied. There was an odd new tone to the other agent's voice that he had never heard before, a breathless excitement—no, *wonderment*. "What is it?"

Cross glanced away from his find long enough to give his superior a look that was somewhere between pity and disdain.

"You don't see it, otherwise you'd know."

"Okay, then enlighten me."

"An apt choice of words." He leaned closer for a better look at the leonine head. "It's an angel."

Rosemont sidestepped to see for himself. "Yeah, I can see that, I guess. It does kinda look like an angel."

"No, you don't understand. It doesn't just look like an angel. It *is* an angel! Exactly as described in the Book of Revelation! Chapter four, verse six—'Four beasts full of eyes before and behind. And the first beast was like a lion.' And there's more: 'And the four beasts had each of them six wings about him.'" He crouched, the water sloshing up to his chest. "There's something written on its side. I know what it says."

"You can read it?" asked Rosemont, surprised.

"No—but I still know what it says. Revelation 4:8—'And they rest not, day and night, saying "Holy, holy, holy, Lord God Almighty, which was, and is, and is to come."' They aren't literally *speaking* day and night—the words are written on them. That's what it means!"

"That's what *what* means?"

Cross stared at the angel for a long moment, then turned to face Rosemont. The older agent was momentarily startled by his expression, an almost messianic light burning in his eyes.

"Revelation! God brought me here, so I could see this. The prophecy, it's true! I understand, it's all coming to me. . . ."

"All right, so you've had a vision from God," said Rosemont, his discomfort replaced by impatience. "That doesn't alter the fact that we've got a mission to carry out. This is a job for archaeologists, not the CIA—let Indiana Jones take care of this. We still need to get Kerim's intel on those Iraqi positions."

"You do that," Cross replied as he took out a compact digital camera. "This is more important."

"The hell it is." He sloshed closer as Cross took a photo of the alcove and the surrounding text-covered wall. "You're coming with me, right now—"

"Mike!" Arnold's shout came from outside, both men turning toward the entrance. "The chopper, it's coming back!"

NINA WILDE AND EDDIE CHASE
MEET THEIR MAKER

Andy McDermott: Hi, good afternoon. It's great to finally meet you both in person.

Nina Wilde: Thank you—you too!

Eddie Chase: Yeah. It's a bit weird, though. Meeting your maker's normally the last thing you ever do.

AM: You don't need to worry about that just yet. You've got more stories still to come.

EC: How many?

AM: Moving swiftly on—

EC: Oi!

AM: —you've now made it through your tenth epic adventure, making this an anniversary of sorts, and in the not-too-distant future you'll be beginning a new kind of adventure when you have your first child. How does that feel?

NW: I couldn't be more thrilled. We've been talking about it for a while, but then I was infected by a biotoxin and couldn't risk having a baby. So discovering not only that the water from the Spring of Immortality had cured me, but also that I was pregnant, was incredible. Even if . . . it did come on the back of an absolutely devastating personal loss.

EC: Can I just ask you something, Andy—how do you live with yourself?

NW: Eddie!

EC: What? It's a reasonable question. Everything bad

that's ever happened to us is the fault of *somebody* not a million miles from here, innit?

NW: Everything good too. I wouldn't have met you without him, we wouldn't have gotten married—and I wouldn't be having a baby. Ah ... now, Andy, the baby *is* going to be fine, right?

AM: What am I, a monster?

EC: Good question!

AM: Yes, the baby will be fine.

NW: Thank God. And nothing else terrible's going to happen to us or anyone we care about?

AM: [silence]

EC: Oh, for fuck's sake!

AM: Going back to your previous exploits; Nina, what would you say was your greatest discovery?

EC: [sotto voce] Don't change the bloody subject. . . .

NW: Wow, that's actually quite a tough choice! Atlantis was my first big find and the one that made my name, obviously, but then there have been things like the Pyramid of Osiris, the city of El Dorado, Valhalla, the Vault of Shiva ... and the ones we've had to keep quiet about for various reasons, like the Garden of Eden or Excalibur, and the most recent one, the Spring of Immortality. It's hard to choose! So on balance, I'd have to say ... this guy. Edward J. Chase.

EC: Aw, thanks, love. Huh, funny how nobody ever remembers the Tomb of Hercules.

AM: And what about you, Eddie? What would you say is your greatest moment?

EC: Out of everything I've been through? Just still being alive! I've been shot, stabbed, bones broken, left half bloody deaf. . . . But no, meeting Nina. We've had our ups and downs, but it's been a hell of a ride.

NW: So what's going to happen to us next? If you could give us a hint, we'd be better prepared for it—

EC: Buggeration and fuckery.